First published in the United Kingdom in 2006 by
Manuscript & Publishing Agency Ltd.
The Forge, Hewish, Weston super Mare, Somerset, BS24 6RS
This edition published 2006.
Printed and bound in Great Britain by Manuscript & Publishing Agency Ltd

A Cataloguing-in-Publication Data catalogue record for this title is available from the
British Library

ISBN 1-905412-14-2

The Glass Pig

Barbara J Swanson

Manuscript Publishing Ltd

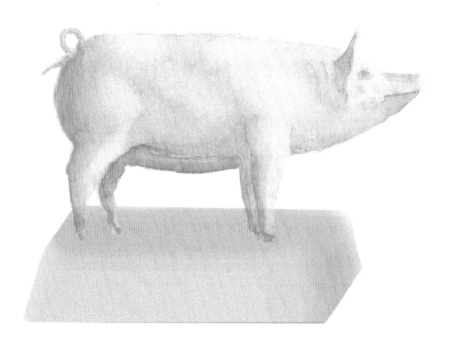

Illustration by J. Chapman

The Glass Pig

The Glass Pig

Chapter 1

Isabel's mind was becoming numb with the churning of her thoughts. Shock was setting in. She twisted around with a shudder that almost threw her off the old kitchen chair. The ghostly scent of that morning's discovery seemed to have followed her back into the cottage.

There was no one there, of course. How could there be? She returned to the work she had started to keep her hands busy and mind occupied. Not that the peeling away of earth-encrusted skins from leeks and onions was all that exacting, but keeping busy made her feel better. She looked behind her at the old Welsh dresser that propped up the wall of the ancient cottage and considered the whisky bottle on its sloping shelf, then shook her head. No way was she going down that road. She'd seen the results of that too often amongst Paul's staff. She had lost count of how many of them he had ordered her to sack when they hadn't mended their ways.

She asked herself yet again if she'd done the right thing, coming here. Did she miss the familiar, daily comfort of humming computers, the plaintive yet strident voices asking for attention - or the baboon-like shrieks of laughter as one of the workers sent a crude joke out into the re-cycled air? And the open-plan offices with not an ounce of dust or mud to be seen anywhere. Had she really given all that up for the company of cawing crows and the smell of horse manure?

The little flat she'd been so proud of was jettisoned once her mind was made up and she lost no time in getting things moving. Paul's behaviour had made the delight in that achievement melt away like sugar on a steaming bowl of lumpy porridge. What on earth had possessed her? She was far too clever to be taken in by flattery - or was she? He had managed to convince her - against her better judgement, she reminded herself - that she was more than just a pastime; that his marriage was finished. She should have known; ought to have seen the signs; particularly when his wife continued to visit the office. A vision of him arose in her mind. His pedantic dress-sense, his thinning hair combed forward to save his vanity, eyes which could hardly stay still - and ditto his hands - all so obviously due to lack of any sort of admirable character that she was, in a strange and inexplicable way, comforted. She was well rid of him. The ghost was laid.

Isabel gasped as another, far more recent, vision reappeared. She shook her head back and forth as if that would send the spectre away. She wasn't going to think about it, she determined. Not yet. There was probably some innocent explanation, in any case. Not something she should allow herself to dwell on - or have nightmares about.

She'd had so many *good* dreams; she was damned if she was going to let them go. Dreams of a new life where she would be in command of her destiny, not trying to please others all the time. It hadn't happened quite as she had hoped. Before two months were up in her new home each night's sleep was being punctuated with confused pictures of un-dug earth and panic that the fruit and vegetables would wilt and die before she had a chance to put them to a good use. Mentally viewing her fast-decreasing bank-balance did nothing to comfort her either. But most mornings, after a large mug of tea, and especially if the sun was shining, she was relieved to find that she could cope with the upheaval of volcanic proportions that were currently happening in her life.

A loud thump resonated throughout the small cottage making her skin goose-pimple with shock. There was someone banging on her front door with alarming determination.

Her imagination skimmed in panic-ridden haste over all sorts of horrors. Nobody ever used the front door so it must be a stranger. It couldn't be Paul; she'd finished with him. Forever. But the thought didn't pacify her. It could be Thom, she reminded herself. She'd told him not to use the front door but he had paid no attention to her request on his infrequent - and unwanted - visits. She ignored the embryonic flame of hope that was battling for life in her chest that it *was* Thom and nobody else. She'd sorted out that business with his silly little ornament and Hannah; was it likely that he'd visit her again in a hurry?

With legs that felt like rubber and sweat dampening the back of her neck, Isabel pushed herself away from the table and stumbled across the cobbled floor towards the heavy oak door at the end of the hall.

Letting it swing open a few inches she was just able to prevent a gasp from erupting from her when her eye lit on the tall man standing on the paving stones of the wooden porch.

It was Thom. And in his outstretched hands were shards of pale blue glass.

Fate, it seemed, was taking great pleasure in making the day worse than it already was. Isabel's mind was so overcast with clouds of renewed shock that she was unable to speak. She stood frozen as her confidence - or what remained of it - flowed like a stream in flux towards the hard floor beneath her feet.

Chapter 2

SEVEN WEEKS EARLIER

Isabel hadn't been in the cottage a week when she came to the conclusion that the place looked more like a left luggage office than a kitchen and something needed to be done about it. Boxes stood like soldiers on the dark grey flagstones cutting down even further the reticent beams of light struggling through the tiny casements. Her bits of china stood in rows on the old sideboard, while the large wooden table was covered with papers and books. She planned, there and then, to improve matters - do a 'make-over' with fresh paint for the cupboards, new plaster for the walls and a nice rich stain for the crumbling beams above her head. Perhaps she was being a bit over-enthusiastic, she told herself, but surely she could manage some curtains to frame the creepers that danced against the glass of the window above the old sink. The old sink; she was proud of that. A good scrub for it and the wooden draining board had made such an improvement that the old boy wouldn't recognise it now. He hadn't managed to do much house-keeping it seemed.

'The wife, she be dead now, these past four month,' he had told her, leading the way up the narrow staircase to the bedrooms on that first visit.

Isabel noticed how careful he was not to put his hand on the rickety and grubby rail which served as a banister, despite his unsteady step. 'But jes' nothin' a bit of scrubbin' an' polis' cain't put right.'

Isabel's better judgement had been overcome by her sudden enthusiasm. The vision of a blissful, fulfilled future almost had her gasping for breath; so much so that she paid only fleeting attention to the lack of decoration before rushing back to her solicitor to get him to complete the sale as soon as possible.

Having managed to carve a passage-way around the boxes and tea-chests in the kitchen she had now determined to start on the two upstairs rooms.

It had been a cruel surprise to find that the previous occupant had decided to leave most of his crumbling furniture behind, giving

10

her even more stuff to sort out. The very first thing she wanted to chuck out was the big iron bed with its rusty headboard and claw-like feet in the larger of the two rooms. This would take some planning, of course, but she'd find a way to get rid of it. For the moment the room could be a temporary store and she'd use the one piece of her own furniture she had brought with her, the new single bed from her London flat, in what she had already labelled her 'guest room'. Not that she anticipated many guests. Silas would want to come and see her new abode. And maybe her mother, if she ever came to her senses and they were on speaking terms, might wish to visit. Isabel had hustled the memory of their last meeting out of her mind; too many other things were clamouring for her attention at the moment.

She decided that a visit to the unfamiliar nearby town was called for. She was surprised by Shilliton's size, expecting it to be a little larger than her village of Shinbridge but not quite as stylish as it now revealed that it was. There was one very long main street with countless smaller ones branching off it. Ancient roofs now looked down on bright, glass-fronted shops filled with quality goods. Georgian houses were homes to solicitors, accountants and countless small businesses, the grey of their stonework accented by myriad dyes. Some of the brightly painted ancient buildings did look good, she'd admitted reluctantly. Just took a little getting used to. The town's prosperity had gone to the heads of the local councillors, it seemed, as they permitted it to broadcast what a pretty, successful town it was. She didn't comment on this as she asked for permission to put out the old bed for rubbish collection. It cost a fiver but that was a good investment, she considered, even if it would be hanging around for another month. In a further attempt at the improvement of her new home she'd asked for directions to a builder's yard.

'You can't miss it. It's next to the station.' the woman in the newspaper shop had told her. Isabel wondered why the shopkeeper had found this so funny.

She understood as soon as she turned down the road that was signposted for the railway station. A great, white barn covering several acres of space appeared like a vision from an extraterrestrial movie. Pushing her trolley along lines of every conceivable boon for the DIYer, she went a little mad, she decided later. Disallowing any vision from entering her head of the dilapidated gloomy shed she was now calling a bathroom, she chose luxury bathroom fittings, matching tiles and flooring and warm peach paint for the walls. She deserved some comfort in her life, didn't she? She was going to transform the small room off the kitchen from a grotty, tumbledown storage room into something she could be proud of. No more perching above a cracked wooden toilet seat, quivering with fear at the myriad of germs swimming beneath her in the rust-stained water or dreading that the aged overhead cistern might decide the moment was ripe for a rapid descent from rusted fixings.

On her return Isabel was turning into the small area she had designated for parking when she became aware of the tall man standing half-hidden by the wooden porch that concealed the front door of the cottage. Isabel hadn't had the chance to try and open that door which looked as it had forgotten how to function many years before. And she certainly didn't know who the visitor was.

The man walked across the unkempt grass at the side of the cottage to the gate at the back as Isabel climbed out of the car. Reaching her he held out his hand and introduced himself. 'Thom,' he said in a concise manner as if she should recognise the name. He then embroidered the information by saying, 'Spelt with a 'th',' as if that would clarify matters. She thought she already knew the answer to her unspoken question as to his identity. But didn't he have a surname?

With the automatic reaction of a well-mannered person Isabel took his hand briefly, deciding not to comment on how he spelt his name. She glanced up at the tall, muscular figure standing before her with a roll of crumpled and string-tied newspaper in his hand. Mid to late 30s, she decided, with little interest. Not bad looking, but she'd already determined that she was finished with all that. No man was ever going to walk into her life again however he spelt his name.

'I've brought you a small 'welcome' gift,' he said.

'Come on in,' she told him, just managing to conceal her reluctance as she led him towards the kitchen door. She had a vague feeling he looked familiar, but couldn't place him. This made her feel strangely nervous of handling badly any overtures of friendship in this unfamiliar environment. So she said the first thing that came into her head. 'I'm not sure that one opens,' she told him nodding towards the front porch.

He didn't bother with a reply. Holding open the stable door that led to her kitchen he marched through it as if he were a regular visitor.

'Thought someone ought to show a modicum of welcome,' he told her in his curious, stilted way. He dropped the newspaper bundle onto the large wooden table in between piles of books and tinned food she had yet to find a home for.

The old table was the one thing she was going to keep, Isabel had decided. Her friends - 'acquaintances' she should now call them - in London would give a week's salary to own something so large, so antique, to show off in their urban kitchens. Even if it was just a twenties' reproduction rather than the Victorian original it pretended to be, Isabel reasoned during the two hours earlier that day when she had been scrubbing and oiling it - before replacing all the clutter that seemed unable to find a better home. But she didn't want any package oozing water onto it. She picked up the roll of soggy newsprint and dropped it onto the sloping wooden draining board, muttering a few words of polite gratitude. She would deal with it later. From the shape and feel of it she guessed she had been given a bunch of fresh leeks. As if she didn't have enough of those already, she told herself prickling with irritation. She bit her tongue so as not to make any remark she might come to regret.

'What are you planning on growing?'

He doesn't waste any time in small talk, does he? Isabel told herself, the irritation recreating itself as annoyance. The 'modicum of welcome' had just been an excuse. She recalled then what the old boy had said. It was something about her neighbour being a farmer.

'Han horganic man, 'e be,' the elderly man had said. Then he'd added something about him being a teacher, too, or so she had understood. 'But 'e 'as all these boys all runnin' around. Cain't think 'ow 'e manages 'is farm. 'An a big un it be, too. Near on a tousand acre o'er there.'

'Growing?' With shock Isabel stopped thinking about the old man who'd sold her the cottage - smallholding, it had been advertised as - and turned back to her guest. They were standing in her small, and still grotty, kitchen, two strangers facing each other as if they had just been introduced at a large social event, and he was immediately interfering in what was her private business. Was she ever to be free of male chauvinists? But that intrinsic courtesy, firmly instilled by a strict mother, kept her from speaking her mind.

'I'm already growing,' she said, emphasising the word. She nodded towards the window and the fruit trees beyond it. 'I've taken on a going concern.' In case you haven't noticed, she added silently.

'A few garden veg.' The sneer was unmistakable.

She had been on the point of offering her visitor a drink, rapidly listing in her mind what her meagre stores contained. One thing was for sure, she wasn't going to waste any of her precious Scotch on this unfriendly person so decided on tea; then dismissed even that idea.

The old boy - she felt that as a substitute for a name the expression deserved capital letters - The Old Boy had given her a few, hitherto undigested, nuggets of information regarding the local 'comoonity' as he called it. One such fragment was to beware of 'tha' ther Harley Thommoson' along with the mysterious mention of '"is gang of prizone fodder'. The two people were just one and the same. She no longer believed the man standing across the table was some sort of philanthropic teacher. Isabel had asked Ben what he meant but he just shook his head so that his aged jowls wobbled like un-set jelly. 'Yu'll be findin' ou' soon enou,' was all he proferred. Apart from, that was, the comment that her future neighbour's name was enough to make 'uz laugh'. ''Is da was tha' keen on the motercycles he named 'is son affer one! Clever man 'e be, too!' he added as if there was something mysterious there.

'I'm your neighbour.' The man - Thom, with an 'h', Isabel reminded herself - spoke as if words were costly and their expenditure had to be carefully budgeted.

'I'd guessed.' Isabel wasn't going to waste words either, if that was the way he wanted it.

'Thought we should have a chat sometime,' he continued unaware, apparently, of her slightly sarcastic tone. 'About your garden.' He spoke as if the final word was some undigestible morsel caught in his throat.

'Garden?' Isabel repeated wondering whether he'd read the wrong books on winning friends. Her precious three acres were a 'farm' to her, not a garden, and the land was going to produce a life-style that she had never imagined while living in her third-floor flat overlooking the fume-laden Hammersmith road. In her dreams she could see herself growing the most succulent and natural fruit and vegetables any of her contacts in town had ever had the good fortune to buy.

'You know what I do, don't you?'

Thom's voice, Isabel noticed unwillingly, was a firm, rich baritone with overtones of a strict schoolmaster. But the question, she felt, was purely rhetorical. She was going to be told what he did whether she wanted to hear it or not. She wished now that she'd got more information out of the Old Boy, before he had disappeared to his twilight home.

'I hear you run some sort of home for delinquents,' was all she said. Let him think what he liked; that's what old Ben had inferred, she was now convinced.

Isabel wished she had a camera at hand to record Thom's expression. She realized she had, unintentionally, managed to get a small sliver into the man's pompous self-esteem. She felt good about that. Briefly.

Thom threw his head back and filled the small kitchen with echoes of loud laughter. 'Good old Ben!' he barked. When his amusement subsided he looked across at Isabel as she stood leaning on the back of her chair. 'I run a strictly organic farm,' he told her, his voice quieter now that he could see that she wasn't sharing his amusement. 'And it's very successful. It's taken me years to build up and I'm not about to let someone spoil it all for me.' He paused as if surprised at the amount of words he'd used. Then he looked across at her again to satisfy himself that she had understood them.

Isabel, her wits nicely whetted by the thought of a good old verbal conflict in which she was to be the victor, answered, 'Oh good. Just what I intend to do.'

'That's the problem.'

Speaking through gritted teeth, she asked, 'What problem?' She heard the echoes of many boardroom speeches in her head and wished for a short moment that she was back in her old life, where people were careful not to cross her; who paid the penalty if they did. All except Paul, of course. Her ego deflated like a crinkled balloon at the thought.

'I can't have you growing things,' her neighbour began and then stopped. 'What I mean is... it's too dangerous to have someone so close to my land growing things which are not totally organic. GM free,' he added as if he believed she had no idea what he was talking about 'It could ruin the whole of my crops.'

And your income, no doubt, Isabel added silently. She was beginning to wonder how she could, without being overtly rude, bring this unwelcome, uninvited meeting to a close. She would have had no trouble in the old days but she was discovering - and very fast - that things were different in the countryside; almost as if rural areas were not in the same land as the one she was born in. Now she was wondering which she preferred, that organised, soulless existence in the world of business or this new life where everything seemed to run on different rules. It wasn't as if she'd walked out of her former life without giving it all a great deal of thought. She'd had a good job and a reasonable salary. Not as much as she should have had as Paul's CEO but that had been her fault, she realized now, for not asking for more.

Then one night when she was waiting for Paul to turn up she'd turned on the TV for something to keep her occupied. The pathetic programmes gave her little choice so she ended up watching something called 'New Education'. She'd thought it was something about educating children *not* to depend on computers and things and actually start reading a book for a change and that she'd find the concept amusing - and totally impractical. One item had stayed with her long after she had gone to bed accepting that there was going to be no company for her that night - as so often happened. A group of children were being interviewed in the playground about food.

'And where does a pineapple come from?' one eight-year old was asked.

'Tins', was the prompt reply.

'Do you know where milk comes from?'

'Of course,' the boy had answered as if the interviewer was a bit soft in the head. 'From farms!'

'Oh, good,' the poor girl, who was just doing her job of junior reporter, replied. Then hope appeared on her face. 'Have you ever been to a farm?' she asked.

'No,' the boy answered with a sneer. 'Who wants to go all the way on a bus just to see machines. We see lots of those in our factory visits.'

The shock had subsided leaving Isabel feeling sad and disheartened. Were children really so ignorant of what kept them alive? The question had made her think long and hard.

So here she was planning to put all her energies into providing good food for people and in the process educate them and their children about where it all came from or would do so when she got organised - and if neighbours didn't come knocking on her door to infer that her efforts were useless. But she knew better now than to kowtow to yet another bully.

She pushed herself away from the chair, drawing in a deep breath as she stood to her full, not-inconsiderable height. Using her best Chief Executive voice she said, 'I think I can grow what I like on my own land.' She wasn't going to let herself down by being defensive. In fact, she wasn't going to argue at all. She stood waiting, hoping it was obvious that she wanted him to go.

Thom took the hint. 'I'm an important person in this area,' he told her. 'And I have a thousand acres of land to worry about. Not just three.'

He turned and marched - there was no other word for it, Isabel thought later as she re-ran the mental video of their, rather unsuccessful, first meeting - through the open door. Isabel stood listening as his footsteps drummed a decreasing beat on the uneven flags of *her* footpath. She couldn't know the reason why, but suddenly she felt disappointed and let down. There was going to be no friendship in that quarter, she found herself thinking.

What if there wasn't? She hadn't expected or wanted any. All she wanted was peace, quiet and the chance to fulfil her ambition of making something worthwhile out of her existence on earth. And alone; not dependent or committed to another person.

Resolve making her straighten her shoulders Isabel picked up the newspaper parcel and threw it, still wrapped and tied with coarse string, into the small ribbed dustbin.

Chapter 3

Marion Hart rang Isabel as promised.

'Yes,' the woman said, as if it was a foregone conclusion. 'I definitely want to place another order, thank you.' She must have heard the note of nervousness in Isabel's voice when she answered the phone. 'I thought everything was well up to Ben's standard,' Marion assured her. 'Don't really like to say so, but it was all so much cleaner,' she chuckled.

Warmth entered Isabel's heart as she listened to the words. Something good at last, she thought.

The tall smart woman in country clothes, which, while down-to-earth still shouted their haute couture genesis, had been walking her dog, a long-eared, short-legged hound of indeterminate breed, a few days earlier. She stopped when she saw Isabel working away in her garden. Introductions weren't necessary, it seemed, as easy conversation grew between them as they faced each other over the rickety gate.

By the time Mrs Hart –'please call me Marion' - had left to allow her dog, Ruffian - an affectionate name for a well-loved creature, Isabel gathered - to enjoy its daily exercise Isabel had obtained her first order. Now a second batch had been requested, so she must be doing something right.

'They'll be with you before mid-day,' Isabel promised. And she was determined that this second box would be as nicely packed with freshly picked fruits and vegetables as the first. She had refused Marion's offer to fetch it herself as her home, she considered, wasn't quite ready to bear the scrutiny of someone as smart as Marion, despite her sincere and amiable ways. She could hardly just pass the big box over the gate without inviting her in, added to which she had an ulterior motive. She was curious to see the inside of the historic building whose stonework reflected in the calm waters of the unruffled mill-leat on the edge of Shinbridge village.

'It was a corn mill,' Marion had told her in their earlier conversation. 'Converted into four apartments about twenty five years ago. It is *not*', she emphasised, 'a 'block of flats' as I heard

18

someone call them!' It hadn't taken Isabel long to decide who that might be. 'And it's a Grade 2 listed building,' Marion added with a modicum of pride, 'so no one can mess about with it.' She laughed then as if they'd had some fun in the past deterring people from doing just that.

They met again in the village outside the old shed which had been converted into a post office and shop so many years ago that it still had the coal merchant's name in fading gold script above the door. Isabel had managed to get the irascible post-mistress's permission and was about to pin up her list of produce behind the glass of the narrow cabinet which hung on the wall to one side of the entrance. A finger tapped her on the shoulder. She turned with a nervous start to see who it was treating her in such a familiar way, imagining all sorts of unpleasant surprises. She was pleased - and relieved - to see that it was Marion Hart.

'Have you got any, shall we say, exotic veg, I can give to my dinner guests?' she asked.

Isabel ran along the small lanes of her vegetables in her mind. 'Would some courgette do?' she offered tentatively.

'Lovely,' answered Marion. 'And some of your luscious vine tomatoes, please. Supermarket ones just don't taste like tomatoes, these days,' she remarked.

Once they had finished discussing several additions to Marion's order and the non-existent problem of Isabel delivering it once more, the older woman turned and went into the post office. But not before she had said a few words which left Isabel's confidence soaring as if she'd been given a gift.

'I do like doing business with you,' Marion said. 'It quite makes my day!' And with a wide smile she left Isabel to complete her promotional exercise.

Later Isabel wondered whether her reaction was that of a child being given a treat. She felt a bit embarrassed at the idea. No, she told herself firmly. The woman was so genuine that she should accept the compliment in the spirit it was given. Now she had to get on with gathering her vegetables and fruits or there would be no more compliments coming her way. She felt a shiver run down her back as she remembered her neurotic response to a friendly pat on the shoulder. Did she really feel that it might have been foretelling some unwanted and menacing encounter? She pushed the thought away and turned her mind back to her work.

Isabel dipped her bucket into the cool water of the stream and carried it back to the bed of leeks, letting it dribble across the small mounds and into the trenches made by Old Ben before he'd sold up and left. She didn't know what else she should do to loosen the earth to enable her to pull out the vegetables without spoiling them. She still had so much to learn. She'd gained a lot from her reading but she was sorely in need of practice - years of it, probably. And the fruits and vegetables needed rescuing before the interminable heat caused them to collapse completely. If she worked quickly she could fill the small dark wooden shed under the fruit trees with a good store of winter food. She'd read how to preserve the apples by scattering them loosely onto the slatted shelves of the hut and how to keep her potatoes fresh in a pile of soil. But all the gem-like soft fruits needed different treatment. Her next investment, she had already decided, would have to be a damn great freezer like those in Shilliton's frozen food centre. Where she'd put it she had no idea but the solving of tricky problems had been one of her strong points, hadn't it? Paul had always been only too ready to drop them onto her shoulders so she'd had plenty of practice. She wished she hadn't thought about him. Paul's name was like a persistent bug which wouldn't go away, she decided with a shudder, attempting to slam a mental door on her unenviable and recent past.

Like an echo from a more recent life Thom's visit reappeared to her. His sermon - there was no other word for it - had cut deep into her satisfaction at her accomplishments, but she was determined that he should never have an inkling of that. She wasn't stupid. She would show him. Just wait and see. Apart from all her other produce her herb garden was going to amaze him; make him take back some of his disparaging words.

On that first visit to the eight-mile distant town she'd taken a list of seeds of all the herbs that could be bought in any good store in London. She had wanted to grow something *different* in her smallholding. The idea of herbs had come like an inspiration from the summer air. She'd got as far as thinking that these could make her name as a provider of good, fresh produce for all those dinner parties taking place in the metropolis as well as letting the country people have the pleasure of buying them locally. It was like a gift that herbs had blossomed into a cult just as she was preparing to leave the capital. She would be able to charge her London contacts a good price which would subsidise those things she was planning on selling locally. Good marks in her higher degree in business management would stand in her stead even in the country, she encouraged herself more than once - especially when the enormity of what she had done threatened to overwhelm her. Once established as a provider of those more esoteric foodstuffs that would grace any table, she could forget about labour intensive potatoes and beans, peas and sprouts, and really enjoy her growing. And be getting more in for it, too. She liked to be able to think of herself as a farmer. Three acres seemed rather a small amount of land to be called a farm, she had to admit, recalling Thom's caustic comment; but the title 'gardener' made her feel like she was growing acres of Arum Lilies ready for the next funeral. Not until she could tack the word 'herb' in front of 'grower' would she consider herself satisfactorily labelled, so she was really going to push herself to get to that point. Who knew what other outlets there might be in the locality for well-grown herbs – the aromatherapist whose ad she'd seen in the local free sheet might start buying from her. Perhaps she should set up her own mini processing factory and sell the woman oils ready for use.

Was she getting carried away? She told herself she should stop wasting energy in dreaming up new ventures before the old ones had borne fruit. Visions of Paul spreading himself too thinly - with the resultant lack of success - wafted through her mind. Perhaps she had learnt something of value from him, after all.

She rescued the trug from under the pea plants where she'd left it earlier and filled it with a dozen large - and still succulent, she noted with relief - leeks, then strode along the path to the beans. She plucked several pounds from the overloaded plants and placed them on top of the leeks before making her way to the raspberry bushes sheltering from the outside world, and unknown predators, in their bungalow of green mesh. She would put a couple of pounds of these in the Hart's box and not charge them. Her PR skills, useful when working with Paul, were not going to be allowed to go to waste; the Harts might recommend her to a friend or two if she treated them well.

'Some nice redcurrants, too, if you have them, please.' Mrs Hart had added with a laugh during their earlier conversation: 'Friends for supper. Roast lamb and all that.' So Isabel was taking things a little further and providing some nice fruit for a desert.

As the red fruit passed from stem to basket, Isabel thought about her other neighbours in the village. It might take months, if not years, before she could consider herself an integrated member of their community. She remembered what a pleasant surprise it had been when the smart woman had asked if she could give an order on that first meeting.

'Old Ben Tyler used to keep us supplied with veges,' Marion had said with a smile. 'I hope you're going to be able to do the same?' It was less a question than a statement of fact.

Isabel's mind vaulted back to the present at a muted sound like that of some far distant car screeching to a halt. There it was again. She reached the overlapping mesh of the fruit cage's entrance when she heard the sound again. It was more like a muted scream now. She stood listening for a moment but it wasn't repeated. All she could hear was the stream gurgling like a contented infant with a bottle in its mouth, its song muffled by the tall arches of the bean poles to her left, and the faint sound of youthful voices in the distance. None of which was worrying enough to send such a rush of adrenaline through her veins.

But then she heard it again. More muffled, this time it sounded as if leaves were being swept up by a frantic gardener; a gardener who was growling in frustration or anger. She had an intruder in her fruit cage, it seemed. Not a furious, large wild animal, however, more like a small young thing that had got itself entwined in green mesh from which it couldn't escape. Isabel stood silent, unmoving, waiting for the beast to free itself. A sudden movement followed by a flash of brown and orange made her step backwards onto the rhubarb plants behind her. She ignored the squelch of squashed fruit as relief filled her and her limbs were able to move again.

It was no more than a small cat, with matted fur and scared eyes. She grabbed it preparing to put it outside its green plastic prison. It clung onto her arm as if its claws were talons, a pathetic mewing streaming continuously from its throat. She pulled it close to her chest and held it tightly as she pulled back the overlapping netting. The claws relaxed their hold, to Isabel's relief, as the animal decided that this wasn't some ogre come to gobble him up but a person wanting to help him. Isabel's tense shoulders relaxed. She sighed and lessened her hold on the kitten. Like a body shot from a cannon in an old movie it leapt away, disappearing into the wilderness of the wide hedge which made a border between her land and the small lane at the side of her property. She was surprised to find herself feeling rather sad to see it disappear so soon. For a moment there had been another creature on earth that had needed her; a creature she might have loved and cared for, given half a chance.

Her first fearful imagining seemed to be materialising, however, as her self-indulgent reverie was shattered. She stood listening in shock at the wild screeching of real car brakes, this time, followed by a sinister shushing sound as wheels slid across the loose surface of the ill-kept lane.

Too late, she told herself, feeling numb. The post-lady it must have been. She was the only person who'd be visiting her at this time of day. Demolishing a small creature might be a common thing these days, but she knew Kate would be devastated to have perpetrated that minor, innocent crime. Isabel untangled herself from the cords of green mesh and went out to speak some words of condolence. But the girl was already back in her little red van and driving away, leaving behind only the ends of white and brown envelopes overlapping the edge of the old American-style letter box. Of the kitten there was no sign. Isabel decided that Kate must have scooped up the remains of the squashed animal and taken them away for disposal. She was a little surprised that the girl hadn't stayed around for some sympathy, or moral support. She must be tougher than she appears, Isabel thought. The vision of a small heap of squashed fur remained with her, on and off, for the rest of the day.

She looked at the letters she had taken from the box. On the top of the pile was a large white envelope with a chillingly familiar postmark. Her nerves still somewhat weak from their recent battering she tore open the envelope, all the time exhorting herself not to panic. The first few lines of officialese, however, had her scuttling towards the old black telephone in the tiny dark hall dropping the rest of the letters onto the cluttered kitchen table as she went.

She dialled Silas's number keeping mental fingers crossed that she would find him at home. There was no way she wanted to have to cope with this on her own. While she waited for him to answer she glanced at the remainder of the short letter. It was just as bad as she feared. Silas's phone rang a dozen times or so before she decided he was out. She was just about to replace the old hand-set when a breathless voice shouted a brief 'hello'.

'Sorry,' Silas apologised when he'd discovered who was at the other end of the line. 'The fellows and I were just putting together the final touches to the plans for the new marina.'

His words made Isabel think of her time as part of big business schemes and she sighed with relief at the thought that she was now completely free of any longing to be part of it again. There were more important things for her to worry about now.

She read the letter to her brother after he had assured her she wasn't interrupting anything; that they had finished their business. A clink of coffee cups - or even glasses - in the background seemed to bear out his words.

'She's up to her pranks again,' Silas said. 'That's obvious.'

'Yes,' was all Isabel could say. Her mind was clogging with visions of what the letter threatened - for her *and* her future.

'She gave you the money,' Silas reminded her, 'with no strings attached, didn't she say? And you repaid her. What does she want now?'

'Me to look after her,' Isabel reminded him, waving the letter in the air as if it could be seen at the other end of the wires leading from the ancient instrument. 'I don't like the way they are now reminding me I signed something to that effect should it ever be necessary. I never got that document back although it was promised I would once I'd repaid the full amount. Which I did.'

'Well,' said her brother in a comforting tone, 'you can't look after her. If she's ill enough to need looking after she has the means to pay for a nice home.'

Typical male, Isabel groaned inwardly. Didn't he read the newspapers, watch television, or listen to the radio? Surely he knew how difficult it was to find good accommodation for a person who wasn't yet senile but needed help and care. She couldn't bring herself to put a name to her grandmother's dilemma; had never imagined that any of her own family could ever be stricken by such an ailment. And the family was supposed to look after them; were made to feel morally obliged. With Father gone, they knew not where, and both Silas and her mother having opted out of any responsibility for the poor old woman she, Isabel, was the only 'family' that remained. She had always known that the day would arrive when *someone* would have to take responsibility for her paternal grandmother but she had managed to push it right to the back of her mind with all she'd had to cope with in the past few months. Isabel wished, for the hundredth time, that she had refused the offer of a loan for her university fees. She had not recognised that there was an element of blackmail in the seemingly generous offer. She had thought it was over and done with once she had repaid everything straight into her grandmother's bank account.

'The solicitor said she's not *ill*,' she reminded her brother. 'And the hospital can only keep her for a few more days. The usual story – not enough doctors, too many patients and hospitals having to close wards because they haven't got enough nurses to run them.'

The enormity of the letter's message now made her feel as if she was encased in concrete with no mind, no will and, certainly, no right to live the life she wanted to. But she couldn't just ignore the old woman's fate, could she?

'She'll have to go into a home,' Silas repeated.

It cheered Isabel a little to learn that he didn't expect her to take all the responsibility for the difficult, bad-tempered old woman her grandmother Lilian had become.

'She's refusing to, remember?' The conversation was going round in circles. Her voice must have conveyed this.

'She's done this before,' Silas said in a tone which was meant to sooth. 'Just a brief lapse of memory. Any old person can get on the wrong bus and then accuse the driver of going the wrong way. It's nothing to get too het up about.'

It came to Isabel like a rather garish and nasty light turning on that Silas did not know what was wrong with Lilian; he seemed to think she was just getting absent-minded. So she told him.

The momentary silence at the other end of the line told her just how shocked he was. He could usually find the apt word to fill any gap in a conversation. 'How far on?' he asked abruptly.

'Early stages,' Isabel told him. 'Could be months before she's incapable of looking after herself. There's nowhere that would accept her at the moment.'

She heard Silas sigh. At least he wasn't telling her that she had to give up her new life and move to Northants to look after their father's mother. *Her* father's mother, she reminded herself still finding it difficult to absorb that recent piece of information.

'Look,' he told her. 'I'll come down and we can discuss all this. Not tomorrow, we've got to finish the prelims. The day after.'

Isabel wanted to tell him how wonderful he was and how grateful she was to have saint for a brother, but all she said was, 'Phew! Thanks, brov. You're a brick,' she joked heavily. She knew it was only a short reprieve; the day might still be lurking around the corner when she'd have to consider rearranging her whole life once more. That she would have her brother's support made her trials seem a tad less weighty than before.

Having put down the telephone and lost the comfort of her brother's voice her mind began its tumble-dryer act as her thoughts danced around her brain in some mad mazurka. Could she manage to have Lilian live with her here? Not a hope, she told herself, looking at the clutter still waiting to be organised. What would an elderly, although physically unimpaired, woman do with her days? Drive the local community scatty with her little escapades? She squared her shoulders and instructed herself not to imagine such unnerving scenarios, allowing her commonsense to come up for a long-awaited breath.

It was a good thing she did for just then there was a knock on the old oak front door. Only a few feet away from the telephone it sounded like the thunder of the gods coming to claim her. She guessed it was Thom, and he was angry as usual.

It wasn't exactly a tirade that came her way. He was too parsimonious with words for that. But he managed to belittle her efforts once again.

'How can you cheat people by telling them your fruit and vegetables are organic?' he asked her after the statutory - brief - greeting.

Isabel didn't bother to tell him she wasn't trying to do anything of the sort. It hadn't taken her long to decide that it was easier, and quicker, if she allowed him to complete his speech without interruption.

'Do you know how much damage you can do?' he asked, his tone as chilly as a March breeze. 'Putting notices in the post-office window saying you have *organic* foods for sale?'

When he finished she might point out that she'd written no such thing. However, with all the troubles the day had brought, for the moment she just wanted him to stop getting at her and go. She might, if she felt like it, clear it all up later.

'It's worse than Foot and Mouth Disease,' he told her, leaving her slightly bemused at how plants could get that. 'The way it spreads,' he bothered to explain to his dim-witted listener, obviously having seen her quizzical expression.

Isabel was too tired to get angry and couldn't be bothered to tell him not to come and trouble her with his concerns when she had enough of her own. Silently she looked up at him. What she had considered as a strong and indestructible tree she now saw as no more than a reed waving in the wind and for some reason she felt bereft. Standing before her was one frightened man, she told herself with yet another quivering arrow of shock. She could not forgive him his rudeness - and she now knew without any doubt that she would never be able to convince him that her 'growing' would never affect his - but he now appeared less threatening, a little less awesome.

Having had his say he dropped a pile of books and papers onto the floor by the door. 'These might show you what's what,' he told her. 'Have a good read and then we can discuss what we're going to do about your little garden.'

Isabel was pleased to see that he wasn't expecting any response. She would look forward to a real barney with him some time in the future, now that she had seen the man behind the facade of an all-powerful Greek god. But, for the moment, she had to busy herself getting the Hart's box ready to deliver.

Thom had turned and marched along the rough, untended path to the little-used front gate and disappeared from sight amongst the trees before she listened again to the echo of his words in her mind. They stung, but she took pride at not having risen to his bait.

On top of the pile were several booklets, all by Earth Savers - all ones she had already perused and made notes from. Under these was a larger book. She picked it up and looked at its spine. This was one she wouldn't mind reading again. She'd had to return her copy to the library before she moved. Yes, she told herself, she would read his literature - she was always willing to learn. Then maybe on their next meeting they could discuss things like two intelligent adults. But she didn't hold that hope too close to her heart whatever revelations she had received.

At least, she told herself later, the mildly stormy visit had fully occupied her mind for a few minutes, and in some strange way was helping to put her other problems into perspective.

Chapter 4

Isabel cast the line as far as she could hoping she was reaching a deep part of the water. If her father was around he'd have taught her how to catch fish; he was bound to have acquired the knowledge and added it to his many accomplishments. Part of his problems, she thought now in a brief interlude of forgiveness, was being too clever; an expert - self-denoted, perhaps - at too great a variety of skills. Another person would be successful, wealthy - and honest, she hoped – with all his talents. Was there something congenitally wrong with that side of the family? she asked herself with a shiver, her thoughts turning again to the problem of Granma Lil, as she had called her when a small child. She hoped not, because, despite the years forever trotting on and her apparent bad luck with men, Isabel hoped one day to hear the patter of little feet in her daily life. Not just yet, she hastened to tell herself; she had far too much she wanted to achieve before dealing with wet nappies and sleepless nights. Just the thought of setting up home on a permanent business with *anyone* made her feel weak with panic just at the moment. Maybe she wasn't cut out for motherhood. Her own mother's life hadn't been exactly wonderful, had it? It was no wonder she upped and disappeared, possibly never to be seen again. That was unlikely, Isabel reassured herself. A more maternal person than her mother would be hard to find. Except for the very un-maternal way she had vanished. Isabel was still a little bemused at the fact that her mother had seemed less than thrilled when between them she and Silas had discovered where she had gone, taking the family yacht with her. And it wasn't long before she disappeared again.

Isabel watched the string with its moribund worm as it lay at an angle to the gentle current. Further out the water was deeper and faster but for the moment she was content to sit on the bank of her own little river, trying to catch her own little fish, at the end of her own not-so-little garden. The sound of light aircraft buzzing around in the sky like mildly demented flies comforted her; reminded her of the pleasure she'd once had doing just that herself. When she got settled - a euphemism for having an income - she might even take it up again. How blissful to be floating around in a little tin box following road and railways like lines of a mobile map, at peace away from all stresses of life down on land.

The still, dry air allowed the sun to cast uninterrupted shards of white light on the moving water, the hum of insects sang soprano to the baritones of the heavier aircraft as they took off from the nearby military base. She hadn't chosen the place because it was near both a large airfield which might offer something in the line of amusing social life and the small one where she might meet like-minded people. But it was nice to still feel part of that world, even if only from a distance. Maybe she would pay it a visit soon...just to have a look around...strange how the song of the little river seemed to be echoing the hum of the small airplane...almost as though it was trying to tell her something...and the river was widening, now split in two by a large island on which was the house of her dreams...long, low, luxurious...all her own with room for friends...a distant mountain...sheltered, small pools in the rock-filled river just right for floating away all the ills of life...a drawbridge kept up until she wanted it down...no trespassers were allowed....

Isabel awoke with a start. What was that noise? It had nothing to do with her, she hoped, but it was definitely too close for comfort. The muffled sound of a car door being closed came from the lane. Stealthy footsteps followed making a shiver run across her sleep-numbed brain. She sat up with a start letting the line slip through unheeding fingers. There was only one person in her acquaintance who had perfected that sly way of moving. But it couldn't be, she told herself, now wide awake, her ears listening while her mind churned. He didn't know where she lived. She'd made sure of that. There were all sorts of means he could put at his disposal to find her, of course, but he'd made it quite clear that she wasn't to be the only woman in his life. And what would he be doing in the area? Unless it meant more money in his hands. He wouldn't be coming to see her for old times' sake, she was quite sure.

The tap of leather soles on the rough flags of the footpath grew louder. She would have to go and see who her visitor was. The open door to the kitchen would have given the game away that she was at home. At least it wasn't that awful Thom. He would have made his presence felt in a way which would have been loud and demanding and not think it necessary to use the almost furtive manner of her current visitor.

Isabel pushed herself upright, the scent of the grass flattened by her weight following her as she stood. Unwilling to hurry towards an unwanted meeting she strolled up the grassy path towards the cottage. She glanced at her fruit cage as she went by. All was well, there. She glanced over at the small orchard on her right. Yes, everything was fine there, too. At last, she took her courage by the scruff of its neck and gave it a good shake. She could delay no longer; she had to face what she already knew was waiting for her at the door of her kitchen.

A dark suit, even on a day like this, thought Isabel. All too familiar were the shoes, as smart as ever, the thin mouth trying, unsuccessfully, to bend itself into a simulacrum of a smile and hair which no breeze would dare to ruffle. The only concession to the heat was the tie, which had apparently been whipped from a hot neck and stuffed into the top pocket of the suit jacket. As debonair as ever, Isabel sighed. She had thought she'd seen the last of him; wanted to be away from that heart-ache forever more. It had taken all the courage she could muster to break away from the relationship and she didn't want her resolve to be tested so soon.

Paul stood gazing at her for a few moments, obviously waiting for her to speak first. Then they both spoke at once.

'What on earth are you doing....?' Isabel began.

'Pleased to see me?' Paul asked.

Isabel shrugged, her past training telling her to be cool-headed, that she could cope with any emergency without fuss or fear; that she didn't need to show what she was feeling. A sudden lack of emotion surprised her. What had she seen in him? Was it just the enthusiastic sexuality that he was exuding even now that she had found so attractive? Had she had been too grateful that anyone, just anyone, had wanted her? Whatever it was, or had been, it was no longer there.

'I had to be in the area on business,' Paul was saying, her lack of warm, gushing welcome seeming to have flooded past his attention. 'A new contract, you know. Big one, this time.'

Whenever had it been anything else but a 'big contract'? Isabel asked herself. And the next one had always been bigger and better than the one that had gone before. With a sudden flash of insight she recognised some of the same traits in Paul as she could now, after so many years of blind worship, see in her father. She just hoped he would never go down the same road as her parent. It had been a pity about the marina, she conceded. Paul's firm might have done a good job there. She didn't blame herself for his losing the contract. When she'd mentioned it to Silas it was already a *fait accompli*, she discovered later. The company Silas worked for had already been awarded the contract and not Paul's firm. In any case, Paul's company had no experience in building a multi-million pound marina, 'affordable housing' for local councils was more his mark.

Having got that clear in her own mind, Isabel felt a little more disposed to being friendly with her ex-boss and - very - ex-lover. She would have to be careful, though.

'You'd better come in,' she said, walking past him into the kitchen. Once she would have worried what her present visitor might think about her home. Paul had been very good at finding things to criticise, wounding her with cutting remarks that would fester for days. He'd done it to keep control over her, she realized with a jolt, and she had been silly enough to be intimidated by it. But not now, oh no, that sort of thing had been thrown out with the detritus of her past in countless boxes and black bags when she moved from her previous artificial life-style. Anything for a peaceful life, she realized now, had been a pretty a silly maxim to live by.

'How's Meredith?' she asked. She hadn't meant to sound sarcastic but there were certain feelings that weren't under her control, even now. She pointed to the second of the kitchen chairs, indicating he could sit down if he wished.

Paul's expression changed from one of satisfaction at finding her to one of deep, indescribable thespian hurt and sadness. If she didn't know him so well she would have thought he was about to burst into tears. She hadn't appreciated what a consummate actor he was.

'That's why I came to see you.' Paul spoke slowly, his words etched with pathos. 'Meredith and I have broken up.' After a pause he added, 'Because of you, of course.'

Isabel sank down onto the chair on the opposite, disregarding the bundles of dry washing draped across it back, and the bag of clothes pegs crunching beneath her as she sat. 'What did you just say?'

'She's understood at last just how much you mean to me.'

Isabel wanted to shout 'rubbish!', but the old training of not arguing with him on the subject of his wife came back to haunt her. 'Huh!' was all she could find in a vocabulary severely limited by the shock which was setting in.

'And you do.' He reached for her hand across the piles of folded sheets and towels which covered the surface of the large table. 'Can we try again?' he asked.

The false wheedling tone disgusted Isabel so much that she was ready to show him the door. She opened her mouth to tell him just what she thought about his behaviour - past and present - before insisting that he go away and lose himself, but he was speaking before her lips could form the words.

'We were so good together, and,' he added, as if this would convince her, 'you were fantastic at your job.'

Isabel knew his words were not sincere. She had been good at her job and knew she was responsible for a great part of any success the company had had but he never admitted it. She had worked hard to help him make Seymour Construction into a damned good company. But she was thankful now that Meredith - once called Charlene, Isabel reminded herself - had discovered about their relationship outside work. His wife was, Paul had said, going to take him for all he had if he didn't drop Isabel and remain the good, family man he had been before she, Isabel, had moved - that woman's words still hurt - into his life.

'Hannah has been,' he paused, briefly, 'rather, um, upset, by all that has gone on.'

The shock of his words made Isabel forget about her intention to get him out of her house as quickly as possible. He was insinuating she was somehow to blame for the behaviour of his difficult, teenage daughter. Isabel had seen her a couple of times, wandering around the open-plan offices as if looking for some mild mischief to get up to. She wasn't bad, Isabel had decided. Just bored. Maybe she'd been on her best behaviour at the time. Best behaviour, however, that didn't stop the teenager from filching a cigarette from the desk of an absent staff member and smoking it in, her, Isabel's, smoke-free office.

'She liked you,' Paul told her, a small, pleading smile playing around the corners of his thin-lipped mouth. 'Was a bit disappointed when Charl...Meredith made all that fuss. 'Lives with me now, of course.'

Isabel wondered about the 'of course' but diplomacy won the day so she didn't ask. She did wonder why they were talking about Paul's daughter, however. Was it some sort of convoluted message he was trying to pass across to her? Like daughter, like father, for example? She was beginning to think she had lost the drift of the conversation.

'You could give up all this,' Paul was waving a hand around the kitchen, seemingly indicating he knew how pleased she would be to leave behind the large old-fashioned deep sink, the even older range, the rough wooden furniture, the stone-flag floor. Even in her eyes things changed from romantic to basic as he spoke. But, then, he wasn't hearing the creeper tapping its gentle tune against the open window, the scents of summer, the hum of bees in the flowers of the plants and the distant, refreshing sound of flowing water.

'I don't want to 'give it all up,' she told him, surprised that her voice sounded so firm. She found that standing up to him, contradicting his pronouncements, was strengthening her self-esteem. His tone of voice inferred that she was 'slumming it' because she couldn't afford anything better and that had stung.

'Come on,' he said. 'You're used to better than this.' He paused. 'It won't always be summer, you know.'

'Maybe not, but I'll cope with that when it arrives.'

'And I do need you,' he continued, ignoring her words while he patted her arm as the only part of her he could now reach. 'We had some good times together.'

He wasn't asking her to agree, Isabel noticed, unclenching her hands from between two rigid knees, just stating what he considered was a fact.

Paul stood up, pushing the chair across the uneven floor with a rattle of its elderly legs. 'I'll tell you what,' he said, looking down at the top of her head, avoiding her eyes. 'I'll give you a bit of time to think things over. I know you'll see sense.' He drew himself up into his usual chairman stance. 'You'll have your old job back, of course.'

Was this what it was all about? He needed someone at his beck and call, who wouldn't argue, on whom he could depend for loyalty - whose skills and experience he could milk to his own advantage.

'And,' he added as if this clinched the matter, 'We'll be back to what we were before. A jolly good partnership.' He looked straight at her this time. 'At work and at play!'

Isabel made no comment. It was obvious that he expected none.

'Think it over. I've got to get back now. Report to write and all that. I'll see you shortly.'

He was now, it seemed, in a great hurry to get away, but Isabel was not overly concerned. He had always been keen to state his case and then depart before anyone had the chance to demolish it. Also Silas was due shortly. For him, she would tidy up, make the little cottage welcoming. Her heart dropped as she remembered the reason for his visit.

Isabel didn't rush to follow Paul to his car. He was in it and had the engine running before she reached the little gate that was swinging closed behind him. A brief wave as he reversed into the turning space that usage had created over the years, and then he and his large car were off down the track.

Life, thought Isabel using one of her mother's favourite misquotes, was either fruit or famine. Fruit, however, had the tendency when unripe to be indigestible. To be honest, she thought she really preferred famine.

Chapter 5

'What kept you?' Isabel hadn't meant to sound so serious. She made herself smile before kissing her brother on the cheek.

'Some of us have to work for a living!' Silas was looking around at the mass of greenery amongst which peeked jewels of magenta and scarlet. 'Apparently that means you, too,' he joked. 'I know you said it was an 'established' smallholding, but I didn't expect it to be quite so luxuriant.'

Isabel liked the word; she could do with hearing many more of the same. A warm bath of praise was just what she needed after experiencing so many moments that weren't exactly full of kindness.

Silas hadn't seen the inside of her new home. She'd dragged him down to view the exterior as soon as she'd got the estate agent's details, but they didn't go any closer than looking over the front hedge. She wasn't going to commit herself until she had had a good long think about what it would all mean. Now his reaction was of the utmost importance to her. She needed his moral support in this great change in her life.

'Give me the guided tour, then,' her younger brother ordered.

Isabel led the way through the open kitchen door and into the tidied kitchen. Whatever she had felt when Paul was there, with his demanding presence and unspoken criticisms, it hadn't spoiled the small pleasures she did manage to indulge in occasionally. Like breathing in the childhood-invoking scent from the sun-dried linen lying on the table. She pushed it into a neat pile onto the old dresser as Silas followed her into the kitchen. Turning at a short shout from her brother she remembered she had forgotten to tell him to duck as he came through the door. She had almost forgotten how tall he was. Height hadn't been of great relevance in their old life of large offices and vast open acres of constructions sites. She wasn't short, herself, but in the tiny cottage he seemed to tower over her. How he'd ever managed on the boat while staying with their mother all those months, she couldn't imagine. What a long time ago that felt now. She felt a cool shiver of shock when she reminded herself it was only a year since they'd found their mother and the boat. Before she disappeared again, of course, their parent having proved that she was quite capable of looking after herself.

'What are you dreaming about?' Silas asked with a grin. He was standing looking down at her across the kitchen table, rubbing his forehead where it had hit the old lintel. 'As if I didn't know!'

'Sorry.' Isabel brought herself back up with a jolt. She had been on her own a great deal but should have taken more care not to descend into the self-absorbed life of the loner. She let her thoughts rest momentarily on their current problem - and the reason for Silas's visit - their eighty year old and ailing grandmother, Lilian Vine.

'Before we start any discussions,' she told her brother, 'I'll take you on that tour! It won't take long,' she laughed without amusement.

'OK. Fine with me.' Silas ran his hand across the scrubbed top of the old table. He looked as if he liked what he was touching which pleased Isabel.

Isabel remembered to warn him to watch his head. But he hadn't forgotten about height restrictions and crept up the narrow staircase with an arched back.

'What's that room?' he asked, nodding over a bent shoulder down towards the hall. 'Sitting room? Parlour, as they used to call it?'

'Office,' said Isabel tersely. She'd had such plans of using it to keep her books up-to-date. The computer had been the first thing she'd unpacked. One small problem, however. She had, so far, no books to keep. Her time, in any case, was totally absorbed by matters outdoors. She continued on up the stairs not wanting to see a look of surprise on her brother's face. It would become her office. One day. But for the moment she didn't want to hear any comment about 'what goes on in your 'office'?' or some such joke.

'You're going to run this thing as a proper business, then?' Silas surprised her by saying.

'Of course.' She would tell him all her plans later. For the moment, however, she just wanted to indulge in the enjoyment of showing him her home.

'Here's your room,' she told him, pushing open the creaking door of the room to the right of the stairs. She'd been using it herself, but thought she could bear the big old bed in the larger back room for a night or two. She felt cheered when she remembered that it would soon be gone to the amenity centre for recycling and she could go out and indulge herself in the purchase of something comfortable and single, she added, reminding herself of her good intentions for the future.

She watched as Silas prodded the mattress on the small bed. 'Don't worry, the mattress is new,' she told him with a smile. 'Or almost!' 'Not like this one,' Silas teased, as they turned into what was, for now, her bedroom. 'Those feet alone must weigh a ton.'

Silas wasn't demonstrating any surprise or disapproval at anything she showed him. Isabel realized with a warm rush of affection that her younger brother had made up his mind to accept her new life-style and was keeping his opinions to himself. The memories of his own unexpected upsets - instigated, she accepted now, by their father - would prevent him from belittling her efforts at trying to get her own life onto an even keel.

Back on the landing Silas appeared to be looking for a third or even fourth door. He gave a good impression of being totally puzzled.

'Don't be silly,' Isabel pre-empted his question. 'It's downstairs, off the kitchen.' She paused. 'You'll have the surprise of your life when you see it!'

'Yes, you're right. I am very, very surprised,' Silas admitted when he saw her bathroom.

'My one luxury,' Isabel told him as he stood in silence, his mouth ajar. The avocado corner bath with its button for a jacuzzi, the golden taps and shower head took up half the space of the small room which had once, Isabel informed him, been a back kitchen. 'A soubriquet for 'junk room with toilet,' she laughed. She told him how, within a couple of weeks, she'd transformed it, 'with the help of the builder's merchants in the nearby town, of course!' into the little ceramic palace it now was. The wash basin, toilet and a bidet - Silas didn't seem to be surprised that she'd brought some of her sophisticated ideas with her from the city - and floor to ceiling tiles were all in harmonizing colours, the floor itself a luxury of waterproof carpet tiles in a deep burnished bronze.

'Phew!' was his only added comment.

'I had to have some comfort.' Isabel was aware that her tone was becoming defensive. In the short time that it had been installed she had managed to take just one bath.

'I like it,' he said. 'A lot!'

'Drinks,' Isabel told him. She wasn't sure whether he was teasing her or not. She shut the door on her Aladdin's cave and turned back into the kitchen. 'On the terrace. Take those out for me, will you?' she asked, pointing to the two old cane-seated chairs by the table. 'While I get some glasses.' She didn't want her brother to see that her cupboard store held only two. He might begin to think that her extravagance over the bathroom should have waited.

'No need,' Silas told her. 'Be back in a minute.' He disappeared through the door and clattered down the path. He was back in moments, two dark green garden chairs resting on the top of his head like some giant cartoon character's helmet. In one hand was a large cardboard box labelled '*Home Barbecue*' and in the other a couple of supermarket carrier bags clanking with the sound of bottles.

'Couldn't think of anything else for a house-warming present,' he told her. 'Not at this time of year.' He didn't add, but Isabel could hear the unspoken words, 'and you weren't likely to have anything as countrified as a barbecue set'. 'And I bought this to cook,' he added proudly.

Isabel, despite lacking knowledge of country living, wasn't sure that a pizza was exactly the right thing for a barbecue, but said nothing.

It worked, however; even if it was a bit burnt on the bottom.

They demolished the pizza and garlic bread and most of the first bottle of wine while covering all the problems Silas was having with the new contract.

'*Another* marina,' he'd said. 'Can't seem to get away from the things!'

'You shouldn't have done so well on the last one, then,' Isabel sniggered.

Silas took a sip from the dregs of wine in his glass and appeared to be considering his next words. 'You've got nice neighbours,' he said, then. He had a small smile lurking around his lips.

Isabel was surprised at the twist the conversation had suddenly taken. He must have met some interesting villager, she suspected. He was always on the look-out for eccentric beings. Probably because he considered himself one. It was quite possible he had asked someone the way as an excuse for stopping to talk.

'That chap on the farm next door,' Silas said.

Isabel sighed, realizing her mistake. 'He isn't,' she said abruptly.

'Isn't what?' Silas asked in a slightly bemused tone.

'Nice.'

'Well, he seemed so to me when I stopped to ask the way. His lad called him to the door when I was asking how to find you. I'd forgotten that your track was tricky to find.'

The look of disappointment on her brother's face puzzled Isabel slightly. Did he know him from elsewhere? That was unlikely. 'He's a know-it-all, patronizing....' She sighed. Why was she getting so heated? He was nothing to her and had no authority over what she did with her own land. 'Thinks he's the only person who knows how to grow things,' she ended lamely.

'Oh ho,' Silas grinned. 'Trouble in't mill, eh?'

'He doesn't want anyone else to make a go of growing natural,' she emphasised the word, 'food. Thinks he's the only one who has the knowledge. I've read enough about it, for goodness sake. And I tell you this,' she wagged a finger up and down towards Silas, 'I know that my fruit and veg will match anything he can grow. And they'll be organic, too. Once I'm organized.'

'Organically organized?' Silas quipped and wished he hadn't.

'Don't you laugh,' Isabel snapped. 'I've got customers already.' She didn't bother to say that her enormous outlet numbered exactly two at the moment, and they were one married couple.

'Feel better?' Silas asked her with a grin. 'Got it all off your chest?'

Isabel shook her head as if in exasperation. 'I can't expect you to understand.' But she did feel better. Better enough to try, now, to face the major problem that had brought her brother to her side and which they had both been ignoring while they enjoyed themselves.

As if reading her thoughts Silas said, 'You told me on the phone you'd been in touch with the solicitors about Gran. What did they say?'

'That I should go up and look after her. What did you expect?'

'But you can't do that,' Silas told her.

'They said the hospital was letting her go home tomorrow. Couldn't keep her in; didn't have enough beds for the sick, let alone for someone who was perfectly well physically.'

'What are we going to do?' Silas asked.

'I thought *you* were going to tell *me* that,' Isabel retorted.

The sun was getting low in the sky spiking the darkening sky with fading shafts from its descending crescent. The crows had settled into their high-rise homes. Even the little river appeared to have decided it was time to rest, its voice now no more than a tired mumble, and the ash in the barbecue was murmuring its last moments before they had made any plan as to what they should do about their grandmother.

'I spoke to the nurse, too,' Isabel had told him at one point. 'She said she was quite capable of looking after herself. Many, much older people manage to do that.'

'But not with what she's got,' Silas said.

'No,' agreed Isabel. 'But it's only early stages, yet,' she added as if attempting to convince herself.

'Yes, but for how long?'

Isabel had wanted reassurance; she didn't feel she should be giving it. But, let's face it, she told herself, Granma Lil is nothing to do with him, is she? Not now; not since their mother had told them her secret. She, Isabel, would have to cope alone, it seemed.

'Listen,' said Silas, his voice that of a fatherly appeaser, 'we'll do something about it. You and me. When the time comes. For the moment let's just leave it. She's got a nice little home, there are neighbours near by and the health visitor will be dropping in most days. There is really nothing much more we can do. For the time being.'

Isabel felt ashamed of her earlier fears. Silas hadn't said but she now guessed that he, too, had been making a few phone calls. In her business days she had never been frightened of facing unpalatable situations; she'd made uncountable decisions without becoming emotionally involved. How strange it was when one of those situations was suddenly about close family?

'How I wish I hadn't accepted that money,' she declared.

'We've all done things which we've regretted later.' Silas spoke the truism as if it was from the top drawer of his own philosophies, but it comforted her nevertheless.

With a start Isabel realized that he wasn't using a cliché at all. He was remembering his own rather sordid experiences when he'd got mixed up with that smuggling. Having been put up to it by his 'father' had made it hurt even more. He rarely spoke about it these days; not since he had climbed several rungs up the ladder of success. She was flattered that he trusted her enough to speak about it now. Having learnt about his parentage had probably helped.

'Come on, Izzy,' he said. 'You looked exhausted. And I want to test that lovely bed!'

Isabel smiled. If only he knew what she had given up for him.

He was right, she was exhausted. But once in the old lumpy bed, sleep was reluctant to come. When she did manage to doze she had the most awful dream. A nightmare, she told herself the next morning. All she could remember, before it faded away in the manner of most interesting dreams, was that it included a horrifying picture of her father, Ken, strung up on the cross trees of a magnificent - but stolen - yacht, hanging lifeless and white above a deck where her mother, Maggie, was wandering around in a bikini, her body that of a teenager, her face that of a raddled, but happily smiling, old woman.

Chapter 6

Isabel was awakened by a strident ringing reverberating against the wall of the small hall. At first she'd thought it was her alarm telling her it was time to leave for work. The round face of the small clock on the floor beside the bed saying it was only 5.15 in the morning helped her to orientate herself. Her nerves were beginning to become like taut lines again after two days without her brother's soothing presence.

She ran down the stairs, her bare feet rubbing on the wood of the uncarpeted treads. Who on earth would be telephoning at this hour? Her heart felt like a ball of unleavened dough as she listed the two or three people it could possibly be.

'You took your time answering.' The voice at the end of the line filled her with foreboding.

'Hello, Gran,' she said as her heart settled in her stomach. She wouldn't say anything about the time, she decided. Having tried it once and had the old woman bursting into tears saying she was all alone, had no friends, couldn't even ring her granddaughter without being told off, et cetera, had left Isabel feeling so guilty that she didn't want to go through all that again.

'Hello yourself.' Even from this distance the self-pity was evident. 'I thought you were coming up to see me.'

'I did, Gran.' Isabel lied. 'And you weren't home.' She kept her fingers crossed that the old woman wouldn't ask her exactly when she had come up.

'Wasn't home?' the elderly voice almost cracked on the words. 'I'm always home.'

Isabel felt the dread of an argument with her grandmother oozing over her. It was strange that when the occasion demanded that the old woman be fuddled-headed, her thought processes appeared to be as clear as the proverbial bell. Isabel wished she hadn't lied now, but there was no going back. All she could do was to try and deflect her gran's thoughts. In this she was doomed not to succeed.

'I want you here. Now,' the old woman demanded before Isabel was able to say anything. 'I can't manage on my own. The place is beginning to smell,' she added in a voice that was suddenly plaintive and beseeching.

Isabel felt the tide was against her. If she wasn't careful she'd lose control, lose everything that was important to her - mostly her freedom. The clamour of the chorus in her mind telling her at one moment she was being very selfish and the next telling her she had a right to do as she wanted was becoming as painful as the anticipation of loss that was already threatening to drown her.

'Gran, I can't just up sticks and leave everything just like that,' she managed to say in a tone which was far calmer than she felt.

'You're a selfish girl, you know.' The voice had lost its pleading quality and was more like an elderly parent talking to a naughty child. 'It was all very well when you needed my help. Now that I want some little repayment you can't be bothered to give it.'

Isabel remembered only too well what she'd felt like shortly after she had accepted what she had thought was a very generous offer from her paternal grandmother. She had been scared, so scared when a friend had told her of a conversation she'd overheard between her mother and Isabel's grandmother who happened to be friends.

'She expects you to care for her when she's old,' Sally had said. 'She told my mum that just the other day. It's the reason she's willing to lend you the money. She doesn't expect you to go off and get a good job once you've qualified. Thinks you'll be able to find work you can do at home while you look after her.'

Isabel had felt trapped; had wondered how she hadn't seen for herself all the strings that had attached themselves to her grandmother's apparent generosity. It was too late now. Unknown to Sally she had already accepted the money and paid her university fees in advance. Four years later she'd thought it was all over, that the chains had been loosened and she was free when she had sent the final cheque of repayment. She had scrimped and saved, allowed herself no luxuries in order to reach this peak of achievement and had relaxed for the first time in years. Now here it was all back again, that horrible feeling of being pulled in like a terrified salmon at the end of a line.

This was getting morbid, Isabel told herself as she listened to a list of her faults, of her mother's faults and even her brother's faults. It made no difference to her father's mother that Silas was no longer anything to do with her.

Remembering the training she'd received on one of her past countless management seminars, Isabel took a long, deep breath before saying anything.

'All right, Gran,' she said in a placatory tone when her grandmother paused for breath. 'I'll see what I can do.'

'Well, just make it soon. Nobody cares about me. Even that son of mine seems to have disappeared....'

Isabel let the voice drone on until it lost momentum. 'Yes, Gran,' was all she managed to say before the receiver was replaced at the other end cutting off any argument.

She could easily have wasted the rest of the day drowned in self-pity, horror, even, at what was being expected of her. She was thirty two, for goodness sake. Surely she had a right to do what she wanted with her life without forever being lashed with guilt. A nightmarish vision of being buried alive in some deep and airless cave arose before her. She couldn't give up this place and go and look after her grandmother. She tried to quell the frightening thought that someone with her grandmother's complaint could go on for years progressively getting worse. She admired people who stood by their ailing husbands or wives but it had never occurred to her that she might, one day, be in the same position. She had her whole life ahead of her. Surely she couldn't be expected to give up everything for the sake of an old woman who, now she dared to admit it, she'd never liked very much.

She wasn't going to do anything in a hurry. Hadn't the nurse said that her gran was quite capable of looking after herself for some time? She had good neighbours, a regular health visitor, so there was no need to worry. Yet.

She'd have another chat with Silas. See what he had to say. Her poor brother was probably irked beyond endurance with the problem of the old woman, but she needed to hear his friendly voice. Not for the first time she asked herself who was the older of the two. She'd have to be careful not to start looking upon him as a sort of father figure! The idea made her smile. Mature he might be but she was still his older sister. And he was on his own now that the strange girlfriend had returned home after her year in an English university. He'd never said anything but Isabel felt he'd been more hurt than he let on when she went off with that art teacher from the school on the hill above the marina. He'd forgiven her, of course, when she came rushing back, gushing with apologies, But Isabel had sensed his feeling of relief when she'd finished her year and returned to Holland.

44

Isabel picked up the phone once more. There was no dialling tone. 'Gran,' she shouted into the black bakelite mouthpiece. 'Gran! You've left the receiver off.' If this was some game to indicate just how badly she needed someone to look after her Isabel refused to play it. There was no reply, of course. The old woman was probably peacefully unaware as she sat glued to the television.

Isabel clicked her tongue in irritation. She would have to go down to the box in the village.

But Silas wasn't at home. The long ringing bell confirmed that. It was, after all, a working day. How quickly she had sloughed off the rules and habits of what felt like a lifetime in a busy office. She was pleased to be away from the false standards of having to drink in the bar of the moment, eat in that magazine-hyped restaurant or end the day partying in the home of the person who just happened to be flavour of the month.

Isabel tried Silas's mobile imagining him up to his rubber-booted knees in a field of mud. Unlikely, of course, during a time of drought. It made a nice picture, however. As did the vision of the successful new development for the particular yachtsmen that that muddy field was destined to become. She got his answering service. It was silly to feel so let down; he had every right to be... wherever he was. She couldn't do any more, she told herself as she finished a brief message to get him to ring her. If she kept rushing around every time the old girl demanded attention she'd have no fruit and veg to sell, and no money to put petrol in the car.

She had just passed the old mill where her only - for the moment! she promised herself silently - customers lived and was crossing the bridge which spanned the same small river that ran along the bottom of her garden. Her gaze was fixed on the water to catch sight of any fishy movement so she didn't notice the man crossing the bridge from the other side and almost collided with him. To her it was an unwelcome encounter with her new neighbour. A fleeting glance at his expression told her that this was not going to be a pleasant, friendly meeting.

'Your visitor find you on Saturday?' He wasn't one to bother with the minor courtesies of life, apparently.

'Yes, thank you.' Isabel made as if to walk on.

'Good.' He turned towards the village. Speaking over his shoulder, his gaze well above her head as if he were reluctant to acknowledge her existence, he said, 'The boys are having a barbecue tonight. You can come, if you want.' Without waiting for an answer he continued on his way.

Isabel almost, but not quite, wanted to laugh at the friendly way in which the invitation had been proffered. Her anger at his lack of any sort of basic manners soon squashed the desire to express amusement, however. She was fed up with everyone taking for granted that she had no mind of her own, no right to live her own life. She would go to the party. Just to show him. Show him what, she couldn't express even to herself. It might be amusing to meet his 'gang of prison fodder' as the previous owner of her cottage had called them. She'd heard their shrill voices as they played their games in her neighbour's fields but, as yet, they'd left her in peace. She would go to the party; show them that she wasn't to be tampered with. It would be a chance to lay down her own personal laws.

'Thank you,' she called to the retreating back. 'Love to.' The back strode on with only a flashing glimpse of a face looking back at her which showed neither astonishment nor pleasure, which made her even crosser.

Isabel was through her gate, down the rough, paved path and into her kitchen before the anger abated. For several moments her brain was jammed with thoughts she would never have put into words, her mind sizzling with all the things she wished she had thought to say. Saying them to the empty air would have done no good, she realized, but just thinking them made her feel better. And she would go to the barbecue. If only to be with other people for a while - and, possibly, enjoy herself. Whether he really wanted her there or not was his problem, not hers.

Isabel guessed that a barbecue would start at about six and was pleased to see that she had arrived at the right moment. One of the boys - Aiden, she discovered later - had romped across a large flat lawn and leapt to her assistance in opening the tall side gate which led from the well-gravelled driveway in front of the large farmhouse to the back garden.

The 'prison fodder' she discovered within minutes of arriving seemed to consist of a dozen or so happy boys of varying ages. They seemed to be in some sort of uniform of dusty jeans and tee shirts, most of which had lost their sleeves. One or two had rings in various odd places, but apart from that they resembled just another group of youngsters who had the wish but not the courage to act as thugs. She gathered later that Thom ran an American-style summer camp for youngsters who were not yet young offenders but who might be on the verge of choosing a life of petty crime to keep up with all those other young people who somehow managed to have all those things they saw advertised on TV. This had made her slightly doubtful about being in their company, but still she felt ashamed of herself as she automatically patted the pockets of her cotton slacks to make sure the contents were still safely there.

Having seen her parked safely in a wooden garden chair, as if she was an elderly maiden aunt who preferred to be outside the circle of activity, Aiden escaped to join his mates. Another lad came up to her, he was about fourteen, she thought, and introduced himself as Dan in a voice which could only have been the result of a very expensive education. 'Thom says I'm to look after you,' he said politely, only just succeeding in hiding the reluctance in his voice. He put one - grubby - hand under her elbow and helped her up out of the chair as if she were his grandmother. He edged her towards the group standing around a table a short distance from a large metal drum with an iron grid across its top. Flames leapt from this as though it was bent on incinerating itself as well as any person who chanced to be in the vicinity.

'He'll be out in a minute,' Dan told her as they reached the table. Having completed his duties he turned and left her.

Isabel was pleased to see that here, at least, were people she might be able to have a decent conversation with. Amongst them were Bob and Marion Hart. Little did they know it but they were helping to keep a very hungry wolf from her starving door.

As barbecue parties went it wasn't very unlike all those that her father had hosted when she and Silas were in their teens. At that time they'd had an aura of unusualness about them; a bit American but enjoyable - as they enjoyed the copious cups of mulled wine, crispy spare ribs, sausages and exotic vegetables on skewers which had sat in a dish of alcoholic sauce for most of the day. Her father, Isabel knew, although he never showed it, was relieved that the people he'd invited had actually turned up. Sucked in by his charm they felt privileged to be at the party. 'Little do they know that he is far more interested in their money than in giving them a good time,' Isabel had heard her mother say to her own mother after one extravagant 'do'. Her quiet comment had contained as much acid as the rich, lemon - store-bought - deserts he served.

Thom's guests were gradually dispersing before Isabel's host managed to find time for more than a casual word or two with her. He would introduce her to someone whose name she soon forgot and then depart.

'I'll show you around,' he told her having satisfied himself that all his guests were happy and well-catered for. Not waiting for a reply he marched towards a wide farm gate at the far end of the large garden. 'Take a look ,' he said, as if this was his sole reason for inviting her to his party. He was leaning on the top bar of the wooden gate pointing to a flat expanse of a field so large it seemed to be disappearing into the distance.

Isabel looked. All she could see was a flat expanse of yellow. Looking more closely she could just ascertain the remains of stalks from harvested grain or cut hay.

'Now look over there.' Thom was pointing towards her own fence many acres away to the right.

Isabel could see that it needed repairing in places but apart from that the fence was of negligible interest. Beyond it her fruit trees held up their heads in the windless air and beyond those was just discernible the green mesh of the fruit cage with tiny jewels of colour occasionally visible. She felt proud at how neat it all looked. Apart from the fence, that was. She was waiting for him to say something congratulatory when he opened his mouth to speak.

'Now you can see why I'm so worried about your cack-handed attempt at so-called organic gardening.'

For a moment Isabel thought he was joking. Then a tiny icicle of fear began to lodge in her brain. He was serious, it seemed.

'A famous writer, a prophet as regards how we treat our earth said: There is an inescapable kinship between farming and art, for farming depends as much on character, devotion, imagination and the sense of structure, as on knowledge. It is a practical art.' He paused. 'In other words we have to be careful not to carry on destroying our world as we are doing now. Do you think our children's children and their children are going to thank us for sterilising our earth, destroying our natural food, our wild life? They might not know it now but this earth will be made up of electrical waves, houses sealed against their poison, children never seeing the outside of their 'homes', learning from moving pictures on a screen and recorded voices. What will have happened to happy childhood then? To friendship? Love of a pet? No animals will be able to exist in that sterile world.'

Isabel stood in silence. Breathing seemed to be difficult suddenly. What was he accusing her of? She knew from all the books, pamphlets and videos she had perused before deciding on this foray into country living that responsibility had to be taken if their world was not to shrivel up and die. It had frightened her at first. Then she'd stopped reading all the fanatical writings and had concentrated on the more practical volumes given over to husbandry. She found her breath eventually, lurking at the base of her lungs but she did not waste it in answering his diatribe. And there was no need to try, it appeared.

'Not only am I trying to make a living,' Thom was saying, 'I am also trying to make that living by abiding by the rules of nature.'

He'd got onto some sort of hobby horse, Isabel decided, relieved to see that she was not, after all, the perpetrator of some horrendous crime for which he was going to run her out of town.

'What good is it for me to try and teach them,' he waved one large hand in the direction of a group of boys still standing around the barbecue, some with cans of pop in their hands, others picking at the remains of food still stuck on the bars of the grid, 'that nature has to be nurtured, looked after before their own lives can improve, when you come and with your urban attitude to the countryside threaten to spoil it all?

'Spoil it....?' Isabel was shocked at the cruelty of the words. 'What am I doing to 'spoil it all'?' Her words sounded like some faltering old car hard-pressed to reach its destination. 'I've taken on a smallholding where everything for years has been grown *naturally* and you think I'm not keen to keep it that way?'

'"Naturally' is not always the same as 'organically,"' Thom told her coldly. 'I've spent years clearing up this place, and there's nobody for miles around who now grows anything that might affect my plants. I aim to keep it that way.'

'But...' Isabel was ashamed to hear herself become defensive so closed her mouth firmly. However she could not resist saying, with a sudden surge of pride. 'I think I know more about all this than you give me credit for.' She was not accustomed to being treated as the person in the dock; was used to being the accuser, not the accused. With sudden inspiration she misquoted slightly something she had read from one of the many books: 'We must take care of our earth as we live by what it can give us,' she said quickly, 'and as we come from the earth so one day will return to it."

'I know all about that,' Thom said with a small, chilly smile. 'And the quote is, to be accurate, 'our bodies live by farming, we come from the earth and return to it." With that he turned and making his way towards the group of youths by the barbecue strode across the large green lawn, Isabel thought with acid humour, except where the big dog currently pleading for titbits from the barbecue, had unknowingly or knowingly spent many happy hours bleaching it with moon-like blotches.

Isabel felt rather like a school child must who was being reprimanded for a crime she hadn't committed, who was a victim of bullying. She stood for a few seconds looking across the golden field to her own refuge while she waited for the vestiges of her anger at the injustice to dissipate, then turned and made her way towards the group. She was not going to add lack of manners to his mental list of her offences. She would say polite good-byes even if she had to grit her teeth in order to do it.

A well-known tune was filtering into the evening air from a distant open window as she reached the barbecue area. Haydn, she thought. The sound comforted her with its memories of university music groups, concerts her mother had taken her to and early days of discovery that she could make therapeutic music for herself on the family piano. The effect of the trumpet sailing effortlessly into its higher registers, the orchestral backing adding the richness of a large group of instruments carefully and lovingly played took the tension out of her shoulders. She took a deep breath. She could cope, she promised herself, with any bad-tempered neighbour. She would ignore him, and succeed, despite his apparent wish for the opposite.

He replied to her farewell with a grunt followed by some garbled words that she was unable to hear. She was damned if she was going to ask him to repeat himself.

It wasn't until she had reached the sanctuary of her little, untidy cottage that the words repeated themselves in her mind, and clearly this time. 'At least you've done some of the right reading,' he had muttered. 'There might be some hope for you, after all.' She didn't know whether to be miffed by his words or flaming angry at yet another example of his chauvinism.

As Isabel crawled into her single, narrow bed that night, she reminded herself that she had decided not to take any notice of her next door neighbour, his non-GM farming or his pack of juvenile delinquents. As long as their actions didn't affect her, that was.

A package had already been left in the old mailbox. It had been delivered by hand, apparently very early, as she had not yet heard Kate and her van arrive or depart. Across the crumpled, brown paper bag used for wrapping were scribbled in large black letters 'THE BIBLE OF THE ORGANIC FARMER'. There was no further message. Inside was a dark brown paperback. It was apparent that he had not given her up for a lost cause, after all, she thought as she opened the cover of the book and saw the name pencilled at the top of the fly-leaf.

The book was one that Isabel had heard about, by an American guru of GM-free farming. The same writer she had quoted - misquoted intentionally, she reminded herself - the day before. She had thought the way she had paraphrased the idea was much more poetic than the original. But, then, her neighbour was obviously not very artistic, would not have appreciated it. The idea of reading the book gave her a tremor of pleasure. She would give it back to him once she had read it but keep it pristine so that he would think she'd not even bothered to open it.

How childish she was becoming, Isabel told herself, with a repressed giggle, carrying the book and laying it down carefully in the centre of the large scrubbed table where her meagre breakfast of crispbread and coffee waited. But the thought made it seem that life had just gained a small touch of much-needed sparkle - a sparkle, whose shine was soon to become tarnished.

Chapter 7

The wheels of the little wagon squealed each time she moved forward to pluck weeds from the earth beneath the heavily laden fruit bushes. Her fingers were working like tiny robots while her mind dwelt on yesterday's barbecue party and the sickening feeling that perhaps she'd given quite the wrong impression to her neighbour. Not that it mattered, she kept reminding herself, but nobody liked to be thought a fool. Paul, even in his worse moments, never dared to shout at her like Thom had. Perhaps 'shout' was too strong a word but she remembered reading somewhere that 'a scream could be hidden in a whisper' or some such thing.

A particularly vociferous complaint from the cane wagon brought Isabel's mind back to the present. She had been going to chuck it out after she'd unearthed it from the outhouse which was now her bathroom but something told her it might be useful. Now she was quite fond of it; she would even buy it some oil on the next visit to town. That and the new rope she had tied to the metal 'U' of its handle would make it quite a piece of rural art; far more valuable - to her - than anything she'd seen in the garden centre. A great plastic and metal barn of a place where the only plants were mere reflections of those in her rural garden. They were growing - growing, that was a joke - amongst tools that were more decorative than useful, surrounded by garden furniture in wood that looked like it had never seen a forest.

She'd had no pressing need to visit such a place; curiosity had just got the better of her. All those television ads with that clever funny couple had made them seem essential places to visit. But she felt diminished now just having being in one. A bit like that man's quote about the link between the soil, the spirit and the body. She'd agreed with him but hadn't been going to admit it. His attitude was that of a teacher talking to a particularly dim kindergarten pupil, for her to do that.

A lot of what he said was good sense, she had to admit. Hadn't she read countless books on the subject? Granted not many of them had been on his particular subject but she'd always assumed that people like him were a bit fanatical - you listened to them, then immediately tried to forget what they had said. She wasn't going to let some big-headed so-called conservationist spoil her enjoyment. She was used to bullies; knew how to deal with them. Feed them the medicine which they found most repulsive - ignore them. They hated that, just as Paul had done.

Unintentionally she gave the wagon a tug, pulling it across a rut in the ground.

It promptly turned over onto its side spilling the carefully gathered weeds across the path. Isabel swore gently under her breath scrabbling around to scoop up the spiked greenery. It smelled just like childhood toothpaste, she noticed despite her irritation; that healthy green stuff her mother used to insist they used. She sniffed again. Mixed with the chlorophyll scent was another; a scent that didn't belong in her fruit cage - that of over-polished leather and laundered shirts, seasoned with expensive after-shave. It came from the other side of the green mesh of the wall of the fruit cage which was a few inches from her nose. Her eyes travelled slowly up from her lowly position; she was in no hurry for her sudden suspicions to be confirmed. She had a horrible feeling she knew what her eyes would find at the end of their oh-too-short journey. She hadn't lived for years – was it really that long? - with that urbane dress sense and over-use - she recognised now - of manly aroma not to recognise them. But what was he doing back here so soon? Hadn't she made herself clear?

When her glance reached his face and she saw the droop of his mouth and the sad crease around his eyes she almost felt sorry for him. Until she remembered what an actor he could be. On a Saturday he was usually out enjoying himself with his pals; going to the races, meeting the right people. He had even been known to take Hannah to the pictures on a weekend afternoon so that he had an excuse for not being with her. Talking to a cast-off girl-friend through the crochet of green plastic would not have been a chosen venue. Unless...

Isabel shrugged her shoulders and suppressing a sigh, brushed the caked earth from her bare knees and stood up. With a little tremor of pleasure she realized she no longer worried about the quips he might make about her appearance; he could say what he liked and she wouldn't care. But, not wanting him to think she might be offering him even a hint of an invitation, she did pull the tight tee-shirt down over her bare midriff.

Having hastened through the minor courtesies, with a few

insincere excuses for her appearance and the familiar act of simulated consideration from him, he told her why he was visiting. Isabel somehow found the inner strength not to recoil in horror when Paul told her why he had come to see her again so soon after their rather less than friendly previous meeting.

'It's Hannah,' he told her. 'She's still very upset over the break-up.'

Isabel recalled the occasions when she met the girl. She would never be a serious contender for the role of Miss Charming, she remembered thinking, but for a moment she was flattered. It didn't take her long to realize, however, that it wasn't her and her father's break-up the girl was upset over.

'I had this idea that she might be able to help you.' He waved his arm in an arc encompassing, it seemed to Isabel, the whole of her garden, the cottage, the river and, possibly, the nearby village as well.

Isabel was stunned into silence. What did she want with a teenage girl who was, it seemed, suffering from some psychological problems because her mother and father had decided to live separate lives? And where was she going to stay in order to do this 'helping'? Despite the warm air Isabel felt a chill run down her spine as she guessed the answer to that.

'She's a good girl,' Paul said with a look which was meant to be beseeching but was in truth just a grimace. 'Really. She needs to get away for a bit. Said she'd love to come and stay with you and learn all about...' he paused for a moment, looking around at the fruit bushes and beyond the green mesh to the lines of runner beans with their scarlet flowers, then at the trees behind him in a quick glance over his shoulder, '..growing things,' he finished lamely.

Isabel did not find out until much later that this was all a fabrication on the part of a father who was willing to say anything to get rid of his daughter in a way that would leave him with no feeling of guilt at his desertion.

'And,' he added looking unusually sheepish, 'I'll pay you, of course.'

Isabel had begun to think perhaps he wasn't so bad, after all. Perhaps he really did care a lot for his daughter and wanted to see her happy. Tiny snapshots of their own happier times together had begun to crowd her mind, dulling her instincts. But those words scattered all the pleasant images into a great invisible incinerator. He was using her, she realized. But she needed money, didn't she?

She let the little devil that was telling her to remember how mean he was fade away into obscurity. She could prove to her neighbour that he wasn't the only one who cared about young people; who wanted to keep them off the streets, give them some self-respect; teach them to respect others, too. She was beginning to feel quite passionate about it all when Paul spoke again.

'She does need to get away,' he repeated as if giving her the chance to practice a little needful altruism.

Isabel's fast-returning doubts must have shown on her face. Get away from what? she was asking herself. Not just the marital split, she guessed. Was it drugs? Bad behaviour? She wouldn't have been surprised. She had to give Paul his due, however. He would never foist on her someone who was like that; he did have some principles, she conceded. Otherwise she would never have stayed with him as long as she had.

'I can't look after her,' Paul told her hurriedly. 'And her mother's gone away with... her new boyfriend. London's no place for a youngster to be on her own all day long. Most of her friends have gone abroad or to family houses in the country.'

Ah, that was it, Isabel said to herself. Mother doesn't want her intruding on her new life; father is frightened that she might go to the bad while he's out at work all day. She was beginning to feel sorry for the girl. Perhaps she wouldn't be so bad, after all.

'Okay,' she said reluctantly after a pause of several seconds which would have felt like hours to a man in a dock waiting for the verdict, which was just what Paul looked like. She was too busy thumbing through her mental catalogue of all the domestic re-arrangements which would, of necessity, occur with two people living in her tiny cottage. So long as the girl didn't mess up her palatial bathroom she could stay for a few days. A single damp towel on the floor, a smudge on the porcelain of her jacuzzi and she would be out!

When she did bother to look across at Paul, Isabel saw that his mouth was turned up at the edges in the facsimile of a grateful smile. She thought, he's always had difficulty in saying 'thank you'. 'When do you want to get rid of her, then?' she asked, suddenly remembering her ailing grandmother. Perhaps she could make this an excuse not to rush up to Northampton for a day or two.

Paul's gulp was almost barely audible but Isabel accepted it as one of relief and gratitude. He was now silently perusing a full diary, it appeared. Or he might even be considering what would be best for his daughter, but Isabel doubted it.

'Would tomorrow be convenient?'

It was Isabel's turn to swallow hard. She knew she was a fool to react as readily as she had always done in the past but she could not help herself. Squashing any idea of pleading for clemency or time, she just nodded her head. The sooner the better, she told herself. Get it over and done with. 'I expect her to behave,' she said to remind him whose home it was and who was in charge.

Paul looked at her as though she was crossing boundaries that were strictly off limits. 'She always behaves.'

Isabel knew he was lying but considered silence could take on a golden hue for the time-being.

'She's got her own transport.' Paul's voice was that of the proud, ever-giving father, as if having the means of getting about was the epitome of good behaviour. 'She'll be with you tomorrow afternoon.'

In Isabel's ears that sounded as if everything had been pre-arranged; that there had never been any doubt as to her acquiescence. At least the girl would be independent, Isabel told herself in encouragement. There would be no running her around - if there was anywhere to run her to. But it was going to be bad enough having someone underfoot. She hadn't had that - apart from the few nights that Paul had stayed in the flat - since she left home. The questions started in her mind, buzzing like trapped bees. What was she getting into? And why? She'd hoped that she had cut free of her ties, but it wasn't so, it seemed. Who said that the past never dies; that it just goes into hibernation?

Isabel shook the panic from her mind. She'd have to get onto Silas without delay. Tell him that she wasn't able to go up and see Granma Lil for some days. Let him deal with her.

Paul seemed to be in a hurry to get away now that he had settled the business of his daughter's short holiday. And unsettled her life.

The telephone began to ring as they reached the kitchen door. Paul seemed to take this a signal that he was free to go - and without delay. She had only time to put up a hand to make a perfunctory wave at his disappearing back before he was out of the gate. As she turned into the house she could hear the engine of his car being gunned into willing life. He had never been one to waste time once he had got his way, she remembered with a hint of bitterness.

She had been planning a lovely long hot bath to ease her jagged nerves. Then a tot of two of...something - she ran over her booze cupboard in her mind and found it sorely lacking - before finishing her job in the garden in the cool of the evening.

With a grubby hand she plucked the old handset off its hook. One day she'd get one of those cordless things she could carry around with her. Not that she got that many calls, but the future might prove different.

At the end of the call all she could do was sigh, but it was a sigh of relief not despair. 'What a day it has been,' she told herself as the exhaled breath seemed to start at her toes and work its way through her whole body to the top of her head. 'What a day!' Life at the moment was like one of those old-fashioned garden swings which had seats facing each other. You felt battered and exhausted once you had stepped off one after a bumpy ride. She envisaged as her first companion on the opposite seat, her gran with all her problems; then it was Paul who had been in the opposite seat pulling harder and harder at the rope that kept them moving; then Paul had been replaced by his unhappy and - Isabel now faced it - wayward daughter. Now her companion, gentler, kinder than any of the others, was her dear, helpful, *wonderful* brother. He'd solved - 'but only for the time being' he warned her - all the problems to do with their elderly grandmother. She could almost have sat on the bottom step of the rickety staircase and cried. But she wasn't that sort was she? And she had a pile of things waiting for attention.

Later she ran over the conversation with Silas in her mind. 'When I've got time I'll come down and tell you all,' he had said.

Isabel had had no idea that he was going to rush off to Northampton and see what the situation was for himself but, momentarily, she considered him a saint.

'Her neighbour was with her.' He had stopped briefly and Isabel had heard the rustling of papers. She was about to rage at him to get on when he continued. 'I'll be sending you all the details in the post but for the moment you've nothing to worry about.'

The neighbour, it appeared, was only too happy to take on the role - paid, it seemed, by the trust on which their gran existed - of carer. She would, until the old woman deteriorated too far, go in every morning, cook her lunch - or at least see that she had whatever she wanted for doing it herself - do any chores that their gran couldn't manage and see her to bed at night, making sure the alarm that Silas was going to get was close at hand should she need it. It sounded too good to be true and Isabel wished she could give her brother a big hug to say thank you. The fact that he'd probably be very embarrassed if she did so was neither here nor there. They'd never been a demonstrative family; in fact, she couldn't remember ever seeing her father kiss her mother or even put his arm around her. As time went on she began to understand why. But some occasions, such as this, demanded the lowering of long-standing barriers.

When they'd exhausted the subject of their grandmother Isabel had told him about Hannah.

'My God!' Silas's sounded shocked. 'I thought you'd finished with that man.'

Isabel's euphoria shrivelled and died. Her brother's reaction was enough to convince her that she'd been a fool to lumber herself, albeit for a very short time, with a difficult teenager. She knew now that she had, as always, gone along with Paul's idea, pushing her own instincts out of sight behind her logic, this time, being supported by the thought of cash in the bank.

'Of course I'm finished with him,' she managed to fight back, knowing her voice sadly lacked conviction. 'It's not him who's coming to stay.'

'Oh no?' Isabel heard a faint snigger from the other end of the line but decided to ignore it.

'Only his daughter. And it won't be for more than a few days.'

'We will have to wait and see, won't we?' was his rather disquieting reply.

Isabel knew how much Silas disliked Paul. She had thought, at first, it was just an indication of professional jealousy. Here was her clever, bright and honest brother who was, as yet, only on the lowest rung of the ladder of success in the construction industry while Paul was right at the top. Or *had* been, she corrected herself, guessing that part of Paul's panic regarding his daughter could be attributable to business worries.

'That's okay, then.' Silas didn't sound totally convinced but his tone was cheery once more. 'Good news all round,' he quipped before ringing off. Isabel decided to ignore any innuendoes and told herself she was imagining them.

She walked slowly back into the kitchen in search of the comfort of a large mug of instant coffee. The jigsaw pieces seemed, at last, to be forming themselves into some sort of picture. A few of the edges might still be missing but she was working on it, she mused as she sipped at the mug till just a sludge of brown remained in the bottom.

Picking up the new reel she'd bought on her last trip into town she ambled down towards the river bank. Her shattered nerves needed the balm of flowing water, the noisy silence of nature and peace from chattering humans. A couple of hours of this and she'd feel whole again.

The line dangled into the water as Isabel watched for the flash of silver skin. She was fast coming to understand the commitment that game fishing imbued its participators with. It had little to do with the catching of a wild creature. It was more than that. She'd have to think about it, she told herself, watching several young trout, frightened by the size of the worm on the hook, take one look and then dash away like children finding themselves in an unusual and frightening playground. She didn't mind; was only too happy to sit in the sun, watching the weeds dancing to the orchestra of the water and listening to the distant chorus of small airplanes as intrepid pilots took advantage of the near perfect flying weather. She wondered if she would be able, one day, to be up there with them and made a promise to herself that she would, come what may. She began to feel much better.

Her peace was destined not to last, she soon discovered.

'I hope you've got a licence for that,' a voice called from across the water.

Isabel looked up startled. A man not unlike her father in size and build, apart from the casual country clothes that Ken would never have donned unless he was on a weekend in some grand country estate, was standing, arms on hips, glaring at her across the sparkling water.

'Licence?' she asked. 'I don't need a licence. This is my property.' She thought that would be the end of the unwelcome conversation. Then she realized who the man was. Old Boy had told her that there were plans afoot for a fish-farm to be built on the other bank of the stream. From what he'd said Isabel had understood that this was to be well away from her property and would cause her no problems at all. She hadn't been at all sure what a fish farm was so hadn't worried overmuch about it.

'I'm afraid you do.' The polite words were etched with sarcasm. 'And I'll see that you're prosecuted for not having one.' The man turned to go. 'My business is dependent on this river,' he added, turning back briefly and waving his hand up and the down the visible part of the water, 'and I'm not going to have all and sundry thinking they can take my fish out of the water if they happen to escape from my tanks.'

Isabel, if she hadn't been so demoralized by the day's happenings, might have smiled at the image of the man's fish taking to their feet and wandering off to pastures new. However, she felt the anger rising. Anger at yet another man telling her what she could or could not do and she wasn't going to have it. She had thought that the country folk would be friendlier and politer than anyone - apart from the Harts - she'd so far met, but it seemed that big cities weren't the only place where people said and did exactly what they wanted without feeling there was any necessity for good manners.

'We'll see,' she shouted at the disappearing back, fearing that the flowing water would cut off her words in mid air. 'We'll see,' she repeated to herself, this time with more confidence and determination. She would find out what her rights really were; get a licence if necessary, although she knew from the deeds she had scanned that she had 'fishing rights' along the bank bordering her property. No mention had been made of any 'licence' but she assumed there was a rule about which she knew nothing. And, for good measure, she would find out about the law concerning any fish that went walkabout from that unpleasant man's 'farm'.

Her peace having been shattered by the confrontation, she picked up the small reel and the plastic bag she had brought in the hope of providing herself with a tasty supper and trundled back to the house.

Reaching the porch of the cottage Isabel almost stumbled over what looked like a small round black and gold stone. But eyes peering up at her from under furry brows and a coat of matted fur proved it to be no stone. She recognised it as the young cat she had 'rescued' from the fruit cage a few days before and who she had believed had ended the day as a moribund pile of squashed flesh and bones. She was relieved to see that it was still alive. She tried to shoo it away from her doorstep so that she could open the bottom of the door but the kitten refused to move. One paw was stretched out as if to protect itself from painful contact with its crouched body.

For the second time in a very eventful day Isabel knew she should follow her instincts, and ignore it, but, of course, she didn't. It looked as if it hadn't eaten for days, its dull fur standing up in the points of a starving animal. She berated herself for being so soft. Perhaps she should open a refuge for unwanted animals and human beings, then she could give up all hope of achieving anything for herself; just be around to pick up the pieces of everyone else's failing existences.

When she looked at her watch a little later she discovered that it had taken her an hour to clean and feed the small, now occasionally purring, animal and see to the injured paw. She came to the conclusion, as she spread a dab of antiseptic cream on a small gash, that it was no more than sprain, a child-like act of begging for attention.

She determined to make some enquiries and Kate would be the first person she'd ask.

She thought that all the happenings of the day would course through her mind like a river in spate all night, preventing her from some hours of healing unconsciousness. It was only moments after she had climbed into bed after the relaxing hot bath she had promised herself earlier, however, that she had fallen into a deep and dreamless sleep. She remained so until the crying of a hungry kitten told her that the sun was up and he was hungry. Fred, she decided to call him. Or Frederica if it turned out to be girl, she decided as she dragged herself from bed.

Chapter 8

Isabel opened the door to let Fred - she'd decided the cat was a male, after all - out into the garden. The heat became steam as it met the interior coolness of the cottage. This dampness might cause her some problems once winter had arrived, she thought. Just another load for her aching shoulders.

She felt low and thought it was reaction from the day before. Then she remembered; today Hannah was coming. The thought didn't cheer her one bit.

Isabel sat slumped over her breakfast - two meagre slices of the bread she'd made the day before in the bread machine she had never used in her Hammersmith flat. Somehow home-baked bread and the country went together like salt and pepper, or peaches and cream. But she still needed practice in baking, she told herself, as she picked at the lumpy, undercooked dough. Perhaps she should try reading the instructions before using it again.

She felt as if she was recovering from a long-malingering flu bug; her arms transformed into weighted bags, her legs unreliable and wooden. She'd be happy to stay where she was and not attempt to stand up, but knew she had to get on. The plants needed watering before the sun was so hot it would turn their drink into scalding liquid, and she had to vacate the small bedroom and make it fit for Hannah. Then there was Alice's weekly telephone call to make. Not that her maternal grandmother demanded that she kept in touch; it was more Isabel needing *her* support than the other way round. And Allie had the gift of finding the right thing to say, words which would comfort. Mostly from Shakespeare or one of the old poets, but apt all the same. What did it matter if the ancient writers would no longer recognise their gems of wisdom? Dates and events of major - and minor - importance were all part of her everyday language and Isabel had always loved this. It made all the difference to the boring history books she had been made to read at school. For as long as she could remember just listening to her grandmother made dull facts come alive, colourful snapshots of the time she was describing. Just thinking of her made Isabel feel better.

What was the matter with her, anyway? She ran over her mental calendar of the past few weeks, and didn't like a lot of what was listed there. However there were things there which she did like. She'd have to concentrate on that. Standing up she put her breakfast things into the bright pink washing up bowl - another recent and essential purchase. Her pretty china was worth nurturing, she had decided in defence of the impulse buy.

Fred, who had been doing his morning ablutions, sitting uncomfortably on one slat of the garden bench at the side of the lawn, joined her as she came into the garden. His expression seemed to infer that, as he was now a member of the family, it was time he got some attention.

'I see you've recovered, then,' Isabel told the cat, bending down and pulling gently at one upright ear.

Instead of trying to escape from the indignity of having his ear pulled and rushing for shelter, he wound himself around the bottom of her bare leg, the injury to his paw now only a distant memory.

Fred tried to help Isabel as she unravelled the hose from its metal wheel, but being bashed on the head by a coiled snake of yellow plastic was not the young cat's idea of fun. He wandered off clearly intent on pursuing his mysterious daily, and more acceptable, activities.

While the water ran from the pipe like a diminutive Niagara, Isabel glanced up at the sky. By the looks of things what she was doing might be unnecessary. Clouds were crowding the horizon like gods joining in a fiendish dance. Ringed with the fire of a now almost invisible sun, they made the blue of the sky above look suddenly sinister. She wasn't fond of thunderstorms and could remember a few incidents in her past when she had wished to be anywhere else but where she was. Just like a scene from the past, two small aircraft, playing chase-me, scooted across her line of vision. She knew only too well what that meant; it was past time to get back to base.

Seeing the planes gave Isabel a bright and cheering idea. She'd promised herself a visit to the local aero club ever since she'd learned of its existence. Today might be the last chance for her to do that for a while - with a guest arriving. And she deserved a morning off. Hannah wasn't due until after lunch - 'sometime in the afternoon', Paul had said. And the weather might just keep some interesting people on the ground waiting for conditions to improve. She wouldn't mind a coffee or two with like-minded people, her diet of kindred spirits being at starvation level. She would love to be close to planes again, too, with their hypnotic scent of aviation fuel.

Isabel felt enormously cheered by the thought. She'd go for an hour, then could be back in plenty of time to receive Paul's unwanted gift. The thought of the money he was paying her removed any sense of guilt at the thought of a Sunday morning drink. It seemed like weeks since she'd been to a party, relaxed among people she had something in common with. Except for the barbecue, of course - but her lasting memory of that was not exactly chocolately sweet. Her spirits slipped a notch or two but she forced any thoughts of unpleasant negativism into oblivion. It was time she exchanged the excitement of going shopping for essentials in the nearby town, currently her only distraction from backbreaking manual labour, for something rather more intellectually stimulating. Her visits to the village hadn't revealed any hidden founts of mental fulfilment. The Old Mill might disclose some drama, but she had yet to visit it properly. And Thom's farm for delinquents didn't exactly fill her with delight. For the moment she was bereft of entertainment and it was up to her to do something about it.

When Isabel left the cottage she was dressed in tidy jeans - those with the legs she hadn't cut off - and a tee shirt she hadn't worn since going down to see her mother in that marina Silas had been working on the year before. She climbed into the little car she had bought to help her move from her London flat to the depths of the country. She wouldn't be without it now. She drove carefully up the short stretch of her rough track, past the lane leading to the village and out onto the road to Shilliton. On one of her trips into the town she had seen the notice for the airfield so she knew where she was going. She had been tempted, then, to call in to see what it was like, but the non-existent jangle of coins in her pocket had forced the temptation into the shadows.

Less than half an hour had passed when she was turning into the small car park behind the low, impermanent-looking buildings which would be concealing a grassy airfield beyond. It was filled with the familiar small, dusty runabouts nestling in unabashed propinquity with the gleaming luxury people-carriers and sleek sports cars. It would be like being alive again, she told herself, once she was back in the normal world of cheerful voices and stridently voiced opinions accompanied by the orchestra of clinking cups and rattling china.

A lightness, as though she'd shed pounds, filled her as she looked around for the appropriate entrance for visitors. There would be a special one for pilots, she knew, and she didn't want to seem pushy – not on her first visit. She'd slipped the black leatherette folder which held her licence into her shoulder bag, ready if wanted; but for the moment she was happy to be just a visitor. In any case, how was she to afford the exorbitant cost of flying? That would come later, perhaps - when her first-class, eagerly ordered, fresh fruit and vegetables were streaming onto the market - or into the market in Shilliton, that was. And then there were the herbs. Mustn't forget the herbs, she reminded herself with a little chuckle of happiness. And it wouldn't be long before someone in the aero club would be trying to persuade her to do a flight. 'Just for the fun of it. Only £60 for half an hour,' she would be told. She hoped her earth-bound boat would soon be sailing in but for the moment she would have to be careful not to be led into temptation.

The sky was now a canvas of purple-grey clouds with streaks of reflected light from a hidden sun etching their outlines. The blue that was left high above the horizon was rapidly fading. Isabel was glad to get into the coolness of the bar; the heat outside had increased with the upwardly mobile humidity. Even the windsock she had caught sight of from the car park, hanging from its pole seemed to be suffering from heat-induced lethargy.

Looking around Isabel was overcome with uncharacteristic shyness. It was different walking into a boardroom where she was well known, respected for her extensive knowledge of the construction industry. Here she was surrounded by strangers where her boardroom skills would not help her.

'Hi. Can I help you?'

The young man - well, boy, Isabel thought - behind the bar was calling to her as she stood by the door. She had been looking around the crowd of both well-dressed and tattily garbed, eager-faced pilots, some with less eager female companions. She also made out that some of the flyers were still hoping to be up and away before the day was much older. Looking out of the window at a rapidly increasing shower, she wondered.

Isabel was suddenly grateful for the boy's attention. It would take her a while to adjust to this new, albeit familiar, environment.

'Coffee?' she asked.

'Sure.' he answered in mock American. 'Sugar? Milk?' The boy had turned toward the gleaming brown and black machine at the back of the bar. To the right of the machine was a serving hatch through which Isabel could see white-clothed tables. A girl was busy scattering china and cutlery on them. Sunday lunch was a popular occasion, it seemed, by the amount of tables she was preparing.

'You new here?' It seemed the boy spoke only in questions but she was grateful for any company. He had turned towards her, a basin-like china cup with a blanket of white foam under which Isabel thought she might just find some drinkable coffee. She still wasn't sure what to expect so far away from London. She took a sip and was surprised and pleased that it was good and deep-flavoured and nodded.

'Come for the flying then?'

Isabel buried her face in the foam so that her stifled giggles wouldn't grow wings and escape.

'Not quite,' she murmured when she was once more in control, wiping the remains of the foam from her face with the square of paper towelling the boy handed her with a grin.

'Hi ya, T. Give us a cup of that stuff you call coffee, then.'

Isabel moved aside as a tall, gaunt man with a rather self-satisfied expression tried to smile down at her. As he was about her height he was finding it difficult. For some reason, Isabel knew, there were men who did not like women to be able to meet them eye-to-eye. She had discovered this shortly after she and Paul met. This man wasn't unlike Paul.... But she was finished with all that. He wasn't a bit like Paul. He wore his hair longer, even had sideburns. But whereas these would have looked ridiculous on Paul they suited the stranger very well.

'You new here?' the tall stranger asked holding out his hand for the cup of coffee the boy had poured for him.

Perhaps they spoke a different language down here in the country, Isabel quipped silently. Give it time and even she might be speaking in this peculiar way, too. She almost giggled again. The expression in her face must have given the man encouragement for he continued.

'You're a pilot, I'd guess,' he surprised Isabel by saying.

How he could know this was beyond her but Isabel felt flattered nonetheless.

'Was,' she answered, her mind on the little black folder in her bag.

'Was?' He looked disappointed for her. 'Was,' he repeated sadly.

'Well,' Isabel hesitated, listening to the uneven waves of conversation around her. They had moved away from the bar by this time and were standing by a window overlooking the airfield, agleam under the persistent thundershower. 'Still am, I suppose,' she told him. She wasn't sure that the licence to fly a tiny two-seater Cessna 152 Aerobat made her a pilot, exactly - not the sort this well-dressed Man might consider to be a fully-fledged pilot. He seemed slightly familiar to Isabel but she couldn't immediately think where she might have seen him before.

'Got a licence to fly one of those?' He was pointing across the grass to a row of very familiar, small high winged airplanes. She'd spent many happy hours on those very aircraft - when her income was good and her time was her own. When Paul had other things to attend to.

Isabel did not notice the glances that some of the people in the crowded café-bar were throwing their way. The men were either winking at each other, she might have seen, or turning away from the couple at the window with looks that could have been described as disgruntled. That many of the women had expressions of envy, some verging on jealousy on their faces might have pleased Isabel in her present state of mind.

'Yes,' she admitted. 'Do you fly?' She thought it was about time she added something to the conversation.

'Got my own plane,' he stated. 'Haven't got time to fly it. Wasted, it is. Not going to sell it, though, whatever anybody says.'

He was beginning to sound a bit angry. Some sore spot she had innocently struck, she decided.

'What do you do?' She knew that asking a man about his job within minutes of meeting him was not acceptable social behaviour but she wanted to get away from the subject of flying as quickly as possible.

'How refreshing,' was the surprising answer. 'Someone who doesn't recognise me.'

'Sorry,' said Isabel, slightly taken aback. It hadn't occurred to her that he might be someone well known. 'I'm new in these parts.'

'I'm Travis Parkin, by the way.' He placed the empty coffee cup on the table beside him and held out his hand to Isabel. 'I cook,' he said.

'And I grow,' said Isabel, thinking he was joking and wanting to reply in the same vein. She withdrew her hand from his tightening grasp.

'Seriously?' he asked.

'Yes, seriously.' She had regained her composure and was now beginning to enjoy herself. Perhaps her wish to meet someone interesting was being fulfilled.

'Where do you...?' Isabel began at the same time as he said: 'What do you...?'

They both laughed. He was quite good looking, Isabel thought, in a craggy, 1950s film-star way. And charming, too. She would have to watch herself; she wasn't so desperate as to allow herself to be picked up by the first man who'd made her laugh. Or was she?

'I say. Look at that.'

Isabel hadn't heard anyone speak like that since listening to one of her grandmother's collection of old radio programmes. She couldn't remember the name of the person but the voice, like Travis's, had been richly redolent of greasepaint and footlights. She'd have to ask Alice the next time they spoke. She looked through the streams of water on the window. Beyond the rain which was pouring off the gutters was - just more rain, falling out of the sky as if a godly hand was emptying a huge bucket of grey water over the land. The small planes had disappeared behind the deluge, lit only slightly in the obscurity by an occasional flash of heavenly light. Then, as they watched, the rain stopped as if an invisible hand was twisting a tap in the sky. Aircraft reappeared brought closer by the telephoto lens of some giant in the sky.

'Well, that finishes that,' Travis said.

'What does?' She was still slightly mesmerised by the power of nature that she had just witnessed. Nor did she want to conclude this encounter, not just yet. She had a lot of questions she wanted to ask.

'I was going to suggest we went up for a spin,' he replied.

Isabel's surprise at the speed with which the express seemed to be moving along its tracks was tempered with disappointment. Don't be silly, she told herself. There was no way we were going to be able to 'go up for a spin. He's just saying that for something to say.

'Some other time.'

Isabel hoped he meant what he said. It would save an awful lot of financial problems if she was able to use his aeroplane, *and* give her some flying hours. Perhaps he wanted her to *hire* his aircraft. But he couldn't charge her when she was flying with him, could he? Her brain was in a bit of whirl. What was all that excitement about the thunderstorm? Interesting, perhaps, but not world-shattering. She began to wonder if the man wasn't just a little bit strange.

'Another day,' he said then. 'Won't cost you a penny,' he added as if reading her thoughts. 'Not when you're flying me around!'

He made it sound like a joke, but Isabel decided to treat it as a serious offer.

She forgot to ask him why he didn't fly himself around if he had time to go out on jollies with her; the thrill of getting some free flying was almost unbelieveable. She remembered with a slight start how friendly her past flying club was; how they all clubbed together to hire aircraft and share hours.

She glanced down at her watch while searching for the right words with which to respond to his generosity. 'Oh, my God,' she gasped. 'Look at the time.' Getting away before he changed his mind might have been a good motive on its own, but she had a packet of things to do before the girl arrived and what with pleasant conversation and coffee too much time had already slipped by.

Travis put his hand on her arm. 'See you soon?' he asked.

Isabel nodded her head, pulling from the flap on the side of her shoulder bag one of her business cards she'd so lovingly made before she moved into the cottage. A little bit irrelevant at present, she admitted, but at least it had her name and telephone number on it.

She nodded towards the boy at the bar, turned and lifted her hand briefly towards Travis and was out of the door before he could say another word. She missed the expression on his face and wouldn't have known what it meant even if she had seen it. But some would say he was congratulating himself on being a very clever boy for landing such a succulent morsel of fish.

Chapter 9

'Allie. What are you doing here?' The childhood name slipped out unbidden.

As she drove down her track Isabel could see a car parked, slightly askew, outside the gate to the cottage. Paul had said Hannah had her own transport, she told herself, as she parked in the space she'd made for her own vehicle in her unkempt front garden, but surely she wouldn't be driving such a traditional bright blue Fiesta of recent make. Not at her age. Then she recognised it and her dipping spirits rose again. Alice stepped daintily from the car.

'Not that I'm not pleased to see you!' Isabel told her grandmother, hugging her. 'But I was expecting a less welcome visitor.'

The older woman had said, long ago in Isabel's youth, that she wouldn't mind being called by her given name, thank you. She wasn't quite ready to live as the shadow of someone else's being and was quite happy to be herself for a few years longer. She was, she would remind her granddaughter, 'the family face' seeing as how her own daughter had upped and left the family home for a jolly tar's existence. She was the only person Isabel had ever managed to show affection for without feeling she was obliged to or the loss would be hers - as she had felt regarding her mother, but that might have been her own fault, she thought with sudden intuition.

'You mean that girl?' Alice asked.

Isabel nodded, shaking her head in surprise. 'She's here, then?'

'She was when I arrived,' Alice answered, her voice unusually cool. 'Didn't stay long. Obviously I wasn't fit company, her with the ring in her nose and hair that looked like she'd just come up from the coalface! Rushed off on a two-wheeled, noisy scooter thing.'

'Oh dear,' sighed Isabel, fearing the worst. 'I'd better get us a drink,' she added smiling at the older woman. The girl sounded as though she'd fit in well with the boys next door, and that's what had worried her most. She hadn't intended starting up her own 'rehabilitation camp', but it appeared she was being forced into it, albeit temporarily. 'We can have it outside,' she said nodding towards the few slabs of paving stone which went by the noble name of terrace.

She left her grandmother to make herself at home while she went into the kitchen to see what her undernourished larder could provide as refreshment after their drink. She hoped Alice would be happily occupied for a few moments trying to fathom what had forced her towny granddaughter to turn into a country bumpkin.

Isabel needn't have worried. Returning with a wine bottle in one hand and the only two glasses she owned in the other she found Alice happily busy. She was wiping the moisture off Silas's two plastic chairs with a rag conjured up from somewhere. The table was already clean and dry and, by the usual miracle-working of her grandmother, seemed to be struggling with the weight of a wicker picnic basket whose lid was propped open. Isabel recognised the prop as the faded wooden ruler that had served her well during her school days. Half-hidden inside the basket were plastic boxes which when opened, Isabel knew, would reveal fresh, tasty sandwiches, some salads and fruit. The routine had never changed over the years, Isabel thought with affection and gratitude.

'I see I needn't have brought any of these,' Alice chuckled. She put a large juicy tomato on each of the two plates she had unhooked from the lid of the basket, having disposed of her rag under a nearby bush. 'Or this,' she added, spooning mixed, creamy salad out of one of the boxes. 'But these might be welcome,' she added pointing to two pots containing something made from chocolate. 'But I didn't know you had a guest, of course.'

'She's not a guest,' Isabel said. 'She wasn't due until later on, in any case.'

'What's her name?'

Isabel understood her grandmother very well. It was Alice's way of asking for a biography of a visitor she found strangely inimical to her favourite grandchild's new and exciting territory. The older woman had already settled on her chair, glass in hand, as if waiting to hear a satisfactory explanation.

'She's my ex-boss's daughter,' Isabel began.

'You mean that awful man you used to go around with?'

Alice was not usually so blunt about what she thought - unless the bluntness would help the other person to avoid a catastrophe. There were many times when it had prevented Isabel from making a fool of herself. She hoped her grandmother's instincts about the girl would prove to be wrong this time, however.

'She was getting bored in London. Her father's working and the mother is away.'

'With some other man, I expect.' Alice's voice was tinged with acid.

Isabel wondered where her grandmother got her information from, correct as it was. Possibly Silas or even her own mother. It was amazing how families seem to think nothing was sacred or private.

'Making use of you, that's what,' Alice told her.

'Ah well,' Isabel said, not rising to the bait. They had finished the tasty picnic bringing each other up-to-date with the small, unimportant happenings in their lives. Alice had always forbidden any deep discussions when food was being digested. That would come, Isabel told herself, with an inner chuckle recognising that it already had. But she wasn't ready to bare her soul. Not yet. And as Alice seemed quite happy sitting looking around, Isabel decided to pre-empt any further mention of the subject. 'I'd better go and get her room ready, I suppose.' Isabel hoped her reluctance was not too obvious.

'Don't be silly,' Alice said. 'What you do with your life is your affair. Sit down and we can have a nice chat about what you've been up to. I didn't come all this way to sit on my own with just a cat for comfort. Not that he's much company,' she muttered. But her tone was uncomplaining.

'Okay,' Isabel said, refilling their glasses with the cool green liquid. 'It has been almost seven weeks since I told you the latest instalments of my oh-so-not-exciting life! My birthday lunch, wasn't it?' It seemed to her more like a century and not just two meagre months. Perhaps her life was more exciting than she appreciated. Interesting it had been, yes, but the only excitement was that morning's activities.

However she put aside her inhibitions and was soon telling her grandmother everything that had gone on since they'd last met. She made few mentions of her next door neighbour - didn't want Alice getting the wrong idea of the area - and some impulse told her not to elaborate on the events of the morning. All she said about this was: 'I've met someone who might want me to supply fruit and veg for his television show.' She couldn't control the smidgen of pride that seeped into her words. Being excessively superstitious about not counting unhatched chickens she did manage to stop herself from adding any details. He hadn't said anything definite, but the hint had been there. She was still amazed at the speed at which it had all happened; it was still just a blur in her mind which she had difficulty in believing in. She wouldn't say too much; not just yet. Isabel crossed her fingers and turned her attention back to her grandmother.

'That's nice, dear,' Alice said as though she, too, would believe it when it happened.

Isabel decided that any mention of having a plane to fly as well would be stretching her grandmother's credulity just a little too far, so she told her about the old boy and her garden, skirted over her contretemps with the fish farmer, even mentioned the Harts, but on the subject of Travis and his - *possible* she reminded herself - plans for her, she said no more.

Mention of the previous owner of the cottage led, strangely, to the subject of their family history. It was never long before Alice managed to turn the conversation in that direction.

Alice, it appeared had got so far with her own research that she was now writing it all down and was having it printed so that she could distribute copies to all her family members.

'Do you know how much that's going to cost me?' she asked at one point. Not waiting for a guessed answer, she said, 'Nearly one and half thousand pounds! But for that I will get a hundred free copies. When you work it out I suppose it's not too expensive at fifteen pounds a copy.' Her laugh inferred that the enjoyment of researching and writing the family history was worth every penny.

Isabel knew that Alice had always been interested in history, whether of the family or the world in general. Whenever Isabel had asked for a historical date she needed for some piece of schoolwork the answer would always come back like a bullet from a gun.

'Theodore Roosevelt. President of the USA. Died 1919,' answered one question from Isabel who had never forgotten the answer. 'Glen Miller 1944,' had given one essay on modern music added colour. 'Television.' This time it was not a question that was asked by anyone, but Alice did like to add interest to any occupation. 'When was it invented? Well I remember the neighbours having one. We were all invited to see this miracle of modern science. 1952-ish was when, I think, the first came into general use. I was equally thrilled with my new electric food mixer your grandfather bought me for our twelfth wedding anniversary.' Alice had got into her stride by now, so Isabel just sat back and relaxed as she enjoyed the images her grandmother was conjuring up out of what could have been dry and dusty facts.

'I always liked cooking,' Alice continued. 'We couldn't do much while the war was on, of course, because of rationing. But we did have a monthly competition at the church. Whoever could make a shilling, that's about five pence in our money now, go the furthest got a prize. I can't remember what the prize was - probably some black market eggs or meat,' she chuckled in remembrance, 'but with my new mixer I was able to make several - six, I think it was - lemon meringue pies with powdered eggs and lemon flavouring and sell them for one shilling and sixpence each. About seven pence today! But if you work it out I made an eight hundred percent profit! Not bad, eh?'

Isabel didn't mind hearing about food; she was in the business, now, wasn't she? And eight hundred percent profit would be just the job!

'Your mother,' Alice was saying, 'grew up to be just as thrifty - and as talented,' she added with false modesty. 'And it looks as if you might be going the same way.'

Isabel was flattered to think that her clever grandmother was comparing her with a mother who was an excellent housewife, a cordon bleu - untrained - cook, as well as being interested in painting and, now, obviously a competent sailor. Or was she? But Isabel wasn't going to allow herself any worrying thoughts about her recalcitrant parent.

'I never liked housework,' Alice was saying. 'I don't know where your mother got her patience and talent for that! I was happy to leave it to someone else,' she laughed. 'But, cooking. I did enjoy cooking. And helping to look after you two when you were babies. That was nice. As long as I could return you to your mother when I'd had enough, that is! By the way do you know why Teddy Bears were called Teddy Bears?' Thinking about them as children had jogged her memory, it seemed.

'I think I know the answer to that,' said Isabel with a laugh remembering her own earlier memory and the added information her grandmother had given when she'd asked for the American president's date. 'Theodore Roosevelt and his not wanting to kill bears, or something like that.'

Alice looked a little disappointed, and then brightened. 'Try this one, then. Do you know when the first Olympic Games - the modern ones, of course - were held and where?'

'No idea!' Isabel was beginning to get a little edgy. She didn't want to be running around like a housemaid when the girl got back. It would make the wrong impression, completely.

'1896 in Athens. Oh, go on and get your home ready for your visitor,' Alice said with a smile. 'I'm just a silly old fool.' But her expression said she was only joking. 'Sad, isn't it, to have such a good memory and not be able to use it!'

Isabel felt a bit guilty. There was no need for her to worry about the girl. It would only take her minutes to make up the bed. She might even make her do it herself. But, then, she was a paying guest and Isabel did not want her telling her father she had to do her own housework. He might decrease the amount he was willing to pay. Which was what? Isabel asked herself, surprised that she'd forgotten to ask.

'Go on, get on with it then,' her grandmother urged.

'No, it's okay,' Isabel said. 'I'm in no hurry. Let me show you the garden.'

'Well tell me about this girl who made your face look like a crumpled sack when I mentioned her, then?' Alice said after they had visited the cage of green plastic and were now wandering towards the stream which was flowing fast after the storm and threatening to reach the top of the bank. 'How long is she staying? And what is she going to do with herself while you're busy in the garden?' Alice waved an arm around the great expanse of Isabel's three acres.

Isabel laughed. Her mother's mother could always make her feel better.

'You don't know, do you?' Alice teased.

'A week,' said Isabel with little conviction. 'And she will have to look after herself while I'm busy.' She felt a small prick of guilt when she realized she had not even considered the girl when the man up at the airfield had made his suggestion. 'She's old enough.'

'How old is that?' Alice asked.

Isabel knew her grandmother was thinking about the time, not so long ago, when she had found her, crouched over a letter, miserable and with a face wet from tears, crying like a child who has just lost her favourite toy. Paul, Isabel accepted, had never been amongst Alice's favourites, and certainly not after she had poured out all her miseries on her grandmother's narrow but sympathetic shoulders. Alice's expression was telling Isabel that her grandmother hoped it wouldn't turn out to be a case of like father like daughter.

'Well, it's life's uncertain voyage, as the poet said, for you. Just take care.' Alice smiled as if she'd now had her say and would forever remain dumb. At least on that particular subject.

'I'd better be off, then,' she said suddenly.

'Off? Already?' She knew Alice didn't care to drive in the dark but it wasn't that far to Bath and this was, after all, not long after mid-summer and it wouldn't be dark for hours. 'Where are you going? Not straight home, that's obvious.' Isabel thought she and her grandmother had reversed roles by the way she was speaking to her; it was disappointment not disapprobation that made her do so.

'Aha.' Alice tapped the side of her nose. 'None of your business,' she said with a smile. 'In truth I think you'd rather meet this girl on your own. Not have your disapproving grandmother making things more difficult than they are!' Before Isabel could speak, she continued' 'I booked a B and B in the village. I didn't know what visitor space you had,' she added. 'And I'm not really sorry, now that I've seen how things are.'

Isabel knew her grandmother well enough to know she wasn't being critical; it was obvious to anyone that three would be considerably more than a crowd in the tiny cottage.

'But,' Alice reached into the large, flat leather bag which hadn't left her side, 'I'm leaving you this to read through.' She handed her a folder of papers.

Isabel could see that it was the typescript of her grandmother's current work by the heading 'Family History' in large letters on the top page.

'I'll pick it up in the morning,' Alice said. 'Wanted an extra pair of eyes to run over it. Say what you like. I won't be offended!'

Isabel ran a mental eye over the list of chores she had to get through before the summer's day ended. The only time she would have to read it was in bed that night. She hoped she wouldn't fall asleep before getting through the inch-thick pile of pages.

Alice was just about to drive off in her bright blue car when she called from the car's open window, '1898' she shouted as she changed gear, 'first motor car allowed on the roads without it's usual escort walking 150 yards ahead. Bet you didn't know that!' And with an expensive-sounding squeal of tyres on loose dirt was off down the track before Isabel could answer.

Isabel turned to go back to the cottage when two wheels making much the same noise drew up at the gate. Hannah had returned from her fun-filled visit to wherever it was, it seemed.

Why the arrival of Hannah should remind her of a cat, Isabel didn't know. But it did and she realised that since his brief appearance at lunch there had been no further sign of Fred.

Chapter 10

Isabel propped herself up against the one meagre pillow which remained after Hannah insisted that she couldn't sleep without at least three pillows.

She opened the plastic file lying on her knees and started to read the typed notes of Alice's memoirs when a weight landed on her legs. Fred had reappeared just after Hannah had returned as if to say he was going to keep a check on things in his new home. At least his appearance had stopped the girl from continuing to extol the - non-existent, Isabel knew - virtues of her distant mother. What message she had been trying to pass over, Isabel had been unable to ascertain. By the way the girl spoke she obviously thought her mother was a much-maligned angel in disguise.

The evening hadn't been completely free of the girl's problems but at least Hannah had appeared to be trying her best to be a helpful guest. She'd even had the forethought - during her mysterious absence - to buy some chops and bacon, along with various other things which she considered were suitable for a barbecue. She'd obviously seen it during her brief, according to Alice, visit to the cottage. Isabel thought it best not to ask any questions about where she had been; she was only too relieved to have the girl back safe and sound. If she'd known Hannah's transport was a dangerous-looking two-wheeled scooter she might have considered asking her father to bring her down himself. But was pleased she hadn't had to do that. And since Fred had come in he'd taken most of Hannah's attention preventing her from continuing her long boring spiel on the merits of her parents.

Leaning back against the hard metal headboard, Isabel tried to put into words how she would describe Hannah to a stranger and found the task surprisingly difficult. I must be getting old, she told herself, as she recalled how startled she'd been at the sight of the bare midriff, over-tight tee-shirt and strangely faded jeans - the back and fronts of the legs were washed-out while the sides remained in the original colour. Must be a new fashion, she thought with a shudder. Even the ring in the girl's nose left her cold whereas she'd have tried that herself, probably, if it had been the latest thing when she was sixteen, going on seventeen. She could just imagine her mother's face if she had. And wasn't the girl's expression familiar? Hadn't all the junior staff worn the same slightly petulant look of the over-indulged child, whatever age they had been? Perhaps her own face had worn exactly the same expression at that age, so she wouldn't judge the girl until she knew her better.

It was tiring, Isabel admitted, having someone invading her hard-won 'space'. She hoped her relief wasn't too obvious when Hannah had stood up and stretched, her mouth a yawning cavern.

'I think I'll have a bath,' the girl said, without asking whether there was enough hot water, or if Isabel, herself, wanted to use the bathroom. 'I've had a long day.'

You're not the only one. But, then, all the days seemed to be 'long ones' just now, Isabel decided. And she'd been looking forward to a soak in her pretty bath. The tank in the attic, sadly, held barely enough hot water for one long, relaxing bath - and that was heated by expensive electricity. The memory of her mother's strict upbringing as regards the duties of a hostess forbade her to comment, however. She would have to have to be patient; it was only for a week.

Isabel had been cleaning up the kitchen - how a barbecue for two could make so much washing up amazed her - when Hannah emerged from the bathroom. Her dark spiky hair, standing on end from washing, her bed-time attire of very brief shorts - 1930's Teddies, Alice would have called them - and a skimpy matching top, made a comic vision for Isabel in the contrasting old country cottage of rough wood, paved floors and scant paintwork. She hoped her visitor wouldn't prance around in front of visitors like that. Not that she had that many visitors, but Alice was coming back in the morning. It might cause an atmosphere if she saw the girl dressed as she was now. Unlikely, of course, knowing Alice. But she was relieved when Hannah, with a brief nod of her head, disappeared towards the stairs and her bedroom.

Isabel shook her head. Thinking of Alice had turned her attention back to the file on her knees which a motley-coloured cat was considering making into a seat. She pushed him off and with a look that spoke paragraphs he leapt off the bed and made for the door. She had left it partly open to let some cooling air into the low-ceilinged room. Soon she heard him scratching on Hannah's closed door.

Gently, almost surreptitiously, the girl's door opened and muffled words were heard. Isabel let a sigh of relaxation escape her. At least the girl was an animal lover, she told herself.

She picked up the file. Most of what was in it she'd already heard from Alice's lips or vaguely remembered herself. It was fascinating, all the same, to read of her grandmother's view of things, particularly her wartime experiences.

'I worked as a radar plotter.' She'd already told Isabel this earlier, but she didn't mind hearing it again. 'In the WAAFs. "Mad Ludo" it was called and we were the Mad Ludoes,' she chuckled. 'We were the first women working in the war and had such fun off-duty. A contrast, I suppose, from our gruelling duties.' She had laughed shortly, remembering, and then became serious again. 'Goering ignored the big masts which were put up for the radar. That was a mistake. He could have won the battle for Britain - as it was called before it became the Battle *of* Britain - if he hadn't. It was fortunate for us that he was so silly.'

Isabel had thought 'silly' was a tame word for a world-renowned bully.

'He died, of course,' Alice had continued with her reminiscences, a faraway look on her face, 'by his own hand a year after the war had ended. On May 1st, the day your grandfather and I celebrated our fifth wedding anniversary. That's how I remember the date so well.'

Isabel was tolerant about her grandmother's predilection for dates, admiring the marvellous way she had of linking them with other things so that she was never inaccurate. Someone just had to mention a certain day and Alice opened up like a brightly illustrated history book.

Isabel wiggled up against the uncomfortable headboard twisting shoulders already sore from the lumpy metal. She was longing for the day when she could say good-bye to the old bed.

She scanned the first few pages - Alice's date of birth, 1920, grandfather Theodore's 1919; Alice's grandmother Sarah, 1871 - the year Livingstone met Stanley, a note said - Sarah and Elijah married 1867 - the year Canada became a dominion another note stated. It was all interesting, historical stuff but Isabel was finding it hard to keep her eyes open. She read about Alice's father being killed on the Somme in 1916 which woke her up. She remembered Alice telling her - sixteen and innocent - about this and how horrified she had been that anyone could have survived that terrible experience.

'They existed on processed meat and dried biscuits, when there was any food, that is. Once they spent seven nights and seven days in their trenches without anything to eat or drink. Can you imagine it?'

Isabel couldn't and had shuddered at what terrible atrocities the enemy had perpetrated. It wasn't till she was much older that she realized that both sides had much to blame themselves for.

Alice had written the whole story down and it all came back to Isabel as if her grandmother were there telling it again. Isabel scanned the notes: 'Theodore in Lord Kitchener's band. 16 year olds. 70,000 men killed in one battle. 180 British graveyards in the area.' Obviously Alice planned to fill it out later. It hadn't taken her long to realize that this was to be her grandmother's *chef d'oeuvre* so she didn't just want to skim through it. But she'd had enough for the moment and would have to finish it in the morning. There was little she was going to be able to add realizing that Alice only wanted her to check the later dates for her.

She settled under the sheet. The scent of chlorophyll rose from trees and bushes earlier blasted by the thunder shower then roasted by a hot sun mixed with dying embers of the charcoal and bath water laden with pungent oils as it lay in the primitive outside drain. Even the thought that she would have to attend to that bit of plumbing could not keep her awake. As she dozed she told herself she should get up and turn off the light. A single bulb, hanging on its wire from the ceiling, with its useless shade which cast no shadows would not help her sleep.

Once back in bed she was asleep in moments, exhaustion letting her lie dreamless until the morning.

Isabel was up, had eaten her breakfast and was out checking the fruit bushes hoping to find that yesterday's storm had not ruined any of the produce she had planned to add to the Hart's basket, before there was any sign of her visitor.

As she was entering the kitchen, looking forward to her mid-morning coffee, the girl wandered in, fully dressed but yawning like a sleep-starved wraith, her white face starved of make-up. And other ornaments, Isabel noted. The black hair was still standing on end as though it had had a fright, its silver streak a rather sinister dagger across the top.

'My dad said he was paying for all my meals,' was the girl's morning greeting. She was standing looking down at the table which was clear of any sign of breakfast, the fruit that Isabel had earlier sorted having making pools of red where her food should be.

'That's right,' answered Isabel. 'Help yourself.' She ignored the girl's sulky look and carried on weighing the fruit on the old-fashioned scales she'd found in the weekly market in Stilliton. The girl's attitude made her hope of any help take wing. It was Paul who'd said something about Hannah 'helping' but Isabel felt she could wait in vain. If she insisted on it she might be forced into accepting less than Paul had promised. Then where would be all her dreams of going flying again.

Hannah confirmed Isabel's fears when, after a breakfast of juice and two slices of toast she announced that she was off to the farm next door. 'To help out with the harvest,' she said.

Isabel didn't know whether to laugh or complain, but she knew now where Hannah had spent the hours of the afternoon the day before. She hadn't wasted any time, had she? Isabel was mystified at how quickly she had stepped into the role of always-welcome guest at the farm next door. Had she known about it before she arrived? Was that why she was here? Had the purchase of the food she'd bought for the barbecue last night had been instigated by some sort of feeling that her hostess might not approve of where she'd been? Isabel was not going to even consider that Hannah might have been given it by Thom; she would have wanted to send it straight back, so it was best if she didn't know the truth.

'And I won't be back for lunch,' Hannah stated.

Isabel didn't argue with her. Alice was coming for her notes; it would be nice to have some peaceful time together before her grandmother returned to Bath. Thinking about the notes, Isabel hastily completed her weighing, wiped the table and placed on it the file which had been resting on the dresser, giving her guilty twinges whenever she happened to glance in its direction. She picked it up. She had to appear to be taking an interest - and she was interested, just lacking in time. If Alice was enjoying a leisurely breakfast at her B and B in the village, she might just be able to glance through the rest of it before her grandmother arrived.

She found the next section much more interesting than all the wartime nostalgia. This was something she could identify with. Isabel read on from the mention of the arrival of television and was reading about how a bottle of whisky - her favourite tipple at the moment, albeit in small doses - cost ten times less in the forties and fifties than it did nowadays and how families started doing their Christmas cooking two and half months before the arrival of the big day - before Alice drove up to the lane, stopping with a skid outside the gate.

'I'm amazed you've got so far,' she said, looking down at the open file, after she'd greeted Isabel.

Isabel hoped her grandmother hadn't noticed her flush of guilt.

Alice settled down comfortably on the seat opposite Isabel and began to quote verbatim from memory the next page which was full of important dates. Isabel let them waft over her head as she thought of the things she had to cope with that day. Until, that was, she heard her own birthday mentioned.

'Your first birthday,' Alice said, 'Judy Garland was singing her famous song from the top film of the year, *"Somewhere over the rainbow"*. You heard it once, and even though you could hardly speak you went around the house singing it all day. And night, too, if your mother is to be believed!'

Isabel knew it was a fond grandmother speaking. No child of a year old could possibly have done that.

By the time Alice left in mid-afternoon, Isabel felt as if she'd spent the whole day reading the saga of a very active family. The fact that the family was her own made it all the more interesting. For once she was pleased she didn't have a television. Watching it would have spoiled the comforting thought that her life-story was as rich and varied as any a writer of fiction could create.

Hannah still had not returned by the time Isabel had made a mixed salad with grated cheese for their supper. 'I'm not going to worry,' she said firmly to the cat that had just reappeared. Fred, it seemed, considered Woodbine Cottage as his nightly residence and what he did during the day was, his attitude said, nobody's business but his own.

'Just like that girl,' Isabel said, laughing at him as he rolled over on his back offering up his furry underparts for a comforting scratch or two.

While she was waiting she phoned the airfield to find out about a trial flight. When she had put the receiver down she was silent for a moment. £60 for the half hour now seemed like a lot of money. Gone were the days when £60 had been little more than pocket money to her, but she needed a treat. She would do it. She knew that that man's offer to let her have 'a spin', as he called it, in his own plane was just one of those things people said in a social situation, and then promptly forgot about. She doubted whether she'd even see him again.

Chapter 11

'3.00 pm Wednesday. That's the first we can do.'

The voice at the other end of the phone had been professional and friendly and like the music of a distant but favourite song in her ears.

'That's fine,' she answered, trying to keep the childish enthusiasm out of her voice. Her heart was doing little leaps of joy. But she'd done it; rung the airfield and booked her flight. There was no going back now. She was stupidly nervous - a year and a few months with no flying didn't mean she'd lost the skill - or had she?

So here she was, turning into a car park which was considerably less crowded than it had been on the Sunday of her first visit. Being a holiday weekend, it shouldn't have surprised her that there was such a crowd. But it had been some while before she remembered that it was a holiday, her life having changed so much in the short time she had been away from the hustle and bustle of office life.

Hannah had deigned to stay at home the day before. The day hadn't offered up any irresistible invitation, apparently. Isabel had begun to regret the lack of that invitation by the time she had shown Hannah around the garden - not that she seemed that interested - named all the fruit, shown her the vegetable patch and encouraged her to admire the tall trees. The girl had no idea about gardens or living in the country.

'Why don't you just go to the supermarket and buy what you want?' She asked at one point. 'My mother does?'

Isabel had taken this as a joke so decided not to reply. She just wished she didn't have to hear quite so much about the wonderful mother. The woman couldn't be that marvellous if she'd gone off with her boyfriend leaving her teenage daughter to fend for herself during the school holidays. Much the same could be said of the father.

'When I was at school we thought everything came out of tins.' Hannah had laughed shortly, looking sideways across to the region of Isabel's chin as if daring her to respond.

Isabel had heard that one before and she wasn't going to rise to it.

Hannah's shoulders had slumped as she realized her joke had

fallen flat on its childish face.

Isabel made sandwiches with some leftover ham and salad greens from the garden for their lunch and Hannah sat at the kitchen table looking bored once the plate of sandwiches was empty and their instant coffee drunk. Her expression told Isabel that she would much rather have had a hamburger and chips, or even a pizza; that healthy food was for geeks.

'Why don't you go for a swim?' Isabel asked feeling inspired.

Hannah glanced out of the window above the sink towards the stream and slowly shook her head from side to side.

'Not the river,' Isabel said hastily. She had enough of a problem to sort out with that man across the water without adding to the list of her iniquities in his mind. 'There's a good pool in Shilliton, I believe.' God, I sound just like some maiden aunt, she told herself.

The girl's face brightened. 'I might,' was all she said. In an instant she was on her feet, however, making towards the stairs, to reappear moments later with a colourful swimsuit which she was pushing into a supermarket carrier. Over her arm was one of Isabel's best towels.

Poor kid, Isabel thought in sudden pity, ignoring the thick towel. She needed someone to bother about her, take an interest, if the sudden lighting up of the dulled eyes was anything to go by. Like a child let out of school, not a sixteen - wasn't she almost seventeen? - year old. Isabel wondered suddenly if Paul had concerns about his daughter that he wasn't going to let on about and if she hadn't suddenly been landed with the role of a carer. That was silly; it was just that the girl had very selfish parents, that was all. She was quite old enough to look after herself. A little gremlin leapt into Isabel's mind, then; Paul had some other reason for wanting to get rid of his daughter, it said. She mentally viewed the idea with icy paws trotting up and down her spine not realizing that her face told of her dread.

'There wasn't another one I could take.' Hannah's face was like that of a child caught out in some wickedness. She looked as though she was going to throw the towel on the table.

Isabel held out her hand, realizing the girl had mistaken her expression for censure. 'I was thinking about something completely different,' she said, pushing the girl and towel towards the door. She felt momentarily guilty at her thoughts. But Hannah wouldn't have known it was anything to do with her; it was just her usual attitude, Isabel guessed.

That was all in the past. For the moment she had happier things to think about.

Isabel was about to knock on the sliding glass partition, then stopped. The sole occupant of the control room was a girl bent over a console of instruments on a counter beneath a wide window. Her moving mouth was close to a piece of equipment which grew like a black metal flower from the shiny surface of the desk. Beyond the window the runway lay from left to right, its grassed area flat and smooth as if recently ironed. As Isabel waited a small plane touched down at the far end. She felt a thrill of pleasure as she watched the two wheels of the Cessna land gently on the grass followed smoothly by the nose wheel. Once the aircraft had coasted past the front of the building any noise from its gently idling engine eerily absent due to the two thick walls of glass and had disappeared from view in the direction of the fuelling pump, Isabel knocked on the glass panel.

The girl's head jerked up and she gazed around as if just awakening. Isabel recognised the sense of returning from another world that she, too, had always experienced when taking her turn at the control desk with all its radio equipment and microphones. The girl smiled, gesturing with a wave of her hand that Isabel should stay where she was and that someone would be out to see her.

Shortly afterwards a door at the side of the control room opened and a tall man in a dark uniform of well-creased slacks and shirt walked towards Isabel. The only thing that spoiled the perfect vision of professional pilot was the dark tie which hung like a miniature shawl around his shoulders and the sunglasses pushed up onto the crown of his head.

Bushy eyebrows looked down at her as he stopped beside her. He only needed a handlebar moustache, Isabel joked silently as she stared him straight in the eye, and the image would be complete. The single gold bar on the epaulette of his shirt signified that he had reached the exalted state of First Officer. She knew that many commercial pilots started this way, but few of them would have stayed on until near retirement, so this was obviously just some sort of honorary title. The thought made her want to laugh for some reason.

'Hi, I'm Rod,' the man said, his voice was recognizable from the phone conversation. He held out a hand. 'Senior instructor,' he told her. 'Are you my victim for the afternoon?' He laughed loudly, smiling across at Isabel before looking down at a clipboard he held in one hand. 'Isabel Vine. Is that you? No relation to the famous con-man, I hope!' Again he laughed loudly as if he found himself very amusing. 'Of course not,' he said, a look of contrition planted on his face. 'Just my joking way! Come on, let's get to work,' he chirped, as if sniffing at his own spring-fresh, golden scent. 'Have you done any flying? Know much about it?'

It took Isabel a few moments to collect her cool which had rapidly melted beneath his pleasantries so she was pleased to find that they were going somewhere else and weren't expected to discuss their 'work' in the public entrance hall. And she was relieved that her own choice of clothing - crush-proof navy slacks and matching shirt - seemed appropriate. She felt she looked like a pilot rather than a pupil; not that there was anyone around to see - the place was experiencing a few moments of peace, it seemed.

'I've booked a half-hour trial flight,' she answered coolly planting a smile on her face. She wondered briefly whether he was so keen on pointing out his own beauty to her that he'd forgotten the reason for her presence.

He appeared to think her attractive expression was meant for him as he allowed a smile to hover around his thin mouth.

Isabel was fast coming to the conclusion that she didn't like the man but knew that if he was going to be passing judgment on her capabilities she would have to take care not to offend him. If he was a good instructor, however, her past training would enable her to cope with that little problem, she decided.

He looked down at the clipboard as he put it down on the desk in the middle of the small office he'd led her into. 'Sorry,' he had the grace to say, 'Thought you were a novice. This was old Sam's slot but he had to go and collect one of our planes over at Barnwood. It had a slight accident on landing,' he added sardonically, without telling her any further details. 'I see you managed to get your PPL, then.'

Isabel did not like the word 'managed'. It made it sound as if she had just scraped through rather than being pupil of the year at her previous flying club. She just nodded.

'Still valid?'

She nodded again, handing him the black folder containing her licence.

'Why go up for a trial flight then? Costs you more, you know.'

'If you look...' she began and then stopped. She reminded herself not to antagonise the man. He would be helping her to re-validate her license when it ran out in a few months' time. 'I haven't flown for some time,' as you would see if you bothered to look, she wanted to add, 'and I might be a bit rusty.'

'Yes,' agreed Rod, 'not all things are like riding a bicycle, are they?' He smiled at his joke, and then copied something from her licence onto the form on his clipboard. 'Do you want left or right-hand seat?' he asked her.

Do you have to ask? Isabel thought. 'Left, I think. Don't you?' was all she said. The only time she had flown in the right-hand seat since she had started flying had made her feel everything was out of order, somehow. And she didn't want him accusing her of being a muddle-headed woman with no talent for getting a small machine into the air, let alone flying it around the countryside.

'I suppose so.' He stood up, gathering his small pile of papers together as if he had just filled out the loading documents for a large, commercial jet. 'I've already planned the flight,' he told her.

Isabel was disappointed to hear this; she had been looking forward to that particular task.

'Saves time,' he said, adding, 'usual on a trial flight. But then I didn't know you were a trained pilot with hundreds of hours on her licence!'

Hardly hundreds, thought Isabel, but enough.

'We'll be following this route.' He pointed to a large aerial view of the local area on the wall. 'Just to let you get your hand in, we'll taxi up to runway 26 and then down to 08 for take off. The wind's veering so you might have a bit of a cross-wind on take-off and landing to cope with. Think you can manage that?' His tone inferred that he hoped she wouldn't so that he would have to take over and prove what a competent instructor and pilot he was.

Isabel nodded her head. If she spoke she might say something she regretted, and her attention was more on a small green area of land and a river on the map which she recognised as home than on his sarcastic comments.

'I'll do the radio,' her instructor told her.

Another disappointment, but there would be other times, she told herself. When she had the money. When Paul paid her she would put aside enough for a weekly hour or two, she promised herself.

She had already begun to fear that the expected week of having a paying guest was likely to develop into more but that there might be advantages to that.

'Frequencies,' he went on, 'are a bit complicated hereabouts. Military aircraft, you know.' He laughed in his special, deprecating and mock-humble way. 'They're inclined to gabble. Sounds like a foreign language. Even I find it difficult to understand sometimes.'

Isabel didn't believe him but let it pass. A doubt had entered her mind as to whether this had been such a good idea. In her previous club everyone did all in their power to give confidence to the most novice of flyers, so that they could forget their unnecessary fears and enjoy the flying. Here she was beginning to feel her own confidence seeping away.

Fortunately for her self-esteem all was different once they got in the air. He allowed her to take control and apart from commenting on the minor misdeed of not pushing in the throttle once the engine had warmed up while they were still on the ground, it seemed that, however hard he looked, he was unable to find much to criticize. He had tried, but soon accepted that he was doomed to ignominy of being proven wrong if he continued. He had even let out a single word of praise - 'good' - as she lifted the small airplane smoothly into the sky, levelled out and flew a complete and faultless circuit which took them over Shinbridge, across the mound behind the village and then over Thom's sprawling land. A brief glimpse of sparkling water was all she was able to see of her own property - experiencing a surprise to see how close, from the air, it seemed to be to the village - before it disappeared from view and it was time to return to the airfield. She even managed to remember the cross-wind and did her down-wind and landing checks without error. Her companion appeared to be stricken into dumbness as she turned towards the runway, lessened speed, lowered the flaps, flared out at the imaginary height of a double-decker bus and landed the Cessna with hardly a bump on the grassy turf of the runway.

'I think you deserve a drink for that,' the instructor managed to say as they left the aircraft in the capable hands of the engineer by the fuel pump and made their way towards the building.

Isabel considered that she should probably translate that into his wanting a drink, but said nothing. She still wanted to be up in that cloudless sky; was exhilarated by the confidence-giving and enjoyable experience it had been but she was, now, beginning to float gently to earth like a balloon which is very slowly and painlessly deflating.

She hit the earth with a thud when he said:'That wasn't bad. For a woman!'

She thought that he had a very warped sense of humour and left it at that. She wasn't going to let him spoil her enjoyment.

To her surprise he led her towards the bar. The fact that he looked as if he were parading a prize specimen at an agricultural show did not deter her from accepting one of the two glasses which had mysteriously materialised. No words had passed between Rod and the barman, so perhaps it was a usual thing that most of Rod's pupils needed reviving after a flight with him. The prize specimen was led from person to person while the instructor extolled his pupil's talents. Fortunately for Isabel's growing discomfiture there were only three people in the bar. One of them she recognised. It was Travis who she'd left in such a hurry on Sunday. This now seemed like weeks ago and not three days. Three days in which she had been able to forget her embarrassing dreams about him becoming one of her customers.

'Don't worry about him,' the man whispered, coming up to her and putting a friendly hand on her shoulder. 'Thinks he's God's gift to women, that one.'

Rod was now talking busily with another man in the bar, leaning over his table to bring his face down to the other man's level. It looked as though he and the man were discussing some important business.

Isabel smiled - in relief as much as in amusement that someone else could see him for what he was.

'Were the trees all right, then?' Travis asked her.

For a moment Isabel wondered what he was on about and then remembered. She had thought it too complicated and too time-consuming at their last meeting to give the real reason for her sudden departure. She had told him some story about one of her trees causing problems and someone was putting himself to a lot of bother to come on a Sunday to see them.

'Oh, yes, thank you,' she murmured. What was it Alice liked to quip? Something about getting the loom out when one lie *had* to lead to another.

'Got quite an estate, have you?' Travis asked with a smile.

Isabel decided to go along with the joke, her spirits still high, although not with the untouched glass on the bar. 'Oh, yes,' she said. 'Quite an estate. All three acres of it!'

Travis smiled again, tolerantly this time. 'I like modest women,' he said with a chuckle. 'What do you do with this 'estate'?'

'Fruit and veg, mostly,' she told him. 'Herbs, too, are on the agenda. You know the sort of thing.' She was getting carried away with her enthusiasm, she considered with an inward chuckle. It must be the sudden injection of high-altitude oxygen. But it had been a long time since she had talked with anyone with sense and intelligence. 'I want to branch out into smoked fish soon.' Wasn't this carrying things a bit too far? She had to find and catch the fish, and buy a smoker.... It was the first time anything to do with fish had entered her mind since her fight with the fish farmer. But smoked fish...it wasn't a bad idea. And the herbs would do nicely for her vegetable baskets - once the small green spikes had become taller than their current four inches.

'Interesting,' said Travis, admiration in his voice. 'And she flies, too!'

'Not so you'd notice!' Isabel answered, nodding towards Rod who was now standing with his hand on the shoulder of a smartly-dressed woman sitting at the table with the club secretary.

'Gave you a hard time, did he?'

'You could say that. But,' she added firmly, 'I showed him!'

'I'm sure you did that,' Travis laughed. 'That's just his way, poor chap. Thinks he's the king-pin of the club, expects anyone who turns up to bow and scrape to him. But don't worry, Juliet won't tolerate that for long.' He nodded towards the attractive young-ish woman in a proprietorial way.

'And she needn't worry about me!' Isabel added silently as she glanced across at the table. 'And Juliet?' she asked, 'I assume she's your property, is that it?' she teased, holding her breath.

Travis just shook his head with a grin. 'She directs my television shows. Come on, I'll introduce you.'

An unexpected image slowly entered Isabel's mind. Like a photo faded from age it told her where she had seen him before and she was suddenly filled with a joyous sense of anticipation.

Juliet turned out to be a bit older than distance had allowed. Mid thirties, Isabel decided with a touch of feline malevolence. She wasn't Travis's girl-friend, it seemed. But she managed to make it clear that another woman in their small entourage would not be made welcome. Only when Travis mentioned that Isabel had a pilot's licence did her attitude change from one of polar ice to that of melting frost, much to Isabel's bemusement.

'In fact,' Travis was saying, his voice a little louder than necessary as if he was asking that the floor be his and not the instructor's, 'I was about to ask her if she'd like to come to Polwyn this week-end,' he added, confusing Isabel even further. 'We might even get a lift.'

His laugh was pleasant, friendly, thought Isabel as Juliet joined in with a slightly frigid giggle. But what was the joke?

'Don't look so puzzled,' Travis said, turning towards Isabel. 'It's only a joke! Thought you might like the exciting experience of taking us somewhere in your plane!'

Isabel decided that silence was, indeed, braver than asking silly questions; it would all become clear eventually. At least, she hoped it would.

'It's just that I'm looking for a pilot,' Travis told her then. 'But not for Polwyn, of course! We were only teasing you. Sorry.'

He did, indeed, look crestfallen, so Isabel forgave him.

'But I tell you what,' Travis continued. 'I'm doing the air show at Shilliton Air Field tomorrow. Why don't you come along and watch? You might be able to suggest what vegetables would be useful for our films.'

And I might be able to sell you some. Were her dreams actually going to come true, after all? Oh yes, she'd go along to see him making his TV programme at the local military airfield summer open day - *and* persuade him to buy some produce from her for future programmes. The day was working out very well.

'And it might give you some ideas as to what to plant on your estate,' Travis said with a smile.

Isabel did not correct him about the size of her growing area. She'd told him the truth and it hadn't made an impression the first time. What did it matter? She thought her three acres were producing as much as any other grower her size.

Even Hannah's sulky attitude could not spoil her mood that evening and she went to bed feeling as she had turned a corner. Her dreams that night were all of floating wings, green vegetables, handle-bar moustaches all mixed up in an unappetising stew before being made into a glorious meal by her new friend and TV cook, Travis Parkin.

Chapter 12

'If I'm to get to the air show,' Isabel told herself as she sipped at her breakfast coffee, 'I'll have to get some work done.' She ticked off on the fingers of her hand the jobs which were most pressing - essential, in fact.

She had tried to work out some sort of routine as soon as she knew what had to be done in the garden and when. Weeding was not the most artistic of jobs, she had decided, but necessary, so she would do half an hour each day and then go on to something more creative. Then the small patch of lawn needed mowing - perhaps she could persuade Hannah to do that, but she wasn't going to hold her breath. And there were new potatoes to be dug for the Hart's box to be delivered that day. Hannah could do the delivery, she decided. She'd enjoy meeting new people, seeing the village at first hand. What a hope!

Isabel had told Travis she could only manage to get to the air base in the afternoon. 'If I don't spend some quality time with my vegetables,' she had laughed, 'they might pay me back by dying!'

'What do you get your staff to do, then?' he'd asked, his eyes widening with amusement.

Isabel had wondered whether this joke about her 'estate' had gone far enough and was about to suggest it came to a dignified end when Juliet had called him to answer his mobile lying on the table in front of her.

Taking her empty cup to the draining board, she was about to go out and get on with weeding the lettuce bed when Hannah made an appearance. Her expression said she objected to being part of the morning world. Isabel's faint irritation at Travis's not taking her seriously she took it out on the girl.

'And what did you get up to last night?' She shouldn't ask her guest such a question, she told herself quickly. But part of the deal with Paul was that Hannah would help her, wasn't it? Or so he had said. One look at the long purple finger-nails and Isabel knew that manual labour was not Hannah's thing. What was she going to help with, then? Isabel sighed, not finding an answer to that question.

'I was next door, if you must know,' Hannah answered, shaking her head as though she had a glossy mane instead of the current past-its-sell-by-date silver-slash crew-cut. 'What else is there to do around here?'

Isabel drew in a deep breath forcing herself not to respond to the seemingly innocent complaint of a spoilt teenager. She also decided that any caustic comments regarding the arrangements with her father would only add conflagratory fuel to slumbering embers.

'Have some breakfast,' she told the girl, 'and then you might like to come and help me pick some fruit.'

Hannah looked taken aback as if she had never had to get her own breakfast before let alone pick fruit. She looked sad, almost as if she was blaming her absent father for landing her in this boring, unfriendly person's house.

Isabel relented. She hadn't had time to give the girl much attention. She thought back to her own teenage years when she had had more of that than she really wanted; she would have loved being in the country away from parental controls.

'I'll get some coffee,' she said pushing past the girl to get to the old range on which a large, heavy kettle was kept permanently boiling. Probably bad for their health, she thought, but it was too useful to throw out. There were lots of things she would have to sort out in her mind eventually; like how could she get so much joy out of polluting the sky with airplane fuel while at the same time telling everyone she was an organic farmer. The two didn't mix, she knew. But she'd sort that out with herself later. 'And you can make yourself some toast.'

'Ugh!' came from the girl as she collapsed in a disgruntled heap on the chair. Isabel thought it was a whisper she wasn't meant to hear so ignored it.

Had she been like this as a teenager? Isabel asked herself tipping the heavy aluminium kettle over the instant coffee. She thought not; her mother would have had a few words to say if she had been. Her father always stood up for her in family arguments so perhaps her mum had been too nervous to intervene. That almost made Isabel laugh. Yes, her father, she realized now, had been a bit of a bully; but her mother had never been a wimp. But you never know what's going on in someone else's head. Isabel let the thought fade. Only good old memories should be viewed in mental slide-slows; sad or bad ones should be relegated to the rubbish heap, she reminded herself. Unless you can learn from them, of course.

'Here we are, then,' she said with false cheerfulness. She had decided that she was going to be nice to the girl from now on; would spend some time with her; try to get to know her. Let her go back to her father with glowing reports of the successful life she, Isabel, had created for herself without him.

'I wish I was back in London. With all my friends,' the girl complained, sending all Isabel's good intentions fluttering away like frightened birds.

'In London,' Hannah continued as if talking to some country bumpkin, 'you have cinemas and clubs. There are all sorts of things to do.' She looked around as if searching for evidence of similar things in the country. Her expression told of anticipated disappointment.

Isabel sighed. 'So why are you here, then?' She considered the question might sound insensitive but she truly wanted to know the answer.

'My father didn't want.... wanted me... to have a holiday,' she ended lamely. 'Some holiday!'

'Well, then,' Isabel said, 'you might as well try and enjoy it.'

'I might,' Hannah answered, 'if you don't keep on invading my space.'

'Invading your space?' Isabel wasn't familiar with all modern terms but she had no difficulty with the meaning.

'If you wouldn't keep asking me where I've been, what I've been doing, this place might just be tolerable.'

Isabel didn't know how to reply to that. She thought she'd been very tolerant.

It was her home, after all; she had a right to know who was coming and going. And when. Or perhaps modern teenagers had different ideas; were allowed any 'space' they wanted or they would make life such a misery for parents - and teachers, too, Isabel feared - that it wasn't wise to go against their wishes. What a horrible idea, she decided from the height of her thirty two years.

Hannah had managed not to mention her mother once. Yet. And the only time she had referred to her father was when Isabel took her down to see the small river.

'My god,' the girl had said, momentarily forgetting the pose of disgruntled teenager she had been wearing like a cloak since her arrival, 'my father could make something of this.'

Isabel had been flattered - for a brief moment. Then the girl spoke again.

'He'd have hundreds of new homes built on all that.'

Isabel realized then that the girl was pointing across the gently murmuring stream at the expanse of mown fields stretching as far as the eye could see on the other side of the river. Isabel felt as if some unseen hand had suddenly anchored her to the ground. But only briefly. She cheered herself by saying silently 'Like father, like daughter, it appears.' To the girl she said; 'Not up for grabs, I'm afraid.' She knew how persistent money-orientated business-men could be once they spied a piece of land they fancied. There was no way this girl was going to try and work on her father's behalf. 'Others have tried,' she lied. 'and spent masses on trying to get planning permission. Sensible people leave it well alone, now,' she added firmly.

'You don't know my father,' Hannah had retorted, but with little conviction.

Oh yes I do, Isabel answered silently.

'I might swim in the river here,' Hannah said then, as if trying to turn the conversation away from a tricky - and unsuccessful - subject. 'The boys next door swim in their bit.'

With a calmness she didn't feel, Isabel said,' Please don't do that. The man across the way,' she waved in the direction of the fish farm, 'is very unpleasant. Has even threatened to take me to court if I as much as leave my own river bank,' she added in an inspired lie. She had enough on her plate concerning him, as it was.

'My father says he... says people don't own rivers, only get licences to use the water. The rest belongs to us.'

Isabel didn't know who the 'us' was intended for, and she decided to ignore the slight hesitation in the girl's speech. For a second she'd had a fleeting fear that Paul might be up to his old tricks again and was appalled at the thought. She then decided that the stress of having a constant reminder of him in his daughter was making her a neurotic woman, so she promptly filed the thought in her mental waste-bin.

'But people who have licences to use the water,' she told the girl, sounding in her own ears just like a school-teacher, 'pay a lot. They don't want other people encroaching on what is - albeit temporarily theirs by right!'

I'm a good one to speak, she told herself with a jolt. She had looked at her deeds for the property, which previously she had only skimmed through knowing that the solicitor would tell her anything that was of supreme importance, after the man had hurled abuse at her for fishing her own water and discovered that, yes, he was right. She did need a licence. She had made a mental note to rectify this matter without delay when in Shilliton but had forgotten. She would do it on her next trip.

'And he's got a gun, I believe,' she added lamely, not knowing whether this was a fact or not.

'So, what am I supposed to do with myself?'

Hannah's shoulders were now hunched, in self-pity or sincere misery, Isabel was unable to ascertain.

'You haven't even got a television. But,' she brightened visibly, 'that nice Thom has made a super place out of the stables where he's got TV, lots of computers - for games, you know - and even a billiard table. It's wonderful!' She sighed as if to say she had been expecting the same from her father's 'friend'. 'The boys are a nice crowd,' she conceded, 'but a bit young for me.'

Prison fodder was what old Ben had called them. Isabel wondered what Paul would say if he knew his precious daughter was hanging around with them. Also, having met them, she thought that even if some of the boys were young others were at least Hannah's age.

She saw no more of Hannah for the rest of the day, for which she was grateful despite the twinges of guilt she felt on and off. If her neighbour had been a bit friendlier she would have rung and asked him whether he objected to his uninvited guest, but she didn't. She could imagine the sarcastic manner in which he would probably tell her that Hannah was far from welcome, and complain about her not keeping her guests under control. She wasn't going to risk that.

That morning at breakfast - prepared in advance this time to save any damage to her nerves or her humour - avoiding all questions about absence Isabel asked Hannah whether she would like to go to the village with her that morning.

'I'm taking a box of fruit and vegetables to some friends there,' she said.

'What friends?'

It was more a matter of Hannah wanting to know their names than a cynical observation of surprise that she had any friends, Isabel hoped.

'They live in the old mill,' Isabel told her, hoping that a vision of an old building would kindle her interest. 'The Harts,' she added, not that the name would mean anything to Hannah.

'No thanks,' was Hannah's terse reply. 'I've heard about them,' she added, then said no more.

Isabel did not ask what she had heard, just accepted the girl's words for the lame excuse it was. 'I'm out for the afternoon,' she told Hannah. 'Will you be okay?'

'Of course.' The girl seemed to have recovered from the slight letting down of the drawbridge the day before.

'Any plans?' Isabel asked, trying to sound friendly without being inquisitive.

'None of your business,' was the less-than-polite reply.

Isabel wondered briefly whether she should make it her business, but she was blowed if she was going to bother about someone who was determined to be such a misery. She hadn't promised to be nurse-maid to the girl. There was one thing, Isabel reluctantly accepted, at least under the beady eye of her next-door neighbour she was unable to get up to mischief. She would hear soon enough if that happened, for sure. And Hannah might even learn a few manners by association. Isabel almost laughed out loud at the silly notion when she remembered who, exactly, Hannah would be associating with. Let Paul reap the benefits of the loving care he had arranged for his precious daughter!

'I don't know when I'll be back, that's all.' She had no intention of leaving a key with the girl but would plan to be back before her - if only she knew when that would be.

'Not bothered.'

Hannah was chasing a square of toast around her plate with the knife as if making a map of her day. Isabel wished she would eat it or leave it alone.

'I'm going swimming,' the girl said. 'In the town,' she added hastily, evidently expecting a salvo of criticism if she didn't offer some information. Her expression inferred that she thought it was a waste of time and money when there was a perfectly good river nearby.

'What about...?' Isabel began.

'They're going on a bus trip,' Hannah sneered. She wouldn't have gone even if she was asked, her tone said, but this was belied by the crestfallen look on her face. 'Then I'm going to see a film,' she stated, 'so I won't be back till late.'

The Harts weren't in so Isabel left the box of produce in the unlocked garden hut at the end of the lawn that sloped to the water's edge. Up here, the river was less powerful than at Woodbine Cottage but just as clear and beautiful, which had surprised Isabel it being so near the village. Being on the ground floor of the old converted corn mill, the couple's property had more to offer than the three flats above, with the lovely garden, their own drive to park in, and a private entrance.

Having completed her errand Isabel drove swiftly to the air base. Shilliton Air Field was a naval station of some importance. Hundreds of cadets entered as no more than children and left some years later fully-qualified pilots, ready to do their job of protecting their country. Not only that, it was the centre for flight-testing of new aircraft. It brought wealth into the area together with a well-appreciated social life. Each summer, the height of that social life was the Air Show which thousands attended. It was the one time in the year when the public who had nothing to do with the base could come in and see for themselves the mysterious activities of an important air base. For Air Day there were visiting aircraft from all over the world predominantly American, Isabel discovered, nestling on the tarmac with planes old and new, small and huge, including the navy's own special fleet of acrobatic small jets on whose red-wings the sun sprayed large intermittent splashes of light. She'd read all this in a flyer which had landed fortuitously in her letter box.

Even without the promotional leaflet Isabel would have known what to expect. The club she had belonged to when learning to fly was associated with yet another large, albeit army, air base. She wished she could sit on the grass at the side of the airfield with the other dozens of happy families and watch the antics of the various airplanes as they went through paces which many of them would normally avoid at all costs. The engines of the planes waiting to take off screamed for attention, accompanied by other aircraft noises which were like the base section of some gigantic discordant orchestra. Some planes were taxiing back to the hangers; others were silently standing on the tarmac away from the centre of activity. These were the veteran planes - the Swordfish, Seafire, Sea Fury and so on - on which visitors, young and old, were allowed to satisfy their fascination by scrambling in and out of.

With some reluctance Isabel made her way to the large open-sided marquee erected next to the viewing area. She was amazed to see how many people were crowded into the hot and relatively airless tent, considering the crowds outside. It must be a bumper year, she thought, and then remembered that this was *the* air show of the season. Many people, of course, came to these things just for the socializing; not necessarily to watch red planes frolicking with danger in a cloudless sky. Even if they had wished to there was no getting away from the hypnotic tang of aviation fuel which mingled with the scent of hot people, spiced with distant aromas of cooking food. Large flower arrangements mixed their cosmetic counter perfumes with the rest of the disparate smells.

She had no trouble finding Travis. His long trestle table, laden with all the tools of his trade, stood at one end of the marquee, away from the noise of the band playing popular tunes on a small raised dais at the other. Juliet was standing to one side seemingly trying to be unnoticed but continuously watchful.

It was some time before Travis noticed Isabel's arrival. He lifted his head and with a smile nodded a welcome to her. He was cooking something in a hot wok over a portable gas ring. From time to time he would turn and from bowls in rows like rotund soldiers, pluck another handful of meat or vegetables. Of herbs there were no sign, Isabel noticed. A crowd had collected in front of the table; free food was on offer and always welcome. When Travis was satisfied that all ingredients were cooked to his standard, he poured a spoonful of each onto tiny paper plates and passed them to the waiting crowd.

Isabel looked around; there was no sign of any cameras so what was Travis doing? Perhaps he was selling something; but she didn't think so. Then she remembered. Juliet had told her that he'd been commissioned to do several half-hour television programmes and as his current appearances on TV usually amounted to no more than ten minutes, he needed practice at keeping an audience fascinated for the much longer time. He was an entertainer at heart, Isabel realized, and was currently helping a grateful navy to entertain its guests. One thing she did notice was a sign standing on a Formica book-rest at the end of the table extolling the virtues of always cooking with organic produce, with a pile of leaflets fanned out beneath it.

While Travis cooked and answered questions from his audience and Juliet watched, Isabel had a good look at the uncooked foods waiting for Travis's masterly hand. And she didn't like what she saw. The plastic-looking potatoes, tomatoes, peppers, courgettes, onions and leeks looked as though they had come straight from the supermarket, while the salads looked wilted. The cubed meat, too, appeared pale and listless - any average cook knew meat had to be larded with fat to cook well, Isabel told herself with a shudder - and the fish looked as if it should have been framed, not cooked. It was not, Isabel considered, a good advertisement for someone purporting to use only naturally grown products. An overwhelming urge to do something about it filled her. She would, she determined, donning once more the cloak of a busy executive, persuade him to use the products of her own 'estate' for his vegetables and she would do some research into finding a good butcher. What could be done about the fish was something she would have to think about. A little voice suggested that perhaps her own fish could become television stars; but not until she had a) learnt to catch them and b) sorted out a licence! But wasn't she allowing her ambitions to trot on before they had even had a chance to learn to crawl? In business she had never been afraid to stride where even the angels might have feared to walk, but she was a novice when it came to television personalities and their programmes. She would have to tread slowly but do something about it she would - and, possibly, she admitted with a tiny, but only temporary, tinge of guilt, achieve something to her own advantage.

Travis was now busy rustling up another batch of freebies so Isabel had a further chance to watch him at work. He was good looking, she decided, in an arty sort of way. His dark, wavy hair was speckled with premature grey making him look as though he should be a member of D'Artagnan's wily group; his build was not unlike that awful Thom's, fit and muscular. But that's where the likeness ended, Isabel decided. Travis had a much better figure, was slighter and not quite as overwhelmingly tall. He had a gift, too; he could hold people's attention while continuing to work well, and smile charmingly at anyone who interrupted with, possibly, an inane question. Even as she watched, he was beginning to take on the role of television celebrity as if he had always known he was born to be well known and well liked.

And, Isabel told herself, he was a great cook. He had to be to make that pile of - rubbish, she was going to say - second-class produce into those well-cooked, attractive - and tasty, if the way they disappeared down fairly intelligent-looking throats was anything to go by! - little dishes. She hadn't spent many years watching her talented mother without being able to recognise a talented chef when she saw one. She wished he were using good ingredients, that was all. Even with her limited knowledge she would guess that these would have shown up as insipid rags under a powerful television camera.

She didn't have time to talk to Travis and was amazed to see that he had been cooking and chatting, and she had been watching, for almost two hours. The small plastic glasses of fruit juice which a white-coated barman had passed around had kept her going. Juliet had made it her business to come over and chat to her, too.

'What do you think, then?' the woman asked, nodding in the direction of Travis who, currently, had been made invisible by the crowd of avid samplers holding out their hands for the little plates.

'Great!' was Isabel's enthusiastic reply. She did not feel totally comfortable with the well-dressed - but somewhat overweight, she thought with delight - TV director. She sensed undercurrents she couldn't, as yet, recognise. 'And,' carried away with her enthusiasm and the awkwardness of her feelings, 'I can see he really needs a supply of good, home grown foodstuffs.' She didn't see the look of surprise that flitted across the other woman's face.

'That's clever of you to notice,' Juliet said after a pause. 'He likes to use only Non G-M foods, of course. That's at the heart of his motivation. Part of his trade-mark, so to speak.'

If she had thought her words might deter Isabel from being too enthusiastic, she didn't succeed.

'Oh, that's all right,' Isabel answered, thinking about her next door neighbour and his organic farming. 'I know all about that. Everything I grow has to be 'natural'. My neighbour demands it,' she laughed.

'Good,' Juliet said in a quiet voice. Then added, so firmly that Isabel suddenly thought she was going to try and put her down, 'We're filming at a fish-shed on Friday'. She surprised Isabel then by saying: 'Why don't you come along and see what it's all about?'

'I'd like that,' Isabel answered. It would be on Hannah's last day, but why should that worry her?

'I'll let you know,' Juliet told her thoughtfully. 'Give me your phone number before you leave,' she said, before returning to her position of guardian to her cooking star once more, leaving Isabel wondering what had happened to the simple card she had given to Travis.

A few minutes later, recalling that she had wanted to be back home before Hannah, Isabel decided it was time to leave. She scribbled her name and number on a page from her tiny notebook and passed it over to Juliet who had just nodded. She wanted to wave good-bye to Travis but he was busy on yet another gastronomic creation. It wasn't going to be long, however, till they met up again, she thought happily.

As she was letting herself into the cottage - there was no sign of Hannah, she was relieved to see - the phone was ringing. It was Juliet.

'I had a sudden brain-wave,' she told Isabel, 'as soon as you had left.' She paused, leaving Isabel squirming to know what this brain-wave was, and hoping against hope that it was something that would be to her benefit, then said, 'About Friday. You couldn't fly us down to Polwyn could you?'

Isabel was shocked into temporary disappointed silence. 'I can't do that,' she said at last.

'Why ever not? You've got a licence, you said so yesterday.' Juliet's voice was sharp as if she had anticipated a response full of gratitude and enthusiasm.

'But I haven't got a plane,' Isabel said. 'And I don't have a commercial licence.'

'Oh, no money would change hands,' Juliet told her as if she had already considered this. 'It would just be a pleasure trip,' she said, 'with us just coming along for the ride. As for the plane,' she added trying to sound as if she had just remembered it, 'Travis has his own Cessna 152, and I know you can fly that.' She stopped as if there was no further argument that Isabel could put forward.

'Why doesn't he fly it himself?' she asked. She was just beginning to think it might work and had had to steel herself to ask the question that might be the end of a rather nice outing. But was she getting into something that mightn't turn out very well for her? she wondered suddenly, deciding that her pleasure would have to give way to good sense.

'Oh well, never mind,' Juliet was saying. 'We thought you might enjoy it, that's all.'

Isabel sighed a sigh which was made up of relief and disappointment in equal measures. But she still had the feeling that she should refuse. This time, at least. She would go to Polwyn in her car - the important thing was to see what she could produce for the show, not display her rusty flying skills to people who could, with a bit of effort on her behalf, become very important to her.

She still didn't understand why Travis didn't fly his plane himself. If he had one of his own it must mean he was as committed to flying as she was.

'Travis...' she began and then hesitated before continuing. 'Why...?

'He's an artist,' Juliet answered shortly as if guessing at Isabel's thoughts. 'Has to keep his mind on his work.' She added then, 'Can you make your own way down, then? The mini-bus we use will be full.'

Isabel had rung off with the feeling that she hadn't handled something well, but could not put a finger on why she felt like that. She'd even forgotten to ask Juliet what time she should be there. Concentrating on her chores in the garden she tried to rid her mind of the mystery. She hadn't succeeded, however, by the time Hannah arrived home.

The girl seemed more cheerful, more amenable. Isabel diplomatically did not enquire after her day and no information was volunteered. After a hastily prepared supper of soup and home-made garlic bread and salad Hannah was happy, it seemed, to have an early night.

Isabel's dreams that night stayed with her well after she awoke early the next morning. She had dreamt of a huge white marquee which had the brightness of a thousand 100 watt bulbs. She and Travis and Juliet were the only ones left in the barn-like place. Travis's face was haggard and tired. Juliet clung onto his arm with one hand, the other running down Travis's wet cheeks. Isabel had not realized he was crying. Then from outside the tent came a clamour of shrieks and screams and the sudden sound of metal being crushed by contact with tarmac. She had wanted to turn and run from the tableau now visible through the open sides of the marquee. But her feet were as if glued to the grass floor. To her amazement the crowds began to filter back into the tent, laughing and dancing in wild, weird pirouettes. When she looked Travis had miraculously lost his distraught expression and had his arm around a magically present Hannah. Juliet standing aside now was glaring at Isabel as if what had happened was a nightmare and Isabel was somehow responsible for it all.

The memory of the dream left her confused for much of the day, until the details disappeared into the mists of reality.

Chapter 13

Isabel managed to find Polwyn on the map and decided it was going to take an hour or so to get there. She decided to ignore her list of chores for that day and start off early. With little traffic to worry about she arrived before anyone else she recognised - or who looked as if they knew that the famous Travis Perkin was making a TV film there that day. She still felt a bit niggled that there hadn't been room for her in the mini-bus with everyone else; she supposed it was because Shinbridge wasn't exactly en route from the studios.

By the way Travis and Juliet spoke, Isabel had thought they were from that television studio famous for its wildlife and nature programmes. She had felt a little let down when she learned they were part of a small, independent film company with offices in the sheds of a disused vacuum cleaner factory in the next county.

After only a couple of missed turnings she found the entrance to the fishing harbour and parked her car in the small pay-and-display at the end of one long, wide quay. Her mind was on the whereabouts of Travis and Juliet and the others so she couldn't really take in all that was happening. To her it was just a blur of large brightly painted trawlers and smaller fishing vessels unloading their catch, all safely protected in red, green and blue plastic boxes, onto waiting trailers. She watched them hurry to the long low building further up the quay before scampering back to the boats to collect more fish. However were they going to manage to film a programme amongst all this noise,? she asked herself.

The cobbles of the quay were slimy with salt water and some black liquid, together with lumps of cast-off ice from the containers of fish, making it as slippery as a ski-slope. She was relieved that she had put on casual clothes and shoes; could even have worn her red gardening boots and she wouldn't have looked out of place. The thought of what Juliet might have to say about that made her smile.

A young man with a long metal bar bent at the end into a hook, returned her smile thinking it was for him. He was standing outside one of the wide sliding doors leading into a shed the size of a Greek amphitheatre; one that was built of tin, however, with echoing high ceilings made of plasterboard. In fact, the theatre idea wasn't a bad comparison, Isabel thought as she looked at the drama being enacted within.

'Will I get shot if I go in there?' she asked.

'Of course not!' he laughed. 'Go ahead.'

If this was the place they hoped to use for their filming, Isabel considered, they hadn't done their research very well. It was a teaming mass of busy people, boxes being noisily pushed from pillar to post, metal flat-bed scales being scraped along the ground from one group of dripping containers to another and an auctioneer shouting his loudest in order to get a top price for the box of oily wet pink, white or dark-skinned fish currently in front of him. But who was she to know? Perhaps it had been chosen to add background colour.

The young man followed her into the shed and hooked his iron bar onto a slatted box the size of a semi-detached's downstair's toilet. Dragging it to the door he loaded it onto a mini forklift truck. He seemed oblivious to the noise and mayhem inside the domed building. Once the little truck was full it scurried away to waiting vans - some with famous names of restaurants, others sporting fish and chip shop titles and other, smaller ones, which advertised 'fish straight to your home from the harbour of Polwyn'.

Isabel could feel apprehension seeping into her as time went on. Perhaps it had all been some sort of sick joke and they weren't coming here, after all. But why should they do that? It wouldn't have been Travis's idea, she assured herself, but there was something - possessive? - about Juliet which had made her take an instant dislike for the woman. And it was Juliet who had rung up and made the arrangements, not Travis.

The auctioneer continued to sing his song, the puller continued to pull his boxes to waiting lorries, the floor continued to have its face washed with a powerful hose, and still there was no sign of the others. She wandered down the length of the fish shed, then turned towards the auctioneer while musing over how long she should stay before calling it a day. She almost tripped over the feet of a chair as tall as a tennis referee's perch. High up a man dressed in black was sitting, a heavy camera perched on his shoulder. She could see that the cameraman was focussing on a large, glossy poster on the wall behind the auctioneer's head. It was one she had studied earlier to keep her mind occupied while waiting. It was covered in colourful pictures showing all the fish that could possibly be found in Polwyn fish sheds – cod, tuna, mackerel, herrings, monkfish, whiting, and salmon of course, and those little flat round things whose name she couldn't for the moment recall, but which reminded her of the word life-buoy for some reason, and countless different types of shell-fish - most of which were being delivered from the boats in large, off-white rattling woven bags. There were other fish she didn't recognise - megrim, hoki, tilapia - but they all looked as if they would provide a tasty meal.

The cameraman looked down at Isabel with an expression that said he was not appreciative of having his perch joggled by some careless woman. Isabel recognised him as one of the crowd at the Air Show. There he had been taking pictures with a small digital camera as Travis worked. Isabel had wondered why Travis kept smiling at him. Now she knew. She learned later that he was now taking shots of the fish auction to use as colour and authenticity in the film he would be taking of Travis at work.

Relief flowed through her as she gathered that she hadn't been made a fool of after all. She felt a bit guilty about thinking that someone as pleasant as Travis could be accused of mischief making. And Juliet was too professional to waste her time at such games.

Calmer now, she moved a short distance from the tall chair. If the cameraman was here, it must mean the others would arrive soon. She would wait until he descended from his great height and ask him.

With a background of the auctioneer's voice sounding in her ear she wandered around the big fish shed taking a deeper interest now. The smell would probably get into her clothes, she thought. But the tang like that of smoked fish - a mixture of fresh fish and salt water - was surprisingly pleasant and refreshing. The black mess on the floor which continuously seeped out of some of the large plastic crates was the ink from 'cuttles', one man told her. She'd never seen it before and dipped one finger into a small pool of the dark liquid. It took her some moments to remove the black spot so she didn't repeat the experiment. Arriving at the door, the puller - as she had heard him being called - was just lifting another box onto the toy-like forklift. A screeching chorus line of gulls - young ones, brown and speckled like hens' eggs, the older ones sleek and grey - surrounded him. As soon as the truck moved away they flew up and perched on the rigging of the fishing boats moored alongside the old quay until another box brought them back to earth once more. Sometimes they were lucky and managed to grab a fish; mostly they went away disappointed.

'Don't get much chance!' The puller grinned at her as she watched the birds. 'But pests they be, those young 'uns. Haven't learned to fish; think we are here to feed them!'

Isabel was about to go back into the noisy jungle of people and fish boxes when a small bus drove past her towards to the end of the quay. She just had time to catch a glimpse of Travis and Juliet and several other people she didn't know before it turned the corner at the end. She turned back into the building, in case they came in by a different door just and she missed them. As she had been invited as just an unimportant onlooker they might forget about her. The fact that she was going to improve on their star's image was still her secret.

She was amazed at how the tableau had changed in the few minutes she had been away. Nearly all the boxes of fish were now empty and being hosed down. The auctioneer was packing up his briefcase and the man with the hose was swirling water around where the fish boxes had stood whilst being auctioned. It looked like a different place altogether.

Just then Juliet and Travis came through the end door. Isabel almost smiled as Juliet had to do a little dance to keep the swirling water from dousing her inappropriate open-toed sandals. They were followed by the rest of the bus passengers carrying tables and chairs, cloths, large laundry baskets rattling with dishes. Some were loaded down with tubs of small bushes growing incongruously amongst cut flowers whose stems were stuck precariously in the earth. These were followed by two men laden with electrical equipment including floodlights the size of air-raid spotters with screens for reflectors, and various other bits and pieces of the esoteric equipment for making an half hour's worth of visual entertainment. Having deposited their loads the first men left the building only to return moments later, one with baskets of fruit and vegetables hanging from each arm, the other with a wine carrier with bottles of white wine, olive oil and balsamic vinegar rattling in his hand.

Visions of her parents came floating back. How her mother had been delighted when balsamic vinegar had appeared on the shelves of the local supermarket. Years of sailing around Mediterranean ports had taught her to appreciate the correct ingredients for the dishes she learned to cook from local restaurant owners, hoteliers and recently made friends.

Her mother had had no trouble making friends, she reminded herself. The idea that she would much rather have been left on her own to do her bits of water colours, her crochet and her cooking, hit Isabel like an electric shock. She would have to spend some time thinking about that. And her father, too. He seemed not to be able to live without the life-giving stimulants of socializing. Why she was thinking about this now Isabel found hard to understand. Perhaps it was that her mind was over-stimulated by all that was happening around her. Perhaps it was because she was lonely without realizing it. The vision of how it all turned sour with her father disappearing and the feeble attempt, Isabel now knew that it was, at appearing to swim to his life's end by leaving his clothes on the beach, filtered unwonted into her mind. And her mother making off with the boat - *his* boat, he'd always called it, though she knew he had put it in her mother's name as something to do with tax - was as extraordinary as any of the other happenings in their family. Silas seemed to be the only sane one. At least he was honest and hard-working and quickly climbing the ladder to success.

The images of her disparate family dispersed as Isabel turned her attention to the activities surrounding Travis who was now standing to attention behind a table. His minions were placing all the things he would need for showing the world what a clever cook he was and how skillful the viewers could become as long as they followed his lead. A girl was trying to dab powder on his forehead but he kept shifting from side to side moving the cooking pots, bowls of pre-chopped vegetables, knives and wooden spoons. Eventually she shrugged her shoulders and moved away. Isabel could see no need for attention to Travis's face; it looked all right to her.

Several supermarket carriers were placed on the long table for Travis to sort through and then, it seemed - if Juliet's frantic flapping of her hands was anything to go by - they were about to get on with the business of making a film.

'Do you know how much it's costing us to rent this place?' she shouted.

'Not a lot,' a quiet male voice answered, thinking he wouldn't be overheard.

Juliet ignored him after throwing a venomous look in his direction.

Just then a tall, well-built man came into the shed. Gold embroidery twinkled on his dark lightweight jacket pronouncing him as a person of authority.

'Everything okay?' he asked Juliet in a friendly voice.

She nodded. 'Don't worry,' she said. 'We're just about to start work. Won't be here longer than the two hours I requested.' She looked around as if searching for inspiration. 'We'll be starting as soon as they,' she pointed to two men who were completing the rinsing of the floor, 'have finished.'

'Oh, I'm not trying to hurry you,' the harbour master told her. 'As you're donating the rent to charity, you can take as long as you like.' He waved cheerfully and left the building.

Nobody looked at Juliet or giggled out loud but the atmosphere rippled with repressed laughter.

A last swish from the hose and there was silence at last. Isabel found it hard to believe that this was the same place she first entered almost two hours earlier. Gone was the cheerful music of the auction, the jokes and laughter which had spiced the salty air, the sense of commercial satisfaction and the friendly bartering after a sale was completed.

The filming soon took her interest.

Travis had decided that, unsurprisingly, fish would be the main course. Spiced up with colourful sauces their paleness would not detract from his art, he told the assembled company before they had started filming.

Isabel could not help admiring him for his cheerful patience as time and again he had to repeat not only his words but actions, too, in order to please the aesthetic demands of his cameraman.

Isabel watched fascinated as he chopped and cooked and chattered simultaneously. Again, however, she felt that the ingredients needed improving on. At one point the young make-up girl was instructed to take a small flower spray and sprinkle water over the wilting spinach, carrots and beetroot that Travis would make his sauces from. He had chosen from a previously prepared tray of fish, four pieces of succulent monkfish to which he was going to add prawns, some smoked haddock and two steaks of unnaturally pink salmon. The dish of the day was to be a quickly made fish pie for four, it seemed. One of her mother's specialities had been fish pie, Isabel remembered. She wondered whether Travis's would match it for taste and appearance. The memory of her mother when they were far from land on the boat making a very good fisherman's pie from tinned fish, dried mushrooms and a tin of condensed mushroom soup so that nobody guessed their dinner all came from the bilges which stored their canned and desiccated foods, amused her.

The allotted two hours - and more - slipped by while Isabel enjoyed herself, learning all the time about what went into the half hour programmes like the ones she used to watch greedily in her lonely evenings in London. She had become quite addicted to programmes on food, on travel, on history, after a hard day's work and to fill the time bereft of Paul's company. She had never, however, allowed herself to become committed to the activities of an east-end square or a pub in the city north of London. Those were not for her, she had decided.

Isabel could see that everyone was getting tired. Travis had promised that he would make enough food for them to have a good lunch once the filming was finished. And they were coming near to the end now, Isabel could see, as the fish simmered in one pan and the sauce gently coagulated in another. If they spent any more time re-doing things the large tray of fish, which on arrival had been heavily laden, would be empty. However, there would be plenty of the try-outs for everyone to eat their fill, it seemed.

They had just finished the wraps - as Isabel had guessed was the term used when at last filming had ended - when a tractor with thick soft tyres drawing a trailer loaded with the containers which had earlier held gallons of slushy ice pulled into the fish shed. It was made obvious by his subsequent action that he had not been apprised of the activities taking place. He had to twist the large vehicle to avoid driving into the group standing outside the poles of lights and large cream-coloured reflectors, just missing the gantries as he did so. The top box was, apparently, not securely fixed to its transport. As if in slow motion, watched by the motionless group, the box seemed to lift itself off its companions, do a giant ballet dancer's arc in the air and land upside down on the floor just in front of Travis's table. No damage would have been done if the water from the melted ice had been tipped out of it earlier. Travis and his companions stood transfixed as melting ice, liberally salted with fragments of rubbish, rose in a fountain-like spray before landing like dirty rain on the long, food-covered table.

The man driving the tractor appeared unaware of the fact that he had just ruined beyond redemption the mid-day meal of a very hungry and tired group.

Suddenly all was action as cameras and lights were pulled out of the way of the still-toppling container. Lunch was ruined but expensive equipment would not be put at risk, apparently.

Stunned at the tableau in front of her Isabel watched as Juliet looked across at the tractor driver, a man with a large red face and ill-tempered expression. Isabel waited for her to throw vitriolic words at the man, had even drawn breath to do so. But Juliet, it seemed, decided that it would be better if she kept silent.

'Worse things happen at sea,' the man said with a demonic grin. Them telly people have got what they deserved, his look said. Juliet just stood like a pillar, her face blanched with anger, as he came over and with massive arms pushed the recalcitrant container through the small crowd and into a corner stacked rafter high with others.

'What about our lunch, then?' one of the gophers asked Juliet.

It seemed strange to Isabel that Travis who was in the position of boss, was not consulted. He had stood in silence throughout the small incident, his face untroubled, as if to say, 'I've done my part of the job so now someone else can take over.'

Isabel wanted to laugh when Juliet managed to say through what sounded like gritted teeth, 'I suppose we'll have to go the pub.'

It was obvious to everyone that as no rent was being paid - and of course, no charity was ever going to be in receipt of beneficence - there was nothing else she could say. It did not take the crew long to pack up their bits and pieces and soon the fish shed was empty once again.

As they were leaving the pub Juliet put her hand on Isabel's arm.

Isabel's immediate reaction was to fear that she was going to be asked to pay for her lunch. But, thankfully, Juliet's parsimony did not stretch that far.

'I'll give you a ring,' Juliet told her. 'You know about what. I think we will make a good team, don't you?'

Isabel did not bother to wonder whether she was being sarcastic. She would have to sort things out in her own mind before they spoke again.

Chapter 14

'I'll drop in and see the Harts,' Isabel said to herself the next day as she closed the door of the village shop behind her. 'See what they need in their next box.' She could also tell them about all the lovely new things which were currently flourishing in her - and, she had to admit, slightly untended - garden.

She needed cheering up. The usual sarcasm from the old woman in the post-office had left her, as it always did, feeling depressed and saddened that someone could think so little of her; almost as though she was an unwanted, self-invited guest at someone else's party. But it always left her feeling slightly guilty, as if she'd offended the woman but she couldn't think when or how. She hadn't been a resident of Shinbridge long enough for that. If she hadn't always considered it a good idea to patronise local traders, she would have waited until she went into Shilliton to do her very moderate amount of posting. All she had wanted today was a first class stamp to put on Gran's weekly letter and she had come away feeling like an interloper.

'Please don't keep everyone waiting,' Mrs Parsons had said, with bad grace handing Isabel her solitary stamp as if it wasn't worth her time and effort. While Isabel waited for her change she had licked her stamp and was about to stick it on her envelope. She looked around. An invisible queue was, apparently, impatiently waiting for her to move. There were two other customers in the shop but they were happily occupied choosing which pastry looked the best as they picked one after the other off the large stand of home-made cakes at the far end of the shop. More went back on the stand than reached their wire basket, Isabel thought with a shudder.

'Sorry,' was all she said, forcing herself to sound more cheerful than she was feeling. The venom on the post-mistress's face should surely have slain her on the spot. It wasn't until she was out of the shop and pushing the letter into the red box set in the stone wall that Isabel experienced the usual desolation. She tried not to let herself be overwhelmed, but, most unusually for her, she was close to tears. She would sort it out one day, she told herself, straightening her shoulders. She had expected too much from life in the country, she told herself fiercely, that's what it was.

The Harts weren't in when she reached the old mill.

'Gone away for the week-end,' their neighbour, an elderly man from the apartment above theirs told her. He was sitting on their wooden bench on the lawn leading to the river's edge, newspapers strewn around him like black and white comforters. It was none of her business, Isabel told herself tiredly; she was sure they would have told him that he was welcome to use their garden when they were away.

And she had forgotten Fred's food, she realized with a sigh, as she wandered away leaving the old man rustling through the scattered sheets of news print.

There was still some of the cat's dried stuff which he didn't like much but would have to put up with. She wasn't going back to the shop. Oh no. A tiny sparkle of inspiration, which raised her spirits, darted into her mind. Perhaps she could make use of her newly gained fishing licence and catch a fish for the three of them. Perhaps just the two of them, she thought, repressing the hope. She had no idea what Hannah's plans were while she waited for her father to come and pick her up, hoped that this would be a soon as possible, then she and Fred could enjoy the as yet, uncaught, fish on their own.

Feeling much better - so much for soul-searing experiences! she sniggered - she wandered back over the bridge and down the narrow road to her own short lane, thinking about the day before. Granted it had been exhausting, but it had been interesting - particularly as she soon determined that it would be her own organic - or, at least, *naturally* grown - produce which would be starring in the next Travis Parkin cooking saga. She grimaced at the memory of the stuff he had used the day before and how the poor make-up girl got it in the neck for drowning the leaf vegetables with her flower spray so that they had to be dried with paper-towelling before they could continue with the filming.

It was no wonder she was feeling a bit down today, Isabel told herself. The excitement of watching everyone at work knowing that she had no responsibility for what happened, her unnecessarily early arrival at the fish-sheds, watching the auction and talking to people involved in the fishing industry must have been more tiring than she liked to admit. And it niggled her that Juliet hadn't said when she would ring her or about what, inferring that she knew and that their plans were a secret between them. Isabel did not like subterfuge;

it always left her feeling uneasy. She hoped it was only that Juliet didn't want to mention the produce she was going to supply, for some reason. Probably thought she would comment on Travis's tatty ingredients. It wasn't very flattering to think that Juliet thought she had so little sense of diplomacy.

Hannah was sitting in one of the plastic garden chairs on the terrace, her feet up on the other, reading a magazine when Isabel arrived back at the cottage. She forced herself not to sound too eager. 'Any idea what time your father will be here?'

'No.' The girl's voice lifted upwards at the end of the short word as if to say she didn't know and didn't care.

'Didn't he say?' Isabel asked, not able to keep the surprise out of her voice.

'No,' said Hannah, firmly this time. 'Because he's not coming, is he?' She didn't move her gaze from the glossy pages of the magazine. Isabel could see pictures of half-naked girls and bronzed men wearing jewellery and little else.

'Ah,' said Isabel, pretending to understand. 'So you're going home on your bike, then.' She hesitated. 'But what about your case?' Her mental gaze wandered to the large suitcase with clothes overflowing from it that had lain on the floor beyond the open door of the girl's room since Paul had lugged it upstairs. Isabel felt like a punch-bag, then, as dismay hit her.

'It wasn't me who said anything about going anywhere on my bike,' Hannah said as if Isabel was somewhat short of intelligence.

The conversation seemed to be going round and round.

'You're quite welcome to stay another night,' the reluctant hostess in Isabel stated.

'One night?' Hannah sneered. 'What happened to all those other nights I'm to be trapped here?'

Isabel pushed up her fallen chin with an invisible hand. 'What did you say?'

'You know as well as I do that my father asked you to look me after for the rest of the summer.' She sounded, suddenly, like some child who knew she was not wanted, while at the same time pronouncing that she was quite capable of looking after herself. 'He's too busy trying to get the business back on its feet after you left it in such a state.'

Isabel heard the shocking words, but she also could hear the underlying reason for the lie. It appeared that she was to act as some sort of battering ram for a spoilt, confused - and unhappy, she accepted - teenager while her father ran around enjoying himself with - and she hated to admit that this hurt, even now - a new mistress. Even so she felt as she had been walloped by a sack full of lead. But that was not the girl's fault.

'Just how long are you staying?' she asked once she'd got her breath back. She was thirty two, for goodness sake, not an old woman sitting around with arms open to receive another person's cast-offs. And she had her new business to make a success of, so how did she ever get into this situation? She could hardly tell the girl to pack her bag and go, could she? Isabel felt trapped and, as far as she could see, with no way of escape. How could Paul do it? she moaned silently.

'I just said, didn't I?' Hannah asked rhetorically.

Calmly now, Isabel advised herself, breathing deeply; she was not going to allow herself to be reduced to petty bickering. 'You mean you want to stay an extra couple of weeks, is that it?'

'Uh, uh,' Hannah shook her head.

At least she had had the courtesy to stop reading her magazine, Isabel noticed through the red haze that was threatening to blind her.

'Dad said he'd discussed it with you. That I could stay here until I go to college.'

There was no hint of gratitude or of asking permission, Isabel noted, through the red mist.

'Anyway, I'm off now.' Hannah climbed slowly up from her semi-supine position, dropping the magazine on the plastic table as she did so. Then, with an air of giving Isabel an unnecessarily generous gift she said, 'Harley.. no, Thom - spelt with an 'h',' she added patronisingly, '... Thom has asked me over for a barbecue.' The little smile on her face was one of pity for an unpopular Isabel who never, it seemed, was invited to the farm next door. 'Don't know when I'll be back, so don't wait up,' she told Isabel as if she, Hannah, were the parent and Isabel the child.

The only thing that would help to quench the fires which were threatening to abolish her peace of mind and self-confidence would be a good, hard day's work in the garden, Isabel decided as, fuming, she watched the girl dance away, a cloth bag swinging from one bare shoulder as she went.

Hot and sweating, two hours later Isabel was lying soaking in her luxurious bath. With a toe she pushed the lever to the left and the water began it's gentle, soothing tumbling, drawing from her the remainder of the taut wires that even the hard work in the garden had not been able to dispose of. The scent of deluxe bath lotion helped the process of relaxation and rehabilitation. 'Rehabilitation', where had she heard that word before? Sleepily she let it play around her mind, the syllables tintinnabulating around her mind like the music of heaven. It was a nice word and one that might become indicative of her new life. She climbed out of the cooling water and wrapped herself in the one towel that remained on the bar on the wall. She didn't even curse her luck in ever having got entangled with Paul - and now his daughter. That, she told herself, was a totally unproductive exercise.

She felt more able to cope with the unwelcome gift that fate had handed her, now. Once dressed she would try her luck with the rod she had bought - along with the requisite licence - on her way back home the afternoon before. He'd been right, her neighbour from across the river, the man in the tackle shop told her - not that she would ever let him know. Also, there was Fred to feed, she reminded herself, feeling a twinge of guilt at not giving the young cat the loving care and attention it obviously expected. It wasn't hers, after all. Just another interloper; but a welcome one, this small undemanding, easy, part-time co-habitee of Woodbine Cottage. In fact, there was usually little sign of him for most of the day; evenings were his time on stage, it appeared. He'd appear once she started to cook her fish, she was sure.

Hold on! she told herself. I haven't caught it yet; in fact I've never caught a fish in my life! And when I do will I be able to kill it? Again the lid of her empty coffers lifted, coming to her aid. Do it she would - when the time came. And, of course, with no fish she wouldn't be able to test the other extravagant buy of the previous day - her fish smoker.

Her luck wasn't in, or, at least not at first. And there was no sign of her neighbour. In a way, she regretted this; would have been able to answer him back with a great deal of pleasure. It wasn't long before she let the regret waft away on the summer air.

After a half hour or so of practicing casting, frenetically throwing her line, laden with the correct fly - according to the tackle dealer - and tugging it back in with hopeful jerks, just as the tackle dealer had taught her, she became as relaxed and quiet as any devotee of angling. It must have been her relaxed attitude because it seemed that she was no longer frightening the fish away. Or perhaps some beneficent ethereal being was trying to make up for the awful day she was having. She almost somersaulted into the river as her rod bent as if a whale had attached itself to it. Then the line slackened and she jerked backwards. Then it all happened again and she was now convinced she had a fish on. After 'playing' the fish - she recalled the term from her father's stories of success after a business weekend in some posh house - she found that the rod was no longer bent or whipping about in her hand. She drew in her line, carefully winding it back onto its reel, and, suddenly, a silver trout lay at her feet. Her courage almost failed her as the sparkling grey fish lay and gasped on the bank, occasionally twisting and leaping about in attempt to get rid of the foreign object in its mouth. It tired of that, soon, and Isabel, now no longer wondering how people could ever say that vegetarianism was the only way to survive, took pity on the creature.

'Kill it quickly,' the tackle dealer has said, selling her a heavy metal instrument he called a 'priest.' Whoever had heard of a murdering cleric, she'd thought with a smile at the time. 'Last rites, and all that,' the man had laughed softly. Thank goodness he'd had the sense not to give her a lecture on hunter-gathering and all that. Like most men he probably thought she shouldn't be out doing the man's work of foraging for food, but wisely stayed quiet on the subject. Now she wasn't so certain that he would have been wrong.

Isabel shut her eyes, lifted the metal bar and brought it down to where she guessed the fish's neck might be. Opening her eyes she found it still gasping and jerking in its death throes. She kept her eyes open on the second attempt at putting the creature out of its misery. Afterwards she could not make up her mind whether she was relieved at having had the courage to kill it, filled with guilt at killing *any* creature, or satisfied with her sense of achievement. But at least she had a fish - and one caught by her own hand. But whether she could now bear to cook and eat it she would have to wait and see. Fred would enjoy it, even if she couldn't bring herself to. But what a waste of a good - and free, she reminded herself - food.

The grey fish with its pointed face was about eight inches long as it lay like a metallic gash in the green of the river bank's grass. She wasn't sure it was edible. It certainly wasn't a trout. After all she'd been through it seemed she had only a nourishing meal for a convalescent kitten.

She could hear in her imagination the post-mistress saying: 'You call yourself an organic grower and then you go and murder an innocent fish!'

Then Thom's voice joined the chorus of one, accusing her of being two-faced.

'Full of chemicals, the fish in your river,' she heard the echoes of him saying. 'Don't you remember that I told you that fish farmer fills his tanks with disinfectant so that the skins of his fish don't go mouldy while living in such unnatural conditions?' It was just many of the things he had had to say to her that evening of the barbecue as they leant on his field gate. 'And where does the water go when he empties his tanks to clean them? Straight into *your* river!'

Isabel knew her imagination was running away with her. Finding out how hard it was to kill a creature in order to eat was exaggerating her sensitivities. Butchers did it all the time, she admonished herself. But, she had to admit, there did seem to be a dichotomy somewhere in the life-style she had chosen for herself. Chemicals and natural growing were soldiers from opposing armies. Just as was aviation fuel, she thought with a jolt, as a jet from the nearby air base screamed across the sky. But, no. She was not going to allow herself to go down that road. She needed the money and that was the bottom line on her personal spread-sheet.

By the time she had reached the end of the fruit cage she had her mental equilibrium well under control and was beginning to gain some pride in the length of pink and silver flesh in the net bag hanging from her forearm - another bit of persuasion on the part of the tackle dealer.

She wasn't prepared, therefore, for being met at her kitchen door by a red-faced - obviously angry for some reason - upright Thom. She could almost see the steam rising from him and briefly wondered what misdemeanour she had committed this time.

'Where is she?' was his abrupt greeting.

Isabel said to herself, I am not going to be bullied by this man. 'Who?' she asked, rather more calmly than she felt, but she couldn't let the seconds stretch into infinity.

'That lodger of yours. That Hannah!'

'I've no idea,' Isabel answered, shaking her head as if puzzled. 'I thought she was coming to visit you.' It crossed Isabel's mind that something serious must have happened for him to have to lose so much dignity by coming to the servants' entrance. The thought almost made her laugh. He'd probably tried the front door first and, not one to take no for an answer, had arrived at the back door.

'Oh, lord!' he cursed, banging a large hand on his forehead. 'Oh, lord,' he repeated, 'that's where they've gone.' He seemed to be answering an unspoken question.

Isabel decided that silence was certainly the better part of valour on this occasion, so kept quiet despite the questions now roaming around her head like a frightened flock of sheep. She waited for the next outburst and, perhaps, answers to some of those questions. She was surprised when Thom turned to go. He hadn't mentioned the fish hanging from her hand. Wasn't worth the trouble probably.

'I've time to catch up with them. Just,' he said enigmatically, twisting around on the uneven flags of her footpath.

Isabel decided that she couldn't just stand by and not find out who 'they' where and where they had gone. 'Just a minute,' she said to the departing back. 'What's this all about?'

Thom half-turned towards her. 'The Glass Pig,' he told her as if expecting that she would already know and was just wasting his time. 'That's what all this is about!'

For some unaccountable reason Isabel could feel the giggles rising upwards from the area of her stomach. Stop it! she told herself. It's just your overstretched nerves. Laugh now and you'll be a black sheep forever. This made her want to laugh even more but the sense that her intuition had just spoken made her calm down. 'The glass pig?' she asked with a hiccup.

'You've no idea what I'm talking about, have you?' Thom had turned so that they were now facing each other.

'No, frankly I haven't,' Isabel replied, shaking her head from side to side. If his face goes any redder he'll explode, she told herself.

'It's a very valuable piece of glass,' Thom said angrily. 'Given to my father in Australia.'

'But why would Hannah want it?' Isabel asked.

'She's been admiring it all week. Said her mother loved things like that, and all that rot,' he said. 'And she's been complaining about her food costing a packet. I should have put two and two together.'

Isabel was shocked into a brief silence. Not only was the girl completely without manners, she was a liar as well. 'How could this piece of glass help her?' she asked eventually. She was fed up with having to defend herself and wasn't going to give him the pleasure of thinking she was doing just that, by mentioning that she provided all Hannah's food.

'Sell it, of course!' Thom was anxious to get away and stood first on one foot and then on the other.

If he had added 'you fool' Isabel would not have been surprised.

'Sell it? How?' She was determined to detain him until some of her questions had been answered.

'Charlie,' Thom answered shortly. 'His father's a fence.'

Isabel remembered Charlie from the barbecue. He'd seemed quite a nice boy for 'prison fodder' she had decided. As nice as any of the dozen or so had been, some had rough speech and boisterous behaviour and a seeming inability to string two words together without the use of cursing, blaspheming and cussing.

Isabel felt the wind leave her sails as if the almost-absent summer breeze had suddenly dropped even further. 'And you think they've taken it somewhere to sell?' It wasn't so much a question as a re-affirmation of what he had already told her. 'But how can you blame Hannah when you don't know for sure?' Isabel was beginning to feel angry, now. Angry because she thought he was probably right. And angry with Paul for putting her into such a situation.

'That piece of glass is priceless,' he almost shouted, momentarily forgetting what a rush he had been in to get away. 'It can never be replaced,' he said more quietly.

If he had been capable of such an emotion, Isabel would have said he sounded sad, bereft.

'Why ever not?'

'You try going to Australia and explaining that the one-off award my father got for the best boar in their major country show had been stolen and, please, could we have another!' He sighed impatiently. 'They only gave him one of the two remaining originals as he was a visitor from overseas - in Oz to learn their ways of superior meat production. The locals get brass replicas.' He shook his head as if he knew it was impossible to try and explain to such a dolt the ins and outs of Australian agriculture. 'It was,' he shocked her by adding in the past tense, 'over a hundred years old.'

'I'm sure you're wrong,' Isabel told him. 'Now, if you don't mind, I have things to do. I'll speak to Hannah when she comes home.' Isabel heard her strange choice of word but ignored it. 'But I'm sure you'll find it's one of...' she was about to use Ben's very politically incorrect soubriquet but stopped just in time, '... your boys who has put it away somewhere.' She had no idea whether that could possibly be true but she now wanted him to go.

He took the hint and stomped down the flagged path but not before saying, glancing at the net hanging ignored on Isabel's arm, 'Jack'll be after you for that.' The unspoken words 'I hope' hung on the summer air as he marched away.

When Hannah came home late that night Isabel did not ask her where she had been. She made no mention of a pig made of glass, either. Serve him right, she said to herself, if between them they've sold your precious ornament. It was nothing to do with her; she had enough to worry about without being expected to....

She was asleep before she could decide what might be expected of her, waking up the next morning refreshed and ready to do battle if anyone should demand it.

Hannah disappeared on her scooter in the middle of the morning filling Isabel with relief that she wasn't going to stay around all day. As she heard the motor of the two-wheeler fade into the distance she walked to the telephone and dialled Paul's number. She had a few things to sort out with him - the rent for one and the length of Hannah's stay for another. She planned to drop a hint as to the sort of company Hannah was keeping. That was bound to bring him rushing down to save his precious daughter from what he would consider a fate worse than death - that of mixing with people that would do her no good, and himself even less. It would be worth having to face him once more, Isabel had decided.

She was disappointed as she waited, unsuccessfully, for the telephone in the Paul's London home to be answered. Not all was lost, she told herself; she could get him on his mobile. A voice of a robot told her that this number was no longer in operation. If her telephone hadn't been old and frail she would have thrown it at the wall of the tiny hall.

There was only thing for it, she decided. She would cheer herself up by going up to the airfield. Travis could buy her a drink and they could have an exciting - to her, at least - conversation about fruits, vegetables and herbs. They would discuss what he would need and when, for his next filming, which she had gathered on Friday was to be in a week's time at somewhere she had never heard of.

At the airfield she had bought herself two cups of foaming coffee before she was forced to accept that neither Travis nor Juliet were going to appear. The only cheering thing was that Rod, fortunately, was on a day off. When she asked the boy behind the bar whether Travis usually came in on a Sunday, she could not understand why the older man sitting a stool further along the bar laughed.

'Not nowadays, m'dear,' he answered for the boy.

He made no further comment leaving Isabel without any knowledge of what his laughter had inferred. She gave up hope and left.

She waited for the phone to ring for the rest of the day. Travis had promised - or was it Juliet? - to get in touch.

Isabel was coming back in from the garden for a cool drink the next morning when Juliet telephoned. She wanted to ask why she'd taken so long but her ingrained PR habits denied her the right.

'We'll talk about that later,' was Juliet's automatic reply when Isabel asked her what produce Travis wanted. 'That's not why I rang.'

Isabel's heart seemed to reach freezing point as the woman's voice paused. Was she to be warned off, told her presence would no longer be required? Was she out of a job before she'd even started?

'You can fly, can't you?' Juliet's voice seemed to have the soft pedal pressing on it suddenly.

Isabel found herself nodding her head in relief. It was not going to be the hangman's gallows, after all. How stupid she was! 'Yes,' she said, 'but I'm a bit out of practice,' she added modestly but truthfully.

'Don't worry about that,' Juliet said.

Worry about what? Isabel asked herself in some trepidation.

'I asked,' Juliet was continuing, 'Rod Smithies only yesterday and he said you were a competent pilot.'

Any feeling of flattery disappeared when Isabel decided that someone was lying. She wondered who.

'You know Travis has got his own Cessna 152,' Juliet was saying. 'And I've made enquiries. As long as we don't pay you to act as our pilot you can fly us in that wherever we want to go.'

'I can't....' Isabel butted in but was interrupted.

'Don't worry. It's quite legal. You'd be doing it as a friend.' Juliet's tone was beginning to infer that she was used to being thanked for giving such a favour and did not appreciate having to argue about it. 'We'll just give you cash when we get home.'

Isabel had been about to say that she couldn't afford to spend days away from her garden; that she couldn't just fly around the country for fun when she should be working. Juliet had, it seemed, recognised this, and Isabel was not about to make a fool of herself this time by asking just why Travis wouldn't do it himself. Instead she said, 'Where are we going, and when?'

Isabel did not hear the sigh of relief from Juliet, exactly, but she felt it was there like a heavy balloon deflating.

'Next Friday,' Juliet said after a moment. 'Haven Bay. Meet you at the airfield at sun-up,' she laughed. 'About 6.30. Can you manage that?'

Isabel thought the question was quite unnecessary as she answered in the affirmative. 'Where's Haven Bay?' she asked then.

Juliet had rung off so could not answer her. It'll be in the road atlas, Isabel told herself, feeling her spirits rise.

The surprising conversation lingered in Isabel's mind. Had she heard a note of desperation in the woman's voice?

Chapter 15

Isabel told herself not to be so stupid. Why did she let herself have a disturbed night - and most of the following day - worrying about what was going to be ready in the garden - *and* suitable - for the following Friday. Hadn't she been a business woman for years, and always able to cope come what may? This was just another business deal and she wasn't going to fluff it by panicking.

There was no way she could ripen the cherry tomatoes, of course, so ordinary, plump vine ones would have to do. Their slightly darker coats would look well on the screen, she told herself. Nor were her round lettuces anything to write home about, yet, so she settled on her experimental Romaines that were looking wonderful with their long, bottle green leaves reaching skywards just pleading to be picked. She congratulated herself for planting them; they were just the sort of thing a TV cook would want to show off to his viewers. Some shiny spinach leaves could go into one of the two plastic boxes ready and waiting on the kitchen table, along with a couple of pounds of freshly dug potatoes. She'd probably come up with a few more things to complement any fish dish that Travis was thinking of cooking before she left. She understood that he didn't cook meat very often!

Isabel wandered around her garden enjoying the peace, the scent of freshly watered earth and the slightly minty odour of the chlorophyll in the runner bean plants, constantly adding more to her mental list of produce for Friday; things that would look good when cooked or just for decorating Travis's worktable when raw. As to which colours would be affected by the strong lights they used she hadn't, as yet, gained much knowledge. She could only keep her fingers crossed. Her self-appointed job was to produce the best-looking, moistest leaves and colourful vegetables that any audience would be pleased to see. A flat wicker basket, she decided, was the thing to use. Some large sprigs of that flat parsley which was attempting to take over her patch of herb garden, with some of her precious basil would be quite artistic. On these she would lay some glowing black and red currants. They would be suitable for any esoteric sauce Travis might be cooking on the day. What a tableau, she told herself with pride. Good enough warm the heart of any budding Cézanne or Van Gogh.

The phone call from Juliet had acted as the necessary motivation for her to get started on her garden. Even her concerns about Hannah and what she got up to paled like a fading photograph as she weeded and watered, snipped and tied. The girl had descended from her room mid-morning, then sped away on her red scooter, returning only briefly during the day for a drink and a change of clothes. She appeared to be, as far as it was possible for the constantly disgruntled girl, reasonably content.

Soon after Hannah's departure that morning Kate arrived with a letter. It was an interruption that Isabel could have done without. The letter - with its usual complaints and self-pity - was from Grandma Lil. But even this could not rumple the leaves of the current chapter of Isabel's life. Silas, she knew, could cope with it. She sighed with gratitude at the thought of how she and her brother had, after so many years, become good friends. How she had maligned him in her thoughts all those years ago, when it wasn't him that was to blame but her father. She pushed the images of the past away; now was not the time to think about what was over and done with.

The next welcome interruption was a phone call from her other grandmother.

'Can you come up for a day?' Alice asked. 'I've had a bit of luck regarding our family history.'

Isabel sighed knowing she would have to refuse. A day in Bath accompanying her grandmother to her newest epicurean discovery where she'd be regaled with info from her colourful past over a tasty and equally colourful meal, would have been fun.

'I've got things to show you,' Alice continued. 'The solicitors were having a tidy up after the senior man retired. You know what lawyers' cupboards are like,' she laughed. 'And they found several boxes to do with our family. I'd love to share them with you. They're fascinating.'

'Ally,' Isabel said her voice regretful, 'I'd love to come but I just can't.' She told her then about Travis and his 'Flying Cook' television series.

'I'm thrilled for you, darling,' her grandmother told her, hiding any disappointment that she might have felt. 'Next week maybe?'

'Yes, that would be lovely,' Isabel told her. As she put the phone down she wondered whether her new commitments were not, after all, threatening to drown her in a sea of duty; that the peaceful country existence was about to grow into a not-too-different type of life from the one she had wanted to escape from.

Wednesday night came and she had completed her written list of all the things she needed to pick first thing on Friday morning. She planned to get up at four so that she could get to the flying club in time to have quick warm-up circuit or two before they took off for Haven Bay. The airfield manager had made a bit of a fuss at having to open up so early, but when he'd heard it was for the famous Travis Parkin nothing was too much trouble. Typical, thought Isabel, remembering her and Rod's first encounter. She found she was able to breathe again once he'd put his phone down; she had been dreading him asking about her flying arrangements.

She wouldn't have admitted it to anyone, but she felt a bit nervous. Not about flying with Travis and Juliet but about her ability to fly any three people, including herself, safely to and from a strange airfield. Images of how well she had done on her trial flight did nothing to sooth her qualms. It was just that things seem to be getting more and more complicated and she was beginning to wonder where she would find the exit to her mounting predicaments. Adding to her problems was, if her dog-eared car atlas was right, the flight would take at least an hour. With the three of them aboard - and she had no idea what baggage the others might bring with them - extra fuel had to be taken into account. It had been an age - or so it felt - since she'd had to deal with this sort of thing. She had been spoiled, she told herself now.

Her musings were threatening to lead to panic when they were cut short by the arrival of Marion Hart to pick up her order. At least that was what Isabel first thought.

'All settled in now?' Marion's pleasant voice was like a lightly scented balm to Isabel's tautened nerves. The casually dressed but elegant woman took coins and notes from her soft beige Gucci purse and pushed them across the table. Isabel had long decided that her faithful customer would not take exception to her lowly life-style. The thought now made her want to laugh. Marion's box was already in the boot of her car but she seemed in no hurry to leave.

'Yes, thank you,' Isabel replied scooping the money into the drawer of the old table. She didn't want her new friend to think the money was *that* important.

'And your lodger?' Marion stood with one hand on the back of the wooden chair. She looked around as if expecting a figure to suddenly appear. 'How's she getting on?' She breathed in deeply as if waiting for the girl to appear.

'I hardly see anything of her,' Isabel answered.

'What does she do all day, then?

'To tell you truth,' Isabel was suddenly grateful that Marion had not left as soon as their business had been completed, 'I'm a bit worried about that. She seems to spend most of her time over there.' She nodded in the direction of her neighbour's farm.

'Oh, does she?' By the expression on Marion's face Isabel gathered that her friend thought this wasn't such a good idea.

'There's not much else for her to do,' Isabel said, embarrassed at the defensive tone of her voice. 'And she likes it there.' Isabel paused. 'I think.'

'Is that what Thom thinks, too?' Marion asked.

'He hasn't said anything about not liking it,' Isabel replied. Any thought of a pig made from blue glass she pushed to one side.

'That's all right, then,' Marion said. 'It's just that I saw her in the village the other day. She was talking to a man I thought was probably her father, from the way they were speaking.'

Paul, in the village? And not coming to see her? Impossible. 'That's not likely,' Isabel told her. 'He's dumped her on me for the summer. Away working.' She didn't want to admit that she had no idea where he was and what his plans for his teenage daughter were. It might sound like a lack of responsibility on her part, and she didn't want Marion Hart to think that. 'I'm sure I would have been told if he didn't like her being over there.'

'Take my advice.' Marion said with a smile that said she was only trying to be helpful. 'Keep an eye on things. It's funny how people say things they don't really mean in order to keep the peace.'

Isabel wasn't sure about the intention of the little speech but said nothing, taking it in the spirit of friendship that was clearly meant.

When Marion departed, leaving a further order to be delivered when available, Isabel was still musing on her words. The idea came to her unannounced that Marion, in a kind convoluted way was warning her to be vigilant about her neighbour's and Hannah's relationship. Horrible images sped through Isabel's mind. No, there could be no reason to think like that, she told herself sternly. As little as she had had to do with the man she knew that he would have no interest in a teenage girl, even he didn't think she was somehow responsible for the disappearance of his precious ornament. Perhaps the reason for all those boys.... Isabel stopped herself abruptly; her imagination had begun to work over-time and she didn't like it. No, Marion Hart wanted to be a friend; that had been made clear on each occasion of their meeting. She was trying to warn Isabel about Thom for other reasons. Isabel sighed, telling herself that only time would solve the mystery of Marion's concern. She, currently, had other things to occupy her mind – like preparing for Friday morning.

The flight, Isabel considered, hadn't quite come up to her expectations. She guessed it was because she was nervous, watched over by the experienced pilot who had co-opted the back seat so that Juliet could sit in the front beside Isabel. Travis did not comment on the two large plastic boxes taking up the space in the small cabin.

Take-off had been good. The engine was nicely warmed up and she had had time to do a couple of circuits and bumps before they arrived. It was the landing that could have been the swan-song for Isabel as Travis's pilot.

The airfield was a few miles from Haven Bay, not far from a military aerodrome. She'd prepared herself by telephoning before they left to see if any recent procedures had been introduced.They gave her a frequency to use once she was in the area of the naval aerodrome. She had written it down on the clipboard lying on her lap. The flight plan clipped to the blue, plastic board was filled in with the frequencies and positions of any small airfield on the way to Haven Bay in case they had to land unexpectedly; also the times and distances between them, estimated flight time and windspeeds. The only thing that worried her was the early morning horizon being etched in a deeper grey than usual. She crossed her fingers that the threatening storm would behave and disappear before they set out on their return journey.

The flight itself went smoothly, just as Isabel had hoped. She wanted to show Travis and Juliet how competent she was. It was also going to notch up her self-esteem if it all went well.

She had done her down-wind checks and had no problem and was approaching the end of the designated runway. During her let-down procedures she was careful to keep an eye on the tower of the church that the book had warned was close to the airfield. She had just reached the point of putting down full flaps when, suddenly, the tower of the church loomed like a ship appearing out of the fog. An unexpected gust of summer wind had caught the small aircraft and was blowing it off the line of the runway. With instinct she slewed the Cessna towards the runway kicking it straight just before it hit the earth with a thump. She managed to keep the nose wheel up until the aircraft slowed and then let it down as gently as the shuddering airplane would allow. The fact that they had landed on the emergency limits of the runway - almost in the farmer's field edging it, someone would be bound to say later - she ignored, in the relief that they were safely, if rather uncomfortably, on the ground once more. She sensed, more than heard, the deflation of Travis's lungs behind her. But to her relief he kept his thoughts to himself. Juliet was impervious to having been in any danger as she watched the airfield buildings approach. Having kept silent throughout the flight - Isabel guessed she was a little nervous - she was now chattering away to Travis, giving him a full commentary of their short journey to their allotted position on the hard-standing in front of the buildings as if he couldn't see it for himself. Isabel was pleased to be left to do the final checks, turning off the engine with a sigh of relief that Juliet's uncharacteristic chatter had prevented Travis mentioning their botched landing.

Once in the bus which had brought the rest of the crew and all the equipment up the day before, Isabel put the incident behind her, chalking it up as just one more tick on her blackboard of experience.

She had loaded her two plastic boxes into the back of the bus, as ordered by the same cameraman she'd met at Polwyn and climbed aboard.

'What's with the secret boxes, then?' Travis joked.

Isabel looked at him. As if he didn't know. 'Just wait and see,' she told him with a quick smile.

Juliet, back to her usual bossy mode, interrupted their brief exchange, and turning to Travis stated, 'I've got one or two things to discuss when we get to the harbour. In private,' she emphasised.

A few minutes drive and they had arrived at an old stone quay. The small harbour was mostly given over to leisure craft. As soon as the bus had stopped Juliet and Travis disappeared into a windowless boat shed at the end of the quay. Isabel had been told that the local harbour master would be clearing it out for their use in case the weather was not suitable for filming outdoors. She learned later that all the people whose places they used were more than willing to be welcoming and helpful; it was a good public relations exercise to have a television film made in a place where income was mostly dependent on holiday-makers.

Tables, as the week before, were standing at right angles to a knee-high stone wall bordering the side of the old stone quay. Being early morning there was only a dribble of water in the narrow, tree-lined harbour, with a stench of fermenting seaweed on a muddy bottom sprinkled with the confetti of pebbles and the occasional human detritus left by the ever-moving tide. As she watched, the water began creeping up the sloping ground as the tide trickled through the narrow gap protecting the harbour from the open sea. She knew that filming had been scheduled for high tide and hoped that no mishap would occur so that the film started with an exciting high water view but ended with the sea having disappeared from sight. The viewers might get the wrong impression of how long it would take to cook The Flying Cook's Quick Cuisine.

At one end of the table was a beautifully scripted notice, large enough to excite the interest of a viewer without looking like an advertisement, announcing that all produce used in the filming of the series was organically produced, that no chemical or pesticides had been used in any part of food production.

Isabel had almost forgotten the reason for her being there as she rushed back to the van; just in time to retrieve her precious boxes herself before they were squashed by heavy, black, camera cases. One at a time she carried them over to a table and opened them ready to release their contents. One of the helpers - gopher, she remembered - helped her by unpacking the vegetables while she unwrapped the flat round basket holding her 'still life'. She was pleased to see that he handled the leaves and delicate fruits and vegetables as if they were made of fragile crystal.

She wasn't prepared, therefore, for Juliet striding out of the shed and with an angry face inferred that Isabel was interfering. Somehow the woman controlled any outburst and even commented that the gopher's arrangement was very artistic. She said nothing about Isabel's basket of herbs and fruits, just pushed the boxes of rather weary-looking produce that had come in the van out of sight under the table with an active foot. Isabel assumed she did not want any detrimental comparisons being made.

Travis mentioned Isabel's name as part of his chat while chopping vegetables prior to beginning the cooking. He made it sound as though the vegetables and herbs - and 'youthfully fresh fruits' he would be using later - had come straight from heaven. She could have hugged him.

It was with some horror that Isabel watched, when half-way through an otherwise uneventful filming, he reached down and pulled some greenery from a box beneath the table, pushing her carefully garnered produce into a plastic waste bag. Still extolling the virtues of 'her' organic vegetables he pretended to be slicing the already chopped limp rags of spinach he had retrieved from their hiding place. He kept his absent viewers' attention away from the greenery while indicating an invisible screen behind him on which, apparently, they would be seeing the ingredients listed for the sauce he was cooking, made in the liquidiser with creamy white cheese, apricots and spinach.

She moved away and sat on the stone wall some distance from the film set. Her view of the action was blocked, thankfully, by the curious crowd of onlookers who had congregated to goggle at a famous - or potentially famous - chef doing his stuff in front of the cameras.

One unscripted episode did cheer her slightly, however.

As the tide came in so the long yacht which had been clasped by chains of sticky mud while still tied to the big rusty rings in the stone wall, only its mast visible, lifted with the incoming tide until its deck was level with the quay. As the boat rose four surprised faces in the cockpit appeared above the small wall. Glasses in hand, they'd evidently been having an early lunch-time party. They did not appear to be exactly over the moon at finding themselves unexpectedly acting as a chorus to the activities on the quay. They treated it as some sort of joke, calling out rude suggestions as Travis tried to keep a sickly grin on his face for the benefit of the cameras.

'What'ya doing, mate? Cooking for chaity?' One man called making the rest of his party roar with laughter.

'Need a hand with that chopper?' shouted another with a loud guffaw.

By this time the sparse crowd of onlookers were enjoying the joke but some of them, to give them their due, Isabel decided, her bitterness waning, were endeavouring to keep straight faces.

Travis who was just about to dissect the large monkfish threw down the expensive French cleaver with such fury that it's pointed end landed firmly on the wooden board, the handle sticking up in the air like some metal butterfly which has closed its wings in terror.

This made the group on the boat laugh even louder.

Travis turned around, tearing off the apron advertising an organisation which promoted organic foods, threw it on the table and disappeared into the boat shed.

'Cut', sighed Ewan, the cameraman. 'Juliet, why don't you go and do something to calm down our star while I talk to these,' he hesitated before continuing, 'these nice people.'

After some minutes of discussion with the group on the boat and with the crowd of onlookers enjoying this unexpected addition to their afternoon's entertainment, the cameraman went and joined Travis and Juliet in the windowless shed, emerging a few minutes later with Travis reluctant and Juliet relieved.

Ewan offering them the exciting roles as extras in exchange for the pleasure of eating the delicious meal that the well-known Flying Cook Travis Parkin was preparing had pacified the people on the boat. They accepted it as being part of a happy holiday on their chartered yacht.

The flight home passed without mishap. Isabel kept any comments she wanted to make on the day's activities until they were safely on the ground. Before Travis and Juliet could leave her and join the happy throng in the bar she asked them to wait a moment. She had something she wanted to say.

'I don't think I can fly you around,' Isabel told them, having rehearsed the words for the entire journey from Haven Bay. 'Nor provide produce for your shows.'

'Oh,' was all Juliet said, fishing in her leather shoulder bag. 'Did you think we'd forgotten our arrangement?' She handed Isabel an envelope which felt as if it contained several notes. 'Hope it's enough.'

Isabel was surprised at Juliet's friendly acceptance of her statement. 'I'm sure it is,' she said, with a note of finality in her voice adding a quiet 'thank you.'

Juliet then turned to Travis and said, 'I think we have a problem,

He nodded his head as if reluctant to admit to any problem in his life.

'You've been advertising this person's 'organic' produce all day. What's going to happen if people find that all the vegetables, et cetera, came from a supermarket?'

'But they didn't,' Isabel said, stung at the injustice. The whole day seemed to crumble around her. Now all she just wanted was to get home but couldn't let the accusation go undefended.

'The ones we used did,' Juliet retorted. 'What would happen if people discovered you had let your name be used on a...' she paused, searching for a suitable word, '...*reputable* programme just so you could reel in the orders?'

Isabel did not answer. She knew, without doubt, she was being black-mailed.

'Also,' added Juliet, a spiteful little smile playing about her lips, 'you've accepted money for flying us in a private airplane. What would the authorities say to that?'

There was no need for Juliet to continue. Without a word she turned and made for the open French windows leading to the noisy bar.

'Sorry,' said Travis with a real look of woe on his face. 'I didn't know about all this,' he told her touching her gently on the arm.

Isabel believed him even though she recognised that there were undercurrents here that she did not, as yet, understand. What she did understand was that she was trapped.

Trapped she might be, she told herself later that day. But somewhere she found the determination not to let herself drown in apathy but just accept the status quo. There were some things she could change and still manage to keep her self-respect. Things that meant she could still have an association with The Flying Cook and his interesting – and possibly for her, lucrative – life.

Chapter 16

Isabel left the cottage at 5.30 even though it wouldn't take her a quarter of an hour to reach Thom's place, but she could saunter.

She hadn't long been in from the airfield the evening before when she heard a tentative tapping on the old front door. It wasn't Thom; she knew that from his previous authoritative bangings on the thick oak. Who wasn't aware that her front entrance was mostly disregarded as a mode of entry? Each time she parked in the small front garden with its overgrown bushes and jostling trees she tried to imagine where old Ben had found it - some castle by its looks, or Dickensian office quarters. It was sadly out of place beneath the small trellised porch of a tumbledown country cottage.

On the other side of the door was a vaguely familiar face. It took her a moment or two to recall it as one of the boys from the barbecue party.

With no opening words of greeting, the boy - about fifteen, Isabel guessed - said in a voice so yokel in tone you could almost smell the manure: 'Marster, 'e be thinkin' as you might be comin' to 'is barb-ee-cue this morrer.' The boy even leaned forward and touched an imaginary forelock.

Isabel had a sudden urge to kick him; or at least, give him a good slap. Not because he was being cheeky, but for causing her to almost choke on repressed mirth. Instead she let the laughter escape and nodded in acquiescence. Who could resist such an invitation!

The boy smiled, then, handing her a book. 'He,' rural English had disappeared, Isabel was relieved to hear, 'thought you might like to read this.'

Isabel took one look at the cover of the book and shook her head. 'Tell him I've already read it,' she said, looking at the familiar brown cover. She forced herself to stifle the wish to add words that would not have been good for the boy to hear and said instead. 'I have my own copy, thank you.' In sudden anger at Thom's persistent patronising she almost told the boy to tell his boss that she would decline the invitation for the party, thank you very much! However, it wasn't the boy's fault so she kept quiet. Maybe she would decide tomorrow whether to go or not.

The youngster smiled again as if familiar with his boss's habits. Clicking his heels together he straightened his shoulders and marched down the narrow path as if he was on parade with the rest of the cadet corps at an expensive fee-paying school. Isabel gathered that it wasn't only boys from the dark and sinister streets of inner London who suffered Thom's administrations.

Later, well into the early hours, she was still thumbing through her own copy of the Association of Land Lovers - A.L.L. for short - multi-printed booklet. She wasn't going to make a fool of herself should her host tomorrow decide to quiz her over it.

Opening the side gate to Thom's garden she stopped. There was not a soul in sight. Was this some sort of cruel joke; somebody telling her she wasn't wanted and would she please go away again?

Distant voices began to filter into her consciousness. She noticed a trail of smoke rising into the sky from the direction of the river and allowed her shoulders to relax, telling herself she was becoming neurotic. For some reason a film-like vision of her mother - before she had upped and left - ran across her mind. Isabel had, until not long ago, considered that her mother was a bit of wimp and that was why her father treated her as he did. She hadn't then seen that it was her father who was at fault. Not until, that was, he had been caught. Then her opinions had suffered an upset of volcanic dimensions. She would have to be careful, Isabel told herself, and not let any man make her as unhappy as her father had her mother. She shooed away the embryonic self-pity that threatened her, recalling how her Mum was constantly going on about how much she, Isabel, was taking on. 'Almost as if you feel people won't think much of you if you don't,' she had said.

Isabel now wondered if her mother, Maggie, had been right all along and that she was now going along the same track. But this was not the time to think about it; the events of the recent past were catching up on her and making her oversensitive. What would her mother say now about her ambitious daughter's adventures: quitting her London job and sought-after flat, moving to a derelict country cottage, attempting to earn a living from an occupation which a few months ago she knew absolutely nothing about and doing the - illegal, Isabel feared - job of pilot for a television personality, while looking after her ex-boss's misfit daughter? The list was exhausting, she told herself. And to be ignored. She wandered towards the distant slacks, shirts and blouses helping themselves to glasses of liquid from frosting jugs of liquid on the table beyond the small stile leading out of the garden.

She was amazed to see that both Travis and Juliet were members of the party, as well as the rest of the TV crew. She couldn't imagine what they were doing there, and hoped her sudden blush would be taken for heat after a quick walk and no more. Juliet was dressed in her usual, expensive, clothes, standing close to Travis as if she owned him. For all Isabel knew, she might possibly do so. Travis was looking as if he didn't agree, however, as he turned away from the vision in pink, looking across at Isabel with a wide welcoming smile creasing his face.

Isabel only had time to smile back and nod before her attention was taken by Marion Hart tapping her arm. 'How's it all going?' she asked in a friendly tone.

Isabel could not prevent her shoulders from lifting in a small shrug. Marion Hart was like that; you never felt you had to pretend.

'Like that, is it?' Marion chuckled. 'Never mind,' she said, patting Isabel's arm again. 'You're a bit of fresh air. Just what we need.' With that she wandered away, led by her husband, Bob, telling her, with a smile of apology towards Isabel, that she was wanted elsewhere.

Isabel wondered what, exactly, Marion had meant by that remark.

To her horror, but not really unexpected, she spied Hannah milling around the barbecue area with the boys, making as much noise as they were. This time Isabel looked at the group of 'prison fodder' and saw individual people. Previously they had all melded together in a moving picture of youth and noise and flushed faces, some with the war paint of tomato sauce on them. Now there were three, at least – Dan, who'd come with Thom's message the first time, then Aiden who'd greeted her at the previous barbecue and now cheeky Charlie - that she could put names to. Looking at them she decided it was time to stop calling this group of healthy, happy young hooligans 'prison fodder.' At least they were keeping Hannah happily occupied; at worst...but she didn't continue with that thought; it might spoil her evening.

Apart from the Harts Isabel recognised only one other of the dozen or so guests, the old boy she had last seen sitting on the Hart's lawn and who she now remembered was called Fred Reynolds. She had been hoping to enlist him as a new customer but he looked as if he existed on meals-on-wheels rather than having any interest in cooking. As did the delicate old lady crouched in a wheeled chair next to him who was introduced to Isabel as Emily, his wife. She did no more than look up and snort. Isabel was aware of the hint that she need not waste her time with them. She was introduced to the rest of the party as the evening progressed but she did not take in names, just that they were mostly village people and that this barbecue was an annual event that they all looked forward to. She decided at one point that Thom must be the village diplomat as she spied the odious Mrs Parsons lurking in the background peering into a glass of murky red liquid as if afraid it was going to explode in her face.

Isabel had been sipping continuously at her own glass which contained, she found, a delectable mixture of fruit juice and red wine, and which Dan kept leaving his position at the barbecue to keep topped up for her, as if he'd taken her under his fledgling's wings. The drink relaxed her enough for her to realize just how tired she was. So exhausted, she felt suddenly, that she just couldn't face any more socializing.

Without being conscious of leaving the happy group, Isabel found herself, glass in hand at the water's edge, the noise of the party now a muted accompaniment to the river's music - spiced liberally by young voices shouting out modern words to each other as they played some game. Some of these might have sounded aggressive and unfriendly if there hadn't been a lot of laughter accompanying them. Isabel was familiar with such words as 'wicked dingbat' and 'you're a prat' from the youngsters who had come on work experience during their Easter and summer holidays from school.

Isabel sank down onto the bank and was watching the ever-changing story of the water's life when she felt, more than saw, a heavy shadow beside her. She looked up at the large figure silhouetted by the lowering sun and thought it was Travis and was pleased that he had bothered to come and find her. To her disappointment it was the great man. Her host, she had to remind herself. He'd come to berate her on some subject or other, she was sure. However much she had enjoyed seeing her new friends and meeting people from the village - and eating his food and drinking his drink - she wished she hadn't bothered to come to his party. She was too tired for yet another lecture.

Thom sank down on the grass beside her. Without preamble he stated, 'You've got yourself into a pretty fix, I gather.'

Isabel was a little stunned at the gratuitous cruelty. How sad it was that he could think of her small-holding as a 'pretty fix'? Wouldn't the friendliness of the Harts show that she was doing everything she was capable of to make sure her produce was good - *and* environmentally friendly?

Thom was not getting onto his high horse about his fear of her meagre acres contaminating his somewhat larger estate, it seemed, when she turned her attention to him. 'I know Travis,' he surprised her by saying. 'We were at school together.'

'That's nice,' Isabel murmured still not sure if she had been let off the environmental hook.

'He's a nice chap...'

'Oh, good,' Isabel said in quiet sarcasm.

'Very talented,' Thom continued as if he hadn't been interrupted. 'And very charming.'

Isabel tried to work out whether there was a message secretly lurking in his words but was unsuccessful.

Thom was saying, 'But he's had a... a run of bad luck just recently.'

Isabel wondered what the hesitation inferred but only came up with the answer that as Thom was so unused to speaking nicely about anyone the words were sticking in his throat.

'He's desperate to make a go of this television series of his,' Thom said.

As if she didn't know that already, Isabel thought. What was he trying to tell her? Was he trying to warn her off for some reason? Was he, in some way, involved with Travis's activities and didn't want her sticking her - business-trained - nose into things? If so, why? His next words belied any belief that Isabel might have in his being a friend of Travis's even if they did work together occasionally.

'Desperation is the operative word, I think,' Thom said. 'Take care you don't get too involved in his activities, that's all.'

'Why?' Isabel had learned, during all those years in 'big business', that sometimes a single word used with scepticism, elicited answers for those questions she did not have the courage to ask. She was irritated, too, that he seemed to think she was unable to make her own opinions.

'That's all I am going to say,' Thom answered. He got up to go and join his other guests leaving her sitting to muse over their brief - and puzzling - conversation.

Weird, Isabel thought, looking over her shoulder to the bend in the river where a group of his protégés now sat in the chilly water. If she hadn't felt so ruffled she might have laughed at their creation of a star like pattern of bare legs stretched out like drumsticks, feet meeting in the middle. The music of modern language wafted across to her: 'You prick, you almost pushed me over,' was shouted with laughter. 'Thick skull, get lost,' was the happy reply. 'It's a war zone,' another said with a sigh. 'Yeah mate,' agreed another. 'Mate' seemed to be name of the day for all and sundry, Isabel decided as she let her thoughts drown the sounds of the river party.

Thom, she reminded herself - was obviously doing some good but things were a bit spoiled by his well-developed ability to find fault with... probably everybody, not just her, Isabel thought returning to the previous puzzling subject. He seemed popular, she admitted, listening to the social sounds floating towards her from the small crowd of guests chatting and eating and drinking away behind her. Would the Harts have anything to do with him if he wasn't a straightforward and honest person? They were nice to her, too, so that wasn't much to go on. And now here were Travis and Juliet and the rest of their crowd. Where did they fit in? She thought she might know the answer to that but it would take some working out. What a complex character he was turning out to be, not one that she could tolerate spending much time with. This would be the last 'invitation' she would accept from him.

She really was feeling out of sorts with exhaustion. She wasn't really worried if the crowd enjoying themselves up in the garden were thinking she was being bad-mannered by not joining in. She hoped they might think she was keeping an eye on the boys.

She must have dozed because the next time she looked the youngsters had disappeared as if she had dreamt them, and the shadows of the trees overhanging the river were reaching further across the water. And the shadow at her side was much longer and narrowly then earlier.

Thom handed her a plate of food and a glass of red wine before sitting down beside her once more.

What did he want this time? Isabel asked herself. More nagging? She didn't ask him why he was neglecting his guests in favour of socialising with his unwanted neighbour. Was he making it an excuse to take the weight off his own feet for a moment or two? She soon wished he hadn't when he began quizzing her, like a school teacher, about the book he had sent over for her to read. The boy hadn't repeated her message, it seemed.

'I hope you understand now why I'm concerned about what goes on so near my own property?' he told her. 'My parents established this farm as a totally organic concern and started these summer camps for children who needed something that society wasn't giving them.'

Isabel wasn't sure what the connection was but instinct told her to say nothing.

'And I want to carry on where they left off,' he told her with more of the stern teacher in his voice than she cared for. 'We are responsible for children, whoever they belong to. Not only for their welfare but their happiness, too. And, on the whole, kids are miserable at the moment. Some of us are willing to work hard to make sure their lives become happy and well-balanced.'

So that's what they were, Isabel told herself. This was more an American-style summer camp than a place for dangerous misfits, she was relieved to learn.

Isabel let her mind range over a variety of non-connected topics-her next batch of beans, the lovely sound of the running water, and the softness of the warm evening - as he lectured her on how modern agriculture was based on economics and not on finding ways to feed people in a healthy, supportive way.

'And children don't just need good food to develop into rational, happy adults. They need a certain amount of danger, too.'

Isabel found her attention forced back to listening to his preachings.

'They are over-protected these days,' Thom said as if he had begun a speech to a crowded room and nothing was going to stop him. 'It's all this political correctness rubbish. If they never experience danger they'll never learn how to cope with it. They might get the odd kick from a cow here, but no one has ever refused to do the milking again when that has happened. They've learnt that it is their responsibility to take care the next time.'

Isabel was about to speak but Thom was still on his podium.

'If they're not given challenges,' he said fiercely, 'taught how to face danger, they turn to other things such as petty crime. Petty crime leads to more crime and ultimately they get hooked on the excitement and then comes the added excitement of using drugs.' He sighed. 'And do you know why? It's because they are *bored*, bored out of their minds. They leave their minds behind because they can't face what's in them.'

Isabel realized he was over-simplifying in order to make it easier for a mere woman to understand. But she was impressed with his passion, his obvious sincerity.

'And the glass pig....'

Oh here we go, thought Isabel. Here is the real reason for all this.

'... stands, not just for good farming, but for the ethics of a happy, healthy existence. Something I try to instil in these kids is respect for themselves, for others, and for others' possessions.'

Isabel kept quiet. She wanted to justify herself, show that she was innocent of the, as yet unstated, crime of which he seemed to be accusing her.

'Children,' Thom said in a quieter voice, 'are just like plants. Feed them the proper chemical-free food, give them space and air and love in a country where the cuckoo stills sings and insects still pollinate the food they eat and they will develop into broad-minded, healthy and happy adults and, eventually, loving parents.' He let out a deep sigh and was silent.

Isabel sensed more than saw his shoulders slumping. Was she not to be allowed to correct his assumptions about her? She had done her reading; had been converted as she sat at her window three floors above the polluted roads of Hammersmith and watched pasty faced children munching hamburgers and slurping chemically-coloured drinks as they wandered home from - as she knew from a couple of visits to schools to talk about her career - over-heated, airless classrooms. Schools where the playgrounds were no longer used, tennis nets rotting and hanging like spiders' webs from rusty poles, the grass on the football pitches pitted and furrowed from the wheels of joy-ridden cars. Not all schools were like that, she knew, but there were far more than should be. She, even if he would not accept it, was trying to do her bit, too, but she knew she would never be able to convince him of that.

In a calmer voice, Thom surprised her by saying, 'I apologize for my ill-temper the other day. I realize now it was nothing to do with you. Except, of course, we *are* responsible to a certain extent for what guests in our homes get up to.'

Isabel was experiencing a new and astonishing sensation. She was being *apologised* to by no less than her patronising and sanctimonious next door neighbour. The words echoed and re-echoed in her mind, mixing with the sounds of a summer evening - water pouring gently over the submerged rocks of the river's bottom, birds returning to the nests calling out like happy, exhausted children, young voices letting off the small fireworks of affectionate insults, adult voices providing a muffled chorus. She couldn't remember a time when she had last sat and listened and hardly responded to such a long conversation. She found her voice, at last.

'About Hannah,' she began, 'I've been meaning to ask whether you mind her coming over here all the time.' She turned to see if she could catch the truth from the expression on his face in case he decided to revert to his haranguing ways.

'She doesn't bother us,' he replied shortly.

Isabel decided he was still angry about the ornament, even if he had absolved her house-guest of the blame, and sighed. Was she ever going to be able to like this man, let alone tolerate his attitude to her?

'Sorry,' Thom said. 'Am I boring you?' He pulled himself up off the ground. 'I'd better go and join my guests. The boys are inclined to get a little over-excited if I'm not around.'

There it was again, his boys.

'Don't you like them?' Isabel asked in some surprise.

'Of course I like them,' he retorted. 'They wouldn't be here if I didn't.'

'You should have some of your own,' Isabel could not prevent herself from snapping back 'And perhaps a wife to help you keep house!' She didn't know why she said that. It was none of her business, after all.

'I had one once,' Thom told her.

Isabel waited from him to tell her all about a short marriage, an acrimonious divorce and how he would never enter the state of matrimony again.

'She died,' Thom said.

In her shock there was nothing that Isabel could find as reply to that. Whatever she said would sound insincere.

'Her father was a sheep farmer,' Thom said, in a tone which inferred that his life story was nothing to do with her and he was just indulging her base curiosity. 'We met when I was lecturing at a college in the north of England and she was a teacher at a secondary school.'

Isabel wondered whether all these details about his past were leading up to something which was, to him, important for her to know.

'She died,' he told her, 'eight years ago. From the effects of the chemicals her father used on his animals. She used to help him with his sheep dipping,' he added as if doubtful that Isabel would know what he was talking about. 'And our baby was still-born.' He turned and walked away as if the feel of the earth beneath his feet was the strength which had helped him live so far and would go on doing so for the future.

Isabel felt as if she had been kicked in the stomach by one of those far-off sheep, her mind numbed by the onslaught of information. A completely different picture of her neighbour was forming in her mind, answering many bewildering questions that previously had never occurred to her.

After a few minutes she decided she could not face the merry band around the barbecue; not at the moment. She did not bother to glance back at the laughing, happy group as she scrambled onto legs that were not yet prepared to take the weight of her body. She stumbled slightly as she walked across the uneven grass of the river bank in the direction of her own property. Fifty two days, every one feeling like a century, she worked out, since she had left her old life behind her. In her sensitised state she wondered, for the first time since she had set out of this adventure of alternative living, whether she had made the right decision.

Chapter 17

'That was a nice pudding you made yesterday,' Isabel said. Hannah had just wandered into the fruit cage followed by a young cat eager to catch the twig she was dragging along the ground behind her. 'I didn't know you could cook.'

Isabel was weeding, throwing scraps of grass and broken branches into a pile on the path. It was time she made some attempt at friendship with the sullen girl, she had decided in one of her calmer moments. She had to admit it was more her not wanting to lose the chance of getting money from Paul, than any fondness for her visitor.

'Yeah, sure,' Hannah answered, throwing the twig under the over-hanging branches of the currant bushes. Fred thought this was lovely until his fur caught on the tiny thorns of the blueberry bushes growing in amongst the currants. He gave up the game as a bad idea and wandered away.

The cat had been an intermittent visitor over the past couple of weeks, but he seemed none the worse for his absences. Isabel had accepted that he'd become a second-home owner in a not-too-distant part of the area. Like a rabbit emerging from a magician's hat he was always on the spot when Hannah was enjoying one of her infrequent appearances, though. Isabel was honest enough to admit to herself that she was just a bit jealous of this. It was she who'd rescued him, wasn't it?

'That's what I want to do. Cook,' Hannah surprised Isabel by saying. Even her voice seemed less morose than usual.

Then Isabel felt as if she had become a reluctant viewer of some badly written film as Hannah's complaints against the world and how badly it was treating her then poured out like a stream muddied after a summer storm.

Isabel forced herself to go on with her work, trying to show that she was listening despite the constant movement on her hands. She did not want to interrupt the girl in case she started back at the beginning again.

'I don't want to go to college,' Hannah said, after bemoaning her fate of having had to leave her home and her friends for the whole summer. 'I don't want to do business studies. I want to learn to cook - properly - so I can get a job in some restaurant.'

Isabel wondered if all spoilt teenagers were like this. She was sure she hadn't been at that age.

'He wants me to work for him and I don't want to.'

By 'he' Isabel understood that she meant her father.

'Why couldn't you have stayed,' Hannah moaned. 'Why did you have to leave?'

A whole young life of bitterness seemed to grow from the seemingly innocent words. Isabel opened her mouth to reply, forgetting the injunction to herself to keep it shut, but didn't have time to utter a single word before Hannah was once more singing her lament of misunderstood youth.

'Having got rid of my mother, the least you could have done was stay and help him out. Get him off my back.'

Isabel felt as though she had been struck by a sack of garden compost. Get rid of her mother? Snapshots of Paul and his sad story flashed before her eyes. Not being able to leave Meredith - Charlene, that was - and all that; of how she was ill and needed him and so on. She was embarrassed to think she had believed it all. At first, that was. Sorting out the truth had helped her stop making a complete fool of herself, she reminded herself. She didn't know what the girl was on about. In a flash it came to her that perhaps Paul's wife had had the good sense to move on; leave him to his own devices. That might account for...a lot of things. That was it, she decided; the girl had been told all sorts of stories so she wouldn't learn the truth.

Isabel sighed into the silence that was hanging expectantly between them, pulling yet another weed from the clinging embrace of the dry earth, not noticing that it was a shoot from the bush beneath which she was working. She wished she had not encouraged the unwanted conversation now. Hadn't she got enough churning around in her mind without having Paul's daughter haranguing her for wrongs of which she was innocent?

She'd been woken early that morning by the telephone shouting for her attention. It was Lilian with her usual bucket of complaints about being ignored, being cast-off now she was useless, how she didn't get enough to eat, and so on. A new subject was a diatribe against her neighbour.

'Never leaves me alone. In the house day and night. I think she's after my money.'

Isabel had dug deep into her reserves of patience and had managed to soothe her grandmother, telling her how kind the neighbour was, how she was delighted to be able to be her companion (Isabel congratulated herself on this) and that the woman would be very sad if Granma Lil was not satisfied with her efforts. It was like talking to a sulky child, she decided, exhausted with the hard work of calming her ailing grandparent. Isabel offered further appeasement by promising to visit as soon as she could.

Lilian then offered up one of her increasingly frequent surprises by saying, 'Don't you say anything against Gwen,' she ordered. 'She's a lovely lady. Not after anything at all. What a thing to say. I don't know what I'd do without her.'

Isabel held back any retort that a normal person might expect. Sudden pity for her grandmother overwhelmed her. She sighed knowing there was no more she could say.

'You ought to learn to be a better judge of people,' Lilian said, banging down her receiver.

At this moment in time, as her mother used to say, she had Paul's 'lovely' daughter to cope with. She'd been letting Hannah's grumbles buzz around like demented bees while her mind had been on her grandmother. It seemed that the train of the girl's thoughts had changed tracks.

'At least you could say something to him,' Hannah was saying in a cold, hard voice which strove to hide its wavering edge. 'Not let him force me to do something I don't want.'

Oh that she had the power, Isabel thought. If she had she'd have her money by now, wouldn't she? However, she wasn't going to start a discussion on the power she had or did not have over Hannah's father. She felt a bit sorry for the girl, the cliché of an aggressive and insensitive exterior hiding a very unhappy person passing through her mind. How awful to feel as Hannah did. Isabel had never been forced to do anything she didn't want. Or, in retrospect, is that exactly what had happened over the years? Had her adoration of her father made her want to emulate him? Conversely, maybe it had made her into a strictly honest businesswoman – one whose integrity was the magnet to those less trustworthy. She didn't dare think about it. Not now, anyway.

The incipient wound of Isabel's reluctant sympathies was cauterised almost immediately by the girl's next words.

'It's so *boring* here, I could die. I can't think why you would think I'd enjoy myself.' She turned to go. 'I'm going over to Thom's.'

Isabel noted the use of the name and just accepted it as a modern way of speaking.

'At least there,' Hannah flung over her shoulder, 'I can have some conversation.'

If the exit of the fruit cage had been a wooden door it would have been flung off its hinges. As it was the green net on its bamboo frame just did an Asian dance in the air, reflecting the midday sun as tiny shards of jade, coming to no damage.

Isabel worked in the garden until her tee-shirt was soaked with sweat. She should go down and have a look at the patch of lumpy ground between the fruit cage and the river bank. It could be just the place for her new batch of herbs. Once it was dug and smoothed over, she told herself. It flitted through her mind that it was the only really untidy bit of old Ben's garden.

The need for a cool refreshing shower was stronger, however, and she was amazed when the old-fashioned clock on the kitchen wall - a legacy from the old boy - told her it was mid-afternoon. It was hours since she had had her lonely breakfast. Now she had things to prepare for the next day.

She could hear mother saying: 'Issy, you are always trying to do a hundred things at once. Why don't you take a break?'

A break at this juncture was not something she could afford. Later, maybe. To leave at six the next morning in order to be in London on time was going to take some organisation; especially if she wanted time afterwards to do what she had planned.

The thought of returning to the centre of her previous life's activities - her many triumphs too, she reminded herself with pride - should have filled her with pleasure. However, for a moment the length of a flash of lightning she allowed her thoughts to slip into the negative ones concerning her personal life. But not for long. It surprised her to realize that she was beginning to look forward to being encapsulated in a tiny tin box on a hot summer's day for as long as necessary. But next year she wouldn't have to chase after things that she would be growing herself. With pleasure she mentally viewed the small, temporary patch she had dug for the herbs and the tiny greenhouse she had tidied for the less hardy ones she would be bringing home with her.

Springfields Market was humming with voices and motorised carts and the now-familiar song of an auctioneer by the time she reached it the next day. She knew it was famous for its Monday herb market and had planned to be there nice and early so as not to miss any special offers that might be going.

The traffic on the M4 had different ideas, however, even at six in the morning. And finding a parking space forced even more time to trickle down the drain. She wondered briefly if the much-hyped congestion charges would really make any difference and thought not. Anyone who wanted their car nearby would be willing to pay for the convenience, she decided.

She had arrived at Springfields at the same time as everyone else, it appeared. The early birds had long since disappeared, their small vans and cars laden with the bargains she had hoped to buy, she assumed. Since the demise of Covent Garden as a market garden, Springfields had been developed as a partial replacement for it - the larger companies with their heavy lorries now having to go out to somewhere near the airport. Situated on the site of a demolished warehouse - not far from Inigo Jones' classical original which Isabel considered was a bit silly on the part of the planners - the new market, a palace of chrome and glass, was teeming with a disparate multitude of white-coated traders looking like doctors as they tended their green and growing patients. For Isabel it was not a comfortable place to be, as from most of it she could see the grey concrete and smoked glass windows of Paul's place of work.

Isabel shrugged that off and hurried homeward revived by the pleasure she had gained from her 'shopping'. She had bought a good selection of herbs for growing in the garden - various mints, bay, rosemary, sage, French tarragon and, as a last-minute inspiration, some horseradish. For the little greenhouse she'd made a selection of basil, dill - which she would transplant into the garden as soon as it had gained some strength - and several varieties of parsley and chives. It didn't seem much but, when she calculated the cost, she refused to let herself drown in her enthusiasm. There were so many other things inviting her to spend her money she had to be disciplined. Her building society account - opened to keep her cash safe for use on re-furbishing the cottage and garden - would soon be empty if she wasn't careful. She packed her new herb family into the car and was ready to leave the metropolis by mid-day.

Her plan for the day was working out. She could visit Alice in Bath on the way home and still be back at Woodbine Cottage before it was exhaustingly late.

Alice had been delighted when Isabel had rung her the evening before. 'Stay the night,' she had said. 'You're bound to be tired after a day in London.'

Talking to her 80 year old grandmother always managed to prise her spirits off the ground, making life seem wonderful once more. But she had to remind her grandmother that Woodbine Cottage - 'Brookside', Thom had caustically told her, 'but Ben didn't want it named after a silly television soap, so changed its name.' - was her business, her gold mine - *eventually* - and, also, she had a guest to look after.

'That girl's still there, then,' Alice had scoffed.

She hadn't sounded too down-hearted that her favourite grandchild - she had, how many, eight or was it ten now? - wasn't able to spend the night with her. She was so self-sufficient, she never took offence; was always able to accept the status quo without sounding martyrish. Unlike Lilian, thought Isabel.

Isabel was hardly through the door of the tall, narrow, Georgian house on the short hill leading from Milsom Street before Alice was galloping along on her hobby horse. 'I've got some new - and interesting,' she chuckled, 'tit-bits about the family.'

'Ah, yes,' Isabel teased, 'the famous family history. Just when was it due for the publishers?'

Alice waved a hand in the air making Isabel fear for the heavy rings which decorated her wrinkled hand. 'Fuff,' she said. 'What are a few weeks between friends?'

Yes, thought Isabel, possibly the publisher had become a friend, but he was also a businessman. She would have to see what she could do to get her grandmother, who had consistently refused to race through the work, at least to trot towards the winning post.

'Almost 100,000 words,' Alice said in apparent appeasement. Her eyes took on the veritable appearance of twin lighthouses as she said, 'I can hardly believe it myself.'

Isabel could believe anything of her lively grandmother, she thought, as she followed the miniscule, smart little woman into the room - too large to be called a sitting-room, too small for the dignified soubriquet of drawing room - on the first floor of the tall house. Large casement windows - now open at the top to trap any stray breath of air that might escape the mist of dust and smoke that clouded the streets - looked across the time-scarred roofs and stone walls of the famous city as if framing a careful reproduction of a familiar picture. The elegant untidiness Isabel always found comforting. Large damask-covered cushions were stacked, as usual, against the fronts of chairs and settees, making comfortable seats for those who wished to sit on the floor.

'If you can't sit with your feet above your heart,' Alice had once bemused Isabel by saying,'you can at least stretch out your feet in front of you. It's much healthier than sitting crunched up on a saggy couch,' she'd said.

Alice had always believed in trying out any new thing that was purported to improve health, retaining only those things which she had proved did actually do as was stated. The large eighteenth century bureau, converted into a gracious drinks cabinet, often proved itself as improving ones' health, too, it seemed, remaining open at all times. And today's, yesterday's and, possibly, the last decade's newspapers were stacked like striated cliffs on every available surface. All in all it was a very relaxing and welcoming room. Isabel always left her grandmother's presence feeling that she had had an all-too-short a time in a reviving health spa.

First things first were, apparently, the order of the day. Food and drink were enjoyed, leaving the subject of the other grandparent as a somewhat less digestible morsel to go with desert.

'Listen, darling,' Alice told Isabel after hearing about the latest outburst. 'You have my permission to pack me off to the securest of old people's prisons,' she used the word intentionally, it seemed, 'if I should ever get like her.'

Isabel knew she was not being unkind; to her it was the most sensible thing to do - as hard as it might be to put it into practice.

'I've plenty of money put aside,' Alice continued, 'for it to be a five-star prison, of course. This house must be worth something by now.' Alice laughed shortly. 'I daresay she's not exactly poor, is she?'

They had had this conversation several times and each time Isabel promised herself she would investigate her other grandmother's financial situation without delay; find out exactly how much Lilian did have put aside - she was going to say, for her old age, and changed it to, for emergencies. Silas and she must look into things as soon as they both had a moment.

Once the unpleasant subject had been combed for clues, and discussion had taken place as to what should or should not be done, Alice was able to return to her favourite subject - her family history and all historical events relevant to it. She loved to quote dates, such as, 'Do you know who was the pop idol of the time when you were born?'

Isabel smiled as she settled back against the large cushion and stretched her legs out in front of her. She knew, of course, but was about to be told again, that was certain.

'She wasn't exactly a pop-idol, of course, and died soon after,' Alice said. 'Judy Garland, of course. With her famous song *Somewhere Over a Rainbow.*'

'I know who Judy Garland was,' laughed Isabel. 'I can't count the times I was taken by you to see *The Wizard of Oz!*'

Alice seemed pleased with her remembering. Then she added, 'But Silas won't be so happy that I can't remember who was singing when he saw the light of day! All I can remember was there was a funny poet who was all the rage. You know. Peter something or other. Or was it Richard? Wrote verses about mundane things like windows and weddings. Didn't like them myself, but, then, I don't know many that did!'

'You're not going to put all this into the family history, are you?' Isabel asked in amazement.

Her grandmother's face looked as though she thought her granddaughter had suddenly turned into a - temporary - philistine.

'Of course, I am. I want this book to be readable by all sorts. Not just our own family!' She chuckled as she said, 'It all adds colour, you know!'

Isabel listened to Alice as if her words were all part of a long and soothing dream. She heard again about her great grandmother being born at the same time as the first car being allowed on the road without an escort; her great great grandmother being born in the year that Stanley had presumed that he had met Livingstone and that Isabel's grandfather had been killed on the Somme at the beginning of the First World War. And so on, until Isabel felt her attention fading, the words becoming a happy, caressing murmur.

'You're not listening to a thing I say,' laughed her grandmother eventually.

Isabel felt wakefulness flowing into her as if a breath of fresh air had suddenly wafted through the open windows.

Alice laughed again. 'Don't worry, darling, you'll be reading it all very shortly. And I know you must be tired. Glad my meanderings did some good at least,' she teased. 'Now tell me about all those other worries you've gathered about yourself since I last saw you.'

That seemed a long time ago, thought Isabel, but it was, in fact, exactly two weeks; two weeks which felt like two years. What a lot was happening in the peaceful, bucolic existence she had chosen for herself. Regardless of whether she was repeating herself, like an upturned jug of liquid it all poured out; Hannah, Travis, the Harts - and Juliet; she hadn't forgotten the occasions when Juliet had seemed just a little less than friendly.

'Jealous, my dear,' Alice murmured, as the flow continued like a river in spate.

And Thom. Isabel didn't linger too long on her next door neighbour, but her grandmother found a word or two to say about him, despite that.

'I think he's being protective,' Alice said.

'*Protective?*' Isabel almost screeched the word. 'Him? Protective?' she snorted. 'Of himself, may be, but not me. He's just a bully.'

'Men have a strange way of coping with situations which are beyond their control,' Alice told her. 'And I reckon that having an attractive, lively - and lovely! - woman moving in next door has made him feel very insecure. Add to that the fact that this particular young woman is obviously on the road to success, is popular with the locals, held down an important position in the City and is leading an exciting life ferrying a celebrity around in his own plane, it's enough to make any poor male feel apprehensive. His way of coping is to make himself the protector. Anyway that's my way of seeing it!'

Isabel felt that the conversation had been going on long enough. She hadn't told her grandmother about his wife and baby. She could just imagine what she might be warned against if she did.

'I must be getting back.' Isabel stood up. She was reluctant to leave but knew she had to. 'To my old maid's existence,' she laughed. 'Dear Hannah is probably swimming in my river and scaring all the fish!'

On the way back to her village and small home, the scent of the herbs - albeit well-covered with soaked newspapers - almost drugged her with their aromas. It was a drug that vitalized not subdued, however. That and the therapy of being with the one person in the world who consistently refused to list her faults, as so many others seemed to be doing, who truly cared for her and her happiness, was all the medicine she needed.

She was even able to cope with Hannah's verbose misery that the wonderful day she had spent with Travis and the boys on a trip to the local wildlife park was over and she was back in the boring old cottage.

'Never mind, dear,' Isabel surprised herself by patting the girl on the arm, just as her grandmother might have done, 'It won't be for long.'

Hannah's face brightened, but Isabel did not disillusion her that she hadn't meant that little time would pass before she was with her friends again. Isabel had determined to get in touch with Paul, if at all possible, and remove this delight from her life.

It wasn't until the next day that Isabel, hunting for a copy of a booklet on herb growing in the pile of cardboard boxes still littering the dusty floor of her 'office', realized that all the boxes had been opened. The contents were no longer in the tidy piles that she had so carefully packed when leaving the flat. It wasn't until she was in bed that night that she recognised with a start the box which had had more rifling done to it than the others; the one which contained all her personal papers - including letters and notes from Hannah's father.

Chapter 18

'I would love to know what I've done to offend you.' Isabel's nerves were still stretched like violin strings after a conversation with Hannah. She was in the mood to be difficult herself and wasn't going to stand any nonsense from an aging, envious postmistress.

Mrs Parson's face was just like a crumpled piece of paper, Isabel decided. Her regular customers would never have spoken to her in such a fashion, her expression said. Her hands continued to put buns into plastic bags which she then sealed with a piece of sticky tape.

'What do you mean?' The postmistress snapped without looking up. 'I've never said that you had.' Her voice was muffled by her downward glance. Obviously no one had ever stood up to her before and she was not quite sure how to react.

'You didn't have to,' Isabel told her, beginning to feel that she wished she hadn't started the conversation now, had heeded her mother's oft-quoted maxim of never saying two words where none would be a better response.

'The likes of you come in here and demand what you want without ever considering what it might cost me.'

'When haven't I considered you?' In her present mood she didn't mind that her words were not exactly grammatical. Before the older woman could answer, Isabel added, 'I don't think it's very professional of you to make *anyone*, whether they live locally or are just visitors, feel as unwelcome as you make me, each time I come into the shop. Without customers you wouldn't have a shop. Isn't that right?' She took a deep breath, and telling herself to calm down, picked up her stamped letter and turned to go.

'And who are you to talk about 'professional'?'

Mrs Parsons' words halted Isabel in her path towards the open door.

Isabel told her. She didn't bother to choose her words carefully just gave the woman a truncated CV of her experience - *and* successes, she emphasised - in business life. And how she was going to put all that knowledge into her new job of running a successful, environmentally friendly, small-holding. That it had elements of the many business seminars she had run on behalf of Paul's large company, she ignored. She spoke from the heart as she had learned to do many years ago as a young and keen office consultant, soon finding that this was the only way to influence the new arrivals into considering themselves as professionals. Apparently her words were having the same effect as then.

'Is that right?' Mrs Parsons asked. 'You, a big business person?'

Isabel listened for the sarcasm which she was sure was present. Surprisingly, it was absent.

'And am I a 'professional'? Mrs Parson asked in a surprised tone. 'Just like you?'

Isabel nodded not allowing herself to speak. Words at present might just destroy any good she had done.

'And you haven't come here just to make a mint of money by refurbishing Old Ben's cottage and then selling it on to some Londoner who will only want to use it for holidays? Swanning around as if they were kings and queens, demanding this and that, never a thought for people who live here all the time?'

Isabel refrained from letting a whistle of surprise escape from her mouth at the unusually long-winded speech. The question was rhetorical, she thought. Mrs P's face said, however, that she was genuinely in search of an answer.

Isabel found a tiny remnant of her earlier courage and took a deep breath. Was she about to spoil this new and fragile rapport that had somehow arisen between her and the post-mistress by saying the wrong thing?

'Yes,' she said, thinking hard, 'you are a 'professional'. And no, I'm not giving up Ben's cottage.' God forbid, she prayed, after all I've been through.

'If that's the case,' Mrs Parsons had reverted to her former caustic tone, sending a chill through Isabel, 'why aren't you bringing me some fruit and veg to sell? Ben always did. A basket, he'd bring, every Friday evening. Now my customers are complaining that they have to go to the supermarket to get their fresh fruit and vegetables.'

Isabel drew in her bottom lip in a brief and painful embrace. She was beginning to understand and wasn't about to spoil things by defending herself. Nobody had told her about Ben and his basket.

'I would like to do that,' she said calmly. 'What would you like?'

The look of surprise on the shopkeeper's face was worth the

miniscule return Isabel thought she could expect from the sale.

'You'll have to provide your own basket,' Mrs P told her, surprise defeating the usual sarcastic tone. 'Ben took his with him.'

Isabel thought of the pile of dusty, grime-laden wicker work in the garden shed and decided to let the woman believe she was right. 'Of course,' she replied.

Mrs Parsons handed her a list. Had the woman been waiting all these weeks for her to make her offer?

Isabel promised to bring a basket with all the fruit and vegetables on the list late on Friday afternoon. Having said that she had the awful feeling that it was quite possible she would not be back from filming in time. She would have to do something about it, ask Hannah, possibly, or bring the basket in early on Friday morning. What a way to start a new business venture, she told herself; Mrs Parsons would probably grumble that they would be past their best by the time she put them on the her counter on Saturday morning and she didn't want to risk that. Asking Marion Hart to bring them in for her later in the day seemed a much better idea.

Mrs Parsons seemed to have undergone a change of personality, then. Even offered Isabel a couple of the succulent apple pasties she had been packing into bags throughout their conversation. 'For you and your visitor,' she said. These, too, were local produce, she had assured Isabel, but couldn't help spoiling things by reverting to her former self and saying, 'Not that I think that girl of yours deserves any treats, of course.'

Isabel wondered briefly what Hannah had done to offend the postmistress cum shopkeeper, and then just put it down to the older woman having a particular sensitivity about temporary residents and left it at that. On quitting the shop she felt she had gone through some sort of operation; the dislike of the elderly woman and her dread of visiting the post office cum village shop had been cut away leaving her free of some nagging, minor illness.

Now all she had to do was sort out the conversation she had had with Hannah that morning. It confirmed that the girl seemed set on antagonising anyone she came into contact with, Isabel had decided. Except for Thom and his boys, that was - a mystery which Isabel had neither the time nor energy to try and solve.

It had sent a cannon of shock through her when she had gathered from a veritable quagmire of words and complaints about life in general, and herself in particular, that she was, once more, being blackmailed. In amazement she asked herself whether she really did look so stupid that people thought she was easy prey, open to manipulation for their own gains. Perhaps she was. That idea had shocked her even more. She recalled her years as Paul's girl-friend, mistress, whatever it was called, and how he had dumped her just when his business was taking off - mostly due to her efforts - and decided that perhaps she was, after all, a dupe. There was the Juliet business, as she was calling it. Travis had nothing to do with it, she was sure. For the moment that could stay in the cauldron of unanswered questions, however, along with all the others that seemed to be erupting on a daily basis.

As soon as Hannah had started talking that morning - for once prepared to join Isabel for breakfast - the reason for her sudden 'friendship' was not exactly the pleasant surprise it could have been. Isabel knew now that the girl had spent the evening before, alone in the cottage, going through the papers in the office. That she had even managed to get the computer running was apparent by her comments about information that was contained only on Isabel's back-up disks - mostly disks labelled 'Paul'.

'I know all about you and my dad, now,' Hannah said. 'Disgusting, I call it.'

Isabel sat in frozen silence for a brief moment then asked, 'What exactly do you know about your father and me?' She should have been telling the girl off for touching her things, not entering into a conversation which, she knew, could lead along a rutted and dangerous road.

'You were his *mistress*,' she girl spat at her. 'You were the woman who made my mother go away,' she added. 'And my father lied. I heard them arguing. He said he didn't have a girl-friend, but he did. It was you. How could you do it? You broke up my parents and didn't even bother to stay and help my father with the business when he needed you.'

Phew! thought Isabel. She knew that Paul was not always straightforward in what he told people but she didn't know until then that he was a liar. And the girl was totally confused which was borne out by her next remark.

'Where's this man you're supposed to have given up my dad for? What about him, then? Gave him the boot as soon as you'd got his money, too. Is that it?'

Isabel had never said anything about another man in her letters — letters which, she now realized, were all there on her back-up disks. She might have mentioned Silas's name and the fiasco over that marina and hoped that was what had sparked off that particular little arrow of disgust, but she wasn't going to bother to set the girl right. But what money? Was Hannah inferring that she'd made off with Paul's money? Suddenly she wanted the conversation to cease; tell the girl that none of this was her business, but she didn't have the chance.

'And why did you have to blackmail him?' Hannah shot at her. 'Wasn't it bad enough that you broke up their marriage without demanding money from him to keep quiet?'

Isabel felt the frown furrowing her forehead. This was getting a bit too much.

'Your father decided that your mother was more important than anything in the world,' she told the girl, in an attempt to halt the diatribe. 'And as she was so ill he wasn't going to give her anything more to worry about than she already had.' Isabel heard herself preaching but was unable to stop.

'Ill? My mother ill? Don't be silly. Okay, so she had some sort of problem when she went to a clinic somewhere, but she was never really ill. Not until you made your demands, that is.'

If that was what Paul had told his daughter Isabel felt she was well out of the situation.

'I'm going to tell him you're on your own now and can go back and work for him. It's not as if you're making any money here.'

Isabel sighed, speechless in her confusion, feeling defenceless and put-upon.

'And we won't need all those house-keepers my dad has had to employ since Mum left.'

So the girl thought she was going to be her father's domestic help, did she? That almost made her lose her composure but she stopped the snort of laughter, born of hysteria, before it could erupt into the laden air. The thought of being discussed by Paul and his daughter nauseated her. It was the cure she needed for the final getting-over of a non-torrid, mostly spasmodic, love affair. That he'd been in love only with her capabilities was something she should have recognised many months - if not years - ago.

Hannah apparently felt she had done her job of blackmail. The small smile on her cold face inferred she had slipped into a dream-world which was happier than the one she currently inhabited. After a few moments she rose from the table and taking her ever-present cloth bag from the back of her chair made for the door.

'You won't get away with it, you know,' she said, pushing the bottom half of the door open with a foot. 'That money you made him give you, you'll have to give it back. If you don't, I know where to go. You won't get away with it,' she repeated as if she had just discovered a really fitting expression before disappearing down the path in a quick trot.

The money she was talking about was what Paul owed her when she left. And, like Hannah's board and lodging, she had never seen – what was it mother used to say? - neither hide nor tail of it. But the thought that Hannah might go to the police and accuse her of extortion could lead only, at the least, to confrontations and problems that she could well do without and, at the worst, to far more.

Once the girl had gone Isabel had let her anger rise to the surface. She was so incensed at all the innuendoes and accusations that she had still been fuming when she got to the post-office to post Lilian's bi-weekly letter. Now all she could do was hope that having got it all off her chest, the girl would be happier. But she wasn't going to put any hard-earned coinage on what would prove, she feared, to be an out-side bet.

That was yesterday morning. After a couple of hours working hard in her garden she had felt her nerves slacken and her anger diminish. She even felt ready to forgive the girl. She was being childishly upset over her parents, that was all. Isabel refused to allow her mind to wander into the realms of Paul's make-believe.

Isabel felt an expected surge of pity for the girl. Unattractive - personality-wise, that was - she might be, but her world as she had known it had crumbled and her sense of security demolished; at her age she needed support and not to be scarred - irrevocably, possibly - by the actions of her elders. Isabel knew she was not going to meddle, however; let her parents straighten the girl out, it wasn't her business, especially as the meagre amount of keep offered by Paul had not been forthcoming.

No mention was made of the previous day's conversation at their brief encounter that morning. Isabel was determined that that was how it would be. As it happened Hannah was happy to grab a handful of digestive biscuits and a glass of fruit juice without even bothering to sit down at the table before setting off on her scooter to an unnamed - but guessed at by Isabel - destination. Isabel felt only a surge of relief.

As she had descended from her bedroom that morning the telephone had started to ring. It was Alice.

'I'm going down to see John Robinson,' she told her granddaughter. 'Thought I'd divert and come and see you. I've got things to show you.' The fact that Alice had to divert by as much as thirty miles to visit her en route to the publishers meant that the 'things' had to be important.

Isabel rushed her chores in order to be able to give all her attention to her grandmother and was just finishing putting a snack together for their lunch when the telephone rang again. It was Juliet.

Isabel had been anxious about when she should be at the airfield on the coming Friday, but didn't want to give Juliet ammunition to use against her if she telephoned at an inconvenient time so had waited for the producer to get to her first.

'We won't need you on Friday, after all,' Juliet said without preamble.

Isabel told herself not to be neurotic; there had been no hint of glee in the woman's words. But what had happened? Had she lost the job before it had hardly started? Her mental cash register rang up a series of noughts as she shivered at the thought. 'Oh,' was all she managed to say.

'We've got a celebrity guest,' Juliet was saying. Was there just that hint of supercilious pride in her voice that she had grown to dread? Isabel wondered as Juliet mentioned a name that was familiar to all watchers of television cookery programmes. 'He's got his own transport, so we're going together.'

There was no mention of compensation for her, Isabel noted, but at least it sounded as if this was just a temporary arrangement. Even so she felt a surge of relief when Juliet spoke.

'We'll expect to see you at the airfield, same time next week as arranged,' she said curtly before replacing her telephone.

Aha, thought Isabel, they don't want anyone taking Ambrose Watson's attention away from them. 'As if I care,' she breathed aloud. She did, of course; like anyone else she wouldn't have minded being in the company of the flamboyant and good-looking television personality for a few hours but would never have admitted it.

Alice arrived at that moment, all cheerful and laden with goodies and an airline pilot's large briefcase so full of papers that the top would not close.

'What's all this?' Isabel asked with a smile, trying to ignore a slight sinking feeling in her stomach. Her grandmother, by nature, was considerate of other people's time, always careful not to be a nuisance. The sight of all the papers, however, inferred that she expected Isabel to spend some time reading her notes of research on the family history she was writing.

'Don't worry, darling.' Alice, it appeared, had read her expression and interpreted it. With a most un-grandmotherly wink she added, 'I haven't come to bother you. I want to sort out my papers before I get to John Robinson's. It looks a bit unprofessional, wouldn't you say?' she laughed, looking down at the over-flowing case. 'There are now just one or two things I wanted to verify before I get there,' she said. 'Like your father's information. I don't know much at all about his history, despite him being my son-in-law.'

Isabel found it strange that her grandmother always mentioned the publisher by both Christian and surname. Hadn't they become friends, after all? But she decided it wasn't worth asking about. 'Why do you have to put him in the book?' Isabel did ask, having guessed many years before what her grandmother had thought of her daughter's husband. Alice had been the first to conjecture that he had disappeared, taken the chance to escape, and had not committed suicide by walking into the sea.

Isabel thought for a moment. 'Date of birth - April 16, 1944. They got married in 1967, the year before I was born - September I think it was. His father was called Ernest - Ernest by name and horribly earnest by nature,' she laughed. '1916, I think and, of course, there's Lilian whose birthday is the 10th of February,' she paused, then continued, '1919.' She had had to fill in several forms just recently so the date was etched on her memory. The thought had made her stumble a little.

'What else do you want to know?'

'If I was just going to put in a list of dates,' Alice told her with a hint of asperity in her voice, 'it would be a very boring book. However, I suppose I can drum up something to give it colour.' She sucked in her cheek and then nodded. 'His grandfather was a soldier, wasn't he? I remember wondering how a brave man could ever produce....' She stopped abruptly. Hastily she continued. 'He must have been in the Boer War, the second one that started in 1902. He would have had something interesting to say about his time in South Africa, I'm sure.'

'Of course,' Isabel said quickly. 'I've got some letters he wrote. If you wait a second I'll try and find them.' She left her grandmother happily scribbling at the large wooden table while she went into her tiny office. Fortunately, Hannah's foraging had been confined to the boxes labelled 'Personal Papers' and the others were still intact. Finding what she was looking for easily and without undue effort gave her the courage to glance at the riffled boxes of personal letters and papers with less pain than she had imagined possible. She would have to sort everything out, but not just yet.

'Here we are,' she said to Alice putting a heavy file full of plastic pages stuffed with hand-written sheets on the table in front of her.

Alice's eyes lit up. 'You're a miracle, do you know that?' she said, thumbing her way through the leaves of plastic. She read from one of the letters: "...rode about forty miles... got within six miles of the Boers but did not attack them.... For the last six days we have been living hand to mouth, getting sheep and what bread we could from the farm houses..." She continued to read. 'Here's another: "Flags flying half mast high and I asked a man for whom the flags were flying. He said "the Queen"...We had not even heard the Queen was ill..." I can see I'm going to have some fun with these. Just the sort of thing John Robertson will be delighted with; might even commission you to make a collection of the letters,' Alice said with a delighted laugh.

Isabel experienced a small thrill of excitement. Not at the thought of having something published - that would be fun and might even bring in a bit of money - but at the thought that her eighty year old grandmother had beaten her to it. She determined to turn up some more material for her. Surely her grandmother's publishing friend would be a little lenient over time?

'His name was Roger, I see. I hope he wasn't the original for that naughty rhyme about a lodger.' She giggled like a school girl. 'But it does say here on a note in the margin that he died of syphilis. Who would have written that, I wonder?' Isabel, until she did some paper tidying was unable to give her any answer. 'He must have been forty when your grandfather Ernest was born.

Isabel heard the unspoken words that Alice was too polite to speak. She knew her father was no saint, had probably inherited all sorts of characteristics from his forbearers; the fact that he was a serious criminal was something she did not want to be reminded of it. Strange how an innocent occupation like writing one's family history can turn up stones revealing all sorts of unwanted nasties if one wasn't careful, she mused. It would all figure in her gran's books, she knew, and she would accept that; there was no way she was going to stop Alice from producing an interesting and publishable book but she might skim over the bits she didn't like when the time came for seeing it all in print.

Alice was bundling the papers into the already over-crowded briefcase, trying to clear a space for the lunch Isabel had prepared earlier when there was a crunch of footsteps outside the kitchen.

Isabel wondered what had brought Hannah back so early. She did not want her outspoken guest finding her match in her outspoken, but so much more polite, grandmother. It would be too much for her overstretched nerves.

Isabel almost fell back into the kitchen when she saw who it was. Thom's bulk was framed by the half-open door, a strange expression on his face. He did not apologise for appearing just as they were about to have lunch, Isabel noticed. In his opinion it was probably well over an hour past the usual time for a mid-day snack. Also, he gave no reason for condescending to come to the kitchen door and not, as he usually did, to the front door.

'I didn't think you would have visitors,' were his first words. 'But I'm not stopping. Came to see if you were all right. After your abrupt departure from the barbecue.'

He'd taken long enough, Isabel thought, having got over the shock at the sight of her difficult neighbour. What if I had been taken ill at his party? she asked herself, remembering the way she had crept away; I could be dead by now.

'Who's your visitor, darling?' Alice called. 'Aren't you going to ask him in?'

There was little else that Isabel could do, without seeming churlish and unneighbourly, so she stepped back and silently indicated that he could step into the kitchen if that was what he wanted.

He stepped carefully over the slightly raised doorstep and then drew to an abrupt halt. 'So you're a regular visitor here, then?' he said to Alice.

'Not as much as I would like to be,' she answered. 'All this you know,' and she pointed a finger at the brief case which was just visible to the man at the door.

Isabel stood looking from her grandmother to Thom and back.

'Do you know each other?' she blurted out finally, watching as Thom bent forward with an outstretched hand which Alice took with unwarranted warmth.

'We've met a couple of times, haven't we Alice?' Thom's voice was different from usual, Isabel thought.

'He writes books,' Alice said.

'Book,' Thom corrected.

'Ah, but that's only a beginning.'

'I've said all I can about the farm. Don't want to bore people!'

'Is there anything you don't do?' asked Isabel feeling that she was being left out of the conversation.

'Darling,' remonstrated her grandmother, 'that's not very polite.' But she was smiling as she said it. 'We met at John Robertson,' she told her granddaughter.

'The boss thought we might be able to help each other. You know, proof-reading, editing, that sort of thing.'

Thom nodded, then turned and left as abruptly as he had arrived, but not before kissing Alice affectionately on the cheek and saying, 'I'll leave you two ladies to enjoy your lunch.'

Isabel was stunned. So many questions she wanted the answers to but didn't know which one to ask first. She didn't get the chance to even start.

'I have something I wanted to discuss with you,' Alice said, before Isabel could speak.' I saw something the other day in a magazine,' she told her granddaughter. 'It might be of some help with your other grandmother.'

Isabel shook her head briefly. She would have to sort out the bewildering puzzle in her brain later. When she had a chance to think.

Alice passed over a cutting from a magazine. It was all about dietary supplements. Isabel was aware that her grandmother put her own health down to proper food, exercise, friends and, of course, dietary supplements, saying she was a walking advertisement for her good life-style. Isabel was tolerant and, despite herself, believed that Alice was probably right. Isabel accepted the cutting and promised to read it later.

Packing herself and the big briefcase into her little sapphire vehicle as soon as lunch was finished Alice was soon speeding away into the distance. In the rush Isabel even forgot to ask her the answer to the riddle of her seemingly friendly acquaintance with the man whose appearance had been so brief.

Alice had been gone only a couple of minutes when Isabel had her next visitor. This time the shock was equal if not worse than seeing her awful neighbour being affectionate to her grandmother.

Paul did not wait to be asked in. He marched to the table, set a bottle of wine down heavily on the wood and then looked around as if expecting glasses and corkscrew to materialise out of the rather dusty air of the cottage kitchen.

Isabel found herself from habit following his unspoken instructions and then turned to speak.

Paul held a finger to his lips. He'd always done this when he wanted to impart important news - or, more often, instructions for her - and wished to keep his train of thoughts running along their tracks without disruption. He gestured her to take the chair Alice had recently vacated and he sat down opposite and poured out two glasses of wine.

Isabel watched as he appeared to be collecting his speeding thoughts.

'I want you back,' he said after a few moments.

With difficulty Isabel prevented a gasp from escaping her. Not at the suddenness of the idea - she had Hannah to thank for that - but at his downright cheek. Hadn't she made herself transparently clear - how many was it? - eight weeks ago. 'But...' she began.

Paul held up a hand as if quelling a rising mob. 'No buts,' he said. 'Hannah tells me what a mess you're in.' His expression as he looked around the cottage kitchen as if judging her haven of peace and tranquillity said he found it sorely wanting. 'You can hardly afford to feed yourself, I hear. You just eat what you can from the garden. That's not enough for a young girl to exist on, let alone someone who is considerably older and should know better.'

Isabel ground her teeth together as she forced herself to keep silent. She would have something to say about Hannah's food - or lack of it, it seemed - later, when she was calmer - or when she was given a chance to speak. She got this sooner than she expected, but the subject was nothing to do with Hannah's food.

Paul seemed to be cogitating on what to say next or, more likely, waiting for her to fall at his feet with gratitude. 'What about her mother?' Isabel asked, knowing she was trying to skate on an only-partially frozen pond. 'Why can't she look after her daughter if she's no longer ill?'

For a fleeting second Paul looked as though afraid that he had been found out. Then he said, 'That's neither here nor there. In fact it's none of your business. I want you back as a worker, not a girl-friend.' He almost stumbled over the last word as if he was using it just to appease her. 'From what I can gather from Hannah - who, I might say, has been very upset that you have to send her to a neighbour to get food - you are getting yourself into a very dangerous situation here. Something about flying someone around illegally?'

Isabel drew in her breath. What had the girl been saying? 'She's wrong,' she managed to say in defence.

'If you say so,' Paul answered as if not believing her. 'But then there's the tiff between you and that neighbour you've forced her on. Says that he runs a rehabilitation camp for young offenders. Do you think that's the sort of company I want my daughter to mix with? You might be able to close your eyes to his activities, but she's too young to do that.'

She was shocked into silence. How confused her life was becoming; everyone wanted something from her but was unwilling to recompense her for the time they demanded she spent on their demands.

'I think you will find it best to leave the area and return to where you belong.' Paul said then as if it was already agreed between them.

Isabel was relieved to see him get up and prepare to leave. She did not have the strength to fight him, another of her mother's much-used maxims. His attitude only confirmed that her decision to leave London, the job - and him - was the best thing that she had ever done.

Hannah she would deal with later - once she returned from that neighbour she so despised. In the meantime she had the article that Alice had left her to read. It would take her mind off things for a few moments.

Isabel had only to read the first few words and then she was drawn into the subject as if by a powerful magnet. It was, it seemed, a miracle cure for Lilian's complaint. She read and re-read it, marking with a pink highlighter the names of the various supplements that were proven to work. As soon as she could she would go into town and get whatever was needed. Her trained business brain told her to be sceptical but she was willing to try anything. As long as Lilian agreed to take them there could be a psychological effect if no everlasting cure. Anything was worth trying. She would even take them up to Granma Lil's and explain what she had to do. And leave instructions for their use for the helpful neighbour, too.

Perhaps there was a benign being somewhere looking over her, Isabel mused as she was dropping off to sleep that night; there were miracles waiting to happen, after all. Once asleep dreams were of little Chinese people rolling around like round pink and brown balls, bright-eyed, laughing and energetic. Standing at one side was large, queen-like Lilian with an arm raised in a regal wave, smiling and nodding her head in time with the movement of her hand.

Chapter 19

A break from all the minor evils that seemed to be plaguing her like an infection which just wouldn't clear up, was very much needed. And now she could cut back the currant bushes so that the fruit hiding in their forest of greenery could get a bit of sun and ripen. She might even have time to dig over that rough patch near the river for her precious herbs. So much time, effort and money had been spent on them she couldn't let them spoil through lack of attention. They weren't going off in the greenhouse, shaded by sheets of newspaper stuck onto the windows with blue sticky patches, but she wanted them to join her growing garden family as soon as possible. It felt like a month ago that she'd rushed up to Springfields to buy them, not just three days. Her life was like that at the moment. Who would have been able to convince her - three months earlier as she scuttled around the barn-like office, supervising the secretaries, the architects and, even, Paul himself - that the days in the country would seem to have double the amount of hours of those in the city. Today was free, however, as her little job - as she termed her post of flying chauffeur - had been usurped by another. A few plans could be made and she'd also catch up on those things she'd been neglecting.

Isabel was putting her herb plants and seed trays from the greenhouse onto sheets of newspaper on the large kitchen table when the telephone shrieked its self-important demand.

'Why aren't you here?' Juliet's voice was sharp; full of panic, a person who didn't know her might have said.

'Where?' Isabel was stunned yet again by the peremptory tone of the woman's voice. What was she being accused of now?

'Here. At the airfield,' Juliet's voice sounded like the screech of some frightened barn owl. 'Where else?'

Isabel drew in a deep breath. She wasn't used to being talked to like this; particularly as it seemed she was being accused of not keeping her part of a bargain. A bargain which had been cancelled, she reminded herself, remembering the prepared box of fruit and veg which was now in someone else's larder. She heard Juliet calling to someone, then.

In a moment Travis's voice came over the line. 'Sorry about this,' he said in a placating tone. 'I do apologise.'

Did she hear a snort from an invisible Juliet or was she imagining it?

'It's just that we screwed up,' Travis said.

'She did, you mean,' the distant voice yelped.

'We thought we were going with Ambrose. Now it appears that he wants some shots of the airplane arriving and me actually getting off it,' Travis said apologetically.

That was going to be a bit difficult, Isabel told herself. As Travis would be sitting in the back seat while she flew the airplane how could he leave by the pilot's door? The pantomime of changing seats once they'd landed wouldn't fool anyone. But they had solved that little problem, too, it seemed.

'I'll have to sit in the front,' Travis told her. 'You can fly the plane from the left hand seat,' he said. 'Good practice for you.' He seemed to find that very amusing.

Good practice for what, Isabel wanted to ask.

'Could you get here as quickly as possible?' He paused. 'Please?' he asked like a child flirting with a mother who had been holding the sweet packet out of his reach. 'Ambrose doesn't mind working on a bit later than planned.'

If Juliet had asked her, Isabel, in her present mood, would have refused. She found she could not refuse Travis, however. Having got to know him from their occasional meetings she felt that he found Juliet a bit of a drag, too. There was something she wasn't able to fathom about their relationship, but couldn't put her finger on exactly what it was. She liked Travis, thought him talented and nice to be with, so she would obey like a good little girl. She could always hope that her good-natured tolerance would make Juliet flaming mad. She felt much better after that thought.

'Okay,' she assented. 'I'll be there as quickly as I can.'

Telling herself she could do nothing about the seeds and herbs now dripping their moisture through the newspaper onto the stone floor, or the pile of washing in the red plastic basket waiting to be fed into the washing machine under the old draining board - none of it which, she knew, would bother Hannah who was still in bed - she grabbed the small flight bag from where she had dropped it beside the tall Welsh dresser. She glanced into it to check that nothing was missing - her clipboard was there, together with her Pooley's Flight

Guide, Cessna checklist and the chart that covered both her local area and the one she had already put in together with her plans for the very short flight. It had all been a bit of mystery when she'd been told that they would be going *back* to where Juliet and Travis came from; that they were using their 'studio' for this week's filming. A mystery, that was, until she remembered that part of Travis's fame was as 'The Flying Cook' and shots of the airplane at each venue were essential. She hoped the flying cook would have had the sense to do all the outside checks while she was on her way to the airfield.

Not for the first time Isabel asked herself why Travis didn't fly himself. Surely his job as a televised chef was not so creative that he had to store up all his energies for it and not dissipate them in flying his small aircraft around. As she enjoyed doing it, however, she wasn't going to enquire too deeply. At least hours were accumulating on her licence - if not much money in her bank account as she'd decided she must refuse any further payment, even in kind. Until her job of ferrying Travis and Juliet around came to an end, that was. Then she would ask for some recompense for her time. Surely that wouldn't be considered 'illegal use' of her licence?

Once at the airfield Isabel didn't delay in passing her flight plan through the sliding window to the girl at the control desk. She hurried through the swing door to join the others who were hovering around Travis's grey and red-striped airplane sitting on the tarmac bordering the grass runway. She had glanced at the weather sheet on her way in and had seen nothing to give her any concern. The wind at their destination was light, which was what she always wished for. So what could happen in 20 miles? Not a lot, she told herself as she reached the other two. They would be at their destination within minutes. She hadn't noticed the tightening isobars on the weather map she recalled later.

Travis, in a moment of relaxation, had described their 'studio'. It had been made by their predecessor from one of the large hangers on an airfield once used by the military and which was now an exhibition centre of antique aircraft. There were all the usual ones, some flyable others just grounded museums open to the public. She was quite looking forward to the day's trip; it would be nice to see again all those aircraft with names her grandmother often quoted when regaling her with yet more information on her family's past.

Travis had the engine running when she got to the aircraft. 'All outside checks done,' he told her as she trotted towards the aircraft. 'Oil, fuel, everything ready.' Travis knew what he was doing, that was obvious; otherwise he would not bother to own a complex and very expensive piece of machinery. It was just his generosity, Isabel decided, that let him give over the fun of flying it to other less fortunate mortals. She would have to consider, one day, if she should indulge herself so much; her time could be spent more lucratively, she was sure. For the moment, however, she would carry on. Especially as it was quite legal for her to sell him produce from her garden. That was nothing to do with her piloting the plane. The thought hovered for a moment - what produce? And when was she going to start providing it? And when would they start using it? she thought with a quiver remembering the earlier occasion.

As pilot, Isabel had made the decision to fly at 2000 feet. Any wind at the height would be light enough not to delay them and speed, it seemed, was of the essence if they were not to offend the great man who had deigned to be part of their programme for one episode. That he was using it as a publicity stunt had not occurred to either Juliet or Travis, but Isabel had a second-sense about these things born of many years of experience.

She found it a bit strange sitting in the left-hand seat. Whenever she'd flown in somebody else's airplane she was usually a passenger in the back. But she soon settled down, the map and clipboard with the frequencies she would need on her lap, Travis in her usual seat and Juliet, for once, relegated to the single back seat. She judged it would take them no more than twenty minutes to reach their destination once they were airborne. Wasting no time she taxied to the end of the runway, ran through the checks, put on full power and they were in the air before ten minutes had passed.

It was the first bump as if she was running over a tyre left in the middle of a road that drew her attention to the fact that all was not as it should be. A quick glance over her shoulder told her why. She regretted immediately not taking a closer look at the weather bulletin back at the airfield. What was Travis doing letting them fly when a thunder storm was just over the horizon? Then she remembered that she had just assumed that he'd read all the necessary notices. Now she realized he was, like a boy with a toy, only interested in playing with his airplane, rather than doing her job for her. There was no excuse; she had properly messed up. But there was no time to go into that now.

The clouds to her right seemed to be growing upwards as if part of an animated film put on fast forward. Again the plane bounced, but harder this time, causing it to lose altitude - but only of a non-worrying amount, she reassured herself quickly, as she heard a quick gasp from the seat on her left. Anxiously she scanned the sky. If she turned to port a few degrees she might just get to their destination before the storm hit them. It would put a little time on the journey but it was worth trying; anything was better than bouncing around the sky waiting to be struck by lightning. She knew the wings had static wicks to protect them from being hit but she was not going to try and prove they worked.

She watched Travis's left hand as it crept towards the control. If he dared to touch it while she was in charge she would whack his fingers with the hard edge of her clipboard, she decided. Just in time he withdrew his hand and placed it between the tight clamp of his knees, making it easier for Isabel to breathe once more. There wasn't a sound from Juliet at the back, nor did Isabel care what she was feeling. She was intent getting them to their destination without mishap and was not going to use mental energy in considering her passenger.

Isabel watched from the corner of her eye as the darkening clouds billowed, throwing out the anvil shapes for which they were famous. Her hands were becoming slippery with the sweat of tension mixed with fear. She wiped them quickly one after the other on the dark trousers she'd thrown on before leaving the cottage. She had been in a thunderstorm before, hadn't she? And had sworn never to be again.

Keeping one eye on the compass and altimeter she banked to port. To try and climb above clouds that were fast approaching was not even worth considering. She must try and get to the airfield as soon as possible. In banking she gained speed. Pulling the nose up slightly gave her more control while still maintaining height. She fancied she could just see the two converging runways of the ex-military airfield. To land too early would be risky with the end of the concrete runway making an unforgiving ridge in the grass before it.

Isabel said to Travis with clenched teeth. 'You do the radio,' she ordered. 'I'm going to have my hands full getting this thing down.'

He was relieved to have something to occupy his hands, it appeared, as he grabbed the microphone.

Isabel could hardly hear the answers from their destination airfield over the noise of the engine but she gathered she had been given permission to take a direct approach, which Travis confirmed shortly after.

Never were landing checks so welcome, Isabel thought, as she breathed the acronym for all the things she had to remember before lining up with the runway. Grasping the control with both hands she managed to keep the small plane going where she wanted it to while being buffeted by the uneven gusts of wind. With only a few minutes left till landing she let the aircraft down to the lowest safe level at a speed just above the minimum that she knew she could manage with. The wheels touched the runway with seconds to spare before the rain enveloped them in blinding cloak. With a sigh of relief she let the nose of the small airplane lower as gently as she could, but even so the plane skidded slightly as the rain made grease out of the dust on the concrete. Cutting the speed to a crawl she managed to find the way onto the stand beside the hangars that Travis was indicating and then stopped the engine. The three of them sat, immobile and silent, while the rain beat its tattoo on their metal shell.

As suddenly as it had arrived the storm departed, leaving the hard surface beneath them steaming as if water had been poured over a mammoth kitchen range. Isabel and Travis sighed in unison. They turned towards each other with twin smiles of relief. Juliet gave a short cough, whether in relief or disgust Isabel was not sure. Her attention was taken almost immediately by the sight of a cameraman, a large black plastic coat covering him and his camera trotting towards the airplane.

'That was wonderful,' the man shouted. 'Can we do it again?'

Travis said a couple of words under his breath that Isabel thought would not have been part of his vocabulary. When he realised the cameraman was joking, his face resumed its usual pleasant expression.

It took a few minutes for the cameraman to fulfil the brief he had been given by the guest star who was lurking in the crack made by the large sliding door of the ex-hangar. Travis was then allowed to descend from his pilot's seat, followed by a somewhat disgruntled Juliet, to make his way slowly towards the hangar, pretending not to notice that his shoes were getting a good soaking on the way. Isabel was to stay in the plane until the others were safely inside, Juliet told her, whispering through clenched teeth.

Isabel's hands were shaking, she was ashamed to see. She was happy to stay were she was for the moment, But not many minutes had passed before she was longing to get out of the now-stifling metal box and find the ladies' toilet without being seen. She had no wish to meet Ambrose Watson, to have him shake her sticky hands. In fact, she cared very little if she met him at all, but she had to be prepared.

Once in the cupboard-like and windowless cloakroom she splashed her hot face with cool water. Pulling a minute plastic glass from a water machine, she downed several cupfuls after which she began to feel better. She wasn't going to let herself down by giving away just how frightened she had been. Even Juliet's face had had a grey tinge lurking under hastily re-applied make-up. Travis had said nothing as he pushed his door open to descend from the plane, just reached behind him and patted her arm before posing for the cameraman - who by then was bending beneath the wing of the Cessna in order to aim upwards to get a picture of Travis leaving the aircraft. 'Well done,' he had breathed between unmoving lips as he smiled for the camera.

Having returned from the cloakroom Isabel decided that, instead of sitting watching Travis and his team at their antics, she would go for a walk. She didn't get far before an enthusiastic club member invited her to see over all the antique airplanes. She began to tire of climbing into one old and dusty airplane after another but considered this was a better way of passing the time than being a sycophantic guest at Travis and Co's party.

Half way through the afternoon, Travis came to find her. 'We're just about to have a break before the final filming. You must be starving.' The glass of wine he held in his hand rocked slightly as he laughed. 'You could do with one of these, too, I dare say,' he told her, waving the half-empty glass towards the sky as if she might need reminding.

Isabel hadn't thought about it but now he mentioned it she was, indeed, very hungry, but not particularly for wine. She didn't know what was on that day's menu for filming - she'd had no time or opportunity to ask – but anything edible would be welcome. It seemed like an age since her early breakfast and the water was all she had had to nourish her since then. The rest of them had probably been nibbling throughout, but it was nice of Travis to think about her. She wouldn't take up the offer of a drink, however; her nerves were still too much like fine wire to risk it going straight to her head. Also she knew the rules; was a bit surprised at Travis for suggesting it.

She was happy, too, to be able to sit and relax for the short time that the filming still needed before the customary 'wraps'.

Isabel, her mind on the return flight, barely took in the actual happenings on the hangar floor under the huge lights that made the building into some gigantic igloo. She took in that the two of them had been cooking a starter, a main-course and a pudding - at the same time, with the same ingredients - and had been striving to out-do the other by finishing first, accompanied by the usual muted canned laughter and applause as there was no audience in view, Isabel had guessed. Now that the filming had been completed Ambrose climbed into his large, customised coach and was driven away. The mess that was left was, apparently, for the benefit of keeping the minions occupied, Juliet's angry expression confirmed as she ordered the young man and girl who had been scurrying back and forth clearing away pots and pans to take them and all the dishes and implements the two cooks had been using out to the small kitchen at the back of the hangar.

'And the floor will need a wipe,' she ordered as they went off with their piles of dirty dishes.

Travis had wandered across to Isabel's side, wiping his face on a damp towel with one hand as he did so. In the other hand was a frosting green bottle and two glasses held dangerously by their stems. "Now perhaps you'll join me,' he laughed.

Isabel shook her head. Would he never take 'no' for an answer? Not unless you want to do the flying?' she quipped.

She was amazed at his response to her invitation. His face, under the half-removed make-up, first was a pale shade of parchment then purple blotches began to appear. He'd been rubbing his skin too hard, Isabel decided then. It was nothing to do with what she had said.

Travis sighed, and then his face immediately regained its usual smooth, friendly expression 'I wouldn't want to spoil it for you,' he said with feigned sorrow in his voice. 'But perhaps we could have one at the club when we've finished?'

'Juliet might want to get straight back,' Isabel reminded him.

'That's okay. We won't hold her up.'

Ever the pragmatist Isabel asked, 'How will you get back here if she's got the only car?'

Travis looked disappointed, as if he hadn't considered this particular point. Or was he expecting her to ferry him home from Shilliton? She was in no mood to put a match to Juliet's uneven temperament by upsetting any of her plans.

'Sorry,' Isabel apologised, shaking her head. Maybe he was just lonely and wanted to spend some time with someone who made no demands of him. She would try and make it up to him later, but for the moment she had to fly an airplane and get them all safely back to Shilliton. The late afternoon air was clear and the sky denied that it had been anything but clear blue and cloudless all day long, as they flew an uneventful twenty minutes back to the club airfield.

With a sigh of relief Isabel watched as Juliet and Travis drove off, then climbed into her own car to make her way back to the haven of peace and tranquillity she had hoped her new home in the country was going to be.

It was still early evening when she turned into her front garden parking area. The birds were still calling to their friends and family to come home to roost, a distant goose was singing for his mate and a single lonely bee was taking advantage of human absence as it buzzed around the creeper hanging across the top of the old door. Sad, she thought, looking at it, almost an endangered species; just another example of what we're doing to our world, she mused, shaking her head.

She plucked the single letter out of the old mailbox on her way through the gate. As it was typed and its postmark said it had come from some local office, she did not anticipate that it contained any nerve-bruising news. On the contrary, the brown envelope contained a flimsy sheet of paper confirming that she now had the right to fish in her own stream and no one would be able to tell her not to unless she leased the fishing rights to them. Not a chance; she'd been looking forward to this too much to even consider doing that.

There was no sign of Hannah, of course. Thom, she feared, would get tired of her spending so much time over there and send her packing. She shivered at the thought. What would she do with the girl if that happened? Perhaps a letter from Thom - a stranger, maybe, but now very involved in the girl's activities - would force Paul to take responsibility for his daughter.

The telephone rang as she entered the cottage. As if conjured up by her thoughts it was Thom at the other end, his voice broken up by the use of a mobile. 'Thought you might be wondering where your girl was,' he announced. 'We've been out all day and we're only now on our way back. We'll be there in a couple of hours,' he told her.

Isabel could hear the murmur of a large engine in the background and assumed they'd been on one of their coach trips. These were a weekly item on the agenda, it appeared. He pressed a button and the sound died.

For a moment Isabel wondered whether she was being totally irresponsible in letting Hannah spend so much time with Thom and his gang – as she was now calling them. She hardly knew the man but felt that he wouldn't let any youngster in his care come to harm. But what about the boys? They might try all sorts of things. But Hannah, she thought, wasn't likely to allow them get away with any nonsenses. Feeling mollified she decided to make good use of the time and continue with the work she had begun that morning.

The wheelbarrow was where she had left it, just outside the kitchen door, which, she was pleased to find on her return, was securely locked and the key in the upside-down plant pot on the left of the door. Some of the things she said to the girl were registering, it seemed.

She retrieved a spade from the small wooden shed outside the window of her glamorous bathroom and chucked it into the wheelbarrow where it landed with the noise of a cannon going off. She put a couple of hand tools in with it, although she was convinced that they would be of little use in digging over the neglected patch of ground. She wheeled the lot along the path, past the fruit cage and onto the patch of neglected land next to the river.

The top layer, due to the absence week upon week of earth-softening rain, was like concrete. For an hour she pushed the sharp end of the spade into it, pressed it down with an increasingly tiring foot and pulled up squares of hard earth, weeds and stones. Once she got beyond the top layer - whose earth she piled to one side having removed all the detritus that no young plants would thrive in - she piled the wheelbarrow high with the stones and weeds and broken branches and wheeled it to the river's edge and upended it over the accommodating water.

A glance at her watch told her she would have to hurry if she wanted to get the herbs, still resting on the kitchen table, into their new bed before nightfall. As she placed the spade once more into the earth she felt something, neither hard nor soft, clink against the metal plate of the spade. Curious as to what she might find she looked down at the shallow hole made by her tool. Some dog had been busy here, burying its bones. This would have been some time ago, she realized; Old Ben had had no pet as far as she knew. She bent down and picked up the bone ready to throw it into the wheelbarrow.

It lay on the palm of her hand overlapping her fingers. She felt the truth scorching her as if the piece was alight and burning her hand. This was no dog's bone, she realized. As she turned over some more of the earth other bones appeared, and more and more, all lying like a large animal asleep on its side. Isabel was frozen with horror as the truth began to ooze into her mind. These were the remains of a human being.

She left the piece of ground, the wheelbarrow, the shovel and the horrendous skeleton it had unearthed, and returned to the cottage. Her limbs were those of an automaton, her mind feeling as if it were full of cotton wool. The numbness gradually thawed as her usual, well-honed, common-sense took over. She had some thinking to do - and fast.

Chapter 20

'You're both strong characters.' Alice leaned across and patted Isabel on her bare arm before picking up her glass of lemonade again.

They were sitting on the terrace enjoying the fresh air before the late morning sun turned the stones into coals and the plastic chairs into enveloping saunas, the iced drinks frosting their glasses of home-made lemonade sitting on the table between them.

Alice had telephoned the evening before and asked whether she'd be welcome as she was on her way to her publishers. Isabel was still so stressed from the events of the previous forty eight hours that she didn't think of asking her grandmother how she could get a businessman to see her on a Sunday. Added to that her mind had suddenly become diverted to the happier thought that someone up there might have just sent her a miracle. Allie was just the person to help her sort out her ever-increasing problems.

Isabel poured into willing ears all her worries, including the ongoing ruffling of her feathers by her neighbour. But she restrained herself from mentioning her find in the earth on the riverside. She *might* come to that later.

'That's what all this is about,' Alice was continuing on the subject of Isabel's neighbour. 'You both know your own minds.' She had always been perspicacious, Isabel told herself. Didn't usually make such snap decisions about a person she'd met only on one brief occasion. But hadn't it seemed that they had met somewhere before....

Alice's voice broke into Isabel's thoughts. 'You're like two trains rushing along on parallel tracks destined never to meet!' Long ear-rings sparkled as she laughed at the thought. 'Perhaps one day you'll meet up in a station!' The older woman was silent for a moment as if she was adding skin, bones and, possibly, clothes to her mental picture. Using a more serious tone she continued. 'That girl is really none of his responsibility. He had a right to be cross when he thought she'd broken his precious ornament.'

'Cross' was hardly the right word, Isabel told herself thinking back to that evening two days earlier when he had visited with a handful of little shards of glass.

She was surprised by a further visit the next morning. While she waited for an apology, he started on a long rambling explanation which even she thought was out of character.

'One of the boys said he saw Hannah handling it just before we set off on our outing,' Thom told her. 'I didn't notice that it wasn't in its usual place until last night. She was planning on trying to sell it, he thought. Even had a friend who could find a buyer for her,' Thom paused as if searching for words. 'The story should have struck me as being all too slick. I normally take what that particular young man says with a degree of scepticism. He's had a tough life, father in prison, mother ran off when he was still a baby, he and his older brother in care since I don't know when. He's liable to tell stories to make himself feel equal to the others.'

Isabel wondered who he was trying to justify. 'It's nothing to do with me, what your boys get up to,' she told him curtly.

'I know, I know,' Thom said, surprising Isabel with his placatory tone. Her surprise turned to astonishment when he added, 'I've come to apologise.' He paused. 'It was nothing to do with your Hannah, apparently. The boy they call Dil,' he told her, before she could speak, 'the one who's musical, knocked it off the shelf with his guitar. A complete accident, just youthful carelessness.' Thom's voice had thickened with sadness. 'It's irreplaceable, of course.'

Isabel felt sorrier for the boy than she did for Thom. The youngster must be feeling awful, she thought.

There was no time to thank him for having let Hannah join them for their trip before he was telling her off then in his more usual teacher-like way, for always leaving the girl unsupervised. 'So that you can go swanning around with that so-called cook,' he had added surprising her with his change of tone.

'I think that's none of your business,' Isabel said, stung into defending herself. She wanted to lie to him that it was financially in her favour to 'swan' around with Travis and Juliet but she feared that might bring forth further maledictions.

'And Juliet is not exactly fond of you, I gather,' Thom added.

The remark was somewhat incongruous, Isabel felt, but he was probably right as the feeling was mutual. Where he'd got the information from, however, was a mystery, unless the woman had bent his ear at that barbecue party.

Then it struck her, like a sudden shaft of sunshine cutting through the clouds. He was jealous; jealous of Travis for being attractive to women. That was it. He had decided Juliet would make a good surrogate mother for his boys. And maybe a wife for him? Whether his 'boys' would like her was an uncertain concept which he might not have considered.

'Her father dumped her on me,' Isabel said, returning to the subject of Hannah, 'and I'm coping as well as I can.' She hoped that didn't make her sound pathetic.

'That man,' Thom snorted, 'didn't look the sort who'd just drop his daughter and walk away!'

Men, Isabel sneered to herself, they always stick together.

'He's probably paying you a packet,' Thom said then, confirming Isabel's thoughts.

That hurt. Isabel whipped her stinging reply into obscurity by saying, 'He's not. And that's the major problem,' she added, in a way that anyone less insensitive would have taken as the end of the conversation. Thom was one of those people who never had to worry about a minor thing like a bank balance; there was always plenty in it, she was certain.

'And aren't you rather neglecting your...' he looked around the garden as if searching the plants and trees for an appropriate description. '... your garden?'

A better word would be 'business', Isabel told herself, hoping she had not heard a hint of irony in his voice. But at least the anger seemed to have taken up its bed and walked. 'I'm not neglecting it,' she said, remembering all the early hours and late evenings she spent slaving away in it. 'It is my business,' she said, emphasising the word. Despite his apology she was still angry at the way he had spoken to her the evening before.

She let her eyes wander around her 'business', ingrained upbringing telling her she should offer him a seat in the shade of the old Bramley tree. That reminded her that she should pick some nice cookers and fresh beans to take with her on her next trip with Travis – if that came to pass, she warned herself, remembering the recent trip. If it did, she would insist that he used her produce and not that horrible, plastic stuff from the supermarket.

With a start she turned her attention back to her neighbour. His unexpected words had filtered through her thoughts.

'I don't mind Hannah joining in with the boys,' he was saying. 'It does them good to have her around. She can keep them in order better than I can.' His chuckle was sudden and surprising. The earlier anger had dissolved, it seemed.

His face was completely different when he laughed, Isabel noted. The usual lines of discontent seemed to disappear and his eyes had become bluer than any man's had the right to be. It appeared, too, that, having had his say and proven himself in the right, he was now able to relax. 'We'll get you sorted out, one of these days,' he told her.

Isabel felt little arrows of ice entering her; things were not to be so different, after all. She had been duped into seeing her neighbour in a new light which now turned out to be distorted and artificial. And she had just decided that he might be the one to help her with the problem of - she could hardly bring herself to say the words - the bones. Disappointment flooded her. She sighed quietly before saying, 'As much as I've enjoyed our chat, I've got things to see to. My 'business', you know.'

Thom glanced at her. The look on his face appeared to be asking what he had done wrong. He shrugged slightly and then pushed himself away from the chair back he'd been leaning on. He bowed his head in a slight nod. 'You're not the only one,' he said, turning to go.

Isabel could not understand why she should feel disappointed as she watched him disappear through the gate. She had stood still, mulling over their slightly puzzling conversation, until she heard the aged engine of the red landrover fade into the distance. For a short moment it had seemed that they might become at some time in the future, if not friends, at least allies. That was not to be, it appeared, but she had too much to do to worry about it, she told herself firmly. Just to show him that he had no right to judge her - or her house guests, whoever they might be - she would do nothing to discourage Hannah from joining his 'boys' whenever she wished to.

She turned to go back into the kitchen when, to her surprise, she saw the dusty red vehicle doing a u-turn on the track and rushing to back to slew to halt beside her. 'There's something I wanted to warn you about,' he said jumping from the vehicle.

One thing he had said in passing earlier which bothered her a little. It had been while she was admiring the shiny round green globes on her Bramley tree and wondering how she would reach the ones at the top without a ladder, so she hadn't paid much attention to it. What did he mean when he said, 'When she's not around they behave just as they always do.'? He had made a joke of it. 'They missed her when she didn't turn up for the trip to the wildlife park.'

Hannah had gone on that trip, hadn't she? It must have been some other time he was speaking about. The girl had been full of the day's excitements; could hardly stop talking when she got home that night. She felt a chill enter her stomach as she wondered what exactly he had to warn her about Hannah.

Alice's voice broke into Isabel's thoughts.

Isabel turned back to her grandmother with a grin of apology. 'Sorry,' she said, 'I was thinking about something else.'

'A lot of something else's, if you ask me,' her grandmother chortled. 'You should have seen your face!'

Isabel heard echoes of what Alice had been saying to her. She had been extolling - if that was the right word - the virtues of her next door neighbour. 'He's bound to be a little bitter after his hard life,' she was now saying.

Isabel almost laughed at that until she recalled what she had told her grandmother about Thom and his late wife.

'Look at all the good work he does with those boys,' Alice reminded her. 'He had a good job once; gave it all up so as to continue with his parents' good work.'

'You know a lot about him, it seems,' Isabel joked without humour. 'Have you been researching his family history, too?'

That might have started Alice on one of her spoken essays but instead all she said, her mind still on Thom, '"A person cannot be whole alone. Conviviality is healing."'

What that had to do with Thom, Isabel was unable to guess. 'I see you read the same book as I have,' was all she said.

'And,' Alice continued, '"Why dost thou pine within?" as the bard said, "painting thy outward walls so costly gay?"'

Isabel looked around at the unpainted cottage behind her, the small greenhouse whose wooden slats were stained with rust, the garden path that needed weeding and wondered what her grandmother was on about.

'You've always been able to hide your feelings,' Alice told her. 'Pretending to be jolly when your heart is breaking! He's a nice chap - behind that rather austere exterior.'

'Alice,' Isabel said firmly, 'He is not my type.' And how do you know he's so nice, she asked silently. She then emphasised each word as she said it. 'It's unfortunate that I'm landed with him as a neighbour, that is all.'

'That's all right, dear,' Alice soothed, not sounding convinced. 'You could do much worse - a farmer with hundreds of acres and a nice house. Of course he'd have to give up his chicken farm.'

'Chicken farm?' It was the first that Isabel had heard of this.

'Chickens, dear,' her grandmother said pursing her lips as if concerned for her granddaughter's sanity. 'Little children. Little naughty children, if what I hear is anything to go by. Now tell me what was worrying you when I called yesterday.' Alice said, making an excursion into one of her usual divergent paths.

'Me? Worried?' Isabel heard herself stumbling over the words. 'Nothing,' she answered quickly. 'Nothing at all.'

Her mind was wandering today. She was thinking about the way he had taken her by the arm and marched her through *her* garden towards the river. They were going at such a pace she had no time to ask what he was up to. Just trusted that he hadn't suddenly gone completely bonkers. She was amazed when he burst out laughing as they reached the patch of up-turned earth.

'Oh dear,' he sighed, amused. 'I see you were warned, then.'

Warned about what? Isabel asked herself. Warned that people had been murdered and buried in her garden? The thought made her feel sick. This had, apparently, shown up on her face which she could feel was suddenly cold and clammy and, probably, pale grey in colour. 'I wasn't warned,' was all she could manage to say.

'Don't look so worried,' Thom had then ordered her. 'It's nothing to get all steamed up about,' he added, not seeming in the least concerned.

Isabel took in a deep breath. If he was that sort of person she might as well stop talking.

'You should have been told,' Thom said in a quieter voice. 'Old Ben,' he said, 'got permission to bury his wife in the garden. He told the authorities that's what she wanted.' He paused. 'What he wanted was to save money, I do not doubt!'

'Aren't you going to tell me what it was?' Alice now sounded a little concerned for her granddaughter's mental health.

'It's all over and done with,' Isabel told her, feeling the weight lifting from her shoulder. She then told her grandmother an abbreviated version of her various conversations with Thom.

Alice sighed, the relief obvious on her face. 'I sensed it was something important when you jumped at a chance of a visit from me!' She smiled. 'Thank you for telling me. Now you can forget all about a pile of old bones – and all your other worries, I hope.'

'Didn't you infer you had something to tell me?' Isabel asked. She had gathered from their brief telephone conversation that the need for more information had been just a ruse for a visit, and that her grandmother had something more on her mind that she did not wish to discuss over the telephone.

'Oh, yes,' Alice said thoughtfully. 'What was it now?'

Isabel had never known her grandmother to forget anything. 'Come on, Gran,' she said, 'out with it.'

'Not so much of the 'gran',' Alice exclaimed with a grin. 'I just cannot recall what it was,' she said. 'I think I told you I am having trouble with my memory. My age, you know.'

Isabel laughed not believing a word of what her grandmother said. There was no one she knew who had a better memory than Alice. Apart from her mother, that was. But, then, she too seemed to have forgotten that she had two children, albeit grown-up and independent. Briefly Isabel wondered where exactly her parent was before deciding it was a waste of effort. Her mother would get in touch. She was still smiling at the thought when the telephone sent its tinny tones through the cottage and into the garden.

'Hello, Sis.' Silas's voice was cheerful if slightly rough around the edges, but that was due to using his mobile, Isabel decided. 'Is Alice with you?'

'Yes,' answered Isabel. 'How did you know?' She felt a bit put out that her brother was more bothered about his maternal grandmother than about his sister.

'Never you mind,' he said. 'Just put her on the line, please.'

Whatever it was, the call was not for her it seemed. She wondered if it was something to do with their mother and then told herself Silas would have told her immediately if it had been.

Isabel tried to listen to the distant conversation from her chair in the garden . She had not been able to find any excuse for staying in the kitchen and eavesdropping on the conversation, sadly.

When Alice returned from the call her faced was unusually flushed, almost as if she had been found out in some misdemeanour. Most unlike her grandmother, Isabel thought.

'That's all right, then,' Alice said, her voice rich with satisfaction.

'What's all right?' Isabel was beginning to tire of all the secrecy.

Alice let herself gently down into her chair before she replied.

'Lilian,' she murmured as if trying to remember the details of her telephone conversation with her grandson. 'Silas has managed to find a nice, warden-assisted flat near her friends and where there's twenty-four hour nursing if needed.'

Isabel did not know what to say as she felt warm, shameful relief rush through her. 'What have you two been up to,' she asked at last.

Alice tapped the side of her nose with one heavily-laden forefinger. ' "In vain with lavish kindness the gifts of God are strewn," ', she admonished her granddaughter cheerfully. 'As the old bishop said!'

Isabel accepted that she would hear no more on the subject of the telephone call; she was to be silently grateful, she gathered. 'And is that all you had to tell me today?' she asked with a short laugh. 'Are you sure there's nothing else?' She felt as if she had been given a present of such value that she could not think of what else to do but joke. She knew, had to accept, that Lilian needed the help and nothing she could do would make any difference. For a moment she silently thanked the benign being she thought of as God for what he - and Silas and Alice, of course - had done for her.

'Of course not,' Alice said in her usual firm tone, if a little faster than Isabel's joke had demanded.

Why was it then, Isabel asked herself later that day, long after Alice had departed to see her publishing friend, that she had the feeling her grandmother was not telling her the whole truth? When she had tried to urge her, Alice had taken her usual refuge in quoting passages from the Bible which, for her, were relevant to the occasion and could not be stated better. It had been a change from talking about the family history and ancient wars and illness that had decimated earlier branches of their family as Alice said, ' "I went by the field of the slothful, and by the vineyard of the man void of understanding. And, lo, it was all grown over with thorns, and nettles had covered the face thereof, and the stone wall was broken down. Then I say, and considered it well. I looked upon it, and received instruction; Yet a little sleep, a little slumber, a little folding of the hands to sleep; So shall the poverty come as one that traveleth; and they want an armed man." It's incredible what I can remember from childhood Sundays of having nothing but learning of pieces from the Bible to do! No radio, no books, no games. Just learning, learning, learning. But ask me the name of the man I met yesterday and I couldn't tell you it however hard I tried!'

Isabel did not bother to argue with her grandmother; just let her go on her travels in peace. As soon as the metallic blue car had disappeared along the narrow track she remembered that she had not quizzed Alice on how she had persuaded John Robertson to give up his Sabbath rest in order to see a - very minor, Isabel was sure - client.

Chapter 21

Isabel stepped into the kitchen to get a cooling mid-morning drink just as the telephone began to ring. For once she didn't feel the shivers running up and down her spine. It was her grandmother, yes - but the easy-to-deal-with one.

'Do you remember that discussion we had about your father?' Alice asked.

Isabel remembered that they had covered - yet again - his dates, his ancestors and, briefly, his disappearance which most people - including the police - accepted as his demise.

'Dear Alex told me yesterday the story of that bank chairman who disappeared. You know, Henry something or other.'

Isabel didn't know who Alex was, let alone recognise the Henry name. Alice was waiting for a response, she knew, but there was a question waiting for an answer first. 'Who on earth is Alex?' she asked, still surprised at the warmth in her grandmother's voice when she'd said his name.

'No, not Alex, dear,' Alice's responded tolerantly. 'He's was alive and breathing the last time I saw him, thank you,' she chuckled. 'Oh!' she laughed suddenly. 'You don't know who Alex is, do you?' She didn't wait for a reply. 'Of course, you don't. You think my friend's called John Robinson, don't you?' Again she laughed cheerfully. 'Alex is the MD of the publishing company founded by a John Robertson a hundred years ago. What a silly billy I have been!' she said drawing a deep breath. 'However, back to business! Now...um, Henry...Taylor. That's who it was. Alex said he'd done the same sort of thing. Left his clothes on the beach as if he'd swum out to his own Abraham's Bosom. Just like your father.'

Isabel had noticed before that her maternal grandmother never called her son-in-law by name; almost as if she didn't wish to acknowledge him as a person.

'He was found somewhere in the West Indies later that year. Do you remember now?' Alice asked.

Isabel did, of course, as much as she had tried to forget the article in the paper about her father's disappearance imitating that particular story. A psychologist would probably say she had pushed unpleasant information into temporary obscurity at the back of her mind. Information that, the doc would have added, was just waiting to explode when it was most unwanted. At least she'd learned who the mysterious Alex was, she told herself with a shrug, her mind going off at a tangent.

'And,' Alice was saying, 'didn't you say something about some boat – a large white yacht I think was how you described it - being stolen from its moorings that same night? Well, Alex thought it sounded just like an...emulation, I think he called it. That's all I wanted to say, dear. Good-bye.' She rang off then appearing satisfied to have passed on the information.

Isabel remembered having mentioned the coincidence to Alice, but at the time she had decided it had had nothing to do with her father's disappearance. She'd had one or two reasons for this, but it was something she hadn't wanted to think about at the time. Now she suddenly wondered whether she had been wrong not to. It was just the sort of thing he would do, she decided, thinking back to the list of his activities which had only come to light some time after his disappearance. She would have a chat with Silas; he would probably tell her to forget about it all as there was nothing they could now do.

Silas did say just that, using almost the same words as hers, when she telephoned him later.

'Let's just leave it, Sis,' he said. 'Do we want him reappearing and upsetting mother again?'

Isabel agreed that they didn't want that to happen - assuming their mother was around to be upset, that was. Her own little pricks of conscience at how she was now deserting her father, in her thoughts at least, she was learning to disregard.

It had taken them both some time to find out exactly where their mother was. Then she disappeared again. They weren't too worried, however. With so many looking out for *Windaru* and its middle-aged lady skipper - coastguards, marina staff, port controls and friends - throughout the UK and France, they were happy to let her get on with her solo-voyaging in peace, knowing that she would have sworn to secrecy anyone who recognised her. Only if she was in trouble would anyone dare to disobey her.

She was up to her eyebrows in mysteries, these days, Isabel decided. Alex was one of them. Isabel tried to count the times his name had been mentioned in the short chat with her grandmother and was unsuccessful. There was something here she thought she should know about, but for the moment her mind was on another mystery. Hannah.

What did the girl get up to when she wasn't with Thom and the boys? She was not responsible for the girl's actions, of course, but she'd been placed in the unwelcome role of parent and was weak enough to think that she had to fulfil that despite her wishes to the contrary. Some evenings Hannah would arrive home full of life and self-centred happiness and chat at length on all manner of things - apart from personal feelings, that was. On other occasions she would do no more than grab any food that was going and take her plate up to her room to disappear until the next activity was due to start the following day. Isabel knew Hannah's life-style was not what it should be, particularly when she heard the girl being sick in the bathroom on a few occasions. She put the hyperactivity down to too much alcohol and wondered how to stop the girl drinking if that was the cause. Not that she drank anything other than sickly fruit juices when she was with her, Isabel reminded herself, but she could easily be dropping into the local on her way back from Thom's. It was the sort of thing a seventeen year old would do - and get away with it, if she looked older than her actual age. Thinking about this, Isabel remembered that Paul had never actually stated his daughter's age. Isabel had only labelled her as seventeen years old from years of buying birthday cards. He had always told her what to get, demanding 'sophistication' and 'not humour', she remembered. The thought that the girl could be younger horrified her, but she slammed the door shut on the idea. She had too much on her mind to add more to the over-crowded cupboard of her thoughts. But it would be a good excuse to have an overdue look inside the local and have a quiet word with the landlord of the pub. When a free moment presented itself, of course.

The next day, being Tuesday, was order day for the Harts. Isabel looked at the note that had been lying in her mailbox when she returned from her weekly excursion to Shilliton. On it was listed only things she was able to supply, she was relieved to see. Whether this was from tact on the part of Marion or because they weren't having any dinner parties, Isabel had no idea. She could still put into practice her PR skills and add extra little bunches of this and that.

Hannah, as usual, had made no appearance by the time Isabel

was ready to go to work in the garden. Fred had returned from one of his long absences and was demanding food as she opened the two halves of the back door.

'You'll have to eat up that tin you started the other day,' Isabel told him, knowing no one was around to rebuke her for her anthropomorphism. That she could treat an animal as a human surprised her. She put it down to loneliness and left it at that. 'It smells all right to me,' she told him. She hoped she wasn't about to poison the little cat, even if the notice in tiny black letters at the bottom of the label stating that it was fit for human consumption would have to be taken with a good helping of salt considering the sell by date on the lid. She wondered if Thom ever fed his animals on something so polluted with un-organic materials, as would surely be his opinion of tinned foods.

He had dropped in the day before with the excuse of a scarf belonging to Hannah left behind on one of her visits. Isabel felt his own visits were becoming all too frequent and wondered what the attraction was. He probably just could not help trying to catch her out whenever he could, she decided, wishing she could tell him to stay away. Whatever she said, nothing seemed to convince him that she was doing all in her power to make her 'garden' - as he called it - totally organic. If he couldn't see it with his own eyes, she wasn't going to point it out to him.

Another cast-off from Shilliton's Superbuy lay on the kitchen table when he called. She shivered at what he might say if he read the story the labels told by the box and not that of the vegetables in it. Nothing you could get in a large, impersonal store could come up to her matchless produce, Isabel was prepared to say if he as much as opened his mouth in criticism.

'Not bad,' he said, looking down at her polished tomatoes, the washed runner beans and the ruby richness of the untreated, unpolished currants nestling against the dusty crimson of her raspberries. These last she had put in as a gift at the last moment. 'Who are they for?' Thom asked. 'The Harts, I suppose.'

Isabel sensed a hint of condescension in his voice, as if he thought she was lucky to have the one customer. She wondered if everyone else thought as he did.

How she wished it was Friday and then she could have put him in his place by saying, 'No. This is Mrs Parson's box,' and, being Friday, she could also say, 'the other one is for Travis.' But she was denied the pleasure of either.

'I hear you're thinking of growing herbs,' Thom then surprised her by saying, no obvious censure in his voice.

Who had been spreading gossip? Isabel wondered before remembering. She'd been chatting to the girl at the whole-food shop and had mentioned her shopping excursion to London. Nothing was secret, it seemed, in the country. At least the girl wouldn't have told him about her interest in supplying herbs for aromatherapy, which was the girl's other occupation.

'That aromatherapist,' Thom said then, sending her spirits into a steep dive. 'It's all rubbish, you know. Rubbing on oils to try and make you feel better. For that's all it does, make you feel better; it doesn't cure disease.'

She wanted to say 'it may help' but decided on silence. She was even beginning to sound like her mother - or was it her grandmother? She busied herself drying up the few dishes propped against each other like a tumbling stack of china cards on the old wooden draining board. He always seemed to want an argument, she told herself. She might find his company a pleasant change from Hannah's if only he would stop telling her what to do. Why did his face have a look of disappointment on it? she wondered as he continued.

'You're just trying to make yourself into an amateur psychologist, that's what.'

Isabel felt her eyes open wide. What on earth was that about?

'A psychologist of the body,' he said then, 'for want of any other way of describing it.' His tone inferred that he could find the words if only she would be able to understand them.

Isabel, for some reason, found that amusing and was hard-pressed not to let a laugh erupt from her. 'I'll pass that on to the aromatherapist,' she said when she could speak without giving herself away. She had decided that she couldn't get involved in that business, in any case. She'd done some research and what the girl in town had told her had only convinced her that the scented road to growing aromatic herbs was not to be her path in life, after all. There was too much involved, including a seemingly enormous amount of investment money-wise, to have the herbs processed, let alone what it would cost her to buy the seedlings that would be required for commercial use. She had decided, long before, to leave it to the experts and had only brought up the subject with the girl in Shilliton as a topic of conversation.

Thom was still standing by the table with his back to the hall door so did not notice Hannah's arrival at the bottom of the stairs a towel and wash bag hanging from one arm. Isabel could see her from where she was standing by the sink. She carefully kept her expression bland as she watched the girl's reaction to Thom's presence. Hannah pirouetted around on bare feet creeping back up the stairs as if she had never descended them. She looked grey and ill, didn't want Thom to see her like that, Isabel decided. She hoped that Thom would go before the girl was sick on the bedroom floor.

'Thanks for bringing the scarf,' Isabel said, moving across the old flags of the kitchen floor with that special way people have of silently influencing another person's actions. 'I have things to do, I'm afraid,' she said, pointing to the box of vegetables as if inferring they were going to shrivel up and die if she didn't get them to their destination as soon as possible. 'Like delivering these to my...' she hesitated and then said, 'customers.'

The rattle of the ancient engine had become just an echo when Hannah reappeared again. The greyness had gone from her face, Isabel was relieved to see. Perhaps the girl had been scared that Thom was after her about the glass ornament. That was it, Isabel decided, as she watched the girl sipping at a cup of herb tea and munching a slice of the dark, almost black, rye bread that Isabel had come across in the Shillingstone supermarket. She was often surprised at what she could occasionally find and put it down to the fact that holidaymakers were around with their demands for esoteric products usually only found in big cities. She was pleased, now, that she had found something the girl liked.

'When's my dad coming?' Hannah asked abruptly, picking at her breakfast.

'I have no idea,' Isabel replied curtly, wondering whether the girl had information that she didn't have.

'You must know,' Hannah said, glancing up at Isabel with her hooded eyes. 'If you're going back to work for him you must know,' she repeated

'Who said...?' Isabel began and then shrugged her shoulders. What was the use? It would only cause an argument with the girl. She was confused, Isabel told herself, as well as feeling unloved and unwanted; just a bundle of neuroses, and she wasn't wanting to add to the girl's aggressiveness. She did want to know the answer to one question, however.

'What do you do when you're not over at Thom's?' she asked, having learned in countless business confrontations that the direct question, one that did not allow the questioned person time to think, often elicited a satisfactory reply.

The girl's face took on the hue of unpeeled garlic. 'Nothing,' she replied, all too quickly. 'I'm always over there. Where else is there to go? There's nothing to do here, and at least over there I have someone to talk to. And Thom has this marvellous games room, and we have lots of fun.' Her defensive babble faded as she realized Isabel was not convinced.

Isabel felt her good intentions collapse into a heap of rags. She had decided earlier not to tell the girl that she didn't feel responsible for her; that would have a bit unkind. And she had felt sympathy for her, but now she just wished the girl was somewhere else. 'Just try to be careful, then,' she said, conjuring up an executive pose from earlier days.

Isabel had wanted to say, 'if you can't be good, be careful' but thought it was already too late for that. Did Paul realize what he was doing? He was neglecting his only child and placing a burden on her own shoulders the weight of which she could well do without. She wasn't flying Travis around - and Juliet, of course - for money, exactly, although she knew she would be rewarded in some way eventually, but she did feel that she might be putting her reputation - and flying licence - at risk in trying to earn enough to feed herself let alone Hannah.

'I've got to go out soon,' Isabel told the girl, hoping that she was on her way to Thom's - or anywhere for that matter. 'Any plans?'

'No,' Hannah answered. 'Can I do some cooking?'

Isabel felt a jolt of surprise. Careful now, she told herself, this might just be the start of something good, but she wasn't going to depend on it. She answered, more cheerfully than she felt, 'Of course. Any idea what you want to cook?'

'I'll make my father's favourite,' she said, her face a little less wan, smiling even and the hooded eyes brighter than Isabel had ever seen them.

'What's that?' Isabel asked conversationally. The box of vegetables on the table was staring at her as if it were a neglected puppy begging for immediate attention. There was something else she had on her mind, too, and didn't want to wait until she had lost her nerve before going off and doing it.

'Vegetable roast,' was the surprising reply.

When had Paul started eating vegetable roast? Isabel asked herself in some surprise. Salads he would eat, especially if they were the artwork of some culinary genius, but she had never known him display any deep liking for cooked vegetables - apart from potatoes, that was and they could come in any guise as long as they were accompanied by a large steak or slices of gravied meat. Well, they would have to do without that, this evening, Isabel thought, mentally casting a glance over the coins in her purse. Perhaps she should spend the money the Hart's box would bring? She quickly discounted that thought as being worthy of a spendthrift who never considered mundane things like domestic bills. Isabel didn't learn until later that the only thing Hannah could cook was a mixture of vegetables cooked in a hot oven for an hour and then served as a complete menu. Her father, it appeared, had always complimented her on her cooking skills so she had carried on producing her vegetable roast until it had become a dish worthy of a dinner party. Or so her father had told her.

'That sounds nice,' Isabel told Hannah. 'Can you pick your own veg?'

'Of course.' The smile had disappeared from Hannah's face and her voice had regained its sneering quality.

'I'll be off then,' Isabel said, picking up the box from the table her spirits lifting at the sight of her handsome vegetables and fruit.

The girl just shrugged.

Isabel was talking to Marion a little later and mentioned her surprise at Hannah's behaviour.

'I think you've been landed with a problem there,' Marion said, with a sympathetic smile. 'What about the parents? Can't you tell them you're too busy to look after their daughter?'

Isabel gave her an abbreviated account of Hannah's life as far as she knew it. 'Her father seems to think I have done something to add to her - unhappiness? If that's the right word.

'In what way?' Marion asked with a questioning smile.

'Her father and I were,' Isabel hesitated, not knowing quite how to put it, 'friends,' she managed eventually. 'He'd left his wife and I'd been working with him for years so we just, sort of, got together.' Isabel found that confession was, if not good, at least refreshing, for the soul. 'When he wanted it, that was.'

'Oh,' said Marion, nodding her head. 'And now you've left him and he's accusing you of making his daughter insecure. Is that it?'

'I suppose,' Isabel admitted. 'But I didn't leave him,' she said quickly. 'He dumped me!' Suddenly she felt better, liberated, and able to see things clearly once more.

'Well, what the hell are you doing then?'

Marion's words shocked Isabel until she looked at her friend's face and found it was creased with affectionate silent laughter.

'It's all nonsense and you know it,' Marion added chuckling. 'I would never have believed it of you.'

And I would never have believed such harsh words could be so heartening to hear, Isabel told herself. 'You're right,' was all she said, smiling at Marion and nodding her head. Someone else had said the same thing to her, and recently, but Isabel could not remember in what context.

'I think I should tell you something,' Marion said, jolting Isabel back to the present.

The words, for some reason, sent little mice with freezing feet running up and down Isabel's spine. What was she in for now?

'That girl spends quite a lot of time in the local pub,' Marion told her, confirming for Isabel that coincidences did exist. 'She meets someone there,' Marion continued. 'I thought, at first, it was her father but now that you have described him I have changed my mind.'

Isabel began to feel that she did not want her newly-made friendship with the friendly older woman to be harmed by anything that might be said. She felt that she was going to hear something less than soothing about Hannah which might reflect on her own reputation. She heard in her head the echo of Grandmother Lilian saying 'friendships quickly made are quickly lost'.

'I didn't think that tight, faded jeans,' Marion was saying with a smile, 'leather jacket and ear-rings in the nose quite summoned up the man you have described!'

Isabel did not want to hear more but her wish was about to be thwarted.

'And from what Don tells me, he doesn't treat her very well.' Marion's voice was serious now, the smile gone.

Don, Isabel knew, was the name of the landlord. She hadn't summoned up the courage to go in, yet. Not because she was frightened to go into a pub on her own - that was for her mother's era, not hers - but because she was not sure she would feel comfortable amongst all the strangers who would be there. They might think, she had told herself, facing the uncomfortable truth, that she was 'up for grabs', as Alice called it, or, to put it another way 'an easy lay'; an expression that embarrassed her now thinking back to how 'easy' it had been for Paul. Marion was saying, 'Often stands her up. And when he does arrive expects her to stay with him till closing time. Comes from London, Don overheard; thinks it's a waste of time to come all that way and then have to stay drinking without company apparently. Something to do with some construction company, if my informant is correct.'

The pieces of the jigsaw puzzle were beginning to fall into place, Isabel sensed.

'There's one golden ingot amongst the silver plate, though,' Marion said. 'It seems that Hannah herself drinks nothing but colas and processed fruit drinks.'

That, at least, was good news, Isabel thought with a rush of relief. Also Marion had saved her an embarrassing trip to the pub. She'd have to wait to have her curiosity satisfied about its interior till another day, she told herself without regret.

When Isabel got back to the cottage, paper and coins rustling comfortingly in the pocket of her cotton trousers, she found a strange car parked, egotistically, in the middle of the track. The track led nowhere, except to a farmer's fields and was little used except by walkers but she always tried to keep it clear. She wondered who it belonged to.

As if she was seeing a film for a second time, the figure standing in her kitchen chatting to Hannah as she pushed vegetable peelings into the bin, was horribly familiar, right down to the expensive sports shoes at the end of the tight, modishly faded jeans.

'This is a friend of mine,' Hannah said, a guilty blush sweeping across her face. Isabel was not expected back so soon, it said.

'Friend?' Isabel was unable to keep the coolness out of her voice. She recognised the type of man, not just from Marion's description, but from long years of passing construction workers on their way to and from Paul's office. She was sure she had seen him before but was not about to acknowledge him. If it was who she thought it was he had a reputation that Lucifer might have been proud of.

The man leaned across the kitchen table as if he were the host and she the visitor and offered her his hand. Isabel ignored it; the picture was becoming all too clear and she did not like what it was depicting. Chance words that she had heard, in her past life in Paul's company, about the character of the man now standing in her kitchen did not endear him to her. She remembered hearing that he was charming, success-orientated, rarely worked a minute more than he had to, and moved from one gullible woman to the next, to pave his way to prosperity.

The worst of the picture for Isabel was right in front of her. Hannah stood silent, biting into her lower lip, her expression one of anxious and unhappy bemusement, her attitude that of a severely intimidated young girl. Who could have thought that the self-assertive spoilt teenager could look so much like a small child who had just been thrashed by an angry father?

'She misled me,' the man was saying. 'We had things to discuss.' The welcome he had been given by Isabel had undermined his abrasive self-confidence, it seemed, and some explanation was needed to restore it. 'I'm just going.'

He ignored Hannah's anguished glance as he turned to go. 'I have to go and see her father,' he said to Isabel as if this was the only excuse for his abrupt departure. 'He and I have things to discuss.' He turned back to Hannah briefly, pointing a figure at her. 'Do you know what they do with your type,' he asked her, the vitriol dripping from his words. 'You'll find out,' he said. He turned back to Isabel. 'Do you know what she told me? She told me,' he repeated as if Isabel was hard of understanding, 'that she was eighteen. And do you know what I've just found out? She's only fifteen. Fifteen years old and sleeping around with anyone who asks her! I find that disgusting.'

At that moment the large glass dish that Isabel used for all her oven cooking crashed onto the stone floor, exploding like a bomb into tiny glittering fragments. Hannah gave a gasp and rushed from the kitchen, her feet making a drum-roll on the stairs up to her bedroom as she disappeared from sight.

The man shrugged, smiled at Isabel as if to say, 'see what I mean?' and made for the door. 'She'll grow up one day. But she'll have to learn not to lead a man on; it could be dangerous.' Then he was gone - forever, Isabel hoped.

She climbed the short flight of stairs as if she was carrying sacks of coal on her back and knocked at Hannah's door. No answer. Only the sound of sobbing. Isabel decided to leave her alone - a good cry was very comforting. She could have it out with her later. The horrible truth had leapt at her like a hungry lion as she had looked from Hannah to the man and then back to Hannah. Hannah's sickness, her increase in weight which Isabel only now realised was remarkable and her sudden changes of mood made it all clear. And she, for one, was not going to allow herself to be made use of and forced to accept responsibility which was nothing at all to do with her. She knew what she had to do.

Paul answered his mobile on its second ring.

'Oh,' he said, sounding mildly disappointed when he heard who it was. 'I was hoping you would ring.' The lie was familiar in Isabel's ears; it always meant he wanted something. He was used to getting his thoughts in order like a shepherd with an errant flock of sheep. 'I knew you would want to take me up on my offer.' Isabel could imagine the self-satisfied smile on his face. 'When are you coming? You'll have to move quickly - get yourself a flat and all that - if you want your old job back. I've got a string of girls waiting for my decision.'

I bet you have, Isabel mouthed silently, waiting for him to stop gabbling so she could speak. 'You're needed here,' she told him abruptly as he drew breath.

'Sorry. No can do,' he answered. 'Just off to a meeting.'

Isabel guessed it was probably a meeting with a glamorous blond or a slinky brunette. 'Don't go,' she shouted, fearing he would not answer her next call if they disconnected now. 'It's Hannah,' she told him, drawing in her breath so that she could sound calmer than she felt. 'I'm afraid,' she began and then decided it was a bad start. 'She needs you,' she amended. 'Now. I'll expect you as soon as you can get here.' She ignored the eruptions of dissent. 'Your daughter's pregnant,' she said putting the phone back on its receiver before she could be led into further discussion.

It explained so much, Isabel told herself as she drifted back into the kitchen. And it was nothing to do with Thom's boys, she was relieved to be able to tell herself. This was why Paul had been so keen to get Hannah away from London. What would his friends say if they knew his fifteen year old was pregnant; how could he face them after that? Isabel did not normally allow herself to be cynical but she felt this particular occasion warranted it. Perhaps he had not known, she then thought. Maybe he was just trying to get her away from a dangerous liaison.

The rest of the day was like a blurred old photograph. She hardly heard Paul screaming at her for letting his daughter down.

'You could have done better,' he shouted at her. 'After all we meant to each other.'

Isabel ignored him. She knew exactly how much she had meant to him now.

'And don't think you can just come swanning back into your old job. The offer's closed.'

Open to anyone with money, beauty and no talent, no doubt. Isabel felt cheered by thinking that. Like Hannah, she knew now she had been duped. Unlike Hannah she had, she realized now, got off lightly. But the girl would cope, she was sure. The worse part was over, now that her parents knew, or would know soon. Paul couldn't keep it from Meredith/Charlene for long. It was those girls who ran off too terrified to tell their families whom you had to pity. Hannah did at least have the good luck of not having to face that fate.

The cottage felt empty, when they'd gone, Paul shouting at her till the last moment. Her little home was not only bereft of unwelcome people it was if the unhappy spirits that had accompanied the arrival of the girl had also departed in the fast black sports that was Paul's latest addition to his status. For the first time in weeks Isabel felt that this was truly her home, her 'soul place' as Alice would call it, and it would become, also, her financial success.

The first thing she had to do, however, was to clear up the mess in the kitchen. She was not too upset about the plate; she could replace it on her next trip to town.

Chapter 22

Isabel laid the trout onto the spread out newspapers on the table with hands that trembled slightly. She told herself not to be silly. It was stone-cold dead and couldn't feel a thing. The smoker with its instruction book lay beside it together with her sharpest knife, matches and a packet of oat chippings.

The evening before she had decided to celebrate her unexpected peace - and the freedom to do whatever she wanted to in her own home - by spending some spirit-reviving, relaxing time on her river bank. She'd taken the rod, with its reel still attached from her last attempt, and the landing net, but she was not bothered whether she fished or not. It was like floating on a calm, soothing tropical sea just to be alone. She could sit and watch the stream moving smoothly past her, the reeds and other water plants waving in harmony with the current like flower-bedecked cheerleaders. Even the family of ducks seemed to be celebrating something as they noisily fussed and fretted their way from one interesting clump of weeds to another. When she saw the circles of disturbed water spreading towards her and then the flash of silver she decided, not really expecting to catch anything, that she should try her luck.

Whether it was because she was not over-anxious for success, or that the fish was not very clever, she hooked it on the first cast. Remembering her instructions from the tackle dealer - and slightly against her better nature - she let her line run freely from the reel then began to draw it in as she felt it tighten. She did this several times amazed at how calm she was about causing another creature pain, before reeling in the whole of her line and lifting the creature from the water with her pristine net. She had switched off her sensitivities it appeared and would never again castigate someone for enjoying a sport where wild animals were hunted for food, as long as those animals were allowed to die as quickly as possible. And, she added, looking at the fish lying lifeless beside her, she now knew how a successful foray for food gave a good, healthy feeling of satisfaction - liberally mixed with pride, she admitted.

Now the silver body lay washed and ready on the kitchen table after a night in her tiny refrigerator. She had dashed out first thing that morning to invest in the smoker the tackle dealer had so wanted her to buy when she purchased her rod.

'Go on,' he had said at the time, 'Your bit of stream is a good'un for those larger fish.' He had smiled as he spoke. Later Isabel recalled that smile as she had her altercation with the fish farmer.

'Can't afford it,' she had answered with reluctance.

'Well, come back when you can,' he told her cheerfully. He had already made a good sale with the rod and reel and box of flies, as well as all the other bits and pieces he had insisted were essential, such as the expensive net and the gruesome piece of metal called a 'priest'.

'For dispatching them,' he had told her. 'Send their souls back to their maker.'

His joke had seemed just as gruesome, in Isabel's ears, as the instrument itself. She had found, however, that it did do its job quickly and painlessly - for the fish, if not for her nerves. So now she had food enough for a family of six, if not more.

As she cleaned the smoker later, Isabel wondered at the unexpected skills she was acquiring in her new life in the country. She looked down at the fish, now beautifully smoked and lying on the oven tray - the only thing large enough to hold it since Hannah had disposed of her one and only glass baking dish. She was going to be eating smoked rainbow trout for at least a week, if it didn't go off before then. What a pity that would be, she told herself. A picture flashed through her mind then - a picture of her beautiful smoked fish lying framed by watercress, tomatoes and lemon slices, with a few new potatoes, boiled and coated in butter and chopped parsley, added mouth-wateringly in artistic heaps around the dish. It would look very nice on television, Isabel decided. She would take it with her the next day; insist that Travis used it, if only for table decoration. He could always say he had caught it on his day off, and cleaned and cooked it himself. She wouldn't mind; he needed any help he could get, she told herself, with that awful Juliet fussing around him all the time.

Isabel's self-congratulation for having such a brilliant idea was interrupted by a knock on the kitchen door behind her. Turning quickly she saw a young-ish man with hair to his shoulders and a camera strung around his neck. He was just withdrawing his hand after opening the top of the door.

At first Isabel thought it was just another coincidence; that he was something to do with Travis. Had come to get some shots they could use the next day. She didn't bother to ask herself what use stills would be.

'Miss Vine?' he asked. He held a well-used strip of card with printing on.

Isabel nodded. It was a long time since she'd been addressed by her family name. It surprised her to realize that, after the initial introductions had been made on her arrival at Woodbine Cottage, nobody had called her by anything but her Christian name. It was weeks, in fact, since she'd heard her surname.

Not understanding why, her stomach gave a small lurch as she looked at the thumbed and greasy card which she had taken from his hand. Isabel read that the holder, a Will Taylor, was a member of some student's union and that he was doing research for a project and would the person approached please assist him in his search for information.

Her stomach returned from its journey to her feet as she told herself he was just a student, couldn't do her any harm. Why was she acting like some guilty person when she had nothing to fear, had done nothing to feel guilty about?

Isabel's first thought had been that he was a journalist. That's when her heart had begun to thump. She had convinced herself that her father's actions were in no way anything to do with her. Except by association, was the thought that had hit her like a hammer in the early days, but she had had some success squashing that idea. No longer did casual acquaintances immediately pluck the name out of the conversation and ask her if she was related to that - refraining with difficulty, she had felt, from saying the word 'dreadful' - fraudster. For weeks after the trial she had avoided any place - parties, business lunches, conferences - where some tactless man or woman would say on being introduced to her:

'Oh... Anything to do with that man who cheated all those poor pensioners out of their life savings?' Some would say it as a joke; others, lacking even more in tact, would ask it with more earnest curiosity. After the first couple of times she almost went into self-imposed purdah in order to avoid having to lie or prevaricate. It all faded, only returning momentarily when her father left his open prison and swam out to sea never to be seen again. And that was more than four months ago, and only made the front page of the local paper. The old story had been vomited up occasionally, much to her dismay, but after a couple of days even those short paragraphs had given way to more interesting, more exciting small stories.

'May I come in?' said the boy.

'What do you want?' Isabel asked not granting his request. She hoped if she wasn't too friendly or welcoming he might go away.

He leaned on the bottom half of the door. 'I'd like to know your side of the story,' he told her with a little smile which did not get as far as his eyes. How like Hannah's they were, thought Isabel.

'What's your subject?' Isabel asked him. She expected him to say that he was studying rural activities, or organic farming, or might even want her to comment on Thom's eccentric use for his family property. She felt the blood freeze in her veins as he said:

'I'm researching the criminal activities of a certain Kenneth Vine,' he said, looking straight at her. 'My grandfather was one of the people he ruined.' His chin was pointed, his eyes hooded slits, his mouth a thin sharp line and two red spots glowed on otherwise alabaster cheeks.

Isabel knew she had to think quickly. He couldn't be sure this was anything to do with her; had probably seen her name somewhere and was hoping for tops marks for successful research. 'What's that got to do with me? she asked, fingers invisibly crossed in the hope that her face wasn't giving anything away secrets.

'I believe he's your father,' he said. 'Or was,' he added spitefully. A young boy had suddenly grown into a dangerous man.

'You believe wrong,' Isabel lied.

'Not according to my source,' he told her, the cold little smile again lurking around the corners of the thin mouth. He reached for the metal bar of the wrought iron door handle.

In two steps Isabel was at the door. His standing on the path and Isabel being several inches taller meant she was able to look down on him. His belief in his information was such that he did not quail before the heat that she knew was in her eyes, however.

'And who might that be?' she asked in her coldest, most managerial tone.

'That would be telling,' he teased without humour. 'All I'll say is that it is someone who knows you very well. In fact, he rang me only last night to suggest I might like to do the story.'

'That's hardly a student's job,' she was swift to retort.

'What's this about a student?' he asked. 'Has someone got here before me?'

'You,' Isabel said, waving the tatty piece of cardboard in his face so that it almost reached his eyes as he leaned forward.

'I'm no student,' he said, lurching backwards, at the same time glancing at the cream card in Isabel's hand. 'I'm an accredited journalist. It says so on the card.' He took it from her and looked down at it. 'Oh,' he said, 'this is just something I use. I find it doesn't scare people like the official one does,' he laughed, without amusement. In an attempt to regain the authority which he thought he'd had, he added, 'I'm always on the lookout for a good story. Where is he now, this K Vine?' he asked, having regained his footing on the crumbling door step.

'I've no idea who you're talking about,' Isabel said sharply. 'I thought you were wanting an interview about organic gardening,' she added, grabbing the first subject that came to mind. After a millisecond's pause she added, 'Not some muck-raking rubbish.' It wasn't until later that the humour of her choice of words occurred to her.

'Well,' Will said, beginning to look as if he was wondering if he had, in fact, make a mistake, 'your friend described this place. 'Couldn't miss it,' he said.'

The penny dropped like a bomb. Who was it said that it was always wise to avoid a scorned woman? It seemed that men, too, could be just as vitriolic as any discarded female.

'Just go back and tell your friend,' Isabel said, trying to conjure up some sort of secret blackmailing message she could send to the perpetrator of her present predicament. 'Tell him...' she said, 'tell him that all businesses have their hidden secrets which are not there for the telling.' It sounded strange even to her, but she thought he would know exactly what she was referring to without the journalist catching on. She was, of course, reminding him of the many scams she had been forced to sort out on his behalf. 'And,' she added, just in case the journalist was as stupid as he looked, 'tell him he's put you on to the wrong person. Kenneth Vine, indeed. Whoever he is.'

The young man shook his head, the long hair bouncing around as is he were in an advertisement for feminine hair colorant. 'I was sure I'd got it right,' he said.

'Well, you didn't,' Isabel informed him, keeping the relief at getting through to him, at last, out of her voice. The invisible ice beneath her feet was still very fragile and if she protested too much she could be in the freezing water beneath it at the first crack. 'Now, if you don't mind, I have a business to run.'

The breath that came from her chest as she watched the man turn and wander down the path still shaking his head, detonated. Instead of exploding in anger at the thought of what Paul had done in retaliation for her not returning to help him out the hole she now knew he was in, it fizzled like a damp squid and died. The realization flowed warmly into her that, through his own actions, she was now truly free of the chains of the unsatisfactory relationship she'd had with him. Lover, she realized, he had never been. She found a deep a sense of satisfaction in knowing that she was no longer the prisoner of other people's demands and desires. Determining never to try again to mould herself to another's conception of her, she felt released and, at last, free to be herself and allowed to live her own life by whatever path she decided to take.

Isabel turned back into the small, shadowy kitchen. The large silver fish lay where she had left it, which surprised her almost. So much had flooded through her thoughts and feelings in the past few minutes that it seemed like a life-time had come and gone. But the freshness of the scaly skin, the mild scent of oak smoke and the perfume of the flavoursome flesh confirmed that it had not.

Still trembling from her near-miss, she wrapped the fish in a sheet of kitchen film, together with some springs of parsley from the pot on the windowsill and placed it back on the baking sheet. Carefully she pushed the lot into the small fridge. It was not difficult to find plenty of space as she had, only that morning, with a degree of venom she did not know she possessed, chucked Hannah's cans and bottles into the bin glad to see the back of such disgusting, polluted, GM packed, chemically sweetened, cancer inducing, health-destroying products. She felt much better as she pushed the fish onto a pristine shelf.

With a sigh that sounded like an exclamation mark denoting the end of an unsatisfactory situation she marched out into the garden. She was going to pick some of her most luscious fruit and vegetables for Travis's use the next day and there would be plenty, too, for Mrs Parsons and her friend, Marion. They all deserved the best she had. She was determined to persuade Travis to use only what she provided, for his programme. She'd heard nothing from the jolly Juliet so assumed it was still on for the next day. She would do the same as she had done with Hannah's junk food, she determined, if they as much as mentioned that they were going to use what they had brought. Poor Travis, she thought, he really is being badly used by that...but she couldn't think of an epithet which truly summed up the bossy woman. She was going to protect him from now on, make sure he had produce that he could be proud of, whatever their budget demanded, or whatever the woman, with her lack of taste, considered necessary.

As she prowled from bush to tree and back to bush, harvesting their gleaming jewels, she could not hold back thoughts of Hannah - and those of her father's latest antics, wondering if she should say anything to Thom the next time their paths crossed. She recalled one of his lectures when Hannah had first arrived.

'This is what I try to get through to my kids,' he'd once said when she had, mildly, complained about Hannah's seeming lack of self-discipline and her lackadaisical attitude to life in general. 'That you've got to have order, self-discipline, before you can get anywhere. Some of them react in the right way; others just carry on as before. But,' he had said, surprising Isabel with the apparent need to justify himself, 'it's getting better as time goes on.' Then one of his rare smiles had made an appearance. 'Even privately educated children have parents who are willing to pay for them to spend the summer holidays with my little council-house thugs!' And then in a more serious tone, almost as if he were reminding himself of the words, he had added, 'You have to have order, be faithful to both human and natural order. Take responsibility for that order before your life or body can be deemed healthy.' There the conversation had ended as he began again on one of his diatribes about her garden and whether it was conforming to - as he saw it - nature's laws.

It wasn't long before Isabel had filled the usual large, flat box. She was proud of the produce, couldn't have wished it better-looking. It did not take long to do a similar one for Mrs Parsons and a smaller box for Marion. This was an extra, a gift for agreeing to deliver the elderly post-lady's to her.

No one being at home when she got to the mill she left the boxes in the shed at the end of the garden. Now she could have a lovely long soak in the beautiful, under-used bath, and after that a celebratory drink. And she didn't want to be late in going to bed with their early start the next morning. They were going to some far-off quay in a tributary of a large Welsh river which she had not visited before. She planned to be, if not up with the lark, at least in plenty of time to do all her pilotly duties in peace and quiet before the others arrived. At least, this time, there would be none of that nonsense of pretending Travis was flying the plane and she was only a passenger; she might even solve the mystery of why that had had to be.

She dropped off to sleep, waking suddenly wondering what time Hannah was going to get home and then remembering she let herself relax back into refreshing slumber.

Chapter 23

The Cessna dipped its nose and glided down towards the small strip of green. It touched down without a murmur from either of the other two. Isabel was pleased that Juliet could find no fault with her planning and execution of the trip. Isabel couldn't think why Travis was so quiet; he'd not said a word during the first half hour of their fifty minute flight. One look at his face at the airfield had told her he was feeling under the weather. She'd hoped his spirits would lift once they were in the air. It was not to be, however.

'Anything worrying you, Travis?' she had asked at one point. They were coasting along at a smooth 125 mph at 2000 feet and she had time to think of things other than steering the small aircraft through the air. Small boats like children's bath-tub toys floated on the waveless - from this height - sea beneath them. Occasionally a seagull or two approached as if to discover the breed of this strange, large bird which was scattering noise and alien smells into their sky, before speeding away in respect to their eardrums. If they had any such things, of course, Isabel joked to herself.

Travis did not even turn his head towards her as she spoke.

'Sh,' Juliet from her seat behind said. 'Can't you see he's asleep?'

Isabel glanced quickly across at the figure in the right-hand seat. Juliet was right; he was sleeping like some over-grown, strangely dressed baby. Perhaps he was coming down with a bug, she thought with a quiver of dismay. That might account for the blood-shot eyes and flushed cheeks she had noticed as he climbed aboard the airplane after Juliet. She shrugged the thought away and got on with the job of taking him and their small aircraft safely to the location for that day's filming, Gunners Quay.

The airfield, the only one anywhere near the small village of the same name, was not one she had visited before. She'd not known of its existence until Juliet had informed her of it during one of her brief, peremptory phone calls earlier in the week. But she had the necessary call-sign for the only available air to ground information centre – yet another military aerodrome - and the telephone number of the club which owned the airfield noted on her passage planning sheet. She could foresee no problems except that it was *tiny*, the club airfield, the chart not even giving it the distinction of a circle denoting a small airfield with no facilities. She had to aim for the village. Next to that on the chart was a large circle with wings in it. Trust Juliet to pick a place that was not even shown on the chart and being in the vicinity of a busy hang-gliding area, too. Isabel felt she might have done it on purpose, then considered that the amount of knowledge Juliet might have about flying a small aircraft would not have made that seem a reasonable assumption, so put it down to ignorance and nothing more. It was just the nearest place to Gunners Quay and that was that. Anywhere further away would have meant one of the crew having to drive the mini-bus down to collect them, forcing them into a much earlier start from their hangar headquarters. The ever-active calculator in Juliet's mind would have vetoed that, Isabel felt sure. Not for the first time she wondered at the significance of Travis being flown around and then told herself she was probably being naive about the importance of the facade any television star worth the name had to put up to increase his value to viewers - and programme makers - and left it at that.

Travis woke up as the wheels bumped gently onto the grass runway. Isabel could see him out of the corner of her eye, glancing around as if slightly dazed. She didn't hesitate, applied the brakes immediately not wanting to use more of the tiny runway than was absolutely necessary.

Isabel felt the usual quiver of pride at the achievement of the successful outcome of any flight, however short, as she guided the Cessna to a halt in front of the hut on the south side of the runway. There was no sign of anyone being present, despite the perfect flying conditions. She recalled that the voice on the telephone had told her the club were taking part in a fly-in somewhere else in the country. Three other small aircraft - one recognisable as a two-seater Piper but the others looking home-made and extremely fragile - were now parallel to the Cessna. She would lock up well before they left, she decided, looking around at the deserted airfield where even the orange sock on its tall pole looked bereft of life.

The mini-bus turned onto the gravelled area next to the small building just as Travis climbed down from the aircraft, obviously still dozy from his sleep. Remembering Juliet's unsuitable footwear and tight skirt, Isabel jumped down to help her out. She knew that Juliet only dressed up to increase Travis's own persona as *The Flying Cook* but she did not want any accident, however minor, to spoil the day. She was a bit of an actress, was Juliet, Isabel had decided long ago. And not one she could admire. Travis, she knew, was different; wouldn't stoop to dressing up just to show off. He didn't need to. Not usually, that was, she thought watching him walk unsteadily towards the waiting vehicle.

After several miles of twisting and hilly lanes they reached that day's location - yet another ancient quay, jutting out into the bend of a river, which at high tide was almost encircled by water, leaving only a small area attached to the land. Isabel was relieved to see that Travis was, once more, the superstar, the television personality come to entertain his distant and future viewers, if not exactly the life and soul of the party. He was saving that for when he was in front of the cameras, she assumed. He would then be chatting and smiling and doing anything that Juliet required in order to make her programme climb up the ladder of television polls. The thought made Isabel feel a bit sick.

She watched them disappear under the flaps of the half-opened sides of the marquee which had been put up for their use and then turned back to the van to retrieve the large, flat, supermarket box of produce she had so carefully culled the night before - and just as carefully placed on the floor of the airplane behind the passenger seat. Despite the heavy, hot midday she felt herself go cold; she had left the blessed thing in the aircraft, forgetting it in her concern over locking up after helping Juliet descend from the aircraft without her breaking a leg. She turned to ask Mike, the bus driver, to run her back to pick it up but he, too, had disappeared to join the others in the centre of exciting activity. She shuddered at the thought of what Juliet would have to say if she asked for a lift back to the small airfield. Once again, it seemed, her role was to be that of chauffeur and on-looker, Cinderella destined never to go the ball; a wilting wall-flower, in fact. Isabel felt the breath leave her in a long, shuddering sigh. Her lovely fruit and vegetables would have to stay in the baking Cessna; there was nothing she could do to rescue them.

Isabel stood leaning back on the hot metal of the mini-bus until the heat seeping through her silky, red top forced her to move. Why she had decided to rummage through her drawer that morning looking for the only smart, summery thing she owned that wasn't redolent of thronged London streets and large, bustling over-lit offices, she couldn't think. Who was she wanting to impress? Clothes didn't maketh man, her mother had told her time and time again - it was the person in them who was important. As long as they were neat, tidy and clean. And she had had no reason to dress up today, unless it was to give herself confidence in front of the over-dressed Juliet. How low she was stooping, she chided herself, with a sudden spasm of revulsion. As she pushed all childish thoughts like those aside, her commonsense took over. It would be much cooler inside the marquee instead of cooking on the narrow road which encircled the quay. And the fumes from the cars as they slowed to see what the excitement was and then revved away around the corner and up the hill made it not the healthiest place to stand. She glanced up at the sky and as quickly turned away again. She was not even going to think about those clouds which seemed to be etching the horizon in pale grey, edged with reflected sunlight. The weather report had been good; a shower later, perhaps, but no wind to speak of and the pressure was higher than normal. She fed that information back into her mind and as she walked towards the marquee, repeated it over and over again until she had convinced herself that the flight back would be as uneventful as the one they had just had.

Isabel was in a quandary now. What could she do with herself for the five or so hours it took to make the half-hour programme? She was no longer excited by being involved, however remotely, with the TV film company; she'd spent too many hours listening to Juliet ordering people around as if they had cotton wool in their heads instead of brains. For a brief moment the thought that the producer would probably make a good shepherdess amused Isabel - if she wasn't likely to scare the sheep, that was. Any amusement of watching the cameramen with their heavy equipment resting on their shoulders like some out-dated machine guns, primed to slaughter a celebrity's reputation, had subsided, too. She told herself she was past feeling any interest in trying to enhance Travis's reputation; it had been only a ploy, a way to find a cheap pilot, that business of agreeing to use her vegetables and the petty black-mailing that had gone with it. Suddenly she felt ashamed of herself. But if Travis wasn't feeling well the least she could was to stick around and offer him cool drinks whenever there was a break. She couldn't see Juliet bothering to do that. She felt better having given herself a job, however menial it was. She wouldn't admit it to anyone else but she was beginning to think that Travis was badly used by Juliet and that he might appreciate having a friend in the enemy's camp.

As she slipped through the gap in the canvas Isabel wondered what all those people looking forward to a nice summer's day outing would think when they found their chosen destination, an old quay where children could safely play and they could have a peaceful drink from the pub across the road, was taken up with some commercial venture. Juliet, it seemed, had ignored any wishes a lowly holiday maker might have. The large marquee covered the entire quay. It was open to the river behind it, the white and glaring canvas making a roof for what looked like a well-furnished restaurant with its small white-clothed and be-flowered tables. Isabel guessed that anyone who dared to be curious would be bullied - with the offer of food and limited drink - into being a member of the audience. If this was unsuccessful - God forbid - Juliet would announce that there was always the canned variety of laughter and applause to add to the menu of the day. At present there was only a small crowd consisting of technicians - including the one who was in charge of the large barbecue standing perilously close to the quay's edge outside the marquee - Euan and his two assistant cameramen, the sound boom man (a term Isabel had found amusing on first hearing it), Thelma the make-up girl, Sam the Floor Manager who would have the job of controlling all the interested audience and a boffer and a gopher. It seemed that this television business had a language all of its own, Isabel had decided early on.

Juliet was marching around as if she had a train to catch while Travis stood quietly at the far side of the same cloth-covered trestle table he'd used at Polwyn. Not quite the same as the smart, custom-built kitchen he had in the hangar, but he would cope, she knew. But he didn't look well, Isabel thought, watching him pick up some implement and put it down in another position, doing the same with pottery bowls already filled with concealed foodstuffs. He looked somewhat bemused, she decided, not at all at home with this makeshift kitchen, as though he was not looking forward to acting as alfresco host. It was all very unlike the first time she had seen him at work, Isabel thought, her concern for his health increasing.

At last, it seemed, Travis was happy with his table arrangements. From her seat at one of the small tables, not too near the front but close enough to see - and be seen - if Travis should need any moral support, Isabel could make out the extra-large chopping board, the row of knives and baskets of fruits, vegetables and herbs - destined never to be used, she knew, along with the pottery bowls which had, by now, disappeared. She knew that under the long cloth was concealed anything he needed, already prepared. On the first occasion she had marvelled at how, with an almost-invisible sleight of hand, he had been able to exchange the small board which he had been chopping on with an identical one with the herbs all finely chopped on it without the audience seeing him do so.

'Quite a character,' a voice said, startling her out of her reverie.

Isabel looked up as a man seated himself on the chair opposite her. He waved a card at her before returning it to the pocket of his creased, summer shirt. She had time only to catch the word 'Press' before it disappeared. Even that small word was enough to make spiders crawl up her spine before she told herself to stop being silly; this was nothing to do with her - or that earlier reporter.

'Local paper,' he said with a slight grimace of fake apology. 'We had a press release. Couldn't ignore it.' He sounded as if he would rather be anywhere else. 'Mike,' he said, holding out his hand. 'Michael Williams, reporter extraordinaire. I don't think!' He said it with a smile, however, as if expecting her to pay no heed to his words. 'Who are you? Co-opted audience of one?' He looked around at the empty tables and chairs and then back at her.

Isabel felt sorry for the man suddenly; it was a day for her to be over-sensitive of the feelings of others it appeared. He must be at least fifty, she decided; shouldn't be doing these minor jobs at his age. Thoughts of her mother fluttered though her mind then. She wasn't so bad, Isabel now decided in sudden recognition of her parent's honesty and integrity. If she'd followed in her mother's footsteps and not continuously try to be a clone of her father she mightn't be, at the age of 32, still trying to find the person she really was; the person who had remained buried for so many years. Perhaps 50 was an age when people for no apparent reason decided to try and recapture a youth whose image had become distorted with the years.

'Isabel Vine,' she answered unthinkingly, her attention returning to the man opposite her. But there was no reaction from her companion, thankfully.

'And what do you do, Isabel Vine?' Mike asked, raising his eyebrows.

'I'm the chauffeur,' she answered, hoping that the lack of humour in her voice was not noticeable. She was disinclined to give him anything in the way of colour to add to his story.

'I thought he always flew to his filming locations,' Mike

said. Hence the soubriquet '*The Flying Chef.*'

Isabel knew he was fishing. 'He does,' she answered, not so quickly as to give anything away. 'I drive him,' she hedged, thinking quickly, 'to and from the airfields.' She knew it sounded a bit lame and hoped he wouldn't quiz her on availability of transport, or ask why he didn't drive himself. It was, to use her mother's words, a bit of a tangled web she was getting caught up in, for sure. She wouldn't know what answers to give to any questions he might ask.

Silently she breathed a sigh of relief as the conversation changed to less dangerous topics, such as the weather - making her want to see the state of the sky beyond the white canvas roof. The muted noise of children as they splashed around on the rocky shore of the river just beyond the quay, dogs barking as they joined in the fun and faint voices of the people on the decks of the two sailing boats moored alongside the quay just yards from the canvas studio, made a background to their desultory conversation. The people on the boats were almost whispering as if they didn't want to get caught up in something as exciting as a television programme being filmed, thus spoiling the peace and quiet they had promised themselves. Somewhat different from the earlier occasion, Isabel reminded herself when once coerced into being part of the film they had had difficulty in getting rid of the, by then, well-oiled yachtsmen.

'I'd heard,' Mike said, veering away from boring subjects, 'that he'd been had up for drunken driving. And the rumour was he'd lost his pilot's licence for the same offence.' He added, forcing his thin lips into an insincere smile, 'And here I was thinking what a lucky chap he was to find such an attractive pilot to ferry him thither and hither! And one who knows how to keep her mouth shut, too.'

Isabel placed her tongue between two clamping rows of teeth and said nothing. The shock of the information helped her keep silent, too. The knowledge that she was quite possibly giving away more than she was revealing by saying nothing, she ignored. She was not going to let Travis down, whatever he had done. No way was she going to add to the porridge of lies that would be served up for tabloid readers to digest with their breakfasts.

The man grinned across at her. 'Don't worry. Chauffeurs,' he emphasised the word, 'are meant to keep their bosses' secrets.'

Isabel was saved from replying to the insinuations by the reporter's attentions being caught by the sudden activity around Travis. Arc lamps were turned on, making war with the bright white light from the ceiling of sun-drenched canvas and the reflections off the water which had, until then, attempted to show they were precious gems and not just splinters of shattered glass.

The reporter stood up. 'I'm going to have a wander,' he told her. 'See what I can pick up from the odd conversation or two!' He winked at her. 'Want to come?'

Isabel shook her head, glad to hear she was to be rid of his unnerving company. It wasn't the first time she had had to fend off the prying breed, she recalled. Anything controversial regarding building large commercial projects where others had always been free to roam had continuously brought out the hacks from newspapers and television like ants happy to change their diet. They would scurry around the large, open-plan offices as if they had a right to be there - until she had sent them away before Paul caught sight of them and said something she - and the company - would regret. And there had been the business of Ken, too - as she now thought of him. Somehow robbing him of his proper title had distanced him - and his antics - making her more able to cope with the past. But neither he nor Paul should be thought of in the same breath as this mediocre, aging hack. She told herself to stop getting so heated and forced her attention onto the activities beyond the barrier of cameras and technicians, lights and all the other clobber which apparently was essential.

Travis, she noticed, with a quiver of alarm, remembering what the journalist had said, seemed to be having difficulty holding the hand-mixer with which he made his sauces. It was wobbling all over the place threatening to shower anyone within reach with beaten egg-white. Euan sighed audibly, touched something on the side of the large machine on his shoulder and gently let it down onto the ground at his feet, the other two cameramen following their boss's lead.

Isabel watched in concern. Obviously the 'flu or whatever it was he was suffering from was getting to Travis. She wondered what would happen if they had to cancel the filming; knew instinctively that Juliet would never allow that to happen. However poorly Travis was, she would make sure that all the expense and planning would not be wasted.

'Ten minutes,' Juliet called, passing her gaze over the assembled crew. 'And then it's back to work.'

Isabel was surprised to see her walking towards her table. Possibly the producer needed to have a break too, but there were many other - empty - tables she could have chosen. She was even more amazed to hear Juliet say:

'That's a nice outfit you've got on.' The wisp of a smile which had floated momentarily around her lips decided it did not like solitary confinement and disappeared. Without waiting for Isabel to say anything, Juliet sat down on the chair recently vacated by the reporter and carried on speaking. 'I'm glad you dressed up for once.' She put up a hand as if to quell Isabel's gratitude for her kind words. 'I've got an idea that will make you some money.'

In time honoured fashion Isabel felt she should scratch her head and look surprised. She was surprised, that was for sure, but she was also somewhat suspicious - as well as nervous - of the woman's motive for approaching her.

'It's like this,' Juliet said her tone inferring that she knew Isabel would be grateful for anything she had to offer. 'We need someone to help Travis. As you can see,' she hesitated for a fraction of a second before continuing, 'he's not well. Of course he's well enough to do his job,' she added abruptly.

Who was it said that thing about someone protesting too much? Isabel asked herself, grateful that she had retained her sense of humour. She was going to need it, for sure.

'He's such a professional.'

Is she trying to convince herself or me? Isabel questioned silently.

'But he does need a little help,' Juliet added, somewhat lamely Isabel felt.

Isabel thought back to her decisions regarding keeping glasses of cold water ready and felt ashamed that due to her attention being taken she had forgotten all about them. She would be happy to help out like this if it was what Juliet wanted.

'And I think you could do it.' Juliet's tone inferred that Isabel knew what she was talking about and would gratefully accept the honour conferred on her.

'Do what?' Isabel asked, with fear in her voice. She had guessed that more things than just glasses of water were being discussed.

'Help him, of course!' The impatient tone of Juliet's voice expressed annoyance at the lack of grey cells this ungrateful person sitting across from her appeared to have. Her PR persona took over then as she realized this was no way to gain another person's acquiescence. 'You're so nicely dressed,' she said, 'so if you do happen to get into a corner of a shot you won't look out of place.'

Isabel felt as if she had just been struck by a wall of concrete. Juliet, it seemed, was asking - no, not asking - demanding that she help Travis while he was being filmed. She was about to shake her head and vehemently refuse the honour of appearing on television when she noticed that Euan, the senior cameramen, had somehow crept up on her and was now aiming the lens of his camera at her face.

'Don't worry,' said Juliet.

When had she recently heard that? wondered Isabel, feeling bleak. She knew that, once again, she was out of control of her own destiny, whatever words to the contrary she was telling herself.

'He's only doing some tests,' Juliet told her as if that was an adequate explanation. 'Thelma's handiwork will rectify anything he doesn't like.'

Isabel was not at all sure she wanted grease and colour plastered all over her face by the make-up woman, but she wasn't allowed to say so.

'And Lucy will be able to twist and turn her little dials if you do happen to say anything when you shouldn't. We can't waste time in re-makes,' the producer added sourly. It was all getting to be a bit like being swept along by a muddy river in spate after a thunder storm. Isabel felt she was powerless, wouldn't be able stop whatever it was from happening even if she wanted to. The only thing that cheered her slightly was the decision to make sure that Juliet did, indeed, pay her for her extra duties. And pay her well.

Her decision made, she followed Juliet to the 'studio' area commanding her nerves to obey her and stop fluttering around like caged birds. She felt a little as though she was moving inside a large, transparent sack which covered her from head to toe, a plastic one which weighed a ton, which she only managed to carry with the help of invisible wheels attached to her feet and set to automatic.

On looking back Isabel had a great deal of trouble, however hard she tried, to remember the events of the afternoon. All she could recall with clarity - after she had discovered that Travis was not experiencing the onset of 'flu but was suffering the effects of being drunk - was that the two boats which had been tied alongside the old stone quay, making a nice back-ground to the domestic scene in the marquee, had disappeared from view by the time they had finished. And the monsoonal rains which then poured down on them like a curtain coming down on a drama, she recalled with no difficulty at all. It was the bits in the middle which were like some faded film.

She had been so busy trying to keep calm and not make a fool of herself she was oblivious to the activities of the nine members of the TV crew, including Juliet who had become but an evil wraith to be dealt with later. She chopped and stirred and whisked as commanded by the slurred words of the star sitting precariously on a tall stool at one side of the film set, pretending to be teaching some enthusiastic amateur cook. She tended the large fish - she doubted it was the salmon it was called - on the barbeque; turned it over and over, finishing by placing it on a huge plate and garnishing it as ordered. Over-garnished, she thought later as she looked at the slices of cucumber and apples, parsley, basil and lemon slices, together with the sauce she had made earlier. She made puddings from melted chocolate, cream, lavish dashes of alcohol and stoned cherries from tins.

It wasn't until it was all over that Isabel had a moment to think. What a shambles, she decided. Nothing usable could come from the five hours of drunken commentary and the muddle made by her having to cook and re-cook, starting from the middle of the recipe, on occasion, using ingredients which by then would be considered inedible to most people. She had not yet been informed of the planned voice-overs to be done later; had not allowed for Juliet's crafty ways.

Isabel, in a moment of clarity, did not need to be told either, that despite the fact that this was only the eighth of twelve planned episodes it was the end of the 'The Flying Chef'.

Viewing the programme later that year Isabel was thrilled to find that she had no need to feel embarrassed at the part she'd had to play. No one could see her dropping that pan, or pouring the chocolate mousse mixture into a wine glass by mistake or even re-chopping some of the herbs that Travis had chopped earlier. Those shots had all been cut and better moments added. Even Travis's voice was clear and distinct as he told her own - totally fabricated, of course - life story. No one, she was sure, would be able to hear muffled echoes bouncing off a high roof which were characteristic of the programmes filmed in the hangar. All in all, she considered, it was quite good.

Travis slept in the plane all the way home, just as he had done on the way down. Juliet sat leaning on the back of Isabel's seat, in a hushed and anguished whisper pouring out all the problems and traumas she had had to suffer over taking on this commission. Several times she'd almost had a nervous breakdown, she confided, over Travis's drinking. So far they had got away with it, but today had been the worst ever. Isabel did not remind her that she had, hopefully, helped it not to be a complete disaster.

Isabel quelled her irritation at the woman's continuous outpourings, managing to listen and at the same time fly the small aircraft. The earlier weather had cleared and the evening was now still and cloudless, so she had no problems where that was concerned.

She began to feel sorry for her until she said, 'I'll manage to get someone else. That's no problem, and I'll be pleased to be without all the hassle.'

She didn't say what was going to happen to Travis, Isabel noted.

When they got to their airfield Juliet held out an envelope and said:

'We won't be needing your services any more.' She held out her hand for the keys to the small plane. 'And Travis will be selling this,' she added, looking at the Cessna.

Travis just nodded his head, his face sad, and said nothing, as if he silently agreed with his guide and mentor. There was more to this couple, thought Isabel, than she knew. I should be brokenhearted, she told herself. For Travis because of what he's doing to himself, and for me because I won't have an aeroplane at my disposal anymore. But that probably wasn't a bad thing, she told herself; she would no longer have any excuse for neglecting her plants. But she was sad to see that Travis was not quite the man she had thought him to be.

Suddenly she felt released, free of something that had been nameless but which she knew had not been quite right. A decision had been made for her and it was the right one.

Later that night, sitting at the kitchen table, she raised her glass of well-diluted whisky and said, as if in good-bye, 'Cheers, Travis.' She then silently wished him good luck, knowing without forming the words that he needed more than luck if he was to survive.

Chapter 24

Isabel was dreaming that she was back in the Cessna, its engines muted to a distant buzz. Then she was awake and in bed and the buzzing continued. It sounded like the kitchen fire alarm she had installed when she first moved into the flat and had been meaning all these years to dismantle and throw away. It wasn't loud enough for that, she decided, rolling over and reaching for the alarm clock which lived on the oak bed-side table. She nearly fell out of bed as her hand searched for the table and the clock on it. Fully awake now, she knew she was no longer in that chamber of loneliness, deceit and unhappiness which her precious London flat had metamorphosed into. She was *here*, in the country, in her own dear - if somewhat shambolic and untidy - little cottage home. And alone, blissfully alone. She sighed and slipped back onto the hard pillow. The first thing she was going to do was strip Hannah's bed and give herself more comfortable pillows and bedclothes, she decided.

Images flooded into her mind as to how she would spend her time awakened her completely, reminding her of what had jarred her into consciousness. It was her mobile, of course, singing its song like some disconcerted bird bringing her a message. It was so long since she had used the messaging service herself that she couldn't think who would have the temerity to re-activate it. Probably Silas, she told herself, or, much less welcome, one of those interminable offers that had plagued her to buy this or that, win the competition of her life, and so on, that had infested her telephone in the early days of her having it. But she'd scotched all that, hadn't she? Her silent questions would have no answers unless she got up and went downstairs to retrieve the instrument from the black flying case she had dropped on the kitchen table the night before.

It wasn't Silas who was tapping out messages at dawn on Saturday morning. Not quite dawn, perhaps, but early enough to disturb her much-needed lie-in. She had to scroll up and down the message before she could take in what it said. Who it was from was an even bigger shock. The message was brief and to the point:

'I am OK,' it said. 'Safe and well. Alice gives me her news. Will B in touch.' It was signed, 'Mum.'

Isabel's kindly feelings of the day before concerning her mother became limp and bedraggled like an old, but cherished garment which could be pushed to back of the wardrobe but never thrown away. At least she had no feelings of anger anymore. She'd sorted that out by telling herself her mother was entitled to have a life of her own, whatever she or Simon thought. Alice had helped, of course.

Isabel pressed the 'reply to message' button and tapped out: 'Where are you? Get in touch, please,' without signing off with her name; her mother would know who it was. She pressed the 'send' button and waited for it to announce it had gone on its way. However, a strange and new message appeared on the tiny screen. 'No facility for replying to this number.' She tried dialling up the 'last numbers' menu and got a similar reply; her mother was well-organised, it seemed, at keeping herself hidden in whatever secret harbour she had found. Isabel shrugged her shoulders. She would get in touch when she was good and ready; was still happy to be away from the constraints of family and domesticity, it seemed.

What was Alice's news and why hadn't she heard it from her grandmother herself? It was obviously something of importance to bring her mother out of her warren and encourage her to communicate with the great world outside her tiny metropolis of plastic boat and garden of water.

Isabel was suddenly filled with alarm. Perhaps Alice was ill and had somehow got in touch with her mother; maybe she'd left instructions with someone on how to do so in an emergency. Isabel almost laughed with relief; that would be the last thing Alice would do. If she contacted anyone it would be her, Isabel, or Simon, both being immediately contactable and close at hand. She flung the grey instrument back into the bag in sudden anger. She didn't need any more mysteries or further hassle, thank you. Calm down, she told herself. She could deal with it later - when the world was awake and ready to receive telephone calls, namely her brother, if she couldn't reach her grandmother.

She flung on a pair of cotton trousers and a tee-shirt with the large letters A.L.L. printed on it, being the only one to hand. Normally she avoided shirts which publicised *anything*, even if it was her favourite charity that looked after their precious endangered land. First she would have some breakfast, and then take a look at her garden. By that time someone might be awake.

Something else called for her attention however. If she didn't get up to Mrs Parson's shop all the meagre pile of Saturday Telegraphs would have vanished and her plan to spend a lovely day struggling with the two crosswords - one day, she was determined, she would finish them both and send them off - would have come to nothing. Another thing she was determined on was to get back into some sort of routine, one that would give her a modicum of quality of life. This was the reason, after all, for her bucolic existence away from the stereotyped and synthetic existence she wasted so many years in.

Without waiting for the kettle to boil for her breakfast coffee she literally trotted up to the village.

'Kept you one, Miss.' Mrs Parsons looked remarkably pleased with herself. She wasn't often quite so polite even if she was much friendlier now.

'That was kind of you,' Isabel said, trying not to sound too surprised.

'And here's your money.'

Isabel looked at the large amount of coins and notes lying on the older woman's palm and wondered what the shop-keeper was on about. Was she being blackmailed yet again? she joked to herself with only the slightest hint of bitterness. 'What on earth is that for?' she asked.

'For the veg, of course.' The woman's voice inferred that, although they might be friends now, she wasn't completely convinced on the matter of her customer's sanity. 'I always like to pay my bills promptly. The total professional, that's me.'

Isabel thought she sounded like one of the many young work-experience people who had wandered about the offices as if the company was privileged to have them there. Then she remembered; she hadn't seen Marion so she hadn't received the money owing for the large box of produce her friend delivered for her. Subconsciously she had accepted that Marion would have passed it on to her eventually, so hadn't even thought about it.

'It looks far too much,' Isabel then said in her most diplomatic way. It was worth encouraging this growing relationship in any way that was necessary.

'Not a bit,' Mrs P responded quickly. 'Worth every penny.'

Isabel felt that she should leave the shop as quickly as possible; she was likely to fall over with surprise if she didn't. She had suffered so often from the elderly woman that she didn't want to do anything to spoil the shopkeeper's change of attitude. So she just nodded her thanks and turned to leave the shop. She didn't get away before the older woman pushed a sheet torn from a stenographer's notepad into her hand, however. On it was a long list - written in impeccable copper-plate, it seemed to Isabel - of fruit and vegetables.

'By Wednesday, please,' Mrs Parsons ordered as she turned to serve another customer who had just come through the door.

Isabel was still a little dazed at all this as she walked back to the cottage. Once she turned into her lane she had reached the stage, however, of being able to accept that it was part of life's rich tapestry, as her oft-quoting grandmother would have said. And, now, perhaps she would be able to carry on with her pleasant plans for a pleasant weekend.

It wasn't to be, it seemed. With his back to her, standing like a misplaced statue on her terrace, was her next-door neighbour.

As the gate clicked closed Thom turned to face her. She was aghast at the expression on his face. Was he ill? Was he, like Travis, a secret drinker - even at 9 o'clock on a Saturday morning? Or was he just enjoying the glee of thinking up yet something more with which to plague her? The look of the wide smile on his face had shocked her to the core, frightening her with its unfamiliarity. His first words made Isabel think that he had, perhaps, lapsed into early senility.

'Thank you,' he said, as she approached the terrace. 'That was kind of you.'

Life was becoming just like one of those films, Isabel told herself, where the scenes, badly cut - she even knew the terminology now - flicked from one another with no seeming coherence. What on earth was he talking about, in his echo of Mrs Parson's words?

'I didn't find it till this morning,' he said.

She remembered what he was talking about then.

'It seems I've misjudged you,' he continued, his voice as cultured as ever, remnants of the strange smile still hovering on his face. 'The boys are thrilled. They're now complaining that I've never given them sweet corn and tomatoes as big as melons. Or melons as big as footballs!'

It was a joke, Isabel decided.

'They're planning a barbeque tonight and want you to come.'

It wasn't a question, Isabel decided. More a royal command which she would not be expected to disobey.

'Do you want to tell me why we've been so lucky as to be the recipients of such a lavish gift?'

The smile was still there, Isabel noted, so she told him about not wanting to waste her precious fruit and veg so had dropped if off at his house on her way back from the airfield. She had been too exhausted to want to meet anyone so had quietly deposited it by the back door and hurried back to her car, knowing its origin would be obvious.

Two pots of coffee later, sitting on the dark green chairs, she had told him all about the events of the previous day as if he were a friend and not just an antagonistic neighbour. It wasn't as if she was telling him any secrets, his knowing Travis since schooldays. It was, in a way, a relief to get it all off her chest.

'You really ought to know about his past,' Thom told her when she stopped to draw breath at the end of her spiel. He spoke as if it was a duty he was compelled to fulfil.

'He was - is - very talented,' Thom told her, the smile gone as if wiped out by the memory of some past sadness. 'A very popular person at school. Always a good friend to everyone - and sincere about it, too. Artistic. Something the average teacher finds hard to cope with so he didn't get any encouragement.' He paused for a moment as if seeing himself and Travis as they had once been - young people with the world at their feet except that, for one of them, the backing of important people was tragically missing.

'He liked cooking, for some reason - inborn talent, I suppose. But, as it so often happened when we were young - education hadn't become quite so liberal yet - his family, backed by our teachers, decided that was not a 'proper' career for a boy so his father - a colonel in some classy regiment - decided he was to join the army. So he did, had no choice, there was to be no money available otherwise, and it nearly destroyed him. Can you imagine someone with artistic leanings being happy learning how to kill and maim?' Thom shook his head sadly.

Isabel sat silent not wanting to interrupt. She wanted to hear about Travis, wanted to know that her feelings of sympathy towards him not been misplaced. Also, in a buried segment of her mind, she wanted it proved that she had had, possibly, a narrow escape from yet another man who wanted a mother and not an equal companion.

'And when his wife walked out on him....'

'His wife?' Isabel was unable to prevent herself from interrupting.

'His first wife,' Thom said, continuing quickly so that she had no time to interrupt with a second and more vehement interjection, 'he adored the kids, thought the world of them and then, just like that, he'd lost them, too.'

Isabel was silent this time; she was too stunned to speak.

'Went to Australia. She couldn't bear the life of penury with Travis, she told him. He'd tried being some sort of businessman to keep her and the kids, but that didn't work. Then he tried writing books. Two were published and then he was accused of being 'un-professional', so gave that up. I hate to think he would stoop so low but it was murmured that he plagiarised someone else's work. He was desperate, must have been to do that.' Thom took a deep breath before continuing.

Isabel was longing to ask questions, but she decided that silence was the best thing in this case. Thom was holding up a peremptory hand indicating that he was about to continue.

'Before the court case he was heralded as a rising star, went to all the publishers parties, mixed with the right people. When the crash came he found that drink was the only friend left.' Thom paused as if to consider whether his next words would be construed as signifying something other than their true meaning. 'Then along came Juliet, the one person in his waning crowd who was not ignoring him. She was going to make him into a TV star. He was working as - scivvy, I suppose is the only word to use - in some run-down restaurant. Learning the trade, was how he put it. He then became Travis Parkin, The Flying Chef.' Thom finished.

'But...' Isabel had so many questions buzzing around in her mind she did not know which one to ask. Thom mistook her hesitation.

'He was plain Barry Parks before that. Saw the name on the back of a lorry and thought that would do very nicely. Just like him to get it wrong; probably would have been sued for plagiarism a second time if he hadn't, of course.'

Isabel could not prevent a sigh escaping through her rigid lips. She thought she knew the rest of the story; had been a part of it. Juliet, too, would desert him and go off and find some other dupe to fall into her web of machinations.

'If Juliet hadn't insisted that they got married it might have worked,' Thom announced, unaware of the effect it had on Isabel.

Her first reaction was of disbelief, the second was the realization of how close she had been to making an embarrassing fool of herself. 'He married *her?*' she gasped. The question was rhetorical; Thom was no liar.

'And he can never leave her,' he said, misunderstanding her yet again. 'Some clever legal thing that says she is in complete control, if not of his life, but certainly of his earnings. She's clever that one,' he added, his voice lacking affection. 'She knew what she was doing, business-wise, in those early days.'

Isabel was not at all sure she was pleased to hear that part of the story, but she was convinced that Thom had no other motive than to warn her off. The warning had come too late, as it happened.

'Don't worry.' It wasn't the first time she had said those words in the past few days, she recalled. 'I was given my cards last night.'

The expression on Thom's face was just another of the surprises that seemed to be littering the morning like autumn leaves. It was one of relief which had turned quickly to - happiness was not quite the right word, Isabel decided - self-satisfaction at a job well done, was a much better description.

'Answer me one question,' Thom said.

Isabel was expecting some intrusion into her inner feelings and was ready to refuse.

'Why the lavish gift?'

She could not ignore the tremor of relief which ran through her. Exhausted as she had been the night before, she was glad now that she had managed to force herself to leave the box on Thom's doorstep. It had nicely taken his attention away from things which she was finding increasingly awkward to think about.

Isabel cut the scene of the box being left in the airplane when she described the goings-on at Gunners Quay. Now she felt he was owed some sort of explanation. She didn't want him to think it was a totally altruistic action on her behalf; he might misconstrue that. He seemed to attach more than necessary importance to her answer. So she told him why he'd been the lucky recipient in as few a words as she could find.

'I'm relieved to hear they all came from,' he waved an arm around, 'here. They're quite up to scratch.'

Isabel felt she was in a Jane Austen novel at the tone of his voice. Mr Darcy couldn't have created a better put-down.

'They're all splendid, in fact. Not a genetically modified piece amongst them.' He smiled. 'I can tell that by their blemishes,' he told her.

Isabel did not know whether to be angry or pleased; angry at his patronising tone, or pleased that he had, at least, accepted that she wasn't trying to ruin his life by growing chemically enhanced produce on his door-step. She decided to be diplomatic and say nothing.

Thom stood up. 'I've got to get back,' he said. 'I've left those scoundrels swimming. A good bunch, this time,' he said with pride. 'Hardly any problems. Except for just that one thing about the ornament.'

Isabel was surprised to hear how casually he was mentioning a subject which had seemed to be so important not so long ago.

Thom leaned on the back of the chair he had just vacated. 'Of course. I forgot to tell you. It wasn't the original. My father locked that away before my mother died, when they left the farm. Apparently she was neurotic about it getting broken. He found it in his office safe a few days ago. Retirement looming and all that,' he gazed across at Isabel as if she knew what he meant, 'he decided to have a clean out. And hey presto! one blue - and intact - ornament of a glass pig.'

'That's good,' Isabel told him, pleased for his good luck but wondering when she would be rid of the scars.

'And it was nothing to do with Hannah,' he admitted.

'I know,' she said abruptly. In her last conversation with the girl she had discovered that Hannah had been covering for someone else.

'I'm sorry.'

To Isabel's surprise he held out a hand to her. Automatically she responded.

'We could be friends, couldn't we?' he asked with unexpected emphasis.

Isabel nodded. Friends, yes, she told herself, but nothing more.

Thom was striding towards the garden gate when he turned and waved to her. He almost bumped into the small woman who was just stepping through the gateway.

Alice smiled at the tall farmer and waved at her granddaughter before offering her hand to Thom. 'Been keeping her on the straight and narrow, I hope, Thom,' she said with the same strange familiarity she had shown on the previous occasions. She nodded towards Isabel who was now standing quietly waiting for the two of them to stop acting as if they knew something she didn't.

'Not much need of that, Alice,' Thom's said cheerfully. 'She's come to her senses.'

Isabel took a couple of steps towards them. It was time she stopped these two discussing her as if she wasn't present. Also, there were one or two questions she urgently needed her grandparent to answer. She took her grandmother by the arm to guide her towards a chair.

Thom waved then disappeared up the track without saying anything further.

'I don't know what you two are on about,' Isabel said to her grandmother with an affectionate laugh, 'but I'm pleased to see you.' She sat down on Thom's chair. 'Are you staying for lunch or is this just another of your flying visits?'

'Questions, questions,' Alice chided, a small, secretive smile lurking around her mouth. 'I'm not stopping, just passing by.' She seemed to find that amusing as she waved good-bye to the back of the disappearing man.

'Where are you going?' Isabel felt her antennae waving in the non-existent breeze. She had been so busy she had not allowed herself time to think about some of the most important things in her life, it seemed. There was the mystery of her mother to clear up. And that of Thom and her grandmother's sudden friendship, too. 'Couldn't be something to do with Mum's message, I suppose.' She had thrown the pebble into the lake wondering what ripples would appear. The ripples threatened to become whirlpools, it appeared.

'She got hold of you, then,' Alice commented. 'When she called me I told her she should. I'd hate for her to turn up out of the blue and give you a fright! Did you call her back?'

'She didn't leave a number, as it happened.' Isabel could hear the affected patience in her own voice.

'Why didn't you try to reply to her message, then?' Alice, her grandmother who shouldn't really be familiar with these things, asked.

Isabel tapped herself on the side the head. She wanted her gran to think she was too stupid to think of that.

'So you don't know my news then?' Alice asked. 'Unless that nice boy has told you, of course. But we told him to keep it secret until everything was ready. We didn't want any well-meant 'advice' to be offered!'

'What news?' Isabel tried to think of something that Alice could have achieved which she wasn't aware of. 'Do you mean that your publisher friend has decided to publish your family history? That's wonderful,' Isabel added, pleased that she had the answer to at least one of her questions.

'I've given that up,' Alice surprised Isabel by saying. She must have noticed the look of amazement on her granddaughter's face so she added quickly, 'Not exactly given it up but Alex thought it would make a good novel. So that's what I'm working on now.'

'Congratulations,' Isabel said firmly, hoping this time her grandmother would acknowledge her good wishes.

'There were lots of things I was finding out I didn't care for,' Alice said. 'I considered it was better to let sleeping dogs lie, especially when Alex said he was interested in the book as a novel - faction, or something, he called it.' She paused. 'Perhaps you could carry on with the family history,' she offered.

Isabel shuddered at the thought of what she might find out about her father's side and thought she was happy not to know.

'He's already given me a generous advance.' She sounded proud of herself, as if to say that she wasn't too old to be just as good as anyone years her junior.

'That is good news,' Isabel told her. 'I assume this visit is just to boast about that, is it?' she laughed. 'And your news is that you're on your way to yet another week-end business discussion!' Isabel smiled to herself as she thought about all these 'business' discussions taking place when the busy publisher had nothing better to attend to. She hoped, suddenly, that her grandmother had not been duped. She gave that thought the push. Anyone less likely to be duped than her grandmother would be very difficult to find. 'Thanks for dropping in and telling me.'

'That's not my news,' Alice told her, a trace of surprise in her voice. 'I was just waiting for your mother to get herself organised and then I was going to tell you. Particularly as you and Silas are to be there.'

'What are you talking about?' Isabel asked, bemused now.

'My wedding, of course! What else?'

With difficulty Isabel prevented herself from tipping backwards onto the stony terrace as she pushed her chair away from the table in shock. She was saved from certain humiliation by the deft movement of her grandmother's hand catching the arm of the plastic chair.

'I thought you'd guessed,' she said, her face a picture of enlightenment. 'You didn't think I've been spending every weekend talking business, do you? What man is going to give up his weekends doing that?' she asked with a girlish giggle.

'And who is the lucky man?' Isabel managed to gasp.

'Alex,' Alice replied. 'Of course,' she added as if she expected Isabel to know Alex and Alice,' she laughed. 'Was meant to be!'.

'But you didn't say anything,' Isabel said, still reeling from the shock. 'Why?'

'You have to be a little selfish sometimes to survive,' her grandmother told her. 'I didn't want anyone to try and deter a silly old woman like me from having a little fun. I've been alone for twenty years, you know,' Alice reminded her. 'And,' she said, a smile on her face now that she had defended herself adequately, 'we all have a bit of Peter Pan in us, if we would only acknowledge it. Why should we grow old before we want to?'

There was no argument that Isabel could find for that.

What a day it had been. Were all her days going to carry on being like this one? She hoped not; she needed a little peace, and fewer shocks and surprises. She was happy for her grandmother, of course she was, but it had come somewhat like a bullet from a distant gun and she was going to feel bruised by it for some time, she was sure. That would go, she hoped. She got up out her chair, her legs seeming to have turned to fragile sticks beneath her, and gave her grandmother a warm hug and a kiss on a fragrant cheek. Isabel had never known her grandmother to be without the benefits of beauty preparations and she now knew how clever she had been.

'I am so pleased for you,' Isabel told her grandmother.

'That's all I want,' Alice said. 'You will be my bridesmaid, won't you?' She wasn't joking Isabel soon discovered. And Silas was going to give her away, although he was not aware of that just yet.

'And Alex's son is going to be his best man. It will be quite a family do, won't it?' Alice laughed. All the plans had been made, it appeared, without the cast knowing anything about the show they were to appear in.

'And when do we meet this man and his son?' Isabel was calm once more; the shock was beginning to subside and the promised pleasure was becoming more and more attractive. Not just her grandmother's wedding, but the thought of seeing her mother again after so many months was an added bonus.

'You know his son,' Alice told her sharply. She twisted her head in a direction which made the blood run cold in Isabel's veins.

'You don't mean...' she stammered as a vision of her grandmother and Thom standing at her gate not so long ago sped before her eyes. This sort of thing only happened in stories, she told herself in disbelief. She suddenly wanted to run away, hide herself, do anything but have to cope with any more surprises. Instead she obeyed her mother's oft-said injunction and pulled herself together, and haltingly offered her grandmother a celebration drink.

'Later, dear,' Alice replied seemingly unaware of the emotions that were threatening to drown her beloved granddaughter. 'I have to be on my way. Alex's got some idea of a special lunch which I'm not supposed to know about! I mustn't be late.'

In a daze Isabel saw her grandmother to her little car and turned back to the cottage. She wanted to get in touch with her mooring buoy, her port in a storm; her younger brother.

As she passed the neat pile of newsprint on the kitchen table which was glaring up at her as if angry at being neglected she noticed the letter she had retrieved from the old mail-box just before she had noticed she had a visitor. The official typing on the envelope told her it was not going to hold any good news. Something else she could tell her brother when they had finished discussing their wayward mother, their adolescent grandmother and anything else that cropped up.

'Silas, now this.' She had been successful for once in getting hold of her brother at the first try, and after their lengthy conversation was ready to throw at him the last thing on her list of predicaments. 'I've another letter about Lilian.'

'Chuck it,' Silas told her without preamble.

'I can't do that,' Isabel told him shocked. What had made him so irresponsible suddenly?

'Yes, you can,' her younger brother told her. 'It's out of date.' He reminded her then about Alice's activities on behalf of a person she need not have bothered about but had taken the responsibility for on their behalves. 'She's very happy in the place Alice found. She even blames you for making her live on her own for so long,' he laughed. 'In that 'tatty bungalow, away from all her friends,' is the way she put it. She's as happy as it is possible for someone with dementia to be now.'

'Thank God...,' Isabel said.

'Thank God...,' Silas said at the same time.

They both laughed. It had been a long-time since they had experienced their twin-like thoughts, Isabel thought with a warm rush of affection for him.

Chapter 25

Isabel stretched her arms above her head and sighed. What a three months it had been – more like a life-time than just one – very busy, occasionally traumatic and often amusing - summer. She pushed the seed catalogues away and picked up the cafétiere; there was plenty of time to order what she needed for the spring. And she wouldn't be without help in getting the right ones, she was sure. The dark brown liquid gushed into her mug as if happy to be free.

Silas came through the door rubbing dust off his hands.

'Well, that's done,' he said with satisfaction in his voice. He grimaced then. 'Fancy anyone doing that!' he exclaimed. 'Anyway they've taken her away to be buried somewhere sanctified and appropriate,' he told her. 'And not before time.'

Isabel smiled up at her brother. There she was, free of that mound of remains which had cast a shadow over her summer - whenever she'd had time to consider it, she admitted. And she was free of her concern for Lilian; even free of her other grandmother, although that was something she would not have wished for. And they certainly were not free of their mother, happily. But for how long Isabel wasn't sure. She said she'd only come back for her mother's wedding and that she would be returning to *Windaru* - where ever that was - as soon as it was over.

'When is she going back to the boat?' Isabel asked, voicing her thoughts.

'Not so much of the 'she',' a voice snapped from beyond the doorway. Their mother stood there, covered in dust just like her son. 'I'll go in my own sweet time,' she added, but smiling now. 'Just as soon as that awful bed I've been sleeping in becomes too much for my aged bones.'

'Huh!' teased Silas. 'Whenever did you worry about comfort!'

'Thank you very much,' Maggie retorted. 'One day you'll see just how comfortable I've made *Windaru*. But not yet. I don't want you two getting any idea of cruising holidays!'

'Where is she, Mum?' Isabel asked, her tone casual. She couldn't fool her astute mother, however.

'Never you mind,' was the sharp reply. 'When I want you to know, you will be informed!'

'Just tell us,' urged her daughter. 'Is she in UK waters or somewhere abroad?'

'None of your business.' Her mother's tone said she was getting weary of the questioning and that they should know her by now; know that if she didn't want to tell them what she was up to they were very unlikely to find out however much they questioned her.

'I suppose you're nervous of Dad finding you,' Silas offered as a way of finding out his mother's feelings.

'Maybe, maybe not,' was all she said.

Just at the propitious moment for Silas and Isabel's parent, a large shadow filled the doorway of the small kitchen. Thom marched in as if he was a member of the family and knew that his presence was just what they wanted.

'Tell them, Thom,' Maggie said, 'to stop nagging me.'

It was strange, thought Isabel, how everyone but her had taken to Thom. Of course Alice had to, whatever she felt now he was her step-son. The thought made Isabel feel strange. There were so many things that she had to adjust to.

Thom smiled across at her - his slight frown betraying that he was having as much difficulty as she was at sorting out their new relationships. His face cleared. 'I'm sure they're only doing it for your good,' he laughed. Turning back to Isabel he said; 'We won't bother about whose related to whom,' he said with a smile, returning to a subject discussed earlier that morning. 'It's too difficult!'

'Well, we've got them safely wed,' Maggie said, diverting the subject from one which was of no interest to her, her expression said. 'And off on their honeymoon, so what do we do now?'

'I have an idea,' Thom said. He was not very amused at the gaping mouths and looks of sarcastic astonishment put on by Isabel and Maggie. 'And while you are here - Maggie,' he paused as he said the unfamiliar name, 'I want you to tell me the rest of Silas's escapades.' He grinned across at Silas who had turned around sharply from washing his hands in the old, deep sink. 'I think we could make quite a story about it. With you and me collaborating,' he told Silas.

Isabel had discovered what Thom did with his time during the winter months when farming was not all time-consuming and there were no naughty boys to see to. He wrote books - not books on farming, or starchy factual tomes but adventure stories for adults, it appeared. Once Isabel had heard the name he wrote under she was grateful she hadn't known it when she bought her cottage. She would have felt patronised, and unable to hang on to any remnant of self-respect when she had felt forced to stand up to his earlier bullying.

They'd sorted all that out, now. A few glasses of champagne and a joyful wedding were very good for divulging what they thought of each other.

Silas shuddered. 'No thank you. That's all in the past now.'

'Pity,' said Thom, glancing at Silas's mother who was mouthing indistinguishable words at him. Words, he thought, which were meant to infer that he wasn't to take 'no' for an answer. He had an ally, it seemed. 'Okay,' Thom said, then. 'We'll leave it. For now.'

So they did. But not forever.